I MARRIED A MASTER

Melanie Marchande

❈ ❈ ❈

For exclusive content, sales, and special opportunities for fans only, plus a FREE romance serial for subscribers only, please sign up for Melanie's mailing list at MelanieMarchande.com. You'll never be spammed, and your information will never be shared or sold.

Table of Contents

Chapter One

Jenna

This had to be a nightmare.

I simply couldn't explain it otherwise. The yawning chasm of silence, except for the *thump, thump, thump* of my own heart - I was sure everyone in the room could hear it. The stares. The growing sense of panic. The fact that all the words on the paper in front of me looked like ancient cuneiform.

Help? Anyone? Can a girl get a Rosetta stone over here?

I opened my mouth, but my throat had closed up.

Any minute now, my grandmother would show up, except she'd look like Beetlejuice, and then I'd be in my underwear in front of my whole high school assembly and I'd be late for my college finals and I'd be missing some flight I was taking because my feet felt like they were stuck in molasses. Then, I'd know.

This had to be a nightmare. There was no other explanation.

Four sets of eyes staring at me. One of them was clearing his throat impatiently, shifting in his chair. One of the others seemed more compassionate.

"I'm sorry," she said, gently. "But we really need to move on."

I worked my mouth open and shut a few times.

"Please," said the throat-clearing one, more firmly. "You've used up all of your allotted time. Thank you, please come again."

When I didn't move, he stood up, with a massive sigh and roll of his eyes. He walked over, grabbed my arm, and began steering me towards the door. My feet shuffled obediently, though the rest of my body refused to move.

I was sitting at a bus stop, and I had no idea how I got there.

Internally, I let out a sigh of relief. The surest hallmark of a dream. Any minute now, I'd wake up in my own bed to the sound of my chirping alarm, waking me up just in time to get ready for my audition.

"Wow, you really choked in there, huh?"

I turned around, slowly.

The girl sitting next to me on the bench - I recognized her. She'd been in the waiting room next to me. She'd've been called up right after me.

Uh oh. This made a little too much sense, for dream logic.

Her eyes were sympathetic, not mocking. "They're never as discreet as they want you to think. I heard them talking about you when I was headed in. Don't worry. It gets better." She offered me a smile. "This your first time?"

I nodded mechanically.

"Oh, don't even sweat it. There'll be other auditions." She waved her hand dismissively.

"No, there won't," I heard myself say. "I'm pretty

sure my career is over."

She laughed. "You know how often shit like this happens? They won't even remember you, let alone think it's notable enough to spread the word to all their secret Hollywood society friends to put you on the blacklist."

"No," I said, shaking my head miserably. "It's not that. It's me. I can't do it. All these years, this was my dream - I've been defending it to everybody who said it was stupid, I've been planning, I've been researching, all for nothing. Because I can't do it. I thought a couple of school plays and some wins at debate club were enough to qualify me for this."

Normally I was more guarded than this. A lot more guarded. But I couldn't stop the torrent of fear and regret - and besides, I was still clinging to that hope.

This was all a nightmare.

"Everybody goes through this," the girl said, patting my arm. "Trust me."

"Not everyone locks up at their first audition," I pointed out. "Okay, so maybe you could name some great actors who did, but that's not the point. What about all the people who choked like I did, and went on to be nothing? The odds were never in my favor to begin with. This is just the final shovelful of dirt on my grave."

"Hey man," she said, standing up and extending her arm as her bus approached. "All I can say is - if you go out there expecting to fail, you're gonna fail one hundred percent of the time."

"Thanks," I called after her, bitterly.

I'd gotten better advice from the side of a Chipotle

cup.

The surreality of the situation had started to fade, leaving me more alert, less muzzy around the edges. I was awake. I was more awake than I'd ever been in my life.

Look, I wasn't stupid. When I came to New York for acting, I knew it was a pipe dream that way too many people share, and not enough people pursue. I knew the work was harder than people imagine it to be. I knew there'd be a lot of hoofing it, spending all day, every day in auditions, doing infomercials until I worked my way up to name-brand products. And maybe, just maybe, if I was really lucky - becoming one of those "hey, it's that chick from the Swiffer ad!" people.

It was just like any other job. Starting out as a fry cook, you don't go into your first day of work counting on being "discovered" by the CEO of McDonald's and pulled to run the company. That was how I treated this. I was going to have to work hard, and scrape by, for a long time. But I had faith in my ability to do it.

And I also had my dream.

Part of me - the part that never wanted to accept anything less than one hundred percent perfection, one hundred percent of the time - had a tiny glimmer of hope that I'd be one of the special ones. A casting director would just happen to be in line behind me at the bank, and he'd see me yelling at the teller (not that I ever yelled at tellers - but shhh, this was *my* fantasy) and he'd just love my passion. I'd find myself cast in a non-speaking role in the next Resident Evil or something, and the director would become besotted, and the rest would be history…

I didn't talk about this dream, of course. Because I knew it was almost offensively ridiculous. It was a childish. It was nothing to hang a career on.

And I didn't. But part of me still wanted it. Part of me felt like if that didn't happen, I'd be a failure.

No part of me was prepared for what actually happened.

Stage fright. I'd never experienced stage fright. Not once in my life had I looked at a group of people in front of me, with cards or a script or notes in my hand, or merely lines in my head, and just frozen up like that. Even the most stringent doubters in my life had always acknowledged that I was good with performance, public speaking, whatever. They doubted the industry, the amount of work - they doubted my understanding of the gritty realities of the job. They doubted by commitment.

But they didn't doubt *me*.

And until now, I never had, either.

Walking down the street, hurried pedestrians pushing past me, I'd never felt more lost. My phone was buzzing in my pocket and I didn't dare answer it. Especially not when I checked the screen and saw it was my mom.

I wouldn't be able to talk to her without bursting into tears. And the last thing she needed to do was worry about me.

I let it go to voicemail, then fired off a quick text implying I was just *so busy* I couldn't possibly pick up the phone.

She answered a few minutes later.

That's my girl! Next stop, Oscars! xoxoxo

I felt sick to my stomach.

My mom thought I couldn't see the worry behind her eyes, whenever I talked about my ambitions. She wasn't much for useful critique or hard-hitting advice, but she was always ridiculously enthusiastic. Sometimes, that was exactly what I needed.

But not now. Right now, I needed to wallow.

I had enough money saved up that I'd be okay for a little while. But the definition of "a little while" was slightly unclear. I knew I'd have to find some other kind of work when I got here, but that nagging, improbable hope in the back of my mind had convinced me to put off my job search for the first few days. After all, wouldn't want to get tied down bagging groceries, only to leave them in the lurch when Robert Rodriguez almost hit me with his car and became captivated by the fire in my eyes.

I would've laughed at myself, if it wasn't so fucking *sad*.

I found myself in the grocery store. It was so crowded, with such low ceilings, the noise of the traffic outside echoing through the wine racks. I wasn't used to this. Even though I didn't exactly grow up in the boonies, city living was relatively foreign to me. I forgot about how little space everything has, how much everything costs.

But you don't get discovered in the suburbs.

With a sigh of self-disgust, I jostled my way to the ice cream freezer. Ben and Jerry's was on sale - it was almost as if they knew I was coming.

As I reached for the door, tunnel vision honing in on Karamel Sutra, my shoulder collided with something. Large. Solid. Warm.

Shit, it had to be a human being.

6

I whirled around to face them, and sure enough, I was inches away from a guy who looked like he belonged on the cover of GQ. Great.

Well, it could've been worse - maybe this was about to become my own personal Nora Ephron style meet-cute.

"Do you mind?" he snapped at me.

Okay, maybe not.

"Sorry," I replied, fully aware of the lack of remorse in my voice. "You were in my blind spot."

"Oh, I was in your *blind spot*?" he shot back. His stormy blue eyes were staring me down, like I'd kicked his grandmother or something. "Maybe you should get some mirrors installed."

Running a hand through his short-cropped brown hair, he blindly grabbed a container from the shelf and disappeared down another aisle.

Well.

Obviously I'd heard the old chestnut about New Yorkers being rude, but this really took the cake. I had bumped into him pretty hard, and maybe I should have been more careful, but it had to be at least fifty percent his fault. Besides, whatever he was going through right now could not be as bad as all of my hopes, dreams, and career aspirations dying a slow and painful death.

Probably.

I finally picked up my Karamel Sutra and headed for the checkout. Picking a line more or less at random, I settled in behind a woman with a full cart of groceries and started scanning the tabloid headlines. *Who* are *these people? What the fuck is Real Housewives of Buena Vista?*

"Excuse me, ma'am?"

I looked up, to see one of the cashiers waving me over to another register.

"I can take you right over here," she said, flipping on her light. I wasn't in any particular hurry, but I figured it would be rude to decline.

As I approached the lane, something pushed past me. Something big, and warm, and solid.

Oh, *hell* no.

"Excuse me," he said, loudly, in a way that suggested it was not so much a request as a notification. "I've been waiting for ten minutes in that line over there, and now the register's broken. This is ridiculous. You have to take me first."

My jaw dropped. He couldn't have been lying more blatantly if he tried.

"Excuse me," I echoed. He didn't look at me, but I figured it was worth a shot anyway. "That's not true. I just saw you at the freezer."

He glared at me. "All right, I'm so sorry I violated grocery store protocol by jumping the line. How can I possibly make it up to you? Bear in mind that every moment I spend defending myself to you, is a moment I'm not using to get the fuck out of here so we can both go home."

It was in that moment that I glanced at what he was holding, and recognized the label.

Karamel Sutra.

Ugh. I already had way, way more in common with this guy than I wanted.

"Excuse me," I said again, pushing past him, and sliding my pint of ice cream towards the cashier. I wasn't going to cave to this asshole, no matter how effective his death glare was.

The poor cashier was like a deer in the headlights. I felt terrible for her, but I could *not* let this guy win. Finally, after a moment's hesitation and glancing between us like she expected an all-out brawl to start, she rang up my ice cream and took my card. I could feel my opponent looming over me from behind, practically breathing down my neck, but I'd won.

"I'm...I'm sorry." The cashier's voice came, very softly and tentatively. "It says your card is…"

I looked down at the screen. DECLINED.

For fuck's sake.

"You have *got* to be kidding me." The man snarled, reaching into his wallet and pulling out a wad of bills. He threw them at the register belt. "That should cover both of us, shouldn't it?" He glared at the cashier, who nodded quickly.

"Good." The man picked up his pint and jostled past me, and I absolutely did not notice the scent of his cologne. "Next time, maybe dig under the sofa cushions before you come out grocery shopping. Some of us have *jobs* to get back to."

Tears stung in my eyes as I stood there, stunned. It was the last straw. Every doubt and hesitation about this city, all those whispering fears that it really would end up eating me alive - it all came crashing down. How dare he? The contempt in his voice was unmistakable. From the looks of him, he was born with a silver spoon in his mouth. Of course he thought the rest of the world was beneath him.

I was still clutching the ice cream in my lap as I sat on the train, riding until the end of the line. Waiting for my stop so I could get out and catch a bus. Too late, I realized that my Karamel Sutra would be half-melted by the time I got home. After growing up in the suburbs, I wasn't used to grocery store trips that took an hour one-way.

A simple enough solution: I'd have to invest in some of those insulated grocery bags. And maybe a few ice packs. But in that moment, irrationally, it felt like just another in a long list of failures that proved I never should have come here in the first place.

As I sat in the plastic seat that was far too narrow for any normal human, my eyes drifted down to an abandoned newspaper on the seat beside me. It was folded open to the middle, one of the pages adorned with blurry pictures of D-list celebrities who'd been unlucky enough to encounter a TMZ photographer while they walked their dogs.

Damn, I was out of touch. Not a single one of these names or faces looked familiar to me, except...

Daniel Thorne out walking with his wife and baby daughter -

Of course I'd heard the name before, although I never saw a picture of the guy. It was his wife who caught my attention.

My jaw dropped as I stared at her.

Maddy?

Chapter Two

Ben

I had a hangover.

Not in the traditional sense of the word. I hadn't been drinking. Much. I'd certainly had more ice cream than I'd had booze. But I felt bleary and exhausted, my stomach tied in knots and a faint taste of regret and failure in the back of my mouth.

It took me a while to remember much of anything.

The wall calendar was the first reminder of why I'd run off the rails last night.

God damn it.

Daria always kept a wall calendar. God only knows why. I kept telling her to use the stupid app on her phone, and she wouldn't need a wall calendar with a Sharpie tied up next to it, because this was the *fucking future* and she was being insane. I hated the grimy string that held the thing in place, just like I hated the little valance curtain that hung above the kitchen window.

But it was still there.

I rolled over, violently punching the accent pillow

on the sofa. Sometimes I still slept on it, for old time's sake.

Certainly not because I fell asleep after watching some Lifetime movie about sadness and death and cancer.

Certainly not that.

Daria's mother was the kind of person who kept fluffy seat covers on toilets. That should have been my first clue. Nothing made of fabric belongs in the bathroom or the kitchen - the two dirtiest rooms in the house. Unless it's a floor mat or an oven mitt, I want it out of my sight.

And Daria was gone.

Every once in a while, it hit me fresh. Like it had just happened. There was no escaping these days, although they came less and less frequently with time. I just had to get through them. Weather them somehow, with the help of my good friends Ben and Jerry.

I didn't even care about her anymore. The Daria I loved as a concept was long gone, and I knew that. I was finished mourning her. It led nowhere, and accomplished nothing. Why bother? Why waste my energy? It was like loving a ghost. Except more pointless, because my concept of Daria couldn't even make pottery with me while the Righteous Brothers played in the background. She was beyond ethereal. She was completely nonexistent, in every possible iteration of every universe.

Here's a fun fact: space and time are the same thing. I know you know that already. You've heard of "the fabric of space-time" or "the space-time continuum." But have you ever thought about what it really means?

Time is just how we conceptualize our movement through space. To put it another way: you already know you can't move through space without moving through time. But did you know that you can't move through time without moving through space?

You might think you're standing still, but you're never really still. The earth is rocketing through the vast emptiness of the universe so quickly you can't even conceptualize it. It's beyond your understanding. Beyond your ability to perceive. Everything we see, everything we feel, is all based on a tiny grain of sand in the vastness of everything we know.

This should be comforting, I suppose. But it's not.

When I meet them, I always think it's going to be different. Every time, I fool myself. That was one of the reasons I lashed out at the girl at the store. I hardly remembered it - I just remembered the exhaustion, the red creeping into the corners of my vision. But the very sight of her made me angry, because of the spark of emotion inside. *Look at her. She's different.*

Like a hero in a Regency romance, I would inevitably fall for the first girl who showed a hint of spirit. Whatever that meant. These days, it hardly meant anything anymore - it was harder to tell who was truly a free spirit in an age like ours.

But I always knew.

There were women who treated me like I was rich, and women who didn't.

Not that it mattered. Not being an idiot, I understood it was inescapable. People would always consider my money when evaluating my personality. If it was down to a decision between me and another man, and I was the billionaire, he certainly wasn't going to win out. To some extent, I'd never really know what any woman thought of me.

And that was all right. It was hardly a true burden, considering where it came from. I'd been rich, and I'd been poor. Rich was better. I just wished I had landed a girlfriend before I had money. It would have made my love life a whole hell of a lot easier.

Instead, I married a woman I hardly knew. When she cheated on me with her *friend from work*, part of me was shocked, but the other part felt the crushing inevitability of this. Had been feeling it for years. We met when we were teenagers. There was no chance for us.

There would've been, if she'd tried harder.

But I was insufferable too. I knew that. As much as I knew I wasn't supposed to blame myself, I couldn't really do anything else. Daria wasn't a degenerate when she married me. I'd turned her into someone lonely and desperate. That was my gift.

I groaned, leaning back on the sofa. The girl at the store was nothing like Daria. But there was something that flared inside me nonetheless, an attraction, a desire that was immediately met with anger and disgust. How could I still let myself start to fall for a woman, when I knew how it would end?

Four years since Daria left. Almost two years since our divorce was finalized.

I was running out of time.

Work went by in a blur. I tried to pay attention, I really did, but it was nearly impossible. All I could hear was the oppressive *tick, tick, tick* of the clock in the corner of the room. Why the hell did we have a clock? Everyone knew what time it was. There were a thousand electronic devices programmed to the atomic clock, self-updating, self-adjusting for daylight saving. Never needing their stupid AA batteries replaced.

Time was my worst enemy now. I gritted my teeth through every meeting, every phone call, trying to sound normal. Probably failing.

Nobody knew my secret. Not even the partners, the biggest shareholders, my CFO - no one. I'd been too ashamed to admit it. Thinking back, I couldn't remember what possessed me to sign that settlement.

You had to prove something. You didn't want her to think...

Being at work was awful. I paced like a caged animal until five o'clock, only because I liked to set an example for my employees. If people saw me fucking off in the middle of the day, they'd resent me for holding them to a normal schedule. Most days, I didn't need to be here at all. It was about appearances.

Every time my phone buzzed, I nearly jumped out of my skin. It was exactly four months, to the dot, until she came to collect her prize. Or so she thought. We hadn't spoken in so long, but I was sure she'd contact me. Just to gloat. Just to remind me - as if I could forget.

But she didn't. And her smug silence spoke volumes.

She just knew. She was confident. She didn't need to taunt me. I was already in hell, and she didn't care one bit. She just wanted what was coming to her.

I found myself in a sports bar, dangerously close to work. Someone might recognize me here. Hell, someone could recognize me anywhere, but that was a pretty rare occurrence. They'd wonder what the hell I was doing in a place like this, but I just needed the noise. The activity, buzzing around me. It was still happy hour, and everyone was acting like it. Forgetting their troubles, drowning everything that bothered them in half-price margaritas and bottomless tortilla chips.

If any of them knew why I was here, they'd probably punch me in the throat.

Boo hoo, the billionaire might have to give up majority control of his company. What a sad story. And it's his *own damn fault*.

Cry me a river.

My eyes swept the room, wondering if I could end my troubles right here, right now. If I asked one of these women to fix my problem, would they agree? Would they slap me across the face? Would they think I was joking?

The last one, probably.

I couldn't understand why this was so hard. It had seemed simple enough, back when I signed the agreement. Just find a woman and marry her. Two years. Two years was plenty of time to fall in love.

Just not, apparently, with someone like me.

At first, I started in the circles that made the most sense. Mentally, I began auditioning all the women I knew. The ones I had regular dalliances with anyway, because what could be more convenient than that? Things might get messy, but we were all adults. We could handle ourselves.

As it turned out, it was much easier to meet a woman for the occasional spanking and rough sex than it was to try and *date* her.

My proclivities seemed to be at odds with my playboy behavior. After all, I was supposed to be into *domestic* discipline - not random discipline with strangers. But this was the closest I could get, until I found the right woman to be domestic with. And that was seeming more and more like a distant dream, every day.

I'd given up on making it happen for real. Now, all I wanted was someone I could trust to join me in the deception of a lifetime.

Daria was no idiot. This possibility had certainly occurred to her - and even if it hadn't, her lawyer would be expecting it. Now, with time so close to running out, I'd have to work very hard to convince them. All of the pieces would have to fall perfectly into place.

I had four months to find a wife.

One of these random sports bar floozies was hardly the right candidate. Not that I had a better option, at the moment. And it wasn't exactly wise to put my trust in some random stranger.

A pair of eyes burned in the back of my mind.

The memory was hazy, and I had to shake my head a few times to identify them. They burned with anger, and that brought it all rushing back. The girl at the grocery store. She was so mad at me, for some reason I couldn't quite recall.

I vaguely remembered being a little combative with her. Acting a little…dare I say it…entitled. I usually made an effort to bite my tongue, because I knew how people looked at me. I knew the kinds of assumptions people made, when they saw someone who had as much money as I did. I'd discovered a long time ago that it was difficult to hide. People always know. The smell of money follows you everywhere, no matter how you dress it down. And last night, I hadn't made an effort to act like I belonged.

No wonder she hated me. Everyone hated people like me, unless they were lucky enough to become one.

The Chase family had been on the top of the Forbes list since before the Forbes list even existed. We were practically the definition of old money. We had the kind of pedigree that hardly even mattered anymore, these days. But nonetheless, I did take some pride in it. Why the hell not? We'd kept our status for hundreds of years, surely that was worth something.

But not to women like her.

For once, someone other than my ex-wife was dominating my thoughts. It was a strange feeling - exhilarating, like taking a deep gulp of fresh air after being cooped up for a long time. Maybe that was my problem. I'd been looking for someone all this time, but my heart wasn't in it. I'd been motivated, I'd convinced myself I really did want to move on. That Daria's settlement contract was actually a blessing. It would force me to get out there, get back on the market, find somebody who could actually make me happy.

Until now, I hadn't realized how much I was lying to myself. Nobody except Daria had dominated my thoughts in a very long time.

I didn't know what it was about that girl. All she did was yell at me, clutching her ice cream in her hand like it was worth a million dollars. Maybe it was, to her. Maybe she was having just as bad of a day as I was. Maybe that was why she didn't put up with my bullshit.

I grinned to myself. Okay, so I liked that. I liked that I hadn't intimidated her. I liked that she didn't back down. All signs pointed to her being a little bit spitfire, determined, unwilling to bow to anyone's authority unless it suited her purposes.

All the same, I wondered if she fantasized about a man who was strong enough to control her. It would be her choice, but deep down inside, she'd feel compelled. She'd no longer be the master of her own desires, driven by a need she didn't fully understand, didn't want to admit. The same need that drove half the high-powered businessmen I knew into dungeons across the city, begging to be humiliated by women in leather corsets. Aching to have their power stripped away, piece by piece. Needing the release of submission.

I wasn't like them. My release was at the other end of the paddle. I admired those women, understood why they did what they did - but their company wasn't for me. I needed the opposite.

I needed somebody like that girl from the store, kneeling at my feet, begging for my punishment.

Gripping the edge of the bar counter, I shook my head. I couldn't keep thinking like that. The last thing I needed was to trade my obsession with Daria for a new obsession with some random woman I'd never see again. In a city of millions, the odds of us running into each other more than once were pretty slim.

Then again, she probably lived nearby. There weren't many other reasons why someone would shop in that particular store. It happened to be right across from my office, and I hate nothing more than going out of the way. Even if it means being able to shop somewhere that doesn't smell like old fish.

She was new in the city. She had to be. I could always tell, the ones who didn't really belong here - who'd come here on the promise of something extraordinary, the magic that was the Big Apple, only to be terribly disillusioned the minute they stepped out of the cab. She was just another one of the many millions who'd last for about six months before they packed it in, headed back for Oklahoma or Michigan or Texas.

I hated the idea of never seeing her again.

God damn it, Chase. Get a grip.

I had to stop this. The more time I spent mulling over some stranger from the grocery store, the less time I'd have to find my pretend wife.

But there was just something about that girl...

Chapter Three

Jenna

After I got home, I did a quick Google search to confirm what I'd seen. Mrs. Daniel Thorne was indeed Maddy, my college roommate, the aspiring painter who ate a lot of circus peanuts and bit her lip when she smiled. I remembered her as being very shy, especially around men - but she'd evidently come out of her shell enough to catch a billionaire's attention.

There was no doubt she'd remember me. We'd lived together for four years, after all - and we always got along just fine, even if we were never terribly close. I always tried to be her wingman, and I'd been successful a few times, but she mostly sabotaged herself. I teased her gently about her awkwardness with boys and her habit of eating terrible candy, and she told me the cigarettes I smoked recreationally would rot my teeth faster than any dollar store confection ever could. She was right, of course. I hated cigarettes. I only smoked them because it attracted the bad boys, and I was desperately stupid back then.

I toyed with my phone in my hand for a long time,

trying to decide what to do. Would she be happy to hear from me, or would she be resentful at the reminder of the old life she'd left behind?

Finally, I dug up the number to the local flagship office for Thorne Industries. Someone answered within one ring.

I cleared my throat.

"Can I leave a message for Maddy Thorne? Just tell her it's Jenn. Jenn Hadley."

"Would you like to leave a call-back number?" The assistant's voice was crisp, but professional. I hoped she wasn't just humoring me.

"Yes, please." I rattled it off, thanked her, and hung up.

It would be nice to have a friend in the city. Or at least an acquaintance. But there was no way I was hanging out with a young Lucille Bluth. If Maddy had turned into some kind of country club stereotype, I'd have to quietly back away.

And if her husband was anything like that guy I ran into in the grocery store - well.

We'd cross that bridge if we came to it.

I wasn't sure how I knew that Grocery Store Jerk was rich. I just did. He had the stink of money, *old* money, in particular - I knew it well. There weren't many people like him left. Not in this country, at least. His family probably hadn't had a whiff of hard work in many, many years.

I'd grown up surrounded by people like him. They only came during summers and holidays, but when they did, their presence was unmistakable. You could feel it, surrounding the whole town, smothering it. After the weeks spent preparing for them, we'd quietly hibernate in our own dingy homes, trying hard not to think about the seven thousand square feet of pure luxury we'd just spent a week cleaning, top to bottom. Fluffing pillows, removing dust covers, vacuuming and wiping down every square inch. When they left, we'd repeat the process in reverse, and if we were lucky there would be some cash on the nightstand.

Every year, every season, it was the same.

When I was young, I'd often asked my parents why we couldn't just live there while the tourists were away. I didn't understand why the houses had to stay empty. They'd never even know the difference. But my mother said something I never forgot:

"These people, they like to own things. Even if they're not using them, they need to know it's theirs. No one else's. They're not good at sharing. It's just the way they're brought up."

I'd believed her, without really understanding what she meant. When I got a little older, I started noticing how sleek and handsome some of the rich boys were. Not all of them were disgustingly stand-offish, and some were actually rather nice. My parents didn't bother to warn me against them - they didn't have to. I'd already learned my lesson, years ago, before I even cared about the difference between boys and girls.

Those kids and I, we'd never be the same. And it might not matter to them, or to me, but it certainly mattered to their parents. I wasn't going to get them in trouble. I wasn't going to be the one who got her heart broken, all because some boy needed to obey his father more than he needed me.

I frowned at my phone. Incoming call, unknown number - typically I'd ignore them, but on a whim, I picked up.

"Jenna?" said a voice I hadn't heard in a long, long time.

"Oh my God." I took a moment to gather my thoughts. "Maddy. I didn't think you'd call back - well, ever, to be honest."

She laughed. "Of course I would, man - how many years has it been?"

"Please don't make me answer that." I groaned, flopping back in my chair. "I've been bouncing around retail jobs since college, I really don't want to account for my time. I see you've been busy."

"Wow." She let out a little bewildered chuckle. "Yeah, I don't even know where to start. Uh, so I started working for a Fortune 500 company, married my boss, got knocked up - you know, the usual thing."

"I feel like I got sucked into a parallel universe," I admitted.

She snorted. "Imagine how *I* feel."

"Pretty damn smug, I'm guessing."

"Actually, most days I still pinch myself." I could hear her shifting in her seat, making little soothing noises to the little girl that was undoubtedly sitting in her lap. "So you're in town now, huh? For work?"

"Hopefully," I said. "Finally decided to chase that dream."

"Really? That's great!" She actually sounded enthusiastic - way more enthusiastic than I felt. "I always thought that was just drunk-talk. But I'm so happy for you. Sometimes you just have to grab life by the horns."

"I think I might've waited a few too many years," I admitted. "But hey. Nothing ventured, nothing gained, right?"

I really hoped that the existential despair didn't come through in my voice.

"Exactly," she enthused. "So, hey - you want to grab a coffee and catch up? I'm sure Daniel can take care of Laura for a couple hours this Saturday."

Weird - I would've assumed a billionaire would have full-time childcare. Maybe Maddy was just a little more hands-on than most. For someone who I never pictured having kids in the first place, her parenting style was kind of difficult to imagine.

We hashed out the details of our coffee date, and I hung up feeling slightly optimistic. Having a friend didn't exactly solve my problems, but it would make my life a little less desolate.

What the hell were you thinking, coming here?

And just like that, the doubt and fear started to creep back in.

I got to the coffee shop early, after a few more days of fruitless headshot submissions. It'd be nice to spend a little while not worrying about the future.

When Maddy walked in, I almost didn't recognize her. It was easier to notice her familiar features in a picture, but in motion, she'd changed.

The anxious, introverted girl I knew in college had all but disappeared. An expensive haircut and recent motherhood had changed her appearance slightly, but more than that, there was something indefinable - like she'd *bloomed*.

She ran up and hugged me, grinning. She smelled expensive.

"It's so great to see you again," she enthused, pulling out her chair. "And it'll be really nice to spend some time with someone who doesn't communicate exclusively by screaming and banging a sippy cup on a plastic tray." She sighed, smiling that particular smile of a new mother. "I love my daughter, more than I thought possible, but I am *losing my mind*."

"How old is she?" I tried to imagine a tiny Maddy toddling around. Back in college, I'd never pictured her having kids. She seemed pretty jaded at the whole idea of marrying and starting a family, but time always changed people.

"Almost two. She's been fully weaned for a little while now, but it's been total hell trying to find reliable help." Maddy flipped open her menu, looking at the words without really seeing them. There was exhaustion lurking behind her eyes, and I felt a pang of sympathy. Before I switched to drama in college, I'd studied early childhood development, and spent a lot of time working in the daycare for credit. No one could run you ragged like a toddler.

"It must be hard. I can't imagine."

"I'd pretty much be happy with anyone who could show up on time and keep her away from electrical outlets," Maddy admitted. "But Daniel's very picky. He's only liked one of them, so far."

"What happened to that one?" I asked.

The corner of Maddy's mouth twisted. "He liked her a little too much."

My eyebrows shot up.

"Don't get me wrong," she said, quickly. "I'm not one of *those* wives. And I trust him. But when someone gives you bad vibes, I figure it's better to be safe than sorry."

There was some of the Maddy I knew. She might deny it now, but she had a wicked jealous streak.

"Sure," I said. "I mean, if I were married to a billionaire who looked like *that*, I don't think I'd let him out of the house."

She giggled. "It's not that bad. But he can be such a flirt sometimes - he pretends like he's so awkward and he doesn't know how to talk to people, but he never seems to have a problem with women."

"Oh, I know that type." Fiddling with my straw, I gave her an appraising look. In some ways, she really hadn't changed at all. "You always did have a thing for those strangely sexy nerds."

"*Obsessive*," she said, a little dreamily. "That's my favorite trait in a man. It's annoying when you're trying to have a conversation and they can't stop thinking about something from work, but once you get their attention…"

I quirked an eyebrow at her. "Single-mindedness in the bedroom sounds like it could have its downsides."

"Oh, probably," she said, with a halfway grin. "I guess that's where the other personality traits come into play."

"Such as?"

"Well, it helps if they're not totally self-absorbed." She stirred her coffee. "I just got lucky, really. I barely knew him when we got married."

I squinted at her. "Are you *sure* you didn't get

replaced by the Pod People?"

"It was a crazy time in my life." She shrugged it off, like it was no big deal - but I couldn't shake the feeling that there was something she wasn't telling me. Back in college, she was terrible at keeping secrets. But things were different now.

Watching her, carefully, I waited to see if she'd spill more of the story. I couldn't even begin to figure out what kinds of questions to ask.

She sighed a little, staring down at her drink. "I guess...I guess there was a part of me, you know, that just figured...why not? You know? How bad could it be?" She laughed softly. "That sounds horrible, doesn't it? But I never thought I'd get married. That was never in the plan. When he told me that he..." She paused, lost in thought for a moment, seeming to recalibrate the story. "...I guess he'd noticed me for a long time. But he didn't know how to get my attention, because he was just kind of...there, you know? He was the boss. He was the person I hoped I didn't run into, because if he had something to say to me, it probably wouldn't be good news. It's hard to just chat somebody up when they're your employee, and you're kind of scary."

Now, she wore a secretive smile. Scary? After getting my fill of so-called "bad boys" in college, I couldn't imagine voluntarily dating anyone who *scared* me. Let alone marrying one.

"It was a whirlwind," she went on. "I realized I actually liked him, you know, as a human being - I felt bad that he had so much trouble connecting with people, and yeah, I know how that sounds. But it's not just his money. He's isolated. Like me. Just, always feeling like he's on the outside looking in. I felt that connection. And when he wanted to get married, I just said yes. Because, why not, you know? Why not grab life by the horns?"

Well, moving to New York and getting married were slightly different levels of commitment. But I just nodded, because I could see the light in her eyes and it made my heart ache.

That was the other thing I just couldn't get together. While my professional life floundered, my love life was even worse. I hadn't had a serious relationship...well, ever, unless you counted that one high school romance that felt like life and death at the time. None of those tattooed scoundrels in college stuck around for long enough to truly break my heart, thank goodness.

"But that's enough about me." Maddy made a dismissive gesture. "How are things going? You get any auditions?"

"One." I made a face.

"That bad, huh?" She smiled. "Well, I'm sure things will get better. I'd offer to work some connections, but Daniel seems to keep his social circles pretty strictly in the tech arena. He can't stand entertainment types. Such a snob."

Her words said one thing, but the curve of her lips, and the look in her eyes - something else entirely. She couldn't even mention his name without looking like a schoolgirl with a crush.

Damn. I never would have guessed she'd do better than me, when it came to men. Sure, I was a trainwreck, but at least I could talk to them without getting the cold sweats.

"Okay," said Maddy, leaning across the table a

little. "Now, stop me if you're not interested in part-time work at all...but didn't you study early childhood development for a while?"

I nodded. "Yeah, I almost finished my degree. Why?"

It took a second for the realization to kick in. Shit, I needed more caffeine.

"I really need some help," she said, that edge of desperation showing in her eyes again. "And in spite of what I saw you do on the trampoline at that one frat party, I actually trust you."

"That's unwise," I said, grinning. "But seriously, if you think Daniel will be okay with it..."

"Oh, he'll be fine." She nodded firmly. "You give off a good vibe. He likes no-nonsense people. And you'd still have time to audition - I'm thinking maybe three days a week? Just so I can get out of the house, get to yoga, do some gallery showings. Like the old days, before I voluntarily turned into a human incubator."

"There's the girl I remember." Laughing, I took her offered hand and shook it. "Gentleman's agreement?"

"Sure," she said. "I'll pay you the going rate for the area." Then, noticing my blank expression - "it's, you know, it's pretty generous. I think you'll be happy with it."

"I'm sure I will," I said, quickly. "I just...uh, I mean, thank you. Seriously. I didn't call to beg you for work, or anything like that."

"Oh, I know!" Her eyes widened a little. "I know you would never. I almost didn't bring it up, I didn't want you to think...but it's a great solution to both of your problems. Can you come by tonight? I'll just let Daniel know, and give him a chance to recalibrate for meeting strangers." She grinned. "Introverts, am I right?"

I laughed. "You're the biggest introvert I know."

"Yeah, yeah. So what do you think? Come have a nightcap, meet the baby? Take the grand tour?"

"Sure. It's not like I've got anything going on." I sighed. "But hey, it'll be nice to meet the man who finally got under your skin."

Maddy was smiling like the Mona Lisa. "Trust me, it was mutual."

Chapter Four

Jenna

Daniel Thorne was a presence.

There was simply no other way to describe him. Maddy answered the door, with little Laura on her hip, but I could feel the man's eyes on me as soon as I stepped over the threshold. He was observing, calculating, trying to figure out what made me tick.

I managed to get a little smile out of Laura, whose big, brown eyes fixed on me much like her father's did. She was very busy trying to understand the world around her, but she still had a little girlish giggle that was Maddy, all the way.

"Hi." Daniel had crossed the room in the blink of an eye, and he was holding out his hand for me to shake. He looked taller in person, with soft, thoughtful features that belied the stern set of his strong jaw, and the firmness of his grip. Radiating intelligence and power, he was basically the exact opposite of Grocery Store Jerk.

Well, that settled that.

His eyes crinkled at the corners when he smiled.

"It's nice to meet you," I said. "Whoever can win Maddy over is obviously an impressive person."

"I'll have to add that to my resume." His smile grew a little. "It really is my most impressive accomplishment."

"Sure," said Maddy, laughing. "Come on in, Jenna. You want something to drink? I've got, uh... well, I haven't really restocked properly since the dry spell. But I've got some Bailey's and Kahlua, and if I send John out for some vodka and almond milk we can make a drink that tastes just like one of those coffee milkshakes from Dunkin."

Daniel looked pained.

"That's fine," I said. "Really, you know, I could do with some sobriety. I should probably start my tenure in New York with a clear head."

"Psssh. Overrated." Maddy waved her hand dismissively. "But yeah, maybe you should get used to Laura while you're sober. Make sure she doesn't drive you insane. That's one strict rule I have for my nannies: no drinking on the job."

"I'll try to keep that mind," I said, dryly. "You were in on the dry spell, too?"

I addressed this question to Daniel, who nodded. "I mean, aside from the scotch in my desk."

He was joking, although it took me a second to realize it. "Right. Like any self-respecting businessman."

I took Laura, sitting down on the sofa and plopping her down on my lap. So far, she seemed like a quiet, serious child. But I knew she'd only need a little trigger to turn into a complete nightmare - and that was my job to figure out.

Taking care of kids was actually a challenge that I enjoyed. Learning to connect and communicate with them, and work together towards a common goal. It was all about compromise and respect - not that different from dealing with adults, except that children were often a lot more reasonable.

Laura blinked rapidly, showing off her father's long lashes. She had his hair, too - his was carefully cut and styled, but it wasn't hard to see how it would fall in loose brown curls just like hers, if he grew it out. But I saw Maddy in her face - the shape of her nose, her chin, more feminine and delicate.

She'd grow up to be absolutely stunning. That was no surprise, really, although I knew Maddy never thought much of her own girl-next-door beauty. Now that she'd gained confidence, she truly looked like someone who belonged at Daniel Thorne's side.

As for the man himself - he wasn't exactly my type, but I could see why Maddy melted. He really was the ultimate fulfillment of all those quiet, thoughtful types she always liked. I still couldn't figure out how he'd convinced her to marry and start a family so quickly, but I supposed it was just one of life's unpredictables.

I tried to imagine what type of guy would be able to light my fire like that, and I came up blank.

Marriage and children wasn't something I objected to, exactly - though it was hard to imagine trusting someone that much. But I just couldn't quite picture my ideal man. Now that the foul-mouthed, cigarette-smoking assholes had lost their appeal, I didn't really know what I was after.

How about a clean, suit-wearing asshole with a

taste for Ben and Jerry's?

Oh, hell. Why was I thinking about Grocery Store Jerk now? I was actually having fun, chatting with the Thornes while I chased Laura across the floor. But I kept going back to our encounter - the flash in his eyes, the way his body hunched over like he was carrying the weight of the world on his shoulders.

Not that that was an excuse. But I was kind of curious. What drove a man to the store for ice cream, and to harass innocent bystanders? Maybe a bad breakup. Probably deserved, but still.

"Can you start on Wednesday?" Maddy was asking me. Oh, hell. I shook myself back to reality.

"Absolutely," I said, smiling. Laura was stacking blocks very carefully, arranged by color.

"We should have one last hurrah before you start your job, though, right?" Maddy glanced at her husband. "You think your dad can handle Laura tomorrow? We can take Jenna out for some drinks that aren't made from Irish cream liqueur, and you'll get a chance to glower in the corner like Mr. Darcy and remember how much you hate everyone." She smiled affectionately. "It's a win-win."

"As long as I can admire your fine eyes." He glanced at me. "Assuming the guest of honor actually wants to go out."

"Sure," I said, chuckling. "You're right, Maddy, sobriety's overrated."

"Good." Maddy got to her feet, nodding like she'd just settled a serious problem. "Bet we can find you a man with some money - I mean, if you're interested."

"Well, I wouldn't say no." I glanced at Laura, like she was going to judge me for being a gold-digger. "But

I'm not exactly on the prowl or anything."

Maddy grinned. "Billionaires can be very persuasive."

I had no idea.

We were at the kind of club that I thought only existed in movies. There wasn't even a line outside; people knew not to bother. Daniel Thorne and company breezed right in, although I was pretty sure the doorman eyed my dress a little askance. It wasn't exactly shabby, but it certainly wasn't billionaire apparel.

Inside, it was clean and quiet, with just the thump-thump of some unidentifiable music keeping a subtle rhythm under our feet. It wasn't quite so dark that I couldn't see people's faces, but I didn't recognize anyone - yet. I had a feeling this was the kind of place that designers and movie stars came when they wanted to be left alone.

"Nice to see you again, Mr. Thorne," said the bartender, as we walked past. "It's been a while."

Daniel waved, but didn't pause on the way to our table.

As we glided past a throng of people, I caught a slightly familiar scent. I couldn't quite place it, but it made my heartbeat quicken a little.

"Daniel?" said a voice from behind me. I whirled around, and my jaw almost hit the floor.

It was *him*.

Grocery Store Jerk, in the flesh. I almost didn't recognize him, at first - but there was no mistaking his face, those blue-green eyes, that air of superiority and the built-in smug in his smile. He looked considerably more put-together this time. His hair was carefully combed, and he'd lost some of the haggard look he had during our last encounter.

He stared at me, and I stared at him. His smile faded, just slightly.

"Ben," Daniel was saying. I glanced back at him - his smile looked frozen. "Fancy meeting you here."

Sidling past me, this *Ben* went in for a vigorous handshake, and I tried to gauge Daniel's reactions. He seemed about as happy as I was to see the guy, which was definitely interesting.

"So this must be your lovely wife." Ben took Maddy's hand and patted it delicately, flashing her a dazzling smile. Oh, sure - a billionaire's wife got the full dose of charm, turned up to eleven. "It's so nice to meet you, finally."

He glanced at Daniel, then briefly at me.

"This is my friend Jenna," Maddy cut in. "She's just moved to the city for acting."

Oh, for fuck's sake. Ben turned to me, shaking my hand with a smile that was clearly stifling a laugh. "It's so nice to meet you, Jenna. Break a leg."

"Right back at you," I gritted, through the fakest smile I'd ever displayed in my life.

"So great to see you all here," Ben said, turning back to the group. "I have to admit, I've been a little bit of a hermit lately."

"Me too," said Daniel, his manner still heavily guarded, cautious. "But I'm sure you've seen me pop up in the news from time to time."

Ben nodded. "I've gotta say, I don't envy *that*."

His phrasing implied there was something about Daniel he *did* envy. I allowed myself a moment to study the two men - both were handsome, though in very different ways. Daniel was slightly taller, or maybe he just carried himself differently. More seriously. Ben's smiles came easier, but I wondered if he meant them.

There were clearly a lot of unspoken secrets between them. If I was judging the awkward silence correctly, it seemed like Daniel was afraid that Ben would spill something he didn't want to be general knowledge.

Interesting.

Judging by Maddy's reactions, she was just as much in the dark as I was.

Interesting.

"Ben, why don't you have a seat at our table?" Maddy suggested, finally. "You two can catch up."

Daniel shot her a look, but she just smiled innocently. As we herded over to the table, I began to ponder the mathematical impossibility of working out a way where I *wouldn't* have to sit next to Ben.

I ended up sandwiched between him and Maddy, and I was pretty sure there was no logical reason why he needed to be sitting so close to me. Once again, I noticed the hint of cologne that clung to him - something sharp and sweet, enticing, in a way that made me resent him even more.

"So, what have you been up to lately?" Daniel asked, still frowning slightly. Ben shrugged.

"You know. The usual. You've obviously been busy, though." He glanced meaningfully at Maddy. "I heard you've got a daughter now - congratulations."

A bit of Daniel's icy demeanor melted, and I saw the proud father shining through. "Thank you," he said. "It's certainly been an adventure."

"I never took you for a family man." Ben beckoned one of the servers in our direction. "Drinks are on me, everybody - what'll you have?"

"I'm good, thanks," I said, resting my elbows on the table. The last thing I wanted to do was accept a free drink from this guy.

"Oh, come on," said Maddy, nudging my arm lightly. "I'm not saying we have to do another Phi Beta Kappa drink-off, but don't be a wet blanket. I've only just started drinking again, I'll be easy to beat."

Her eyes sparkled. She didn't often roll out the persuasive charm, but when she did, she was almost impossible to resist. I wondered if *that* was how you landed a billionaire.

"Maybe just one," I conceded. "Vodka cranberry, please. But I'll open my own tab."

"No, no, no," Ben was saying, as I tried not to look at him. "I insist, Jenna. Please."

I shook my head. "Thank you, but no thank you, Ben." Shooting him a slight smile, I lowered my voice slightly. "You don't owe me anything."

Maddy was watching me, puzzled. Before she had a chance to voice a question, I turned the tables back.

"So," I said, glancing at the power couple. "You guys met at work, huh? That's crazy."

A little bit of color rose in Maddy's cheeks. "Yeah, I was doing the graphic design thing, and I guess..." She cleared her throat, glancing at Daniel, as if waiting for some kind of cue.

"I hired her for her talent," he said, with a halfway grin. "At least, that's what the file says."

"Gets funnier every time," Maddy muttered, rolling her eyes.

"She actually did beat out ten other candidates with her portfolio," said Daniel, glancing at her. "H.R. would never let me actually see anyone until they were past the final interview stages. I think they assumed I was *shallow*, for some reason."

Ben snickered. "I can't imagine why."

Daniel gave him a warning look.

"I got very lucky," said Maddy. "In more ways than one."

Ben smiled indulgently. "I guess it was only a matter of time before someone broke through that shell."

"It'll happen to you, too," said Daniel, with a slight raise of his eyebrows. "Just wait. And I'll be here to make fun of you for a week straight - so brace yourself."

"First of all, I'm not making fun," said Ben. "And secondly - I don't have a shell. I'm an open book. Just haven't met the right person yet."

"Right," said Daniel, quietly, with a private smile.

The drinks arrived, and I gratefully turned my attention to the vodka while the conversation went on around me. I could feel Ben's eyes watching me intently from time to time, but I wasn't going to give him the satisfaction.

As we talked and laughed, I began to learn a little more about Grocery Store Jerk Ben. He owned a company called Chase Pharmaceuticals, which I looked up on my phone to find out that they basically owned the IP to every drug I'd ever heard of. I found myself giggling at his jokes - which I hated, but as my glass began to empty, I forgot exactly why.

That wasn't accurate. I remembered our

encounter, but I forgot why I *cared* so much.

Before long, we needed another round, and our server seemed to have disappeared. Daniel finally declared he was going to the bar himself to put in the order, but he disappeared into the throng and didn't return before we'd all finished sipping the last of our melted ice from the bottom of our drinks.

"What the *hell* is taking him so long?" Maddy twisted her head around, trying to catch sight of Daniel in the crowd of people at the bar. "Okay, hang on. I'd better go rescue him."

Damn it.

I sat there, quietly, waiting for Ben to say something. The tension in the air was palpable, and I knew he wanted to, but perhaps wasn't quite sure where to start.

"Jenna," he said, finally.

I looked at him, reluctantly. I didn't want to talk about it. I wanted to forget about it, to forget about him, but I was starting to wonder if that was entirely possible.

"I wanted to apologize for my behavior at the store," he said. "I didn't want to bring it up in front of everyone, because quite frankly, it's embarrassing."

"I'll say." Raising an eyebrow at him, I took another sip of my drink. "Just so you know, I'm not expecting one. I don't really think it's necessary. You can say you're sorry all day long, but you've already showed your true colors."

Ben shook his head vigorously. "No. That's not me. You have to understand - I hadn't slept in two days. I barely even remember what I was doing. Just that it seemed really, really crucial to have some

Karamel Sutra before I collapsed in bed."

"You probably shouldn't have been out in public," I pointed out, feeling slightly mollified - but not wanting to show it. This could easily all be a lie.

"I *absolutely* shouldn't have been out in public," he agreed. "Unfortunately, I live alone with two cats and neither one of them saw fit to stop me."

I snorted into my drink. "Are you painting yourself as a lonely spinster so I'll feel sorry for you?"

He nodded. "Absolutely. And it's working, isn't it?"

"A little," I admitted, acknowledging his grin with a tiny smile of my own.

I was acutely aware that I had to be careful. People like him were nothing but trouble. All he had to do was turn on the charm for a few minutes, and he could get away with murder. Hopefully not literally. But either way, I couldn't stand his type.

Don't get sucked in, don't get sucked in…do not look him in the eyes…

"So, I'm sorry," he said. "I hope you'll give me a second chance to make a first impression."

I sighed. What did he want me to say? It wasn't like he thoughtlessly cut me off in traffic - he'd been deliberately rude to me in two separate encounters, and delirium or no delirium, I felt like I'd be foolish to ignore it.

"Let me make it up to you," he said, quietly, chipping away at my resolve. "At least I should be able to buy you a drink - right?"

"Fine," I said. "One drink. But for the record, I have a job."

He blinked.

"You said, 'some of us have jobs to get to.' Or something like that."

"Oh." He chuckled slightly. "I don't remember what the hell I said. I'm surprised I even used real words."

He was downplaying it so well. I almost believed him, I *wanted* to believe him, but there was something about the way he talked that made me think he wasn't being completely sincere.

Right on cue, Maddy came back, Daniel and our drinks in tow.

"They're very sorry about the slowness of the table service," she informed us. "They had three servers call in tonight. Apparently some big author is doing a book signing downtown and they didn't want to miss it."

"You ever hear of Natalie McBride?" Daniel scowled slightly. "*I* haven't, but apparently she's worth missing a night of work over."

"Oh, yeah," I said, taking my drink. "Those books. *His Secretary* or whatever. She's supposed to be the next E.L. James. Always been a hermit, so it's kind of a big deal that she's doing public appearances now."

Ben was staring at me.

"What?" I shrugged. "Some people read gossip about reality TV stars, I read gossip about authors. At least they're contributing something to society."

"That's debatable," Daniel grumbled.

"Oh, come on." Ben was smiling. "Think of all the marriages those kind of books have saved. Every couple years, somebody needs to come along and remind everyone that women actually *do* enjoy sex."

"*Nobody* can have sex like they do in those books."

Daniel was irritated; Maddy was amused.

"How do *you* know?" She grinned, picking up her tiny straw and gesturing with it. "*What have you been reading?*"

"Nothing," Daniel insisted. "Because books are a dying medium, as anyone with half a brain cell should be able to see."

Maddy let out a guffaw, glancing at me. "He thinks he can read the future in tea leaves, because he's got Eduardo Saverin on his speed-dial. This is the man I married, ladies and gentlemen."

"I don't have Wardo on my speed dial." Daniel was smiling as he glanced at his wife. "I think that was just another one of your fantasies."

"Damn it," she said, offering him a little smile in return. For a moment, they were completely absorbed in each other, sharing some private joke.

"Nice guy," Ben put in, looking over at me. "Oddly enough, he's a lot more cut than he was in the movie. Maybe I should put in our next drink orders now, you think? We might get them some time this century."

I shook my head. "I think I'm done for the night. Thanks, though."

"Really?" He glanced down at his phone. "It's not even ten o'clock."

"Yeah, but I have to get up early in the morning. Gotta get on schedule for my new job."

"Oh, congratulations." He threw back the rest of his vodka. "What set are you on?"

Damn it. I'd already forgotten that Maddy told him I wanted to be an actor. At the moment, I really didn't want to even *think* about my ambitions, let alone discuss my utter failures with a stranger.

"Oh, some commercial," I lied quickly. "I don't even remember. I think maybe it was a broom, or a new kind of frozen lasagne or some shit. Ads are way too abstract these days, right? It's not like I'm going to know from the copy."

The center of his forehead creased a bit, and I could tell I was laying it on too thick. But I couldn't just admit that I was going to be the Thornes' nanny. Not when Maddy had let my plans spill - I didn't blame her. She had no reason to think I was hiding it.

And I wasn't - I just didn't need to give Ben another opportunity to feel superior.

Not that he was showing any signs of that tonight. At least, I didn't think so. It was hard to tell, with him. Everything about him seemed so disingenuous. Like he was putting on an act. A certain bravado, just saying what he thought I wanted to hear - or what he thought everyone else at the table wanted to hear. He was like a politician. Always pivoting, adjusting, calculating just the right thing to say at the right time. I didn't like it. I wanted him to act like a real person, for just five minutes.

Then again - maybe our encounter in the store was him acting like a real person. Maybe the only modes he had were "politician" and "asshole." He certainly wouldn't be the only one.

"Well, I hope it goes well," he said. "That was lucky, to land something so fast - when did you get into town?"

I shrugged. "God, I don't know, a couple weeks ago? I've lost all track of time, I swear. Things have just been so crazy." I let out what I hoped was a lighthearted laugh. "I didn't start completely from scratch, though. I've got this cousin in the area."

What was wrong with me? Why was I laying down the lies, so thick and fast? Did I really think I could get away with this?

Well, yeah. It's just for tonight. Not like you're going to see this guy again. Even if he's a friend, your job is to take care of their baby when they go out. This'll probably be the last time you all hang out together.

The night started to wind down. After we vacated our table, Maddy and I headed to the restroom, and I ended up escaping the crowds around the door before she did. As I rounded the corner of the hallway, I heard Ben's voice, a little elevated - enough to make me stop in my tracks and prick up my ears.

"...and I don't see why you won't at least give it a chance." Ben sounded exasperated.

"I don't *do* that anymore." Daniel was glancing over his shoulder - not in my direction, thankfully, but I ducked back behind the wall anyway. "At least, not with strangers."

"They're not strangers," Ben insisted. "Don't you miss them? At least come for the social hour. Bring Maddy. I'm assuming she's aware of your tastes."

There was a moment of silence, where I swore I could almost hear Daniel gritting his teeth. "She's not used to...all that. It's private. Between us. Not a fucking social hour."

"I don't know what you're so afraid of." Ben

sounded exasperated. I pretended to fiddle with my phone as people pushed past me, as if anyone cared what I was doing. "Give me one good reason why you don't want to come back, and I won't go straight to your wife and tell her what a pussy you are."

I expected to hear the sound of a fist connecting with a jaw. Instead, Daniel's voice was dangerously quiet. I had to strain to hear him. "If you so much as breathe one word of this to her, I'll have you killed. I know the head of Blackwater, and he owes me a favor."

Ben laughed. "Fine. Have it your way. But if she starts asking me pointed questions, I can't promise I'm going to be discreet."

"And I can't promise you'll live through the night," said Daniel, calmly. "Seems like a fair trade to me."

What the hell were they talking about? What tastes?

My head was swimming. I felt like I should tell Maddy about what I'd heard, but why? Ben seemed to think she already knew, even though she didn't know about him. Daniel must have some kind of wildness in his past that he'd tamed, but hadn't completely left behind.

When Maddy finally emerged, we all gathered by the door to say our goodbyes. After Daniel and Maddy disappeared into their town car, I turned to Ben.

"You come here often?" he asked, with a cheeky grin.

"I'm sure I'll see you again sometime," I said, brightly.

He frowned. "It's a big city."

"Yeah, well, apparently we buy our ice cream in

the same place."

And with that, I turned and walked away, feeling triumphant.

Chapter Five

Jenna

It wasn't long before I saw him again.

My first day with Laura was a delight. Mostly. She threw a fit when I wouldn't let her eat the corner of the rug, but we mostly subsisted in a state of quiet mutual respect. Despite her serious expressions, she was still a kid who cried at the drop of a hat and giggled when I read her favorite storybook with different voices for all the characters.

After lunch, she seemed a little stir-crazy. She kept pressing her nose against the window longingly, and I decided I could use some fresh air too.

"What do you think, want to head out to the park?" I asked her.

Her face lit up. "*YES*," she declared, running over to me.

She was toddling around pretty well, but not quite ready to handle city sidewalks, so I trundled her into the stroller and headed outside. The air was crisp and clear, and we both basked in the sun as we made our way through the crowds.

While I walked, I tried to understand what it was about this city that everyone found so magical. Sure, it was alive - people everywhere, to the point where you could practically hear a heartbeat. But it was exhausting, too. I almost felt like I could hear the buzzing of everyone's thoughts, their worries, the hum of nervous energy that kept everyone swarming around in all directions like so many ants.

The park was a little more peaceful. I walked slowly, enjoying the dappled sunlight through the leaves and letting the noise of the city fade into the distance.

"Fancy meeting you here."

I stopped in my tracks, turning towards the sound. Ben was ambling towards me, hands in his pockets, wearing an easy smile.

"You didn't mention the little bundle of joy." He grinned at me, and I couldn't tell if he was messing with me or not. She was Daniel's spitting image, but he might not have looked close enough to notice.

"Just doing a favor for our mutual friends," I said, forcing a polite smile.

"Hey, now that you mention, I do see the resemblance." He crouched down by the stroller, catching Laura's attention with a little wave. "How's it going, Ms. Thorne?"

She glanced at him, and then quickly back down at her own hands, squirming.

"She can be a little shy around strangers," I said, as Ben stood back up.

"Well, that's no surprise." He shrugged. "But I'm sure she'll do absolutely fine for herself."

Laughing, I gently rolled the stroller back and

forth a little. "That's a fair bet. It helps to have billionaire parents."

"*Successful* parents," Ben said. "Money can't buy ambition."

"Right. I'm sure you were voted most likely to succeed among all the other trust fund babies."

He looked a little surprised. "What makes you think I'm a trust fund baby?"

Rolling my eyes, I didn't bother answering. Let him think that it rolled off of him in waves - he didn't need to know I was basically the Horse Whisperer when it came to sniffing out the idle rich.

Ben folded his arms across his chest, his eyes glinting a little as he gave me an assessing look. Out in the sunlight, I could see the little gold flecks in his irises. "You haven't really forgiven me for the ice cream incident, have you?"

I shrugged. "Doesn't really matter, does it?"

"It matters to me." He had his hands buried in his pockets, shoulders hunched slightly - a posture that was intended to make him seem less threatening. Or maybe it wasn't calculated.

Hell, this was a billionaire businessman I was talking about. What were the odds of that?

I wasn't sure why he cared so much. Unless, of course, it was just the sheer irritation of some plebe seeing him for who he really was. I couldn't imagine that was uncommon for him, but maybe his charisma managed to win people over in spite of the current cultural disdain towards men like him.

"Why don't you like me, Jenna?" He looked like he actually wanted to know. For crying out loud.

I just laughed a little, finding it difficult to believe

that I was really having this conversation. "What's your investment in this? Now that I'm the Thornes' babysitter, I doubt we'll be spending much time together socially. You can just move on with your life and conveniently forget that I ever existed."

"But I don't want to forget," he said, sounding remarkably sincere.

Oh my God, was he *hitting* on me?

I frowned at him. Was it possible? Did he actually think, after the way we met...

His eyes look so much more green today. It must be the tie. They're like emeralds.

I shook my head suddenly, to dissipate the unwelcome inner monologue.

"Trust me, you'll be better off," I said. He'd conveniently glossed over my accidental admission of my real job. Maybe he didn't notice, or maybe he just didn't care.

"Babysitter?" he repeated, as if he'd heard my thoughts. "Thought you were working on a commercial."

"Believe it or not, most commercials aren't ten-month shoots," I told him. "I'm just picking up a few jobs on the side until something more permanent comes up."

He just watched me thoughtfully for a moment, and I kept expecting him to say something else. But after a few minutes, he said:

"Well, I'll let you get on with your day."

Disappearing into the distance, his head was slightly bowed, like he was lost in thought.

Maddy had gone to spend some time in her studio

space after her daytime errands, so Daniel was the first one home that evening. I'd put Laura to bed, and was flipping through the sad offerings on T.V. before deciding to settle for the *Storage Wars: Texas* marathon.

I half-expected him to forget I was there, but he offered me a slight smile when he walked in the door, his shoulders slightly tight, like he was bracing himself for a stranger in his house.

"Welcome back," I said.

"How is she?" he asked, setting down his briefcase and walking into the kitchen.

"She's sound asleep," I said. "Couldn't get her to go down for her nap today, so she's out like a light."

"Excellent," said Daniel. "I hope she didn't give you too much trouble."

"Oh, no." I waved my hand dismissively. "I never argue about naptime. She was a perfect angel for everything else, but she decided she wasn't tired, so she just played with her blocks quietly for a while. I think some kids just naturally have enough steam to get through the whole day without stopping."

"No problem with that, as long as *you* have enough steam." He smiled. "I don't mind admitting that she runs me ragged, but I guess that's normal. Can I have John give you a ride home?"

I shook my head. Much as I appreciated the job, that seemed like a step too far. "My bus comes in another forty minutes or so. It's fine, I'm in no particular hurry."

"Well please, feel free to wait here - you want something to drink, now you've been relieved of your duties?" He pulled two beers out of the fridge, and I shrugged.

"Sure. Might as well." Immediately, I wondered if I could somehow direct the conversation to Ben. I figured there was no chance in hell that Daniel would spill anything I really wanted to know, but I might be able to at least get a sense of what kind of person he really was, underneath that carefree veneer.

Daniel popped the cap on both beers, and I sat down across from him at the kitchen island, taking a sip before I spoke. "So, how long have you known Ben?"

His eyebrows went up, a fraction of an inch. I'd expected him to snap shut like a clam, but he seemed much more interested in my question than in protecting his own secrets.

"Close to a decade now," he said. "We fell out of touch." He cleared his throat and rotated his beer bottle thoughtfully. "It's funny - you know, he asked me about you."

I shouldn't have been surprised, given his behavior at the park. Clearly I had his interest in some form, whether I wanted to or not. But my heartbeat quickened, my throat drying slightly as I tried to process this information. "Really? What'd he want to know?"

Daniel shrugged. "The usual. Where'd you come from, what are you up to, do you have a boyfriend..."

I let out a bewildered little laugh. "What'd you tell him?"

He shrugged. "Said I didn't know. But I have his number, if you want to clarify a few things."

Picking at the label of my beer, I tried to make sense of all the conflicting thoughts swirling around in my head. "Don't tell him I asked, okay? He doesn't need any encouragement."

That earned a grin. "All right, but can I tell him you'll call?"

I sighed. "I don't know, I mean...I'm still trying to settle in. It's so quick."

He nodded, obviously sensing that I wasn't telling the whole story. But I was mindful that whatever I said would probably get back to Ben, and I really didn't want him feeling like he had to prove himself to me.

After a moment of silence, he spoke again. "He didn't leave a very good impression on you, did he?"

I shook my head. "We've run into each other a few times," I admitted. "I don't know quite what to make of him."

Smiling down at his drink, Daniel finally answered me, after a few moments of thought. "Well, I can't tell you what to make of him. I'm still trying to figure that out myself. But I know he's one of the most loyal and trustworthy people I've ever met. He gives you that vibe of someone who'd sell out his own grandmother - but I've never had any cause to regret trusting him."

With what?

I was dying to ask, but I know he wouldn't tell me.

"So the whole insincere thing...it's just an act?" I was suspicious, and understandably so, I thought. "Why would you want people to think that about you?"

Daniel shrugged. "I couldn't tell you, but I do know he's been going through a bit of a messy divorce. He doesn't talk about it much. The fact that he's shown interest in somebody else means he's seeing the light at the end of the tunnel. He's got walls, but they might not be up forever."

The conversation drifted to other topics after that, but on my bus ride home, Daniel's words kept echoing in my head.

I didn't want to be anyone's light at the end of the tunnel. Least of all, a man like Ben. So why was it, when I closed my eyes, all I could see was green flecked with gold?

Chapter Six

Ben

Chemistry.

It's purely elemental, something that just happens. You can't fake it, can't force it, can't do anything except stand back and watch. Put the right ingredients together - or the wrong ones, depending on your point of view - and the results can be explosive.

A lot of people who met me just assumed I was some idiot rich kid who knew nothing about the way my father's company worked. They were wrong - not that they really cared. There were certain things people just wanted to believe about me, and knowing the truth didn't support that. I studied long and hard to understand exactly what it was we were doing. I threw myself into the science of pharmaceuticals, determined to understand the reports from the labs, to actually speak to the doctors and the researchers in their own language. On more than one occasion, I was told it wasn't necessary. But that never mattered to me.

I earned the spot at the head of the boardroom table, even though I didn't have to.

It's true, it was coming to me either way. So I guess I'll never know the meaning of truly striving for something, that fear of losing - which is what people really mean when they talk about "hard work." It's not supposed to be a choice.

In all fairness, I didn't ask to have a choice. And when it came down to it, I wanted to do the best I could.

Chemistry was always my favorite. Put just the right amount of two things together, and watch the results. They were always predictable, and you couldn't fake a reaction.

That was the thing about me and Jenna. She might deny it, but deep down inside, she knew. We had chemistry. I could feel it sizzle and pop between us, and I knew it wasn't just me.

Chemistry's never one-sided. To put it in purely scientific terms, it takes two to tango.

She liked me. She liked me where it mattered - at the base of her brain, in the chemicals deep inside, the things she couldn't change or control. No matter how much she disliked me or distrusted me, up at the frontal lobes where we try to think and reason and understand things, she couldn't change that one simple fact.

She liked my smell. She liked feeling the heat from my body, close to hers. She liked the sound of my voice and eventually, I'd prove that she liked the taste of my mouth.

It was purely elemental. Pure chemistry.

I'd never be able to convince Daria and her bloodsucking lawyer of anything at all - not without real chemistry. She'd know the difference. She'd dig and she'd dig, she'd hire every private detective in the city until she had proof of my deception. She'd take it to the judge and I'd be well and truly fucked.

But it didn't matter if the marriage wasn't real, so long as the *chemistry* was. Daria would feel it - somewhere down deep in the core of that twisted lump of coal that she called a heart.

The more I thought about it, the more sense it made. If I wanted to keep my company, I had to convince Jenna to marry me.

The "how" was a problem I'd deal with later on.

Chapter Seven

Jenna

Just as I'd expected, I ran into him at the grocery store again. I wondered if this was his usual haunt, or if he'd come here on purpose to try and wheedle me into a date. I almost wished Daniel had never told me about his interest; it was more fun when I didn't know that Ben was just trying to get into my pants.

He was frowning at the shelf of peanut butter and jelly, and I could have easily walked past. I didn't even need any peanut butter. But for some reason, I stopped, sidling up next to him and snickering a little when he didn't even notice someone was nearby.

"You all right, Chase?" I nudged him with my elbow, because I felt like it would annoy him. "You seem a little out of sorts."

He snorted, glancing at me. "What, are we in boarding school? Call me *Mr.* Chase if you insist on going by last names."

"I absolutely will not." I laughed, leaning on my cart. "Seriously, what's going on? Can't figure out another meaningless formula tweak to renew your patents? Don't worry, I'm sure you'll find a way to keep raking in those millions."

He looked like he was gritting his teeth. Had I actually found a way to get to him? That was a miracle - and pretty fun, to boot.

"If you have to know," he said, "I'm trying to figure out how to convince somebody to do something for me."

I raised my eyebrow at him. "I have a hard time believing that's a struggle for you."

"Normally, it wouldn't be. But I have a feeling this one's going to be a tough nut to crack." He was giving me a look that I didn't quite understand, but it sent a little shiver up the back of my neck.

"Well, I don't mean to be crass, but a blank check is almost always well-received."

"That's the thing." He was still looking at me in that peculiar way, and I wanted to know why. "I have a feeling this isn't just going to be a question of money."

"So you have to rely solely on your powers of persuasion, with someone who doesn't want to be persuaded? That's a tough one." I ran my tongue along my lips to moisten them slightly, trying not to let my eyes wander down his partially-unbuttoned shirt. He wore expensive tailored clothes like they annoyed him, hanging off of his body as if he weren't meant to be wearing anything at all.

Get a grip, Jenna.

I spoke again: "Why not just be yourself?"

He smirked. "Do you really think that's good advice for me?"

"No, not at all." Our eyes were meeting, we were both smiling, and *damn* if it didn't feel good. The same warmth in my chest that I would've felt looking at someone I actually liked. "I just wanted to see if you'd admit it."

"Tell me, Jenna, are you this brutally honest with everybody, or do I just get the special treatment?" Now *he* was leaning on my cart, pushing his body closer into my personal space. Trying to regain dominance over the situation. He wasn't comfortable any other way, and that irked me.

"A little bit of Column A, a little bit of Column B," I told him. "You just really bring out the bitch in me, what can I say?"

"Aw, I think that's the nicest thing a woman's ever said to me." He reached into my cart, plucking out a six-pack of ramen noodles. "You know, these are cheaper if you buy them individually. They're just trying to screw you over. Worse than Big Pharma, even." He winked, and dropped the package back in my cart.

"How the *hell* do you even know that?" I demanded, feeling more annoyed than I probably should have.

"What, a billionaire's not allowed to check price tags?" He shoved his hands in his pockets, stepping away from me. "Or you mean the thing about Big Pharma? Because everybody knows they're out to get us. That's just common sense. Chase Industries' logo is eerily similar to the Federal Reserve - you really think that's a coincidence?"

I was giggling helplessly. "It's amazing how many conspiracies are predicated on logo designs, right? You'd think some of these sinister organizations would have just hired a new graphic designer at some point to cover their tracks."

"Hey, I'll bring that up at the next board meeting. Thanks." He gave me the *thanks, babe* finger-gun gesture, clicked his tongue, and walked away. I was left shaking my head, and wondering why the hell I couldn't stop smiling.

The more I thought about it, the more I wondered if I was just being too harsh on Ben. I'd made all kinds of assumptions about him based on his wealth, his job, and one bad encounter in the grocery store. Obviously, he had a sense of humor about himself and his job, and he was more down-to-earth than I'd imagined.

Maybe I should give him a chance. After all, I was alone in a new city, and so far most of my social interaction was dominated by a two-year-old girl. Some variety would be nice. I doubted it would be anything long-term, but where was the harm in a few dates?

After a lot of nervous pacing and practice conversations in my barren apartment, I made my decision. The next time we serendipitously just "ran into" each other, I'd mention what Daniel said to me. It seemed like a natural enough opening, and if I managed to sound low-key and flirty enough about it, maybe it wouldn't be terribly awkward.

I tested out a few options - *so, your friend told me you were asking about me.* No, that sounded weird, like I was trying to suppress Daniel's identity in order to protect the innocent. *So, Daniel mentioned you were asking about me.* That was better - maybe. Or should I be more direct? *To answer your question, no, I don't have a boyfriend.*

Should I say *yet*? Or was that coming on too strong?

This didn't used to be so hard. When did Maddy and I switch roles? At what point did I lose my ability to speak to the opposite sex?

I was just out of practice, that was all. I needed to get back in the saddle. And this was the perfect opportunity.

Once I'd made the decision, I threw myself back into my search for acting work. There were way, way too many auditions that were completely out of my wheelhouse, but I was able to find a few that might fit, and a few more open calls I could visit to stay busy for the rest of the week. Whenever I wasn't taking care of Laura, I'd be pounding the pavement.

The first open call was about as depressing as they come.

I ended up sitting in a tiny plastic chair, wedged between two other hopefuls that I could only pray were auditioning for different roles. One of them was a dead ringer for CCH Pounder, so much so that I did a double-take - and the other was a man in his thirties, dressed in a shirt and tie with his sleeves rolled up to reveal full sleeve tattoos that would inspire hatred in the soul of any makeup artist.

He sighed audibly, and I considered telling him that he should roll his sleeves down and cover up the body art. But then I realized I had no idea what the hell he was going for - maybe he was supposed to play a motorcycle gang leader or something.

After a whole afternoon of waiting, I never even

got my chance to read. They had a much bigger turnout than they anticipated, and more than half of us were turned away, filtering out into the streets in a cloud of rejection.

I'd actually been ready, too. Primed for a performance. I'd spent so much time and energy getting myself pumped for the experience, and now I was completely deflated. It was a terrible feeling, and I wandered towards my bus stop with my stomach in knots.

The grocery store, and its array of comforting junk food, beckoned. I hesitated and weighed my options. I could always go to the overpriced convenience store that was closer to home, where I probably wouldn't run into Ben. But they didn't have half of what I wanted. If I shopped here, there was a chance I'd run into him, even though I hadn't seen him in almost a week. I was in no mood to try and seduce a billionaire.

I decided to take the risk. Halfway through the cookie and cracker aisle, I was starting to feel safe.

Then, I heard his voice.

"Day off?" He sidled in front of me to grab a package of Ritz.

"Yes," I said. "Well, no. I went to an audition." I made an effort to arrange my face into something neutral.

"How'd it go?" He seemed genuinely interested - or at least, genuinely interested in *me*. So that was something. I tried very, very hard to remember my resolution from earlier, but with the taste of sour disappointment in my mouth, it was hard to remember his positive qualities.

I shrugged. "Pretty good. I'll hear back from them. But, you know, I don't hold my breath. Once it's over, I just try to move on and forget about it."

Lie upon lie upon lie. I wondered if it showed; Ben might be a lot of things, but he certainly wasn't an idiot.

"That's the healthiest way to go about it, for sure," he said, with a smile. "I'm just stepping away between conference calls to restock my secret snack drawer."

I snickered in spite of myself. "High-powered executives have secret snack drawers? How cute, they think they're people."

"What, CEOs can't stress-eat?" He tucked the box under his arm. "I know, I know, nothing compares to the exquisite pain of striving to be an actor. I won't even attempt to refute that. But sometimes, I need a box full of high-sodium travesty to get through the day. I just hope nobody spots me, because according to my recent profile in Forbes, I only eat non-GMO, gluten conscious sustainably sourced whole foods. Also, activated almonds."

"What the hell are *activated almonds*?" I'd almost forgotten why I was in a bad mood.

"I don't even know!" He threw up his hands. "I'm pretty sure my assistant fills those things out for me, maybe I forgot her birthday or something and that's her idea of revenge. Either that, or she actually thought it sounded good." He frowned. "Or, I got into my *other* secret drawer and hit the booze a little too hard before I answered that email. They're equally likely, I think."

"You need professional help," I informed him. "And for the record, no, I'm not one of those douches who thinks acting is the hardest job in the world. I'm sure you lose a lot of sleep while you're trying to relax in your Scrooge McDuck swimming pool filled with money."

It wasn't my best work, and it came out sounding a lot more bitter than I meant. Damn it. His face changed slightly, an expression I couldn't quite identify darting across his face. But he recovered quickly. "Nah, I gave up on that. Too many paper cuts.

"Well, this is awkward."

It was the only thing I could think to say. I cursed inwardly, hating myself for being so...well, *awkward*, when it came to Ben.

We were face to face, having just nearly collided with each other in the cold and flu aisle. Of course, I couldn't be buying cough drops or Carmex or anything like that.

Of course I was buying hemorrhoid cream.

Ben, meanwhile, was buying condoms. Of course he was.

"It's not awkward," he said, lightly. "I mean, maybe *now* it is, because you pointed it out."

I had the ridiculous urge to shove the box behind my back, but it was too late. I thought I'd be safe here. It was almost four full blocks away from our usual impromptu meeting spot, and I'd never seen him up this far.

I glared at him. He was so fucking carefree, so *la dee da*, and he didn't even understand what I was going through. I'd been up half the night staring at my head shots, trying to figure out what was wrong, and I finally realized that I looked like a crone compared to the fresh-faced ingenue who stared back at me with those doe eyes. In real life, I looked like I hadn't slept in a week. The stress was wearing down on me. I had to do something about it.

Years ago, I had a drama teacher who told us about the old trick - hemorrhoid cream gets rid of those pesky under-eye bags. Supposedly. I'd never had the occasion to test it, but now, I was starting to get desperate. I just wanted to look in the mirror and see some recognizable version of myself, not a Life Alert spokesperson.

Now was probably not the time to flirt with Ben. I was beginning to seriously question why I'd ever thought it was a good idea.

"Fine, it's not awkward," I said. "I live down the street, you work down the street, of course we shop at the same drugstore. Why does it need to be awkward?"

"You live up the street?" he repeated.

"Yeah, at Regal Arms." I made a vague gesture, unsure why the hell I was telling him where I lived. But it was too late to take it back now. "Got a date tonight?"

He glanced down at the box in his hand. "I just like to be prepared," he said. "Just so you know, I'm not going to sink to your level."

His voice was gently teasing, but I could hear a real level of stress behind it - couldn't be about *me*, of course, I wasn't that conceited. Either he was nervous about his date, or - and this seemed more likely, judging by the size of the box - the date was actually a foregone conclusion, and at least partially intended as a remedy for whatever stress he was otherwise going through.

I rolled my eyes. "Very noble of you."

"Fine." He gestured at what I was holding. "You know that doesn't work anymore, right? Not for the eyes. They changed the formula. Get witch hazel instead. They sell it next to all the homeopathic crap, but it actually works."

My face was burning. On the one hand, at least he knew why I was really buying it. On the other hand, was it *that* obvious?

"How the hell do you know this stuff?" I demanded, finally giving in to my stupid instinct to shove the box behind my back.

"I work a lot of late nights. 'Haggard' isn't a good look for meeting with the partners. My assistant taught me all the tricks." He half-smiled. "I mean, uh, not that *you* look tired or anything. I was just making a guess."

"Thanks," I muttered, willing my face to cool down. My tone said *I hope you choke on your activated almonds*, which I realized was horribly unfair. He hadn't actually done anything wrong, except commit the cardinal sin of implying that I didn't look perfect at all times. God, how much of a bitch was this whole situation turning me into?

"Seriously, you look great," he said, raising his eyebrows slightly. "Please don't continue attempting to murder me with your eyes."

"I'm sorry." I sighed. "It's just...this whole dog-eat-dog world out there. I've only got one nerve left, and it's frayed to hell."

His smile turned sympathetic. "I hear that. Well, maybe you could take a break for now. Work on something else. Acting will always be there, right? Give yourself a chance to get settled somewhere new.

Just living here for the first time is enough to drive a lot of people crazy, and you're piling a lot of stress on top of that."

"I've got nothing else *to* work on," I insisted.

"But what's your plan to fall back on? I mean, you're not going to act forever - right?"

He said it so matter-of-factly that I wondered if he even knew what he was implying.

"Sorry?" I frowned, pretending like I hadn't understood. Giving him a chance to dig himself out.

"I mean...come on." He let out a little laugh. "It's not supposed to be a long-term career, is it? What are you planning on doing in a couple decades? When, uh..."

My lips thinned as I stared at him.

"When, uh, what exactly?" I said, finally, as he worked his jaw open and closed a few times. "When I get too old?"

"That's not me saying that," he cut in, quickly. "That's just...that's how things *work*, isn't it?"

He was seriously committing to this. Okay. Fine.

"Oh yeah, sure, I forgot." I laughed a little. "Maggie Smith, Helen Mirren, Judi Dench, you never heard a damn thing from them, once they were out of their thirties. Such a shame. Wasted talent."

"Come on, Jenna." He was raising his voice slightly. "Why do you always have to take things in the worst possible way? I'm just trying to say that maybe you'd do better if you weren't hanging all of your hopes on one thing that's probably not going to work out in the long term. That's just realistic. It's not because you're not talented, I'm sure you are, it's not because you're a woman, it's just...things don't always work out. You should get used to that idea, because trust me, that's one thing not even a Scrooge McDuck pool of money can change."

There was a real bitterness in his voice, and it had nothing to do with me. But I was the one on the receiving end up of his cold glare, and I'd had enough.

I stared down at the box he had clutched in his hand. "Magnum XL? Are you sure that's really necessary?"

"Oh, ouch." He clutched his hand to his chest, smirking.

I gritted my teeth into a smile. "What? I'm just being *realistic*. Statistically, do you know how many men actually *need* extra-large condoms?"

"Never researched it." He folded his arms across his chest. "If you don't believe me, I have several references you could call."

Rolling my eyes, I turned away from him. But I had to give the guy credit for not offering to *show* me A lesser man would have.

God damn it, stop trying to make excuses for him.

"Give me your number, and I'll prove it for real," he called after me as I walked away.

Well, so much for that.

I spent the next two weeks *not* thinking about Ben.

I didn't think about him while I made Laura her lunch, helped her arrange her Little People by profession and hairstyle, and prevented her from attempting to cut off her Barbie doll's hair with a nail file she'd somehow found wedged behind the bathroom vanity. After I told Maddy and Daniel about that, they spent about twenty minutes blaming each other for letting it fall down there and forgetting about it, and I just quietly assured them it was completely normal, that I'd never seen any structure built by human hands that was one hundred percent child-proof, and quietly slipped out the door.

The next day, judging by the tense way Maddy was holding her shoulders, they still hadn't quite resolved the issue.

I didn't think about Ben.

I didn't think about Ben while I submitted to a few more calls, attending more open auditions, showing up earlier and earlier, hoping for a chance to read. Somehow, it never worked out. Somehow, no matter how hard I tried, I never managed to get there early enough. I was always on time for my nanny shifts, but when it came to auditions, I found myself hitting the snooze button over and over.

It was nothing more than self-sabotage. I knew that. The crushing sense of doubt made it so difficult to put the effort in. Best case scenario, if I arrived early enough, all I got was a *chance*.

A chance wasn't enough. I was sick of chances. I wanted something for real, I wanted all of the time I'd spent hoping and dreaming to actually mean something. But I knew that was silly. Conceited. Ridiculously so. Everyone else hoped and dreamed too. That wasn't enough. I had to work for it.

I just wished there was some guarantee. It wouldn't take much. Just an assurance that I wasn't chasing a mythical pot of gold at the end of a rainbow.

Ben might have the stress of a billion-dollar company bearing down on him, but he didn't know what it was like.

Don't think about Ben.

I finally crawled out of my own ass long enough to actually secure myself an audition, and get up when my alarm went off. The first time. More or less.

I had a good feeling about this one, in spite of all evidence to the contrary. It was posted on classified ads instead of the big industry-only site that I'd subscribed to, but there were plenty of indie filmmakers doing totally legitimate projects without going through the normal channels. I just had to have a little faith - that was all.

Besides, the supposedly official, fully-vetted industry-only site was so archaic and slow that it made me want to cry. I always expected to see a dancing skeleton in the corner of the page. It didn't exactly inspire confidence.

The audition was much further uptown than I was used to going, and I walked past the building three times before I found the creepy little cement staircase leading down to the unmarked door.

A quiet little warning bell went off in the back of my head, but all of this was consistent with a smaller, indie project.

I had to stop self-sabotaging.

Inside, everything was eerily quiet, except for a faint mechanical buzz from somewhere underneath the floor. A few other girls were sitting in the waiting room in mismatched folding chairs, at least a few of them looking incredibly strung-out, and the others on the verge of it.

Turn around. Walk away.

The stubborn determination rose up in the back of my mind. *Do you want this, or don't you? Stick it out. No more excuses.*

One by one, we were called into a back room by a guy in a dark hoodie with lank, dirty-gray hair. I stayed frozen in my seat. I waited.

Minutes passed, and I decided I'd had enough.

This wasn't it. This wasn't the time to get motivated, not in a sleazy basement office for a movie that might or might not even exist. I stood up and started to head for the front door.

Right on cue, the door in the back of the room popped open again.

"Hey, where are you headed?"

Clearing my throat, I turned around to face him. "Uh…I just, um, I have to go. Sorry. I hope you find somebody."

He shook his head, gesturing me towards him. "Nah, come on. We can get you in right now."

There was a noise of protest from the other girl who was still waiting, but he silenced her with a look.

"Uh…okay. I guess." I followed him into the back room. None of the other girls left in tears, so whatever was going on, it couldn't be too bad.

The back room was even more depressing than the front, somehow. Before I knew it, I was alone with this guy, and the single flickering fluorescent light didn't do much to make this place not feel like a repurposed closet. He handed me a few pages; they said UNTITLED PROJECT.

He grinned at me, and I was actually surprised that he wasn't missing any teeth.

"Welcome, hon," he said. "You're gonna be reading the part of Nicole, okay?"

There was a creeping sensation under my skin.

Walk away. Just walk away.

But I couldn't afford to. Not if I wanted to keep chasing this dream.

It was really, really sweet of Maddy to offer me a job. But Laura would be in school before I knew it, and I couldn't rely on her mother doing me favors for the rest of my life. I wasn't going to give up, no matter how creeped-out I felt right now, with this guy's eyes glued on me, and not another soul in the room.

Looking down at the script, I couldn't suppress the thought that this was one of the worst things I'd ever read. It didn't even seem like it could be real - it was *that* bad.

"Um..." I said, glancing up at him. "Should I just go ahead and start?"

He nodded.

It was incredibly difficult to inject any passion into the words, but I tried. The guy hardly seemed to be listening. His eyes were all over me, but I had a feeling I could have just started reciting the alphabet.

There was a sinking sensation in my chest. I'd just walked into some kind of scam, most likely, and I wasn't even smart enough to sniff it out beforehand. How the hell was I going to make a career out of this?

"Wow," he said, when I was finished. "Great job. Listen, we had a lot of auditions for this project, and you're one of the best. But there's no guarantees, of course. Thing is, we're always producing something new, and even if we're not, I've got friends who are always looking for talent. If you want, I can make sure to pass your info along. Get you listed where all the big companies really go looking for their talent."

I cleared my throat. "I'm already on Cast Me."

Making a noise of derision, he stood up, his chair scraping against the floor. "Cast Me? Psshh. Nobody looks at that crap. I've got a line on all the best people. Lots of them are looking for girls just like you. I can hook you up - give you a nice discount, even." He grinned. "And for no extra charge, I'll make sure you get on *all* the lists. Including the extra exclusive ones for the really ambitious girls. Those projects are in high demand, but if you know somebody, you can get in. If you ever decide you want to make some real money, it's a useful thing to fall back on. Real classy productions only. No fetish stuff."

Oh, for fuck's sake.

I jumped to my feet. "Does this ever work?" I snarled at him, as I rushed for the door. Thankfully, he didn't try to stop me.

"Sometimes." He shrugged as I walked away. "If you ever change your mind, just call the number in the ad."

By the time I got on my bus back home, I couldn't believe I had any teeth left to grind.

I'd walked right into a fake audition, some kind of porno scam, and I was actually dumb enough to see it through past the first warning signs. What the hell was wrong with me?

I didn't belong here. I never would.

A sort of dark panic was clawing at the inside of my chest. I did my best to ignore it, hugging my knees in close and just staring at nothing. It took several minutes of unusual commotion in the bus, and noticing we'd been stopped for entirely too long, for me to look up and try to figure out what the hell was going on.

"I don't know," the driver was saying, sounding incredibly exasperated. "It's just blocked off. All they're telling me on the radio is the whole neighborhood's shut down."

Whatever. I was only a few blocks away from home. I pushed past the irate passengers and hurried down to the street, stopping in my tracks when I ran up against a sidewalk blockade.

"Sorry, ma'am," said the cop standing watch. "This whole area's closed for an emergency gas repair. They had to evacuate. It's not safe to be around, for at least another six or seven hours."

"Six or seven hours?" I felt like screaming, but it came out in a sort of a numb murmur. "But I live here..."

"What's your cross street?"

I told him.

"Sorry," he said again, shaking his head. "You're right in the middle of it. You might want to see if there's a friend you can stay with, or get a hotel. There's no telling how long this will really go on."

He said that to me confidentially, like that was some kind of fucking help. I took a few steps back and tried to reorient myself. What the hell was I going to do? All I wanted was to go home and take a long, hot shower and try to forget about my own stupidity. Now, I couldn't even go home.

I weighed my options. Maddy hadn't been kidding about my pay being competitive, but I still didn't exactly want to spend my money on New York hotel rates. Of course, if I called her, she'd immediately tell me to come stay in their guest room. But I'd seen how they were orbiting each other since the Great Nail File Argument. I didn't really want to be in the middle of that.

Besides, she'd done enough for me already. I was sick of being helpless and relying on my rich friend for everything.

Six or seven hours. If I was lucky. Well, this was supposed to be the city that never slept, right? Maybe I could just hop between coffee shops and bars until the street re-opened. Enough caffeine and alcohol, and I'd forget all about my ill-fated "audition." Maybe I'd even find a place to spend the night after all.

I smiled wickedly to myself. No, I wasn't exactly ready for a one-night stand. That had never been my style. Hell, though, it sure would be nice to do something to shake loose all those persistent thoughts of Ben that I definitely was *not* having.

"…what do you mean, *nobody*?"

For a second, I actually thought I was hallucinating. My brain must be playing tricks on me, because I definitely did *not* just hear that voice coming from a few feet away.

"I'm sorry, Sir." The cop was sounding more and more exhausted. "I mean *nobody* gets through."

"Do you know who I am?"

I turned around, slowly, like the ill-fated heroine in a horror movie.

"Sir, unless you're an emergency worker or a city employee with the proper ventilation equipment, I don't care who you are. I can't let you through." The cop glanced at me, like *can you believe this guy?*

And no. No, I couldn't.

"What could possibly be so important up in this lowly end of town, Mr. Chase?" I asked the back of his head.

He whirled around, his face twitching almost imperceptibly. "Well, well. What an unexpected pleasure." Folding his arms across his chest, he stepped closer to me, his quest to get past the barrier forgotten. "Once again, you've got that talent for running into me when I'm at my absolute worst."

"Well, you are in my neighborhood." I made a vague gesture. "More or less. Except I can't go home."

"Shit." He glanced at the barriers, then back at me, with a ghost of a smile. "Well, that's pretty terrible. Worse than my day."

"You have no idea. Trust me." I sighed. "I don't even have the energy to hassle you. I just want to go home and collapse, and that's the one thing I can't do."

"Did you call the Thornes? I'm sure they'd be happy to have you."

I shook my head. "They're fighting. Besides, I'd rather not, you know? They've done enough for me already."

Ben cocked his head to the side, slightly, and I tried not to stare. The ever-shifting color of his eyes was stormy blue today, like a choppy, unpredictable ocean. "Would you accept a favor from someone that you don't owe anything to? Except maybe an apology for implying that he has an average-sized penis?"

In the background, the cop coughed audibly and shifted his weight from one foot to the other.

"Depends," I said. "What is it?"

I should have been running for the hills, but I was

just exhausted and off-balance enough to hear him out. Whatever it was, this was a bad idea. We didn't mix. We were like oil and water, and I wasn't even sure whose fault it was anymore. I just knew that my feelings for him were in stark opposition to the way we actually interacted, and the more time I spent with him, the more I wanted...

I didn't even know what I wanted. And that was part of the problem. As much as I hated his attitude, I loved the give-no-fucks attitude that lurked behind it.

"Crash at my place," he said. "It's not far. At least you can have a drink, and make fun of all my rich-person furniture." He winked. "If you play your cards right, I'll let you swim around in my Scrooge McDuck pool."

"Oh, man." I let out a long sigh, looking him up and down. He was still dressed from the office, with a deep purple tie that was probably bringing out that stormy blue in his eyes. I wondered if his suit was custom made, or just bespoke. I wondered if he had his coffee beans shipped in overnight from Colombia on a special plane. He was joking about the money pool, but I just couldn't wrap my head around this guy's day-to-day life.

And in spite of everything, he was still trying to work...some kind of angle with me. I couldn't quite figure out what. He seemed just as frustrated by me as I was by him. Maybe he liked that sort of thing. Maybe he was a masochist.

No, that didn't seem right.

"Is that a yes?" He tilted his elbow towards me, like we were in a Victorian love story. "Come on, Ms. Hadley. Admit it, you're curious if I have a robot butler."

"I am," I admitted, giving up the fight and following him. But I wasn't going to take his elbow. "I'm also curious why you're being nice to me."

He shrugged, giving up on the overly-chivalrous gesture and shoving his hands in his pockets, with all the laissez-faire of a man who doesn't care about ruining the lines of a five thousand dollar suit. "Why the hell not?"

"You gave up awfully easy on whatever your errand was in my neighborhood," I said, thoughtfully. "Right after I showed up. It kinda makes me wonder."

Ben grinned at me. He was squinting a little in the sunlight, and my eyes wouldn't stop drifting to his mouth. "You got me," he said. "I was feeling a little bit conceited, so I decided, hey - what the hell, I'll stop by and see Jenna. She'll knock me down a few pegs."

"I'll be more than happy to provide that service for you, any time you need," I told him. "But I don't really believe you."

"That's very wise, Ms. Hadley," he said, pausing for just a moment before he darted into an intersection against the light. Cursing under my breath, I followed him, even as an approaching cabbie leaned on his horn. Ben flipped him off casually, and grabbed my wrist to pull me onto the sidewalk, and to safety. "A very wise decision, indeed."

Chapter Eight

Ben

Things weren't going quite how I planned, and for once, that was a good thing.

The thing about Jenna was that she was unpredictable. She'd show up out of the blue, her hazel eyes assessing, penetrating, wanting, and *hating* - not necessarily in that order. If I had a talent for photography, I'd want to capture a close-up of those eyes. They looked like a NASA picture of a nebula that exploded many millions of years ago, the sight of it only reaching us just now. Something ancient and terrible and breathtakingly beautiful.

I had been going to see her, although I wasn't about to reveal that now. After the way our last conversation ended, it would seem weird. It was much better that we'd meet by chance like this, and I could play the role of the rescuer after her terrible, horrible no good, very bad day.

I'd much rather have the conversation about my little marriage problem on my own turf. Yeah, this was going to be much better.

It had to go well, otherwise, I was completely fucked.

"We're here," I announced, taking the stairs two at a time up to the front door of my brownstone. Jenna lifted her eyebrows a little.

"What?" I asked, pressing my thumb to the pad and punching in the code to unlock the door. "Not what you expected?"

She shrugged a little. "Where I come from, the idle rich have much bigger houses than this. But I guess that's one of the hazards of living in the city."

I just laughed. She hadn't seen the inside yet.

Stepping inside, she caught her breath. I'd hired only the best to deck this place out, and I was very happy with the results. Even in the middle of New York, it still had the feel of an elegant mansion isolated on a hill.

It was always fun to watch the realization dawn on someone's face - I didn't just have a place in this building, this building *was* my place.

"You own this?" she asked, her hand resting on the glossy banister at the foot of the spiral staircase.

I nodded. "The whole block. But this is the only place I live in."

With a bewildered little laugh, she walked past the staircase and around the corner to poke her head into the library. "This is *huge*."

It was the smallest room I had, but I didn't bother mentioning that.

"You want a drink?" I asked her. "Something to eat? Whatever - just name it. Make yourself at home."

She walked into the library and sat down on the leather love seat, pulling off her elegant stiletto heels.

Her eyes never left me for long. "I know you brought me here for a reason, Mr. Chase, so spit it out. What is it? Do you need me to sign Daniel's birthday card?"

Well, if she was going to play it like that.

"Now that you mention it, there's something I could stand to discuss with you," I said, settling into the armchair opposite her. "Are you sure you don't want something to drink?"

"I'm sure," she said. "Whatever you're about to say, I want to hear it with a clear head."

Damn it. She could read me much better than I was strictly comfortable with.

I began to speak.

"Ten years ago, I was married." I could see her doing the math in her head. "Yeah, yeah, before you ask - I was too young and it was stupid. We both were."

She raised her eyebrows slightly. "I wasn't going to say anything."

"Okay, sure." I smirked. "But the ugly details don't matter. It was great, until it wasn't, and her cutthroat lawyer came up with the most diabolical settlement of all time. I was lovesick, so I accepted it. I didn't think she was serious. The whole thing was like wading through a nightmare. I didn't even think it was enforceable. I don't know what I thought, but I knew I was lucky that she wasn't going after alimony or spousal support, so I signed it."

Jenna's forehead had that adorable little wrinkle in the center, and I knew that meant she was about to say something that would infuriate the hell out of me. "*You* didn't have a lawyer?"

I gritted my teeth.

"Okay," she said, after a moment's silence. "I get it. We all make mistakes. I'm not here to sit in judgment of the way you handled your divorce." She cleared her throat lightly. "Actually, I'm not sure why I'm here."

Right. I still hadn't gotten to the juicy part.

"This does *not* leave this room," I warned her. "You understand?"

She nodded innocently.

"I'm serious," I said. "You don't tell anybody. Not Maddy, not Daniel, not your mom, not your priest."

She snickered. "Do I strike you as somebody who goes to confession?"

"Hell, I don't know your life." Shrugging, I stood up to pace the floor. I couldn't get this out if I had to look her in the face. "I agreed to give her fifty-one percent stake in my company, within two years of the divorce being finalized."

Jenna stared.

"Unless," I said, turning on my heel to begin the epic journey to the other side of the room. "*Unless* I got married, and *stayed* married, for a total of two years. That clock begins on the day the license is filed. If the marriage ended at any point after the original two-year time period, bam. Agreement over. Fifty-one percent to the Wicked Witch of the West."

Snorting, she leaned back in her chair. "Right. I'm sure you were blameless in the whole thing."

I didn't dignify that with a response. "It's been one year, and eight months," I said. "I have this bad habit of procrastinating."

Jenna raised her eyebrow, laughing softly. "Did you even *try*?"

"I figured it would just happen, you know?" I shrugged. "Take care of itself. Well, that didn't work out. Now I'm thinking I need to find another solution."

I eyed her, trying to gauge her reaction. But it was impossible to tell if she was following my logic.

"Or," she said, smirking, with her arms folded across her chest, "you could just admit defeat and give the woman what she deserves. She outsmarted you. And by the sounds of it, it wasn't even that hard. Just accept it."

Was she *serious*?

"*Fifty-one percent*, Jenna," I said, as calmly as I could manage. "I know this isn't really your area of expertise, being a drama major, but if you've ever caught a rerun of *Shark Tank* you'll know that means -"

"A majority share," she said, calmly, cutting me off. "That must really sting, my condolences."

How the hell was I going to make this woman understand what Chase Industries meant to me? She'd never been responsible for anything more important than a toaster oven. I couldn't believe Daniel trusted her with his *baby*.

"Well, as a drama major, I clearly don't understand how contracts work," she said, with a very thin-lipped smile. "But I'm pretty sure, legally speaking, you're what they call *completely screwed*."

I raked my hands through my hair, staring at the wall. I couldn't look at her face for one second longer. Such a smug look, on such an effortlessly sexy and infuriating woman - I could put my fist through the wall.

Or, kiss her so hard that she forgot how to be a smartass. That was always another option. It also sounded like it was a little less likely to end in broken bones.

Probably.

What the hell was I doing? *Focus, Chase.*

"It's not about the money," I said, finally, cringing at the sound of the words.

She wasn't even trying to stifle her laughter anymore. "Of course it's not," she said. I heard the sound of her gathering her things and standing up - no, no, *no*, things was going much worse than I'd anticipated.

"I'm not really sure why you're telling me all this," she was saying. "But unless you're about to offer me a million dollars in exchange for pretending to be your wife…"

It was a joke, but as soon as she said it, all the blood drained from my face. I couldn't help it.

"Mr. Chase," she said, taking a step towards me, her voice soft and tainted with disbelief. "Are you offering to *pay* me to *marry* you?"

Reflexively, I shook my head.

Her eyes narrowed.

"Okay," I said, raising my hands in a gesture of surrender. "Maybe."

"Oh, my God," she laughed. "This is…this is too good. Are you…this is a joke, right? You're pranking me. Please, let's not drag this out any further."

She was heading for the door. Suppressing the urge to jump up and block her way out, which I figured would look pretty bad, I just said: "Where are you going to go?"

She sighed. "I don't know. Somewhere crazy people aren't making me bizarre offers that sound like the setup to an Andie McDowell movie."

"It's not like it's for a green card," I said, spreading my hands open in a vague gesture. I hoped it would read as *come on, what the big deal?* "I'm not asking you to lie to the government. I'm not asking you to commit fraud."

"Actually, I think you are." She wasn't sitting back down yet, but at least she was standing still. "Assuming your settlement was legally binding, if I were to do this with you - if anyone were to do this with you, that's like lying to the courts. Implicitly."

I didn't actually know the law from a hole in the ground, but she didn't know that. "Let me guess - you picked up all of your legal knowledge from *Judge Judy*."

Smirking, she made her way back to the love seat. "Maybe so, but I know the difference between a lie and the truth. And what you're asking me to do - what if your ex-wife challenges it in court? You'll be asking me to commit perjury."

"She won't," I said, with considerably more confidence than I felt. "If it's mildly convincing, she's not going to bother. Trust me. She knows I can outlast her in court, and I'm not going to give up."

Leaning forward in her seat, she looked at me searchingly. "How do you plan on explaining you just happen to be getting married right before the deadline?"

Ah ha. I smiled, leaning back in my seat. I'd actually put some thought into this, and I was rather proud of it. "So, this one requires fudging the truth a little bit. But Daniel's...you know, he's techy, and he's got a bunch of those types who will do his bidding. We'll create a false history of correspondence between us, going back a year or two. Daria and I met online, so that'll be a very believable origin story for us. If I make it seem as though I've been really interested in you for a long time, and we've been slowly moving along in the progression of our relationship, it makes sense that I'd eventually tell you about my dilemma and of course you'd agree to help me. But I waited as long as I could, because I didn't want to scare you off - I didn't want to put pressure on you. I didn't want to ruin what we had."

She was processing all of this, but she didn't immediately laugh it off. I took that as a positive sign.

"So, I only just moved here a couple weeks ago, and we're already talking about marriage?" She hugged her arms close to her torso. "Do you usually move that fast?"

"Like I said - I'm going to create a history. You can get to know somebody pretty well over a long-distance relationship."

Jenna raised an eyebrow. "Evidently not well enough."

Sighing, I massaged my temples. "I lived with Daria for years before I had any idea who she really was. The way we met didn't matter. People who want to hide can always hide, even when you're looking them right in the face."

The irony wasn't lost on me. I was asking for an absurd amount of trust from her, and there was no getting around that.

She was wavering on the edge of a decision. I could tell. Before I could stop myself, I said:

"Do you really want to be a nanny for the rest of your life?"

There was a moment of heavy silence.

"I'm not a nanny," she said, her mouth twisting. "I told you, I was just helping out that day."

"Daniel told me he hired you." I steepled my fingers together, staring at the Newton's cradle on my desk. "I'm not really sure why you bothered to hide it."

"Because. You, and everybody else in the known world, thinks it's stupid to try and be an actor. You all think I'm going to fail, and you can't wait to give me well-meaning advice about it." Bitterness tinged her voice. "I don't need to give anybody more ammunition. Most people work on the side while they're trying to get started with acting. But if I do it, suddenly it's a sign that I need to just *give up*."

I could feel the tide of fear and insecurity behind her fierce defensiveness. There was no reasoning with her - not when she already thought I didn't believe in her.

"Think about it a different way," I said. "Wouldn't this be the performance of a lifetime?"

She let out a soft, humorless laugh. "Sure. But what difference would it make? Nobody except you and me will know."

If I was right, this would eventually sink in. Her own self-doubt would assure that she eventually accepted my offer. She needed to prove her abilities to herself, much more than she needed to prove them to anyone else.

"I'm not asking you for an answer today," I said. "Just think about it. If you have any questions, ask. In the meantime, we can talk about something else. Or nothing. You can go watch TV if you want, and pretend I'm not even here. I just thought it was high time for me to be honest with you." I lifted my hands in a supplicating gesture. "And whatever you say, whatever you decide, you're welcome to stay here until your street opens back up."

She bit on her lower lip. "How long have you been planning to ask me about this?"

"Not long." It wasn't exactly a lie. "You just seem sensible and level-headed, and I think Daria would believe I might fall for somebody like you."

She bit down harder. I'd said it very casually, almost thoughtlessly, but it had the desired impact. No matter how she felt about me, that was flattering.

Finally, she released her now-swollen lip with a little *pop*. "Did you really think that would work?" she asked, with a sardonic smile.

"What?" I said, innocently. "It's true. Come on, Jenna - give me a little credit. Shallow flattery obviously isn't going to work on someone like you."

She laughed, rolling her eyes as she stood up. "You are something else. If I ask where your bathroom is, will you be able to answer me without calculating the best possible wording for the flattery of the human female?"

Why did I think it would be a good idea to marry her, again?

"Down the hall, second door on the right."

As she left the room, I remembered.

No, not because of *that*. Well - not entirely because of that, at any rate.

It was the way I felt whenever she walked away angry at me. Like something was wrong in the world, and I had to fix it.

Chase, you are in deep trouble.

❊ ❊ ❊

When she found me a little while later, I was in the kitchen, fighting a silent battle with myself. I heard her walk up, and noticed her standing in the doorway without actually seeing her there.

"A million dollars? That's lunch money to you, Mr. Chase. You're going to have to do better than that."

I was *going* to offer her two million, but she'd managed to stomp all over my very well-scripted and impressive offer. I was even going to go down on one knee - in an ironic way, of course. I'd never actually marry this woman. One of us would end up dead before the honeymoon was over.

"You drive a hard bargain," I told her. "Two million. But that's my final offer."

She laughed. "How much did you have to drink while I was gone?"

"Nothing," I told her. "I'm as serious as a fucking graveyard."

"I don't think that's a saying." She looked at me, searchingly. "Are you really...I mean, *why me*? And more importantly, did you think this through? It's a terrible idea. I'm not even sure I buy your story. Who willingly signs away a majority share of their business on that kind of condition?"

"A very stupid man," I said. "But I think that's been well established, at this point."

Her face softened slightly. To my utter astonishment, she drifted to one of the stools and sat down. "You still love her, don't you?"

My mouth twisted. "Not even remotely. I promise."

"I don't believe you," she said, softly. "You mean there's not a place, in the corner of your mind, where you're still together? Where you can't just write off? You can't pretend it never happened?"

For the first time since Daria left, I felt that peculiar sharp pain in my chest.

"No," I said, sharply. Too quickly. "I'm done with her."

"That's not what I asked." She cocked her head. "There's what you decide about somebody, and there's the way you *feel* about them."

"Thank you, Dr. Jung." I was walking away from her, without consciously meaning to. I was heading for the fridge, seeking the comfort I'd forsaken long ago. There was nothing but half a box of muesli and some almond milk. Ever since I'd been single, I'd completely lost the ability to control my eating habits. My only option was to buy nothing but whole-grain cereals and vegan milk substitutes - otherwise, I'd be filming my own special for TLC.

"That doesn't even make sense," she pointed out. "Did you ever study psychology?"

"No." I stared at the muesli like it had personally betrayed me. "Do you want to order a pizza?"

There was a moment of silence.

"What?" she asked, barely stifling a chuckle.

"Nothing." I turned around to face her. "If you don't want to, then, fine. I meant what I said. There's no pressure."

"I mean, never say never." Jenna grinned. "I could always go for some pizza."

"I'm not talking about the pizza." With a quiet noise of frustration, I raked my fingers through my hair. "The pizza is off the table. The other offer stands, at least until you stab me in the throat."

"I would never," she said, with a sparkle in her eyes. "You're not worth it."

Well then.

"But I don't know why you're writing off the pizza. I think this conversation would go a lot better over some cheese and pepperoni."

The memory came back in a rush. Daria and I had our first date in a hotel, watching Mystery Science Theater and eating thin crust Domino's with cheese and pepperoni.

I was a different person back then. Everything felt so important, every moment filled with the kind of overwhelming passion that most people only ever read about. We were smugly absorbed in our delirious love, and anyone who told us we should think about gently, gently applying the brakes - well, they just didn't understand.

To put it plainly, we moved too fast.

I wasn't going to make that mistake again. No matter how much Jenna made me wonder - made me want to know how much of a smartass she'd be, once she was crawling across my kitchen floor in nothing but a frilly apron - I wasn't going to rush into anything again.

Sex just confused everything. Sure, when I'd met Daria, I was nineteen - I liked to think I'd matured considerably since then. Certainly, my brain had. I wasn't sure about other parts of my anatomy.

And that was why I had to stay far away from Jenna. Well - unless she agreed to be my wife. But even then, I'd be careful.

You're being an idiot, is what you're being. You really think you'll be able to resist her, once she's living with you?

Doesn't matter. She'll *resist* me.

I liked to tell myself that, but there was absolutely no denying the way she looked at me. Beneath all the exasperation and frustration, there was always that undercurrent - a certain look in her eyes, or a curve to her smile, betraying how much she just wanted to peel off my suits and find out if I really looked as good as the expertly-tailored fabric implied.

Jenna was still staring at me, with something like pity on her face. And I absolutely could not abide that.

"If you don't want to do it, fine," I said, making a dismissive gesture as I turned back to the fridge. "I'll find someone else."

The thought of *finding someone else* brought on that rising tide of panic, the one that welled up in my throat, threatening to drown me. How? Where? It had to be someone I could trust, someone I knew I could live with...

Jenna didn't really fit either of those stipulations, but for some reason, the idea of *her* as my fake bride was soothing. Maybe because I knew I could count on her honesty. Maybe because, as an aspiring actor, she was motivated.

And maybe because I wanted to torture myself.

"Wait." She was chewing on her lip, thoughtfully. "A million five. And I still get to live my life. I'll fulfill my obligations in public, of course, but you're not going to control what I do in my time off - as long as it doesn't undermine the show we're putting on."

I stared at her, my mind racing. "Are you bargaining with me?"

"Yes," she said, archly. "So, go on - what, exactly, would you need me to do? What's it going to take to convince your ex-wife and her lawyer that we're really an item?"

Clearing my throat, I turned back to face her. "Well, there's the obvious. We'll need to be seen together, and frequently. You'll be visiting my office at lunch, and coming to meet me after work - the way any disgustingly love-struck couple would do. You'll come with me to every charity dinner, every fundraiser night. I'll pay for everything, of course, your clothes, whatever you need...that goes without saying."

"I should certainly hope so." She crossed her arms, a gesture of hers I'd grown to hate. And not just because it covered up some of her charming assets. "And that's it?"

I didn't know what she was driving at. "More or less, yes."

"What about..." she uncrossed and re-crossed her legs, delicately. "Public displays of affection?"

"Oh." I shrugged, unable to tear my eyes away from her lips. I really hadn't been thinking about that before, but I sure as hell was now. "We'll hold hands, sometimes we'll kiss, I guess. Just follow my lead."

Jenna let out a little closed-mouthed laugh. "There's kissing, and then there's *kissing*," she said. "Which one are we talking about, here?"

Was she trying to throw me off-balance, or did she actually want to negotiate this ahead of time? All right, it wasn't the craziest thing ever. If full-on face sucking was going to make her too uncomfortable, then we could promise to keep things on the chaste side. But damn, I'd been turning this plan over and over in my head for ages, and it never occurred to me that this might be an issue.

And now, I couldn't stop thinking about kissing her. Not just a dry peck on the lips, either.

Maybe that was what she wanted. My eyes narrowed as I looked at her, trying to figure out what she was playing at. Did she think I'd offer up more money if it meant having my tongue in her mouth?

Would I?

"Is that going to make a difference?" I said, finally.

Her smile was full of secrets and promise, or maybe she was just toying with me. I could never be sure. "If it wasn't going to make a difference, I wouldn't be asking. This isn't a zero-sum thing. I can always ask for more concessions. See what you're willing to do for me, in exchange for what I'm willing to do for you." She shifted slightly in her seat. "*Business*, Mr. Chase. You might be familiar with it."

"All right, fine." I circled the island, coming closer to her, watching for a reaction. She always seemed more confident when we had some distance between us. "So, if you really think it'll be that bad to kiss me - what do you want in return?"

She laughed, color rising in her cheeks. "That's not what I meant, and you know it. I'm sure it's not going to be unpleasant, but it's...intimate." Clearing her throat lightly, she went on, eyes still fixed on my face. "Generally, when people have to be intimate with strangers, there's some kind of concession made."

I really hadn't expected that. Snickering, I slid onto the stool that was furthest away from her. But I was still close enough to notice the minute changes in her body language. "I figured you'd be offended it I brought up that comparison," I said. "Anyway, it's not really like that at all. If anything, this is more like what you want to do for a living. Just acting. Do actors usually get paid more if they have to kiss?"

"Actors don't kiss with tongue," she said, bluntly. Her ears were burning, but she wasn't going to show her embarrassment voluntarily.

Smiling, I leaned on the counter. "You're not watching the right movies. But, okay, fine. You want to put a price on it. Go ahead."

Jenna folded her arms tighter. There was annoyance and disappointment in her eyes. She'd been half-expecting me to offer her a test drive, and she hated that I didn't. She hated it because it meant she was wrong about me, but also because there was a tiny part of her that wanted to.

Maybe not so tiny. She glanced at my mouth, and I was pretty sure it wasn't just because I couldn't stop worrying at the side of my thumb with my teeth.

"If you're curious about my tongue, I can provide references on that, as well." I grinned.

Rolling her eyes, she stood up. "Okay, that's enough of that. I'm going to see if they've opened up my street yet."

She was fumbling with her phone.

"Wait," I said, feeling the tide of desperation rise again. "Jenna, please - I know I've been...flip about this. Hell, I'm flip about most things. But it's serious. Whatever you need to feel comfortable, I'll do it. Just...please, think about it."

I hated being in a position of weakness. Daria had proved how badly I could allow myself to be taken advantage of, when that happened. But something about Jenna made it hard to play it cool. I knew I had the upper hand in a lot of ways - I could offer her money, and security, and a lot of things she wouldn't have otherwise. A job sitting for the Thornes was a pretty sweet gig, but it wasn't going to last forever. I was offering her an actor's dream: enough money to live on while she searched for that one role that would make her a star.

All the same, she always had the power to walk away. And that terrified me.

She looked at me with an expression that bordered on pity. I hated that, but not as much as I hated the idea of her leaving.

"It hasn't been that long," I said, in a more quiet, even tone. "Your street's gotta be closed still. Just stay for a little while longer. We don't have to talk about it anymore. We'll play cards."

Her mouth twisted slightly, with something like amusement. "You want to play cards?"

"Come on." I smiled back at her. "I know there's some tiny part of you that doesn't hate me. Try and tap into that, just for long enough to enjoy a couple hands of strip poker."

God damn it, I really didn't know when to stop.

"I'm kidding," I said, quickly. "I mean, unless you have a pressing desire to get naked."

Thankfully, she grinned. "I think you caught me on the wrong day for that."

Chapter Nine

Jenna

As it turned out, Ben had a whole poker set, complete with fancy chips and a crisp deck of cards that looked completely untouched.

I won the first two hands, through pure luck, of course. Although I always did have a pretty good poker face. And to be fair, Ben was probably a little bit distracted.

Why the hell was I still here?

Well, he was right. There was some not-so-tiny corner of my mind that didn't hate him. Hell, until recently, I'd actually been hoping he would ask me out on a date. Now that possibility seemed to have flown out the window, but I had to admit, I kind of enjoyed the flirtation. It wasn't entirely unpleasant to think about kissing him. Or *kissing* him, for that matter.

I felt slightly off-balance, the strangeness of the day, of the situation, taking a firm hold on me. It was a bit like being drunk, except there was an extreme sense of clarity. I'd started the day with a bold decision, and I hadn't allowed myself to think twice. It hadn't ended well, but that didn't stop the strange head-rush. It was addictive. Full speed ahead, and damn the consequences. Was this how people like Ben lived all the time? Knowing there would always be some kind of cushion to catch them if they fell?

"I feel like I have an unfair advantage," I said, throwing down my cards.

He nodded, that rakish grin showing only a hint of the nerves he must feel. "You do," he said. "But I was going to be a gentleman about it."

"I'm leaning towards yes," I confessed. "But I'm reserving the right to change my mind, if anything seems off."

His eyes were shining with hopefulness, and anticipation. "What do you mean, 'off?'"

"I mean, if it turns out you were lying about anything you told me. The reasons why you need to do this. I don't particularly care why, but if I can't trust you, then I can't do this. It goes both ways."

He nodded. "That's fair. If there's anything you want to ask me..."

Interlacing my fingers, I leaned towards him slightly.

"I want to see the settlement," I said, finally.

Ben blinked a few times, looking relieved. "That's only fair," he responded, quietly. I'd expected more resistance, but instead he walked over to a safe in the wall and punched in a code, blocking the number pad with his body.

He brought me a sheaf of papers that looked and felt official enough. I paged through it, glossed over the legalese that didn't seem to have much pertinence. However, there was enough of it to make me believe it was the real thing.

Then again, if Ben was committed to fakery, he would've put in some effort. Really, this proved nothing. But I felt better holding it.

"I'm afraid I can't let that leave this room," he said, after a long silence. "But if there's anything else I can do to ease your mind, just let me know."

Something furry brushed against my ankle.

"Oh!" I looked down, seeing the bright green eyes surrounded by orange fur. The cat purred loudly, rubbing his body against my leg as I scratched behind his ears. "I kind of thought you were kidding about the cats."

"You're not allergic, are you?" he asked.

I shook my head. "Do you really have three?"

"Believe it or not." He laughed. "Everybody told me you can't have just one, and I didn't believe them, until the first time I walked by the adoption center in the pet store and I thought to myself, *well, I've already got all the supplies...*" He rolled his eyes a little, but he was still smiling. "That's Harry. They found him under a car when he was just a kitten."

The tabby was taking a liking to me. With a tiny *oomph* noise, he jumped up on the sofa beside me and poked experimentally at my lap.

"He's the alpha," Ben said. "If you buy into that sort of thing."

"Sure, he seems like a real killer." I stroked Harry's neck as he curled up on my lap, purring contentedly.

"He knows when to pick his battles. There's no point in fighting with the beings who give him unlimited food and warmth." Ben was grinning. "Cats, on the other hand, are competition."

I glanced around the room. "Is that why the others are conspicuously missing?"

"You'll meet them eventually," he said. "Carl and Lizzie don't have as strong personalities."

Giggling, I rubbed Harry's vibrating ribcage. "You really sound like a crazy cat lady. I hope you know that."

"See, you've got to rescue me from this before I'm too far gone." He was joking, kind of, but there was real exasperation in his tone. It was like he was so tired of being single that he was anxious to just play at being married, even if it wasn't real.

"What do you think, Harry?" I looked down to the cat for advice. He blinked at me sleepily. His green eyes were almost the same shade as his owners', in a certain light. "You want to see a lot more of me soon?"

Ben raised his eyebrows. "Are you hitting on my cat?"

"*Gross.*" Apparently, I was still capable of blushing. "That's not what I meant, and you know it."

"He's not very good at giving advice." Ben looked at me searchingly, his face going serious again. "So can I get a conditional yes?"

I sighed. "Okay. Yes. A thousand times, conditional yes."

"Fantastic." He grinned, gathering up the cards. "Celebratory hand?"

"Sure, why not." I expected the weight of my decision to come crashing down on me, but I felt strangely calm. Maybe that was a good sign. Or maybe it was just a sign of impending insanity. I couldn't really be sure.

"You don't think this is going to look a little bit suspicious?" I bit my lip, glancing at him. "We've known each other for all of, what, six weeks?"

He shrugged. "What's suspicious? I've got money, you're sex on a stick, I don't think anyone's going to question why we're together."

I would've turned bright red, if I had any capacity left for embarrassment. As it was, I just stared at him.

Ben blinked, innocently. "What? It's an expression."

"Yeah, and not one you generally say to a woman's face." I managed a weak laugh. "Even if it's an obvious lie."

Shuffling the deck of cards, he raised his head just enough to glance at me under his eyebrows. "You've *got* to stop that. Learn how to take a damn complement."

This time, I laughed for real. "I hate to break this to you, but that's not exactly a *compliment*."

"What, is it an insult now? I've really lost my grip on modern slang. Kids these days!" He made a dramatic gesture, which doubled as a way to deal me my first card. I felt like my eyes would actually fall out of my head if I rolled them any more, so I just picked it up and leaned back in my seat.

"Generally, yeah, women don't like be called objects." I picked up the next two cards, smirking at him. "That may come as a shock to you, but there it is."

"Sex isn't an object," he protested. "It's a *concept*."

"A stick is most definitely an object."

"Yeah, but I said you were *on* a stick, not that you *were* a stick." He picked up his cards. "I can't believe we're still talking about this."

"On a stick? Like a spit-roasted pig?" Instantly I realized what I'd said, and my capacity for embarrassment came roaring back. He grinned at me.

"I'm going to leave that alone," he said. "Because I'm a gentleman."

I threw my cards at him.

Four hours in, and I didn't want to leave.

How did this happen? I couldn't be sure. I just realized I kept glancing at the time with a growing sense of unease, watching the hours pass, knowing that I'd have no excuse for staying once my street was open again. I should have wanted to run away, to scurry into some quiet corner and try to clear my mind. Start to untangle this mess I'd gotten myself into. But at the moment, nothing sounded less appealing.

It almost felt like an adrenaline high, being with him. I was always waiting for his next move, his next word - some part of me breathless with anticipation, pushing back against the current of annoyance that always came along with it.

Over the past few hours, he had slowly transformed. Piece by piece, he shed his work attire, the jacket now hanging by the door, his tie slung over the back of his chair. He undid his cufflinks - yes, cufflinks, in such a nimble, yet unmistakably masculine gesture that I couldn't help but stare. He didn't seem to notice, or think it was unusual to have been wearing cufflinks on a perfectly average weekday afternoon. Then, he rolled up his sleeves to the elbows.

Oh, good God.

"Inked" didn't even begin to describe it. His forearms were tapestries of imagery and color, words and symbols and intricate designs all intertwining. They were all different, I thought, this was the product of many years' work - but they all told one long story.

A pair of well-toned forearms were enough of an enticement, in and of themselves. It was impossible to look at them without imagining the way they'd twitch and undulate while he touched you. But sleeve tattoos? I might have gotten over my bad boy phase in college, but once you have a taste for ink, it never really goes away.

I became aware that I was staring.

"Yes, my father was angry as hell, and no, I don't need to keep them covered at work. I just prefer it," he said. "To address the frequently asked questions."

I raised my eyebrows at him. "Of course you don't have to," I said. "It's your company. Do you think they'd care if you showed up naked?"

Why the hell did I pick that example? Instantly, I was blushing again. I'd have to remember to cake on an extra layer of foundation the next time I saw him.

"That sounds like a challenge," he said. "But I'm pretty sure the board's allowed to vote on my dismissal if I start acting unstable. Remind me not to appoint my favorite war horse as CFO."

"Caligula didn't do that because he was crazy, you know," I blurted, without thinking. "He did it because he wanted to mock the senate."

"Right, because *that's* a sane way to express it." Ben grinned. "By the way, if I do that, you're also allowed to call your contract null and void. I mean - I have no plans to go insane, but just in case."

I was trying to form some kind of clever response, but all my brain had to offer was: *tattoos*.

This was becoming a problem.

"Not that this isn't a lovely time - but have you checked on your street closure lately?" He coughed quietly. "I know you wanted to go home and unwind, and this isn't exactly the most relaxing atmosphere."

Oh, you have no idea, Mr. Inked Up Billionaire. No idea at all.

"What makes you say that?" I sat up straighter in my seat, trying to act like a normal human who wasn't reduced to a drooling puddle in the presence of sleeve tattoos. "And yeah, I just looked up the DPW alerts. They're..." I was already up to my ankles in a lie, I might as well fully commit. "They're saying not until tomorrow morning."

"Oh." It was hard to read his reaction; maybe Mr. Chase had a poker face after all. Wait a minute, had he been letting me win? That put an unpleasant twist in my chest. "Well, you know, I don't want you to feel pressured or anything, but you're welcome to stay here tonight. I've got...five or six spare bedrooms, I think."

I laughed, even as a twinge of excitement quickened my heartbeat. That wasn't what I meant - I'd just wanted to stay for a few more hours, maybe. Hell, I wasn't sure what I wanted. "I couldn't possibly," I said, quickly. "I mean, I don't want to disturb your..." I glanced around the room for the missing words I couldn't find, my thoughts as blank as the skin on his arms *wasn't*. "...cats."

Ben let out a low wicked laugh, his eyes flashing to me briefly with something that made my throat go dry. "That's the lamest attempt at a polite protest I've ever heard," he said. "You can have your pick of a room, and I'll loan you some clothes. And I'm pretty sure my cats will be fine. They'll just hide in the servant's wing."

He was joking. I was *pretty* sure he was joking.

"We should probably talk about some of the boring practical stuff," he said. "Come up with some kind of plausible relationship arc. We'll have to get our story straight for when we start telling people," he said. "Like your parents, for instance."

Oh, shit. My parents. Somehow, I hadn't even thought of that. The utter strangeness of uprooting myself and starting in a new city must have completely scrambled my brains. I was going to have to lie to them, and I hadn't really done that since I was a teenager.

Well, except for...pretty much every conversation I'd had with them recently. But that was different. Those were little white lies, just to make them stop worrying about me. I wanted my mom to think I was incredibly successful and happy in my new home, lest she and Dad come rushing up from their cute little retirement condo in Florida to rescue me. They'd scrimped and saved wisely for their golden years, and they deserved to enjoy it. The last thing they needed was to worry about me.

And this was going to make them worry. It was completely out of character for me, and I didn't even know if they'd believe it. I wasn't even sure how to make it sound believable.

"You look worried," he said, cautiously - like he was afraid of what I was about to say.

"I just...I didn't think about that," I said. "Telling my parents. I don't even know how to start that conversation."

He shrugged. "Just tell them you fell in love. What's so difficult about that?"

"But my parents already know I came here for acting - not for some guy." My mouth twisted at the thought. "They know how much it means to me. They're not going to believe I left everything behind just to pursue the dream of *getting some*."

"You'll have to tell them you just kept it a secret." He shrugged, unconcerned. "You didn't think it was going anywhere serious at first, and then by the time you realized it, it had been going on too long and you didn't know how to bring it up. You moved to New York for acting, *and* to see if it was worth pursuing something with me. But you wanted to keep things private until you were sure it wasn't going to just fall apart."

I chewed on my lower lip. It wasn't the craziest thing I'd ever heard. It even sort of sounded like me; I'd kept most of my relationships secret from my parents when I was a teenager, because I hated the thought of their well-meaning interest and probing questions. I knew they'd always suspected it to be the case, so they wouldn't be all that surprised.

But they *would* feel betrayed, and I hated that thought. Doing this meant losing their trust, and that wasn't something I'd even thought about when I agreed to it. I was letting Ben into every part of my life, allowing him to affect my relationships with other people - letting him control what I said and did, even when we weren't together. If I let the truth slip out, the

109

whole thing was ruined.

The thing was, I wanted to help him. I couldn't really explain why. There was something in his eyes when he talked about Daria, about his past…it was different. I never saw that look, except when he was thinking about her. It was like Daria was his only weakness, the one little break in his armor where he couldn't hide who he really was.

He still had feelings for her. There was no doubt in my mind about that. For all I knew, this whole thing was just a ploy to get her jealous. Maybe there was no settlement.

Well, if that turned out to be the case, I didn't have to hold up my end of the bargain either. I'd have no qualms against publicly humiliating him, and walking away. Sure, he was a friend of Daniel's, but I was sure any reasonable person would understand.

Looking at Ben, there was one thing I just couldn't deny.

It felt good to be *needed*.

I couldn't remember the last time I'd felt that. My parents were the only people I'd been close to recently, and even that wasn't like it used to be. The first time I came back from college, I felt it. They still loved me, and they were happy to have me home, but for the first time I felt like a stranger in my own house. My room was too quiet, too clean, like a museum. I didn't belong there anymore. When I was growing up, all of our lives were intertwined, but I'd pruned myself away to grow up and strike out on my own. In my absence, they grew back together like ornamental trees, but without me.

They kept on loving and supporting me, but there

was just no room for me anymore. Not the way there used to be.

Something about Ben was magnetic. He needed me, and that simple fact reached out and plucked at something in me. Something unidentifiable, but important.

"Wait a minute," I said. "But Daniel and Maddy already know we didn't meet online, they're the ones who introduced us."

He frowned a little. "So - we'll ask them to keep it a secret. Because otherwise, your parents wouldn't understand. I mean, unless you want to tell them you got engaged to a guy after knowing him for about a month, that's another option."

"Ugh. No." My head was swimming. "They'll probably hold an intervention. Daniel at least knows you, so he'll hopefully tell Maddy there's nothing to worry about, and they won't question it too much. This is getting *way* too complicated."

"Not at all," Ben said. "So, Daniel and Maddy know the truth. Right? Everything except the fact that it's a fake marriage. But they know how we met, and they know why you really came here." He picked up a pen-holder and a solid brass paperweight. At least, I *thought* that was brass. "This is them." He placed the two objects close together, touching slightly. "This," he said, gesturing to the rest of the clutter on his desk, "is everybody else. They're in Group 2. Total lie group. We met online, we got to know each other for a while, you came here to get to know me. So all we have to do is tell *them*," he gestured to the pen-holder and paperweight, "to keep the lie straight. That's manageable. The four of us can get the story straight, and then everyone else will just fall in line."

I slumped forward in my seat. "My head hurts. Can we go back to the drawing board on this one? Maybe it is better if we just tell everyone the truth. I mean, the Maddy and Daniel version of the truth. That we, like, fell in love in a couple weeks and are just horribly irresponsible people. I'll just have to...I don't know, sound convincing to my parents. And not insane. I don't want them to think you're like, David Koresh or something."

He sighed. "I wish we weren't on such a tight timeline. If only I'd met you sooner..."

I let that statement hang, on its own, for quite a while. I didn't know what to say.

If only I'd met you sooner.

Why me?

I wasn't special. If this was a scheme to get into my pants, it was hilariously elaborate. All he would have needed to do was...well, roll up his sleeves, apparently. No, he really needed me, and me specifically, and I didn't know quite what to do with that.

I was standing in a shower that sprayed from *five different directions*.

Ben's bathroom was exactly as posh as I would've imagined, and then some. It felt like I'd stepped into the pages of a magazine, and the thought of getting even one tiny drip of water on the beautiful stone floor was almost too much to bear. This was like some kind of luxury resort that I only could've visited if I won Wheel of Fortune or something, but it was just Ben's everyday life.

Well, I could get used to this. Particularly the heated towel rack, and the huge fluffy bathrobe I could practically lose myself in.

After I was finished, I stared at the pile of clothes he'd given me. No underwear, of course. My cheeks went slightly pinker at the thought of him knowing that I was walking through his house without panties. It seemed...excessively kinky, for a man I barely knew, and didn't actually plan to sleep with. No matter how good he looked with his sleeves rolled up.

I pulled on the workout sweats, which were too long for me, but definitely too tight in the hips and thighs. Serviceable, though, in a pinch. The tee shirt was fairly crisp, from some Chase Pharma corporate fun run five years ago. I guessed he'd thrown it in the back of his closet and never worn it. It smelled vaguely of cedar. Irrationally, I wished he'd given me something that smelled like him.

As if it wasn't intimate enough to have my bare ass pressed against the inside of his old workout pants.

I surveyed myself in the now-defogged mirror. It wasn't exactly runway material, but I didn't look terrible. My makeup was all washed away, and I didn't have anything to touch up with. But I was surprised to see that my face didn't look as pale and plain as I feared. There was a certain brightness in my eyes, my cheeks, and even with my hair hanging heavy, lanky and damp, I looked kind of...pretty.

Not that it mattered. I mean, he was marrying me for the way I looked in public. It didn't matter if I was a complete troll around the house.

Laughing to myself, I hung up my towel and robe and padded out into the hallway. Ben turned around almost immediately, as if he'd been examining one of the paintings across the hallway.

Was he just standing there…waiting for me to get out of the shower?

Weird.

"What's so funny?" he asked, ambling towards me with his hands deep in his pockets.

Red alert, red alert, tattoos on display.

"Nothing," I said. An image of putting one of those shower heads to a *very* different use suddenly flashed into my head, and I was blushing. Again.

He had the good grace not to mention it, but I could tell he noticed. There was always a little smile that accompanied it, his answer to my embarrassment. He liked it. Of course he did.

"Like the shower?" His smile widened a little. I wasn't sure if he was implying what I thought he was, or not - my grip on reality seemed to be coming looser by the second.

"It's incredible," I said, letting the curve of my lips betray a hint of innuendo. Hell, I might as well have a little fun with this. "I wish I could use it every day."

"Yeah, that's what they all say." He was grinning.

The word echoed in my head.

All.

All the women he brought here.

All the women who showered in his home.

None of my business. None. And yet, something quivered inside my chest.

His forehead creased slightly, and his smile disappeared. A moment later, he recovered, and I wasn't sure if he was simply reacting to my stony silence, or if he actually regretted saying it.

"I'm going to have a drink in the library," he said. "Maybe write some dirty words in my zen garden. You're welcome to join me, or I can show you to your room."

In spite of the lingering discomfort from imagining him with all those other anonymous women, I laughed. "Why don't you just write BOOBS on a calculator?"

"Please, that's amateur hour. I'm a professional. I use my tiny sandbox to write all the names I wish I could say to the guy who's running the conference call and won't stop clearing his throat."

He wasn't kidding - he actually had one of those little zen gardens, complete with white sand, tiny polished rocks, and miniature wooden rakes. There was nothing but abstract designs at the moment, so I picked up one of the rakes and used the flat side to smooth out all the sand before carefully tracing BASTARD.

Looking up from his glass of scotch, he lifted his hand to his chest in mock appreciation. "Oh, is that for me?"

"If the shoe fits." I sat down, smiling at my handiwork.

"You have any auditions lined up this week, Little Miss Can't Be Wrong?"

My lips thinned. "It would be great if you could never, ever call me that. Ever." I sighed. "But, to answer your question, no. I was hoping the one I went to today would pan out, but..."

"But?" He raised his eyebrows, silently prompting me to go on.

"But, it was just some scam, and I'm pretty sure the guy offered to put me in porn."

The eyebrows went up a little further.

"No comment?" I said, after a moment.

"I'm really sorry that happened to you," he said, sounding for all the world like he *actually meant it*. Well, okay, that was a surprise.

I shrugged. "It wasn't the worst thing ever. I just, you know - psyched myself up, and then it was nothing. Not even worth leaving the house for."

"But you gotta get back on that horse." He frowned. "That might have been a poor choice of words."

Okay, slightly less of a surprise.

"I haven't even logged back onto the site that has the legitimate ones," I said. "But that'll teach me to hunt for jobs on Craigslist."

"Here, I'll help you pick one," he said. "Why don't you log in, read me the headlines. I'm really good at picking things. Ask Daniel about my March Madness brackets."

I laughed. "That's very generous of you, but their website is a piece of shit. I can't make it work on mobile, and I think I'm done with Craigslist stuff for now."

"You want to use my computer?" he reached under his desk and pulled out a laptop. "Come on. Don't chicken out on me."

I rolled my eyes. "Okay, fine. But I'm not making any promises."

When I flipped the screen open, it blocked my view of his arms. Sigh. But hey, this couldn't possibly hurt. And maybe it would even be productive.

Suddenly, I heard a tinny version of a familiar song, slightly muffled, and Ben dug into his pocket. He frowned at the screen of his phone.

"Sorry," he said, glancing up at me. "It's my brother. I've gotta take this. He's in the middle of one of his famous crises."

"Sure," I said, nodding absently. He disappeared out the door and down the hallway, and I was left alone to browse the listings. *None* of them sounded good. I was hopeless. Whether it was self-sabotage or not, my own brain was terribly good at convincing me that none of these jobs were worth my time. Maybe Ben was right - maybe this little exercise would actually be good for me. In this case, his judgment might actually be more trustworthy than mine.

Something told me the conversation with his brother was going to take a while. Absentmindedly, my eyes scanned the menu bar, noticing his most frequently viewed sites. News, news, science news, medical news, more news, FDA news. It made sense, but did he really not have any extracurricular interests?

He must.

And I could find out what they were, if I really wanted to.

His bookmarks were *right there*. All I had to do was open the window. There couldn't be anything truly confidential in here. He wasn't using it to log into banking or investment websites. The only remotely personal thing I saw was some kind of zombie-killing game that he probably used to blow off steam. Of course, he'd be stupid to let some random person play around on a laptop that might have corporate secrets on it.

Glancing at the door, guiltily, I opened the

bookmarks menu.

There was a lot more of the same boring stuff in there. It was all sorted into sub-folders, including one called "Recipes" that had a few tasty-sounding ideas in it. I still felt like a total creep, but it was somewhat of a relief that there was nothing scandalous in here.

A relief...and a disappointment?

What the hell was wrong with me? Why did I *want* there to be something wrong with this guy?

Just close the stupid menu. There's nothing here worth seeing, and you're being totally ridiculous. How would you explain

There was one folder just labelled "Research." When I hovered over it, there were only a few bookmarks, and each one was just a random string of nonsense letters.

Curiosity overtook me. Feeling like a total creep, I clicked on the first one.

Instantly, my eyes snapped shut. *Just close it, Jenna. Don't even look at it. He probably forgot this stuff was on there, it's not fair to snoop on him.*

I heard his voice raise slightly in the other room. Not enough to pick out words, but enough to indicate the conversation was either going to end very soon, or drag on for a while longer.

I opened my eyes, and I saw the site I'd clicked on.

THE DOMESTIC DISCIPLINE FORUMS.

I stared. The banner at the top of the page was Photoshopped from a vintage newspaper ad, one that portrayed a stern-looking man with slicked-back hair, who had turned his wife over his knee. Both of them were dressed in typical 1950's outfits, and the woman's

look of shock - along with the man's upraised arm -
told me everything I needed to know.

Shit.

I could hear Ben's voice coming closer. "All right,
all right. Listen. I have to go. Please don't do anything
stupid, okay? Just sleep on it."

Frantically, I closed the window and took a deep
breath. I was sure I looked guilty as hell. But why on
earth had he let me - almost a complete stranger - use
his computer? Did he *want* me to find this?

Thankfully, when he walked back into the room,
he seemed too distracted to notice how I looked. He
was pinching the bridge of his nose between his thumb
and forefinger, face downturned. "I swear to God. My
brother. They could make an HBO melodrama series
about his life, and it would fit right in."

"Less incest, I hope," I quipped, before I could
stop myself. Instantly, my face turned an even deeper
shade of red. Why did I say the most inappropriate
things when I was nervous?

Ben just laughed. "Perv."

"Hey, they're the pervy ones. Not me." He hardly
even seemed to notice I still had his computer, breezing
right past me and plopping down behind his desk. He
was searching for something in the drawers and piles
the paperwork. I breathed a sigh of relief. "What's
going on with your brother?"

"I probably shouldn't say," he said. "But
relationship problems run in the family - we'll just
leave it at that."

Laughing, I relaxed into my seat, trying not to
think about what I'd just seen. "They can't be worse
than yours."

His mouth quirked up as he turned to look at me. "You'd be surprised. So - find anything promising in there?"

It took me a few seconds to remember what he was talking about.

Right. The auditions. Shit.

I couldn't do this. I couldn't sit here and have a casual conversation with this man, pretending I hadn't seen what I saw. I needed to know. I had to find out what it was. The room suddenly felt stifling, horrifyingly so.

Swallowing hard, I looked up at him. "Actually, um, I'm kind of tired. Could you point me towards my room?"

Chapter Ten

Jenna

Sleep eluded me.

I had to know what the hell that website was about. And I was drawing the line at sneaking back down to his library and looking at the computer again. I wasn't a complete degenerate.

Was *he*?

Was it some kind of sex thing? Or was it really some kind of lifestyle that somehow revolved around spanking? Was it some combination of both?

I laid there in the impossibly plush bed, staring at the glow of my phone, my thumb hovering over the web browser.

Finally, I typed it. Letter by letter, so slowly, until Google helpfully auto-completed it.

Domestic discipline.

I hit "Search," and immediately wished that I hadn't. The glut of information hit me faster than I could absorb it, conflicting terminology and ideas swarming - *corporeal punishment, spousal abuse, Christian domestic discipline, erotic spanking*. Holy shit.

Taking a deep breath, I tried to focus in. BDSM. Okay, so that was something I knew about - obviously. Not exactly something I'd ever thought about doing, but I knew plenty of people did. I guessed it was normal for them, even if it didn't make any sense to me. But this? This was something different. Weirdly specific. I couldn't wrap my head around it.

The one thing I was quickly learning was that it meant different things to different people. For some, it actually was a reflection of their spiritual beliefs. Ben didn't really strike me as the Born Again type, so I figured that was unlikely to be it. But the motives were unclear. It was all about someone being in charge, and someone else being *taken in hand* - which, as far as I could tell, meant they were treated like a disobedient child who needed to be punished when they stepped out of line.

My skin was crawling. The word consensual kept coming up. Consensual, consensual, consensual. This was something that both people wanted, every blog article and op ed piece assured me. Except for the skeptical ones, which I had to admit I was leaning towards. Was this just some thinly-veiled way to hurt the one you loved? Or, at least, act out unhealthy relationship impulses?

I started scanning through the articles available on one of the biggest websites. I hadn't yet been able to bring myself to seek out the forum I'd seen on Ben's computer, but I was moving in that direction.

The titles of the articles were all I could swallow, for now. My eyes started to glaze over.

When to Stop Spanking - how to tell when your

punishment is effective
   Knowing Your Roles
   Asleep At His Feet

I set my phone down quickly, my heart squeezing in my chest. *This* was what he was into? Were Maddy and Daniel into it, too? That little gleam in her eyes seemed to hint at something, not to mention Ben's not-so-private conversation with Daniel at the club - but I couldn't imagine the girl I knew in college willingly becoming a domestic servant. I mean, what the *fuck*.

This wasn't something people did anymore, was it? I mean, as much as I didn't really understand BDSM, I accepted that it was fun for everybody involved. This didn't seem fun. It seemed way too serious, too reverent of a cultural norm I didn't believe it.

My curiosity outweighed my cringing, and I returned to my search. I kept going back to the repeated use of *consensual*. But how could someone consent to a relationship that was so uneven?

I didn't get it.

How could anyone live like this all the time? I didn't like the idea of roles. What if I didn't want a *role*? What if I just wanted to be a human being? I was seeing stories of spouses who felt like they had to adopt this lifestyle, because it was what their other half "needed" - and they claimed to be happy, but it felt hollow to me.

I mean, how? Why? I wanted to be respected. I wanted to be treated like an adult.

Taking a deep breath, I squeezed my eyes shut for a moment. It didn't matter. The terms of my agreement with Ben had nothing at all to do with his private bedroom activities. But I still felt like I needed to know. Maybe because it seemed to speak to his character. If he really was so attached to the idea of subservient women, could I even pretend to be married to him?

Opening my eyes again, I saw an article called "In Defense of DD." An acronym that - I had recently learned - referred to domestic discipline.

I opened it.

My eyes scanned over the words, seeing them all, but absorbing almost nothing. Then, I reached a paragraph that made me stop.

Look at it like this: people choose to be married. They choose to live as a couple, in the same home, sharing so many aspects of their lives. Raising children together, usually in monogamy. Many women choose to take their husband's last name, and even wear a ring that declares his "ownership" of them. It's only recently that men began wearing wedding rings with any regularity. And even today, it's quite rare for a man to wear an engagement ring - yet it's considered commonplace for women to display this symbol that hearkens back to the days of women as commodities.

These are all choices people make, based on nothing but traditions they feel they should reenact. Those who buck the trends are considered strange. But divorced of cultural context, there is nothing objectively stranger about living in a DD partnership than living in a "normal" one. It's not a 24/7 sex game. It's simply another way to live, and for the people who find fulfillment in it, it's beautiful and natural.

I wanted to believe it. I did. For a long time, I'd

viewed this kind of stuff with a sort of "anchovies on my pizza" philosophy. I didn't want them, personally, but far be it from me to deny anyone else. This, though...it was just too strange to me. It wasn't like wearing a wedding ring, or living in the prescribed ritual of husband and wife. You could do that, and still be equals.

The idea of acting out this kind of fucked-up power dynamic with someone like Ben, who already loomed so large compared to me - what a joke. If anything, *he* should be submitting to *me*.

Right. I managed a tiny laugh. Like I could ever order him around.

I didn't want to. The thing was, as maddening as he could be, I would never change him. I didn't feel like it was my right.

And it didn't matter, not really. But I wished that he felt the same way about me.

I left early the next morning, before Ben had come out of his bedroom. Slipping quietly down the stairs, I found my clothes in the dryer and changed quickly, dropping his into the washing machine and finger-combing my hair as I walked towards the door.

Out on the sidewalk, I felt like I could finally breathe again. It was a cool gray morning, not quiet exactly, because this city never was. But it was a quiet murmur, building towards a dull roar.

Just breathing. I needed to clear my head, to get away from his influence for just a little while. I'd actually joked about him being a cult leader, but I wondered if this was how acolytes started. An inexplicable magnetism. Drawn, against their better judgment.

Calm down, Hadley. You're sleep deprived. Nothing's going to make any sense for a while. You need to get home and rest.

But I wouldn't be able to sleep. I knew that already. How could I possibly forget about this, about everything, and just...switch off my brain?

My mind swirled with all the words and images I'd been devouring since last night, with just a few breaks here and there for fitful sleep. The more I saw, the less I understood, but I *had* to understand. I had to know. How could someone want this?

In some corner of my mind a notion was growing, and suddenly I was assaulted with the image of Ben rolling up his sleeves. But not to relax. Not for fun. No.

For punishment.

I imagined words spilling from his lips, those full, sinful lips with the little traces of stubble just above and below. Not enough to scratch, just to rasp pleasantly against my skin. Except there would be no kissing, no, not now.

You've been a bad girl.

I walked faster, running through an intersection just as the signal was changing. A cacophony of honks accompanied my crossing.

How long did you think you could get away with this? It's time to accept your punishment.

There was a sudden awareness between my thighs, and I stole furtive glances around me, like passing pedestrians would somehow know.

I imagined unspeakable things, and my hazy state

somehow gave everything sharper edges, brighter colors. I paused in a little park to...something. I didn't know. Catch my breath? I was breathing awfully fast, and my pulse felt impossibly quick, like my heart could explode at any moment.

"So that's a 'no' to breakfast?"

The sound of his voice made my heart leap into my throat. At first I thought I must have imagined it, but no, I wasn't that tired. He was walking towards me, in last night's clothes, and those damn sleeves were still rolled up.

Did he even go to bed? I'd only assumed. I never actually heard him come up the stairs again. He must have been in the library the whole time, and my furtive escape must have woken him up.

Stupid, stupid, stupid.

"I'm sorry," I blurted out, hugging myself tightly, fighting the sudden urge to shiver, though the harsh early morning sun was burning through the last of the night chill. "I just kind of..."

"Are you okay?" He stopped a few feet away, giving me my space, but barely. He clearly hadn't slept well either, though that might have something to do with the fact that he'd probably just slumped over on his desk. "Last night, it kind of seemed like..."

I didn't answer, couldn't bring myself to lie.

He actually looked worried, like it mattered what I thought. Maybe he was concerned that I'd back out of our agreement. I honestly didn't know if that was on the table, or not. I didn't know a lot of things, anymore.

"...it kind of seemed like something upset you," he said, finally. His eyes briefly darted around us, like he suspected spies hiding in the trees. "I wish you'd come back so we can talk about it."

I tried to shake my head. I really did. But the muscles wouldn't move. And really, he deserved better than this. No matter what kind of man he was, I should give him more than wide-eyed silence.

"Tonight?" he suggested, and there was a tight burst of relief in my chest. That would give me the time I needed. Time to clear my head.

Finally, I managed to nod. "Yes," I said, ungluing my tongue from the roof of my mouth. It was difficult. "Tonight, I'll come back. I just need..." I sighed. "I just, I didn't sleep well."

He nodded. "Me neither. Then again, I usually don't."

We stood there for a moment, not really looking at each other, not speaking. The air was thick with everything we didn't say. How had this tatted-up, arrogant rich boy managed to twist me around into so many knots, just by existing? Just by asking a favor of me?

Not even a favor. He wanted to pay me to be his wife. It was the world's strangest job proposal, from a man I didn't understand at all. I was beginning to think I never could.

He was the one who ended it, turning on his heel and walking back towards his place. "Sleep well, Jenna," he called, over his shoulder.

I stood there for a moment, still thinking. Just thinking. It was always clearer when he wasn't around.

And then, I began the long walk home.

Chapter Eleven

Jenna

I woke up in the afternoon. My limbs felt corpse-heavy, and I dragged myself out of bed with such a massive effort that my head was swimming at the end of it.

And I was supposed to go and see him. Again. Tonight.

I wouldn't. I couldn't. I had to call him and cancel, but - I realized as I groped for my phone on the stack of boxes that served as my bedside table - I didn't have his number.

I agreed to marry the guy, and we didn't even exchange contact information. Fantastic.

After last night, my shower felt like standing under a dripping faucet. But it was better than nothing. I woke up by degrees, the cobwebs slowly dissipating from my mind. I *could* just stand him up.

Bad girl, bad girl, bad girl...

I almost slammed my hand against the shower wall in frustration, before I remembered that my neighbors were about six inches away. No more wall-slamming, I was in the big city now.

Laughing hysterically, I shut off the pitiful water and reached for a towel. I'd never wanted anything more than to just go home, back to my cozy apartment where I paid half as much for twice the square footage. Where I knew everyone, and everyone knew me.

Where all of my dreams would go to die.

I wouldn't. I couldn't.

I just wanted my life to be simple again.

Well, that was basically impossible at this point. After I'd dried off and dressed, I picked up the phone and called Maddy. I didn't know what else to do.

Pick up the phone, pick up the phone, pick up the phone.

"Hello?" She sounded breathless.

"Hey, um, could you…" I swallowed hard. "I was hoping we could talk. I kind of wanted to…run something by you. Is this a bad time?"

There was rustling in the background, and a series of more abstract sounds that basically answered my question for me. "Yeah, it kind of is, sorry," she said, sounding incredibly distracted. "But, you want to get coffee later? Like in um…an hour?"

"Two hours." Daniel's voice cut in, sounding very close.

Maddy made a little scoffing noise. "An hour," she said, before turning her mouth away from the phone slightly to address her husband. "If you think that kid of yours is actually going to nap for longer than an hour, you're delusional."

"Forty-five minutes for us," I heard him murmur, faintly, in the background. "Forty-five minutes for you to *recover*, and half an hour to get cleaned up, get dressed, and get yourself to the coffee shop." A moment of silence. "Any arguments? *Tick tock*, Ms. Wainright."

I heard her soft, indulgent laugh. "I'm so sorry," she said, into the phone. "Two hours, okay? Same place as before. I'll try not to be late -"

The phone cut off abruptly, and I was left to think in silence.

I should probably feel a little embarrassed that I'd clearly interrupted something intimate, but instead, I was vaguely fascinated. He called her by her maiden name, like they were playing some kind of game. Maybe enacting old workplace fantasies they'd never had the chance to fulfill, when she actually *did* work for him.

That, I could wrap my head around.

There was something about Daniel's voice. His tone. It was completely unlike the way he usually spoke to her, when other people were around. I wasn't sure exactly what I'd witnessed, but even over the phone, I could feel the electricity between them.

I wondered what any of this had to do with spankings, and corrections, and being...*taken in hand*.

I spent the next few hours wondering.

Maddy was late.

She burst into the coffee shop with a furtive smile that she couldn't quite seem to hold back. Her hair had clearly been hastily blow-dried, and she was wearing a silk scarf around her neck in the way women only do when they're hiding love bites. It was impossible not to smile.

"Sorry," she breathed, sitting down across from me. She was glowing, as if she'd just finished laughing at some secret joke I couldn't possibly understand. "And, uh, you know, I'm sorry about earlier. He's usually a lot more, uh...discreet. I probably shouldn't have answered, but..."

"No, I'm glad you did," I said. "Really." A moment later, I realized how that sounded. "Not in a creepy way."

She laughed. "No, I get it. So what's going on?"

I'd been so anxious to tell someone, and now, I realized I didn't even know where to start. We hadn't finalized our story. If I said the wrong thing, I could screw this whole thing up.

The hell with it. I'd wing it, and screw the consequences.

"I spent last night at Ben's place," I confessed. Maddy's eyebrows shot up. "Not like that," I hurriedly added. "I just - look, okay, I'd *tell* you if I slept with him."

She was smiling like the cat that got the cream.

"I'm serious," I said, trying to mold my facial expression into something like sincerity. Already, I was starting to lie to her - I didn't know how long I could keep this up. "They were doing work on my street, there was a gas leak. I couldn't go home. He invited me to stay at his place, so I wouldn't have to spend money on a shitty motel. I just happened to run into him after I got back from my audition from hell."

"Audition from hell?" she repeated, clearly wanting to know the whole story.

I made a vague gesture. "I'll get to that later. The point is, I did it. I followed him home. I don't know why. I wasn't sure what was going to happen."

Once again, she broke into a smile, this time with a little accompanying giggle.

"Turns out, nothing much," I went on. "Just cards. Lots and lots of cards. And...we talked."

"You *talked*," she echoed, meaningfully.

"Yes," I emphasized. "Just talked. But it was..." I cleared my throat. "I don't know, it was...surprisingly nice."

"Huh." Maddy shifted in her seat, watching me closely. She could tell I was holding something back, but with any luck, she wouldn't be able to tell what. "I got the feeling you couldn't stand him."

"Well. He sort of grows on you. Like a fungus." I was no longer sure if I was lying. "It's weird. I've been...I don't know. I've been running into him a lot lately, and every time we talk, he makes me smile." I shrugged. "That's something, right?"

"It *is* something," Maddy agreed. "Jen, are you sure you're not just...nervous, or lonely, or something? I just don't think you should jump into anything you're going to regret."

Excellent advice. How could I deflect it? "I know, I know. I'm not exactly rushing into something serious. I just wanted to..." Taking a deep breath, I tried to gather my thoughts. "I wanted to ask you about something. As one woman to another. It's not exactly something I can run by my mom."

Her eyes lit up. "Okay, that sounds juicy."

"It is fairly..." I laughed a little. "...juicy. I guess. So, okay, let's not get into the details of how I found this out. All right? Because that's just a distraction. It's not important. What is important, though, is how I'm supposed to react to it."

"Wait, wait, wait." Maddy held up her hands, a smile playing on her lips. "Okay. You can't just gloss over that. Were you snooping?"

"Maybe a little," I admitted. "But not really. He wasn't making an effort to hide anything. I mean, who just lets somebody use their computer without at least logging them into a guest account first? Obviously he wasn't really trying to hide anything."

"Whoa, whoa, whoa." Maddy set her drink down so abruptly that it sloshed over the edge of the glass. "Hold on. *What* did you find on his computer?"

"I'm getting to it!" I insisted.

"Not fast enough!" she squealed. "I need to know *yesterday*. Come on, don't hold out on me. I'm dying over here."

Taking another steadying breath, I bit my lower lip. How was I supposed to ease into this? Especially without letting on that I'd overheard Ben and Daniel talking about something that sounded suspiciously related?

I hesitated as long as I thought I could, without Maddy throwing her drink in my face.

"Have you ever heard of domestic discipline?"

The silence was deafening. Maddy stared at me, her face completely blank, before she broke into a fit of giggles.

"Oh my God," she managed, finally, her cheeks pink. "Okay. So. All right. That answers a lot of questions."

My stomach tightened. "Shit. I hope I didn't tell you something you weren't supposed to know."

"Oh, please." She made a dismissive gesture. "I

knew there was a reason Daniel wasn't telling me how he and Ben really met. He doesn't like reminding me that he had a life before we were together. He knows how I get sometimes. But he's really, really bad at judging what's going to bother me, and what isn't. Emotionally tone deaf, these billionaires." She was grinning like she'd never stop. "So, domestic discipline - that's kind of an unusual flavor, for somebody like Ben. Or maybe not. It kind of depends on the person. Wait - *what* was your question?"

"I'm not sure anymore," I admitted. "But I've got like, a thousand more."

"Okay." She took a deep breath, laying her hands flat on the table. "So. Let's see. This is all very top secret stuff, okay? Very private. I don't usually talk about it. I mean, who would I tell? But you're the exception...especially considering the situation."

My head was swimming. "Slow down, Mads. Seriously. I can hardly wrap my head around the fact that this guy probably wants to spank me for speaking out of turn - I don't even know what the hell you're talking about."

"Okay, okay, I'm sorry." Her face flushed a deeper shade of red. "So...BDSM. You've heard of it, right?"

"Once or twice," I said, dryly. "But it's not something I ever..." Hesitating, I watched her face. So she and Daniel *did* do that kind of thing. That much was clear, from her expression. But how? The girl I knew in college would never stand for that sort of disrespect.

Maddy let out a long sigh. "It's not like what you think," she said. "First of all - I don't do *that*. The domestic discipline thing. But from what I see - I mean, it's different for everyone. But someone like Ben, I think, it's just another way of playing with those dynamics. You know. Just a game."

What I saw looked pretty fucking serious, but I couldn't figure out a way to explain that without sounding like an overly-sheltered child. Clearly, Maddy had gone leaps and bounds ahead of me when it came to this stuff. "I don't understand," I said, helplessly. "And I don't know how to ask him what it means. I'd have to admit I was snooping."

"Not necessarily," she said, shrugging. "Just say that something popped up on his computer. He's not going to know enough to contradict you, and he'll be on the defensive so fast he won't have time to question whether or not it makes sense."

"He doesn't need to be *defensive*," I insisted, although I wasn't sure how true that was. "I don't even have the right to ask him about it. I just…"

"It kind of sounds like it's going to concern you," Maddy said, with a meaningful look.

"Stop it," I grumbled, staring down at the table.

"Tell me I'm wrong."

Her eyes sparkled. I refused to meet them, hoping that my embarrassment passed for a genuine interest in Ben. And hoping, more than anything, that it wasn't so convincing because there was a grain of truth in it.

I did *not* want to be treated like a disobedient child. Not by my boyfriend, not by a lover, not by my fake husband. Not by anybody. It didn't matter what I'd agreed to - I would never kneel down for this ridiculous, insulting charade.

Then why are you so anxious to know about it?

"I…I really don't think that's for me," I said,

finally. "It was more...I don't know. I just want to make sure he's not some kind of psychopath."

"He's not," said Maddy. "I promise. I know it seems..." Her eyes went slightly dreamy. "Until you've experienced it, you can't really know. It sounds kind of...scary, or brutal, or something. But it's not. You'll never feel more valued than you do in the hands of a caring dominant. Trust me. The connection is unreal. It's electric. I'm not even convinced we were ever meant to have vanilla sex, you know. As a species."

I blinked. "That might be taking it a little far."

"Maybe," she said, still smiling like a smitten schoolgirl. "Don't knock it till you've tried it."

This was just too much. Suddenly, *I* felt like the weird one for not wanting to be tied up and flogged.

You've stumbled into a nest of deviants, just like Grandma always warned you about when you said you wanted to move to New York.

I had to grin. This probably wasn't exactly what she was picturing. Fifty shades of long-term monogamy.

Resting my chin on my hand, I tried to absorb everything I'd just learned. Part of me wondered if I was being unreasonably prudish. I mean, this stuff was practically in the mainstream now. I was pretty sure I saw fuzzy handcuffs for sale at Target. But if people really needed to spice things up, couldn't they do it without some kind of contrived game about *ownership* and *control*? What on earth was hot about that?

The goosebumps that suddenly appeared on my arms offered an answer, but I wasn't ready to explore it.

"Go on," said Maddy, gently. "I know you want to

ask me something. I'm not exactly an expert, but I'll try to make you understand."

I was massaging my temples, slowly, trying to get rid of the pervasive headache that had been hanging out behind my eyes since yesterday. "I don't know. Just, the whole thing doesn't make sense to me. I have a feeling it's just one of those things. Like anchovies, or caviar."

Maddy grinned. "An acquired taste?"

"I was going to say, some people like it, and some people just don't. And they never will." Folding my hands on the table, I stared down at my fingers for a second before I looked up at her. "The people who are into this kind of thing - can they ever give it up?"

It was pure curiosity, I told myself. But it played well. She thought I was into Ben, and I was feeling out my options. That was exactly what I needed her to believe.

She shrugged, uncomfortably. "I don't know, Jen. I don't think there's always an easy answer for that."

"Sorry, is that...rude?" I turned my gaze back down to my hands, feeling foolish. "I just don't know. I don't know what I'm doing. I'm not saying I'd ask someone to give it up, I just want to understand. Is it recreational fun, or is it part of somebody's sexual identity?"

Maddy half-smiled. "I think you're asking the wrong person."

Shaking my head, I pushed my chair back. "I can't possibly ask him any of this. We barely know each other."

"He doesn't seem very shy," Maddy said, standing up. "I think it's worth a shot, if you really want to know what makes him tick."

Chapter Twelve

Jenna

What makes him tick.

I wasn't sure I wanted to know. But I needed to know, for some reason that I couldn't quite explain. The questions had wormed their way into my brain and wouldn't let go until I had answers.

Later on, I found myself slipping into my nicest dress, brushing my hair, touching up my makeup. Just like I was preparing for a date. Like I had to impress him. Hell, the guy had already proposed to me. What was I after, exactly?

We hadn't agreed on a time, so I waited as long as I could. Staring at the blank wall where I should probably have a TV, but I still hadn't bothered to buy one. When the anxious vibrations in my chest reached a fever pitch, I dumped my essentials into my nice purse and headed for the door.

Halfway there, I saw him across the street. Hands in his pockets, dressed like he was yesterday, before he started slowly unraveling. I wondered if he'd been into work today, even though it was a weekend. Probably.

He certainly hadn't spent the day staring at a blank wall and worrying about what he was going to say when we saw each other.

"I was coming to pick you up," he explained, when I reached him on the sidewalk. "Realized I didn't have your number."

There was something hesitant in the way he spoke, like he was biting back something he really wanted to say. Probably *what the hell*? Because unless he'd dug into his browser history and figured out what I did, what I saw, there was no particular explanation for why I suddenly ran off just as the sun was coming up.

"Yeah," I said. "I realized that too."

I wasn't going to mention that I realized it because I was planning on canceling. It was too late for that now.

He was like something out of a catalog, walking beside me, long strides showing off the perfect cut of his pants. Even though it was still balmy outside, he wore his jacket to complete the look. I had to admit, if he was going to play dominant, at least he dressed the part. There was something about a well-dressed man that primed you to say *yes, Sir*.

Social conditioning. But in his case, there was something more to it.

Even with his tie off and his sleeves rumpled up past his elbows, he exuded a certain authority. Maybe especially like that. Because it was clear, then, that he wasn't just relying on some kind of costume. He was born into this role. He commanded hundreds, maybe thousands of people, on a daily basis. People couldn't say no to him. He snapped his fingers, they obeyed.

He didn't know how to be any other way.

We reached his place in silence, and it wasn't until I was in the massive foyer that I realized I had no idea what to say to him. But apparently, I didn't have to. He headed for the library and gestured for me to follow him - a little twitch of his fingers, but unmistakable, and needing no words.

Without questioning, I followed him.

He sat down behind his desk, and I took my seat across from him. I felt like I'd been called into the principal's office. It was tempting, terribly tempting, to just get up and run away. I didn't want to talk about this. I didn't want to explain myself, or hear his justifications for why he was the way he was.

"I know you left for a reason," he said. "So, just tell me."

Taking a deep breath, I watched him carefully for his reaction. Now or never.

"I saw something on your computer."

There was a moment of heart-stopping silence before he reacted.

He grinned. "You were snooping."

"I wasn't *snooping*." Immediately, I felt defensive, folding my arms across my chest. "I just pulled up your bookmarks. I was curious."

"In what universe does that not count as snooping?" He raised his eyebrows. "A man's bookmarks are private. That's like somebody looking through your purse."

Cringing, I shrunk slightly in my seat. I knew he was right. If I caught him doing something similar to me, I'd kill him. So much for Maddy's assertion that *he'd* be the one on the defensive. I made the choice to delicately ignore his implication that I wouldn't understand the concept of privacy, unless he drew an analogy to something uniquely feminine.

Ugh.

"Who lets somebody use their computer without logging into a guest account first?" I challenged.

He just smirked. "Somebody who trusts his fellow humans."

I couldn't stop myself from rolling my eyes. "Am I supposed to believe that's you?"

"What, do you think I set this up?" He made a *who, me?* gesture with open palms. "You're the one who asked to use my computer."

"No, you offered," I corrected him.

He smirked. "Yeah, I did. Silly me. Thinking you wouldn't go digging through my bookmarks like you were looking for blackmail material." Leaning back in his chair, he looked at me, his face growing serious. "I know what you saw, Jenna. And I know it pissed you off for some reason, because you tried to sneak away at the crack of dawn. But I don't know why, and I can't know unless you tell me."

Really? Was it not obvious to him?

I was still struggling to find the words to explain something so basic. How could he not get it?

"Was I not clear enough about the strictly platonic nature of this arrangement?" he prompted. "It shouldn't matter to you if I'm into balloon-popping or eyeball-licking." He paused. "I'm not, by the way. In case you were wondering. The point being that even if I was, it wouldn't matter, unless you have a policy against doing business without people whose paraphilias don't exactly match up with your own."

I could feel my lips pulling into a thin, disapproving line. It must look terrible, like I was some kind of disapproving schoolmarm judging him for things that were none of my business. But I couldn't just pretend like it didn't bother me.

"At least licking someone's eyeballs isn't demeaning," I said.

He blinked, but his expression didn't change. After a moment, he stood up, walking into the hallway. I stared after him, wondering if he was really just going to pretend like I hadn't spoken.

I followed him, into the kitchen.

Finally, he turned to look at me. He was reaching for something in the wet bar. "If we're going to talk about this, I'm making myself a drink. What do you want? Lemon drop martini?"

I frowned. "That's not what I ordered at the bar."

"But it *is* your favorite drink." That wasn't a question. He turned his attention to filling a shaker with ice. "But for whatever reason, you don't treat yourself often. Maybe you think it's too girly, or it's too extravagant, or too sugary, or too many calories. Hell if I know."

There was a knot of frustration in my chest. This wasn't the direction that our conversation was supposed to go. "Okay, Sherlock Holmes. Fine. Yes, I'll have a lemon drop martini. Not that you seem to be giving me any choice."

I sat down at the island.

"It was the menu," he explained, coming towards me with a glass. "The specialty drink menu at the bar. You were looking at it, and you kept your finger by the 'Skinny Lemon Drop Martini' the whole time." He took a sip of his Jack and coke. "Not that you *need* skinny drinks, mind you."

"I'll drink what I want, thanks." I looked up at him. "Seems like you have a little bit of a sweet tooth, yourself."

"Nothing wrong with that." He sat down nearby, but a few stools away, giving me space. "We can't all drink straight tequila and trap scorpions under the empty glass."

I had to laugh at that. "You think James Bond was into spanking women?"

"Oh, definitely." He smiled. "That's certainly the face of a man who engages in a little rough play every now and then."

"Huh." I was pressing my knees together, protectively, without really understanding why. "I always would've thought that any man who feels really secure in his masculinity wouldn't need to hit a woman."

His face softened a little. "I don't *need* it," he said. "If anyone needs it, it's them."

My heart constricted. "So that's how you look at it, huh?"

A frustrated sigh escaped his lips. "That's not how *I* look at it, it's the truth. Do you really think I'm forcing anybody into something they don't want? Do I strike you as that kind of guy?"

"I don't know!" I insisted. "I don't really know you at all. But I do know that people can hide who they really are. It's easy. And the only time I ever met you when you weren't 'on,' you treated me like I didn't matter." I hadn't intended to talk about our first meeting in the store, but it was all coming out in a rush. "You treated me like I was less than you. Maybe your excuses were legit - maybe you really were just tired and out of your mind. Or maybe that's how you really feel, and you just didn't have the wherewithal to hide it."

I expected him to have a knee-jerk reaction - to be offended, maybe even to yell at me. But he just sat back and re-crossed his legs. I wondered how many times he'd had to have this sort of conversation with a woman, and felt slightly chilled.

"Jenna," he said, "if you *didn't matter*, I wouldn't be talking to you right now. You matter. Disbelieve me about anything else you want, call me a liar, call me insincere, but don't doubt that you matter to me."

His eyes locked with mine, so serious, I had no choice but to believe him. Even if none of this really made sense, I couldn't argue with that logic.

Why I mattered to him was another question entirely - and one that I wasn't prepared to ask.

Taking a deep breath, I fought to hold on to rationality. It was a myth that hurtful, controlling men were just unable to reign in their emotions, that every bad thing they did happened in a fit of passion. Their choices were cold, calculating, meant to entrap and twist the mind into undeserved sympathy. I had to remember that. More likely than not, Mr. Chase was a wolf in sheep's clothing.

"Fine," I said. "So tell me why you're into...*that*."

The corner of his mouth twisted at my tone. "Is there anything I could say that'll make a difference?" he mused, aloud, not really expecting an answer. "Well, I wasn't always. If that makes it better. A woman asked me if I would do it. She liked the idea of the whole

BDSM scene, the dominance and submission dynamic. But the culture didn't appeal. She was sort of...old-fashioned, I guess. She told me that she'd looked into it, and she finally found a version that made sense to her.

"When I started looking into it, my skin crawled, too. It didn't feel right. It was against everything I'd been taught, it seemed regressive, it seemed...well, I don't have to tell you. It wasn't all that different from 'normal' BDSM, but at the same time, it felt like another world. It felt more serious - less like a game. I told her no. It made me uncomfortable. I looked at her, and I just couldn't picture myself acting like some parody of a stern parent. It was distasteful. I respected her too much."

He paused, smiling humorlessly into his glass. "At least, that's what I told myself."

After a moment, he started again, softer this time, his tone laden with the full conviction of his words. "Finally I realized that if I respected her, if I *really* respected her, I'd trust her to know what she wanted. I was treating her like she was fragile. Like I knew better. She was asking me to live out that fantasy of 'Mr. Chase knows best,' but instead, I was giving her the reality. She was strong enough to understand what she really wanted, to admit it, even in a culture that might punish her for wanting exactly what women were supposed to want, just a few generations ago."

I'd expected some kind of impassioned defense, but he was talking like a women's studies textbook. I almost snorted the last mouthful of my martini. "So domestic discipline is a revolutionary act?"

He quirked an eyebrow at my skeptical tone.

"Our culture creates certain desires, cultivates them, and then judges you when you actually want to act them out. You're only allowed to 'know your place' as long as it doesn't bring you any pleasure." His eyes glinted. "I say, fuck that. Fuck them. *Take it back*."

"Oh, boy," I said, looking down at my empty glass. "I think that's the first time somebody's used that line on me."

"It's not a line," he said, earnestly, leaning towards me a little. "I mean it. Every word."

"Yeah, well." I glanced around, looking for some escape that didn't exist. "I think you'll have to find somebody else to help you dismantle the patriarchy through spanking."

Ben leaned back in his seat, a reluctant smile tugging at his mouth. "I wasn't offering," he said. "I was just explaining. It's not backwards, it's just a lot of harmless fun."

This wasn't really a conversation I wanted to have with *anyone*, let alone a near-stranger who wanted me to be his pretend-wife. But it seemed I was stuck with it.

"Look, I get it," I said. "I'm not a prude. I get bondage and blindfolds, I get that a little pain can be fun sometimes. But I just can't wrap my head around making a lifestyle out of it. Actual punishments. Twenty-four-seven crawling around naked in an apron. It's just…it sounds tedious to me."

"Nobody said it had to be twenty-four-seven." Ben twirled his glass around between his thumb and forefinger, slowly, grinning. "I think you might be projecting."

"But that's a thing, isn't it? Twenty-four-seven?

Total power exchange?" I was challenging him with stolen phrases I barely understood, but the sickly-sweet vodka had loosened my tongue and I couldn't stop myself. I wanted some kind of rationale. It was easy enough to see why he might enjoy it, why any man would - but why on earth would any woman willingly become a domestic slave?

He nodded, slowly. "Yes, those are all things. But they're all different. What I do is a playful sort of thing. It's an arrangement. It can be stopped at any time."

An *arrangement*. That didn't sound terribly sexy.

Blowing out a puff of air that caught my too-long bangs and scattered then across my forehead, I glanced at him. He was right. He didn't have to sit here and explain anything to me, but he did. Even if it sounded like he'd just come up with the most over-the-top politically correct excuse he could, whether or not it was based in reality...he was *trying*.

I frowned at the remains of my drink. Maybe, just maybe, he was being honest. Maybe that was really how he felt. It was hard for me to believe, put together with the whole package of Benjamin Chase. He was a contradiction. I wanted my life to be simple.

And yet, I was still considering entering into a marriage of convenience with a billionaire who wanted to spank me. That was...anything but simple.

Hold up.

I did a u-turn on my own train of thought, examining what had just run through my head. *Wanted to spank me.*

Me.

He'd never expressed that. In fact, everything that

I'd mistaken for genuine interest was apparently just him preying on someone desperate enough to agree to his crazy plan. If he liked me - I mean, really liked me, wouldn't he have side-stepped the whole "I have to marry you" thing and made an effort to actually woo me, first?

I mean, probably. It was hard for me to wrap my head around the best course of action for a situation like his.

He began to speak after a long silence. "Once again, to be clear, I wasn't trying to hide it from you, I just didn't think it was important for you to know. The last thing I want is to make this thing more complicated than it already is. Obviously, we're only going to act as a couple in public. I don't expect anything more from you." He glanced at me. "Which I'm sure is a relief, so I won't bother saying that of course it goes both ways."

Laughing slightly, I set my empty glass down. "So that's it? You don't want me to like...go with you to any of those clubs, or whatever?"

He shook his head. "That wasn't part of the deal."

What he *wasn't* saying, however, still reflected in his eyes. He did want me to go to those clubs with him. I could hear the hesitation in his tone, like maybe he'd been hoping to ask me about it later, to ease me into it down the line. Once I was comfortable with him, and let my defenses down. Or maybe I was just imagining things.

"I know you said it was a conditional yes," he went on. "But I hope this doesn't count as a condition."

Even after a long sleep, which should have left my mind refreshed, I still felt tangled up in confusion.

Exhausted, a little raw, wondering if I thought about him spanking me because I actually wanted it, or because the idea had been planted in my head. Because his tattoos made me stupid, and I wanted him to touch me, even if it wasn't the kind of touch I expected.

The things he'd said made sense. His introduction to the world, his reluctance, creating tension in his relationship because he couldn't wrap his head around it. Not so long ago, he'd been like me, standing on the outside looking in.

My eyes were fixed on the polished hard wood floor in front of me, but I dragged them up to his face with an effort.

"I need to trust you," I said, simply. "And I'm not sure I can."

Silently, thoughtfully, he folded his hands on the desk. His fingers intertwined.

"Plenty of women have chosen to trust me," he said. "None of them ever regretted it."

"Not even your ex-wife?"

It was a low blow. I didn't mean it that way - it just escaped, without permission, dangling in the air while he held his face in a carefully composed mask.

A moment later, he shook his head. "She never trusted me," he said. "But I've learned a lot since then."

I didn't know what that meant.

Two million dollars. Was I really thinking about walking away?

I thought about Maddy. How happy she looked, having reconnected with her husband just days after a blowout fight, touching some deep level of feeling that I couldn't even begin to imagine. The quiet authority in his voice when he told her when she was going to meet me, gave her a schedule like he was actually still her boss. And the way she warmed to it, obviously loving his control.

Because she trusted him.

Trust was key. No matter what, I couldn't get around that.

"This is a different kind of trust," I said, at last. "It's one thing to trust a guy not to physically harm you, but this…"

Ben raised an eyebrow. "You think what I do is *easy*?" He paused, as if he actually expected an answer, before continuing. "It's not about accidentally hitting too hard. If you can't avoid that, you've got no business being around other human beings in the first place. My responsibilities go so much deeper. And so does their trust. They have to trust me to know their limits, to read their reactions, to understand every little moan and whisper of their body language like I'm reading a book. They have to trust me to know their fantasies before they know them. That's the most you'll ever trust anyone, in this life. It's not one snap decision, one moment, it's a constant balancing act that I can never let go." He fixed me with a look, and it spoke of cool detachment, but there was always something swirling in his eyes. "If *they* can trust me, you can trust me."

I didn't know about that.

All the same, there was something hypnotic about the way he spoke. It would be so easy, so terribly easy, I thought, to fall under his spell.

Of course it would. I was vulnerable, I was alone, I was looking for reassurance. A place to belong. However enticing certain aspects of these man might be, he wasn't it.

"So what do you think, Ms. Hadley?" His elbows were resting on the desk, hands folded in front of his face, not-quite obscuring his smile. "Don't say no. Not now. I've already bought the ring."

I felt too warm, suddenly, my fingertips tingling with an excitement I couldn't name. "Really?"

He gave a single nod.

"Let me see it."

Lowering his hands, he reached for something on his desk, like he suddenly needed something for his hands to do. "No."

I cleared my throat. "Sorry?"

"No," he repeated. "You're not going to start wearing it yet. We can't announce our engagement right away, that's absurd."

"So? I can still see it." I caught myself before I actually started pouting - what was it about him that brought out my inner brat? "Come on. I want to know what kind of rock billionaires buy for their girlfriends."

"And you will, when it's time," he said, simply. He had the maddening tone of someone who's so used to getting his own way, there was no need to be defensive or to protest. His way was the only way.

Well, one thing was clear. If I wanted to make this work, I was going to have to play along.

"Fine," I said. My tone was full of calm acceptance.

He looked at me with a hint of suspicion. "Fine?" he echoed. "That's it?"

"That's it." I smiled. "Now, are you going to offer me dinner?"

Something in the room had changed. I couldn't define it, but he *chilled*, palpably, some door inside of him slamming shut with nearly audible bang.

"I think we're going to be seeing plenty of each other soon," he said. "Go home and get some rest. Are you taking care of Laura tomorrow?"

I nodded, trying to make sense of his sudden change of attitude. "For the next two days," I said. "Then I'm free until Friday."

Standing up, he started shuffling the papers on his desk. "Good. On Wednesday, I want you to come to the office with me and meet everyone. Keep your schedule clear. Can you do that?"

"Yes."

Yes, Sir.

I answered automatically, without hesitation or question. I thought I saw a slight grimace on his face, but it quickly disappeared.

What the hell did I do wrong?

Chapter Thirteen

Ben

Son of a bitch, son of a bitch, son of a mother flipping cocksucking *bitch*.

This girl had me so tied up in knots, even my cursing didn't make sense anymore.

How I'd managed to keep my cool for as long as I did, I'll never know. When I woke up to the sound of the front door clicking shut, I figured, worst case scenario she must have had an attack of conscience - or an attack of good sense, maybe, about our plans. But that wasn't right. She'd very specifically changed her tune right after I left her alone with my computer.

A ball of panic started to form in my chest, and I sat there with my hand on the closed laptop for a while before I had the courage to open it.

There was nothing on there. I knew there was nothing on there. It was practically a full-time loaner, just for casual use, and I was very careful not to leave anything personal on it. It was safe. I'd let near-strangers use it a thousand times.

There must be something I was forgetting.

Finally, I forced myself to look. If I wanted to catch her before she got all the way home, I needed to know what I was dealing with - and fast.

When I spotted it, my stomach leapt into my throat.

I'd completely fucking forgotten bookmarking that site on this fucking thing. Not that it usually mattered. But I must've been drunk. Did I think I was being subtle, naming it some random string of letters? It stood out like a sore fucking thumb. I should have called it "Carpet Repair" or something.

Carpet repair. Jesus Christ.

Before I had a chance to think about it, I was running out the front door, heading down the sidewalk towards her neighborhood. It was sheer luck that I managed to run into her, and pretty remarkable that she actually stopped to talk to me. Agreed to see me again, nonetheless.

I could see the barely-concealed revulsion in her eyes. She didn't understand it. Of course she didn't. It was one of those things you had to *feel*. Everything I'd told her about my history was true. The first time Daria told me she wanted it, I wondered how I'd managed to hitch my wagon to a mental patient. I was about as judgmental as they come. Then, when I finally had her moaning and squirming underneath my hand, everything started to make a *whole lot of sense*.

It wasn't just about sex. I mean, sure, you'd have to be robot not to get a hard-on with a sexy woman squealing and shimmying across your lap, especially when you can feel her getting hot for you, punishment or no punishment. But the power, the control, it was intoxicating even beyond that. Even though I never had Daria's trust, I had something like it. And with her, I learned that *almost* was good enough.

Of course Jenna didn't understand it. I couldn't expect her to. But that wasn't what bothered me. I'd talked her back into our deal; that was no problem. I was persuasive. Short of her discovering I was the Zodiac killer, there was nothing I couldn't silver-tongue my way out of. That wasn't the reason why my brain felt like it was trying to swallow itself.

She *wanted* it.

Some men, some Doms, they claim they can look at a woman and just *know* if she's a natural submissive. I happen to think they're full of shit. People can put on all kinds of masks, all kinds of performances, during their everyday life. What I do is all about stripping those away, slowly, slowly revealing the person underneath who just craves pure sensation. The submission is just a way to get there. In the end, it's all about feelings. Triggering the right brain chemicals. Pretty soon, you're hooked.

Jenna wasn't hooked yet. But oh, she wanted a taste.

I could tell.

When we met, if she had the desire, it was dormant. It was too deeply hidden for me to see. But once the idea was planted in her head…

Well. Now, it had wormed its way into her brain. There was no way it was coming back out. Even if she never did it, for the rest of her life, she'd wonder.

And I didn't want that for her.

There was beauty in submission, yes. There was comfort. There was happiness, for those who wanted it, they got some kind of gratification they couldn't find any other way. But I'd never been fully convinced that they didn't lose a part of themselves in the process.

While something inside me growled with pleasure at seeing a powerful, independent woman subdued - another part of me still recoiled. I believed everything I'd said to Jenna - at least, I wanted to. Those were the justifications I'd read, over and over again, until I could recite them to myself whenever I had doubts. But that spark she'd had when she confronted me in the grocery store, the way she didn't even think twice, just saw me acting like an entitled asshole and lashed out. I never wanted to see that disappear. I didn't want to see her bite it back, I didn't want to see all kinds of unspoken things flashing in her eyes while she reluctantly bowed her head. It wasn't right. She deserved better.

Better than me, at any rate.

I didn't contact her again until the day before our planned visit to my offices. Thankfully, I'd actually remembered to get her number this time. After some thought, I elected not to mention how I'd practically kicked her out of my house. A proactive apology would be nice, but it also had the potential to breed unnecessary awkwardness. Better to pretend it never happened. Hopefully, she'd do me the same courtesy.

After an hour or so, she responded to my text, just as coolly and nonchalantly as I could have hoped. Yes, we were still on. She wondered what she should wear.

Let me worry about that, I told her, pressing send before I had a chance to stop myself.

Shit, I really had to stop giving this woman orders. But I already had a plan in place, involving a boutique downtown that already had my Amex on file. They knew my tastes, and they knew how to make a woman look good in them. She'd be perfectly dressed for the part. I had to smile when I pictured her going to the door with a frown on her face, not expecting a package, only to find a beautifully wrapped box from a place she'd probably never dreamed of setting foot in.

This was my favorite gift to give a woman, and one I reserved for special occasions. In this case, of course, it wasn't so much a gift as a necessary expense for our facade. But of course, I'd let her keep it. I've always felt that a dress belongs to its owner in some special way. It always carries the memory of her, no matter what happens.

I half-expected a call or a text, the next morning. What the hell? I worried that she hadn't gotten the package, that something had been mixed up along the way. The boutique didn't open for another hour and a half, but I tried calling anyway, and the owner answered on the first ring.

"Good morning, Mr. Chase," she said, smoothly. "How can I help you?"

"I just wanted to make sure that delivery went through," I said. "Haven't heard anything from the recipient."

"It certainly did, Mr. Chase. She even signed for it. Would you like to talk to the courier?"

"No, thanks, that won't be necessary." I sighed. "I appreciate it."

"Anytime, Mr. Chase."

So. Either I'd pissed Jenna off, or she was just going the route of quiet submission to my will. Damn it.

Or maybe she's just being polite, and you're being ridiculously melodramatic.

No, polite would be *thank you*. And it wasn't a gift, not really. It was an order, tied up with a pretty bow, but an order all the same. As much as I tried to act like a normal person, I couldn't help slipping into this role. Especially when it came to her.

It was odd. With Daria, with all the others, I always felt like I was wearing a mask. Every action I took as their Dominant, as their would-be *Head of Household*, was carefully thought-out. I had to consider my every move, lest my instincts lead me in the wrong direction. But with Jenna, it came naturally. I must have grown more accustomed to it than I thought.

My driver, Tim, was waiting for me patiently. Since I asked my employees to arrive by nine o'clock, I always made a point of showing up by eight-thirty so they'd see me settled in already. It was all about setting a good example. This morning, however, time was just slipping away from me. I finally climbed into the backseat of the town car, fighting the nagging sensation that I was forgetting something.

He got us to Jenna's place in record time, and her front door popped open almost as soon as Tim pulled up to the curb. She walked down the stairs quickly, not giving me nearly enough time to appreciate the masterpiece she was wrapped up in.

From head to toe, she looked ready for the red carpet. Her silky dark hair cascaded down, almost unstyled, which suited her best. It was humanly impossible *not* to imagine running my fingers through it. The dress was a rich shade of eggplant, bringing out some hint of violet in her midnight-blue eyes. The neckline dipped just low enough to hint, but not quite tease, while the fabric clung just right to show off the swing of her hips.

My mouth was suddenly dry.

Suddenly remembering myself, I hopped out quickly, almost colliding with Tim as he went to the open her door. "No, it's fine, I'll get it," I told him, trying to jockey past as an irritated driver honked at us for blocking part of the road.

By the time I made it past him, she was already climbing in. I sighed, and returned to my seat. So much for chivalry.

"You should let me open your door for you," I said, as she gave me a bemused look.

"Seemed like there was some confusion," she said, shrugging. "I thought I'd cut out the middle-man."

This was going to be a long day.

I stabbed the button to raise the partition, and turned to her. "It's one thing around here, where no one's going to notice. But when we're going to be seen together, you need to act like my girlfriend. Like you're expecting me to treat you like a princess."

She rolled her eyes. "Oh my God, what is this? Tsarist Russia? Wait, I know, maybe I should sleep on forty mattresses with a pea under it, so I can prove to the commoners that I'm worthy of your love."

The spike of annoyance in my chest was actually a relief. She hadn't changed. "Just trust me, Jenna. I know this world. You don't."

"Okay, well, I'm pretty sure Mark Zuckerberg's wife opens her own door when she gets into his Honda Fit. Just because you're rich doesn't mean you have to act like disgustingly old money."

"We have to get into the habit," I said, firmly. "People will notice. Mentors of mine, people who've been like parents to me. They're old-fashioned. They need to see me taking care of you."

She absorbed this silently for a while, her arms folded across her chest. It was defensive posture, but I could tell it was beginning to sink in. She really didn't know this world, and she was realizing that now. But it was satisfying to argue with her, rather than her just accepting her fate.

"Thank you for the dress," she said, quietly, after a while.

"My pleasure," I said, fighting to keep the innuendo out of my tone. I was almost successful.

"How'd you know my size?"

"You left your clothes in my laundry room all night, remember?" Belatedly, I realized how creepy that sounded. "I promise, I barely touched them. Just enough to read the tags."

She smirked. "Hey, here's a tip, next time you do something like that, just tell her that you knew by *looking* at her. I don't know why, but women seem to find that very attractive in a man. It definitely sounds better than 'I rifled through your clothes.'"

"I'm supposed to know someone's dress size by looking at them?" I frowned at her. "How the hell is that even possible?"

"I don't know, try asking one of those carnies who guesses people's weight. It's in all the romance novels." She sighed, leaning her head back on the seat. "The size-guessing thing, I mean, not carnies. For some reason, they're not so hot."

For a moment, I sat in silence, wondering if I

really should feel creepy for touching her clothes. It seemed like a necessary evil, and I certainly didn't have any size-guessing superpowers.

Finally, she spoke.

"So, what was the other night all about?"

It was the exact question I'd been dreading. I could play dumb, and if I really committed, she'd probably go along with it. That wasn't like her. Even if we were still practically strangers, I knew that much. She wasn't one to bite her tongue. But the other night, when I'd talked to her in that tone...she melted to it. We'd fallen into the exact roles I didn't want us to take, because I knew where that was headed.

It never lasted. Not when I was involved.

I wasn't going to play dumb.

"I'm sorry about that," I said, putting on a remorseful smile. "Just had a bad day. I guess it hit me all of a sudden. I didn't get much sleep either, and you know how that goes for me. It's like feeding a Mogwai after midnight."

She might be poking at my defenses, but she had a wall up herself. I felt it crack, just a little, as she smiled at my stupid joke. "Okay," she said. "Well, good. I was afraid I did something."

"No," I lied, leading her towards the waiting town car. "Of course not."

After that, she was quiet. Thoughtful. Closed off, even, which was good. The more she kept her distance, the easier this would be.

Chapter Fourteen

Jenna

The building was breathtaking.

It felt like something out of a movie - gleaming marble floors, a massive bank of elevators with attendants, and even towering tropical trees in the corner. I couldn't imagine walking into a place like this and knowing that it all belonged to me. That it was *my* responsibility.

"Morning, Mr. Chase," the security guard called from his glass box. Ben waved, and they exchanged brief pleasantries as we headed towards the elevator. It didn't escape my notice that Ben had bothered to retain the names of the guy's kids, and the fact that his daughter just graduated to the next level of Girl Scouts. Unless, of course, it was all bullshit and the guard was just too polite - or too cowed - to say anything.

"Going to your office, Mr. Chase?" the elevator attendant asked with a cheerful smile. He nodded at me in acknowledgement of my presence, clearly not knowing who I was.

"Yes, Dave. Thanks." Ben rested his hand on the small of my back, lightly, just a ghost of a touch. But it was like every inch of my skin suddenly came alive, responding to the warmth that radiated through my dress. "This is my girlfriend, Ms. Jenna Hadley."

Dave took this in stride, as I supposed any professional elevator attendant would. But I thought I detected a hint of surprise. "It's wonderful to meet you, Ms. Hadley. Please don't hesitate to ask if you need anything."

Anything elevator-related, I presumed. I just smiled and thanked him, although I found myself spending the rest of the ride wondering whether he'd get in trouble if *Mr. Chase's girlfriend* sent him on a personal errand that took him away from his post. I hoped not. It was hard not to feel like a bull in a china shop. I was acutely aware that I was upsetting some kind of delicate ecosystem here, a world about which I understood absolutely nothing. And since this wasn't a heartwarming Nora Ephron comedy, I had a feeling it wasn't going to end with everybody deciding things were better when you just cut loose.

The elevator was so quick it made my heart drop into my stomach. Or maybe that was the way Ben's fingers curled against my lower back, just slightly, before he seemed to suddenly realize what he was doing, and pulled his hand away.

When the doors popped open, I took a deep breath and stepped out. The hallway was so long I couldn't see the end on either side, so I waited for Ben to follow, guiding me to the left and down another hallway I hadn't even noticed at first.

"How big is this place?" I muttered under my

breath, mostly to myself. He just smiled, gesturing me towards the huge double doors that evidently led into his office.

I bit the inside of my cheek to stifle a gasp.

The whole back wall was nothing but picture windows, displaying a gorgeous cityscape. I couldn't stop myself from walking over to them, pressing up against the glass and staring down until I started to feel a rush of vertigo. My knees wobbled slightly.

"Careful," said Ben, taking my elbow. "Don't look down."

I wanted to snap that I was fine, but instead, I just turned my gaze upwards. The city looked like an ant farm from up here, everything tiny and inconsequential compared to us.

The rest of the office was skillfully decorated, but it paled in comparison to the view. I walked around the perimeter, while Ben sat down at his desk and started looking through his drawers.

On the wall furthest from the door, there were several plaques and awards displayed, most of them emblazoned with the names of organizations or societies that meant nothing to me. My eyes were drawn to some of the plainer, more official-looking certificates, and I slowly began to realize what they actually were.

Diplomas. He had a bachelor's degree and a Master's of Science in Pharmacology, both from NYU. My brow furrowed.

"Are these real?"

He glanced up at me. "Yes, I really did win 'Most Improved' in Little League. Also, the diplomas didn't come from Kinko's. What kind of question is that?"

I sighed. "Obviously I know they're real, I just meant...I thought maybe they were honorary degrees, or something. I'm sorry."

Shrugging, he gestured to the chairs opposite his desk. "It's fine. Most people assume the same thing. I just wanted to understand at least *some* of what our science department was talking about, so I went to school for it. So you see, I'm not just an empty-headed socialite after all."

I sat down, feeling slightly cowed. At least he took it in good humor, more or less. His desk was massive, solid wood, polished perfectly and organized in precisely the way his desk at home wasn't. Someone else must manage this for him. An assistant, most likely. Hell, a guy on his level probably had six or seven interns at his beck and call too.

As if on cue, there was a quiet rapping at the door. "Come in," Ben said, and the door swung open slowly. A young, doe-eyed blonde was standing there, carrying a cup of coffee.

"Drew the short straw this morning, huh, Claire?" He smiled as she approached, and I could practically feel her stress level ratchet down a few notches. "Thanks. It's perfect."

"You're welcome, Mr. Chase," she said, or rather squeaked.

"This is my girlfriend, Ms. Jenna Hadley."

I was going to have to get used to hearing that.

"It's so nice to meet you," Claire half-whispered, shaking my hand with her cold, clammy one. She swallowed audibly. "I'm sorry. It's my first day. I'm still getting my bearings."

"Please, don't apologize. It's nice to meet you too."

She disappeared out the door a moment later. I ignored the knot in my chest, which was certainly not jealousy. A girl like her couldn't possibly handle a man like Ben, with all his complexities and dark desires.

I couldn't stop staring at his desk, wondering if he'd ever spanked anyone on it. Did that extend beyond the boundaries of *domestic* discipline?

Maybe women in the workplace just weren't compatible with it at all. I suppressed a laugh, sitting down carefully in one of the chairs across from him.

"Penny for your thoughts," he said, glancing up at me as he began hunting through drawers again. "Damn it. I can never find anything once they've cleaned up in here."

"Nothing," I said. "Just admiring your desk. It's very, uh, imposing."

"Intimidating the subordinates is always good," he said, with a grin. "I play good cop, the desk plays bad cop. Everybody wins."

"I don't think people like Claire are afraid of your desk," I pointed out. "They're just afraid of you. It doesn't matter what your personality is. Anybody with as much power as you have is...well, scary. For lack of a better term."

He just laughed. "Do I scare you?"

"I mean, on a personal level? No. But in the sense that you could probably make me disappear without a trace, if you wanted to? Yeah, a little. Rich people are dangerous. They're basically unstoppable."

I was echoing my parents' sentiments, without consciously meaning to. They'd spent so much time and effort drilling them into my head, it wasn't a surprise that a few of them actually stuck. But really, I didn't need them. I'd seen enough firsthand to know that money was power, and power corrupts.

And the closest thing to absolute power was having a net worth of almost fifty billion dollars.

Benjamin Chase could practically run his own space program. He could charter a private jet twice a day just to take him across town. That kind of wealth made you crazy, utterly disconnected you from any kind of reality.

But there was something else, too. It struck me, the more time I spent with him, that none of this was particularly interesting for Ben. Certainly not enjoyable. His money made his life easier in countless ways, there was no doubt about that, but it was just *normal* for him. It always had been. Someone like me could sit and imagine being able to thoughtlessly spend thousands of dollars on a single bottle of champagne, and it seemed like it would be a thrill. And maybe the first time, it would be. But for Ben? It was just like buying a cup of coffee.

I was hardly wallowing in sympathy for the guy, but it was hard to imagine all this excess being so *joyless*. So empty and without any sense of excitement or thrill. No wonder guys like him had to drive race cars around a track until they crashed and caught fire, just to feel something.

Or spank women recreationally. I supposed that was another way to get one's kicks.

"Do you have an assistant?" I asked him, finally. "Or...a secretary or something?"

"*Administrative* assistant," he said. "Yes. She's fantastic, except when she cleans up my desk. I can't figure out her organizational scheme at all. I'm pretty sure it's one of the signs of a budding psychopath."

He glanced up at me. "What's that sour expression? You trying to scope out all the women in the office, so you know who you should act jealous of?"

It was a harmless joke. Nothing more. But an angry heat flared in my chest, and I could feel a flush creeping up my neck. "Billionaires and their secretaries, right? It's practically a cliche at this point. I'm just trying to figure out where I stand." I cleared my throat. "Theoretically speaking, of course."

"Theoretically, you've got nothing to be worried about," he said. There was a glint in his eyes, or maybe I just imagined it. "Theoretically, my assistant is happily married, and would happily flay me alive if I dared to make a pass at her, which I most certainly wouldn't, by the way. Actually, none of that is theoretical. It's all true."

"Yeah, well, nobody thinks they're a cheater until they become one." I glanced over my shoulder. "Theoretically, if I were the jealous type, I wouldn't care about any of that. I'd just see if I thought she was attractive, if I thought you might be attracted to her, and I'd smell blood in the water."

"Are you the jealous type?" he asked me.

"Theoretically," I said. "It lends some credence to the performance, doesn't it?"

"Theoretically," he said. "If you want any tips, just watch Maddy. I hear she's fiercely possessive."

I laughed. "Some things never change. Does it drive Daniel crazy?"

Ben shook his head, with a smile. "He *likes* it, if you can believe that. Makes him feel special. I don't know why. Even animals can feel jealous. It's the basest emotion there is. The most selfish, too. But he thinks it means something, and that's all that really matters. Jealousy signifies love to a lot of people. I always thought Daniel was smarter than that, but…" He shrugged. "I guess nobody's smart when it comes to hormones, right?"

"I think it's kind of sweet," I admitted. "Exhausting, sure, but I don't usually judge how people decide to spend their time. Some people play chess, some people do tai chi, some people get jealous. And hell - I mean, if I landed a guy like Daniel, I'd probably be worried about that too."

Ben's forehead crinkled slightly. "You like him?"

"Not him," I said quickly. "Not him exactly. You know what I mean. Someone…desirable."

The clock ticked very loudly.

"I'm keeping you away from work," I said, after a few moments that felt like an eternity. "Sorry. Uh, should I just…come back around lunchtime, or…?"

"You're not," he said, at last, seeming to untie his tongue with an effort. "I promise. But you don't have to sit here and stare at me all day. I'll have one of the interns show you around, get the full office tour. It might come in handy someday if you need to act like you've actually hung out here voluntarily, from time to time." He cleared his throat. "And after that, well…" He hesitated. "Yes, we'll talk at lunch."

Chapter Fifteen

Jenna

I still couldn't wrap my head around the size of the place. A fresh-faced intern named Greg showed me around the offices, babbling enthusiastically about every department and every feature. I could hardly tune in to what he was saying, but I smiled and nodded, trying to pretend like my mind wasn't back in the office with Ben, trying to figure out what he hadn't said to me.

I was anxious for lunch, but not because I was hungry. In fact, I wasn't sure I could eat at all. My nerves were jangled, my stomach tied in knots, and I really didn't know why. After Greg proudly showed me the fancy employee gym, which included a bank of blood pressure monitors, he got an important phone call and had to dart off for a few minutes. To avoid chewing my fingernails down to the nubbins, I plopped myself down in one of the monitors and stuck my arm in the cuff, just for the hell of it.

According to the machine, I was in Stage 2 hypertension and my heart was racing like I'd run ten miles on a Stairmaster.

Briefly, I wondered if fresh-faced Greg would run and fetch me a damn Xanax.

I quickly cleared the display before Greg came back, lest he insist on driving me to the hospital. If possible, he seemed even more perky than usual.

"So, do you want to tour I.T. next?" he asked me.

"Actually, um, I have to make a few phone calls." I cleared my throat, hoping I didn't look as pale as I felt. "Is there somewhere quiet I can go?"

"Absolutely." He ushered me down the hall, towards some empty-looking offices. "We reserve these spaces for any contractors or consultants who might need a place to work. Please, take your time, and page me if you need anything."

I sat down in the office and closed my eyes, focusing on deep, steady breaths. At first, all I could heard was my heart racing, but eventually I began to calm down.

The place wasn't nearly as nice as Ben's, or as expansive, but that was probably just as well. I didn't think full-length picture windows would particularly calm me down. It was small, and it was quiet. That was all I needed.

I sat there with my phone in my hand, thinking about calling Maddy. Things were rushing forward so quickly, and here Ben was introducing me to all of his employees as his girlfriend. Just last week, I'd told her that I had no serious intentions towards Ben. Of course she didn't believe me, and something told me that she wouldn't be shocked, but I had to play my cards carefully. At this rate, everyone in my life was going to think I'd completely lost my marbles.

By the time I'd calmed down, it was after eleven o'clock. I took a few more deep breaths and finger-combed my hair a bit, then heard a light tapping at the door just as I stood up.

"Yes?"

Greg poked his head in. "Sorry to bother you, but Mr. Chase said you had plans for an early lunch." He looked...flustered? Embarrassed? Something had clearly shaken him. Poor Greg. Frowning, I followed him down the hallway and over to yet another massive bank of elevators.

"Do you need me to show you the way back to his office?" he asked, looking like he wished I'd say no.

"Um, do you mind?" I had no idea where the hell I was in relation to my starting point. It might as well have been Antarctica.

He let out a tight breath. "Of course not," he said, falling silent as the elevator doors closed. I wondered what the hell was wrong, until we reached the right floor and I got close enough to see the look on Ben's face, loitering in the doorway to his office.

"Hello, darling," he said, in a tone that almost convinced me. I let him grab my hand and jerk me close, very close, workplace-inappropriate-close. His mouth descended on mine, and I melted to it like we'd been lovers for years. It felt so *natural*. His tongue sought access and I granted it, forgetting to care that we were being watched, forgetting this wasn't real. My knees buckled, and I leaned against him, feeling his body's unmistakable reaction.

A moment later, he pulled away, and glanced at poor fresh-faced Greg. He was still standing there, red as a beet, waiting for the cue to leave.

I swallowed. Hard.

"See we're not disturbed, Greg. You can go." Ben's voice was husky. Greg nodded, disappearing down the hallway as fast as his legs would carry him.

Ben pulled me inside, shutting and locking the double doors with one hasty, smooth motion. My heart was hammering again. Some part of me really thought he intended to do this - and while my brain reeled at the presumptuousness of it, I couldn't deny that I wanted it. I couldn't deny his kiss had brought my body to life.

He stabbed a button on his phone intercom. "Carol, hold all my calls."

Carol's voice squawked through the speaker. "You already told me that, sir."

"Oh, did I? Something seems to have scattered my thoughts. I apologize, Carol."

"Don't mention it, sir," she said, dryly.

I stared at him, and he stared at me. For a moment, I swear he was almost about to grab me and push me onto the desk. But the wildness in his eyes faded, and he cleared his throat lightly.

"Early lunch, huh?" I said, faintly, lowering myself into a chair. "That's subtle."

"Got to make it convincing." He cleared his throat, sitting down and adjusting his jacket. "Sorry about that display out there, I should've warned you."

"It's fine," I said. "I can roll with the punches."

He smiled. "So to speak."

"What's the, uh...what's the plan, exactly?"

"Well, we'll stay in here for a while," he said. "Then, we'll actually order some lunch. At that point, we should both look like two people who just had furtive sex at work, but are trying to hide it. But not trying *too* hard. It's a subtle art. But I'm sure you can give me some pointers, with your training."

I laughed, then I realized he was serious. "What, you want me to...finger-tease my hair?"

"Sure," he said. "Whatever you call it. Look disheveled, but not *too* disheveled. Don't worry, after lunch you can go home and try to wash the stain off your soul."

He wanted a performance? Well, I'd give him one hell of a performance. I buried my fingers into my hair and ruffled hard, then rubbed in circles with a flat hand on the back of my head, to create the illusion of sex-hair. Purposely smudging my lipstick with my hand, I was struck with inspiration. I dug into my purse. Ben was undoing his tie, looking at me with vague interest.

"Come here," I said, holding up my lipstick.

"Seriously?" He grimaced as I approached, dabbing some into my finger and smearing it along his jawline. "Nobody's going to notice that."

"Not consciously," I said, trying hard not to notice the feeling of his stubble on my skin. "But the whole is greater than the sum of its parts. It's like how they handmade all the chain mail for *Lord of the Rings*. Seems like overkill, but it's what you *don't* notice that contributes to the overall effect of realism."

"Hmm." He still smelled good. And expensive. "You might be right."

"Do you have some of that cologne here?" I asked him.

He hesitated for a moment, then smiled. "Yes," he said. "In the bathroom. See, I knew you'd be good at this."

I hadn't even noticed the door in the corner, designed to blend into the wall. Inside, it was almost as nice as the one at his apartment, but not quite as big. There was a shower, though, which I imagined came in handy for those all-nighters. I wondered how often he ended up sleeping here.

The beautiful mirrored medicine cabinet had a little bottle in it. I lifted it carefully, and unscrewed the lid.

"Wait," he said, following me into the small room. "Let me do it. Otherwise it's just going to smell like you're wearing it on purpose."

I rolled my eyes.

"Someone's skin chemistry completely changes the smell," he insisted, dabbing a little bit onto his fingertips. "Didn't you just say it's the little things that count?"

"So I did."

"Where do you want it?" he asked, without a hint of irony.

I stared at him for a moment.

He raised his eyebrows, expectantly.

"Um - well - where do *you* wear it?" I countered. "Because, you know, if the idea is that it rubbed off on me, from you, I need to figure out what the most likely..." I cleared my throat. "...uh, mode of...you know, transmission. Was."

"Sure," he said, his eyes sparkling. He gestured vaguely in his chest region "So..."

"So," I said, my pulse fluttering again. With hesitant fingers, I reached up and touched my collarbone. "About here, then?"

"All right." He looked more serious now, stroking gently along the edge of the bone, dipping slightly below into the soft skin. The scent rose as it warmed to my body, and he rubbed it in, gently.

"Normally," he murmured, "you just dab, but in this case we're trying to create the illusion of…" His eyes flicked up to mine, briefly. "…friction."

My breath caught audibly in my throat. "Right," I said.

His fingers drifted down to the neckline of my dress, tracing along, leaving a trail of sensation along my skin. I shivered. He wasn't putting the cologne on anymore.

"Your lipstick's not right," he said, quietly. "I think you'd better put it back on, and start again."

I swallowed hard. It was still clutched in my palm, but I didn't think I could steady my hand enough to avoid looking like a clown.

"The…the lighting's terrible in here," I said.

"Let me." He reached for the lipstick, pulling it from my fingers. I didn't try to stop him. I stood there, with my lips already parted, while he leaned forward and gently painted me with color. "You know," he said, his breath so close I could feel it on my face, "I read somewhere that the whole point of lipstick was to remind men what you look like when you're aroused."

He finished, and I smacked my lips gently. "Yeah, and have you ever noticed what your tie's pointing to?" I smiled.

"The more refined we try to be, the more animal we are." He was still standing close, so close, and all I could breathe, all I could see, all I could smell, was him. "Isn't that always the way?"

I lifted my hand to my face, but he stopped me with a gentle touch on my wrist. "What are you doing?"

"Smearing it," I said, breathlessly.

He shook his head, loosening his collar. "Didn't you ever hear of killing two birds with one stone?"

It was a dare. A challenge. I stared at him, and he stared at me.

I wasn't going to let him win. Not this time.

Stepping forward, closing the distance between us, I went up on tiptoe and pressed my lips to his neck. It wasn't a kiss, not at first - until it was.

I felt his whole body react, his arms flexing automatically as if to grab me and pull me closer, before his brain kicked in and remembered what we were really doing. My lips trailed down to his shoulder, seemingly on their own. A moment later, I managed to yank myself away.

His eyes were hooded, slightly downcast. As he raised them to my face, I felt the tension in the room pulled to the breaking point, ready to snap.

Chirp chirp. Chirp chirp.

For a moment, his face blanked with confusion. Then he shook his head, reaching into his pocket hastily.

"Shit." He fumbled with the screen. "I have a meeting in half an hour. We've got to order lunch now if we want to get caught on schedule."

I let out a sigh of relief - at least, I hoped that's what it was. He fled the bathroom and I stood there for a moment, clutching the edge of the sink, trying to reorganize my thoughts into something passable as sanity.

"What do you want?" he called out, from the main part of his office.

It took me a few seconds to remember what he was talking about. Right. Food.

"Whatever," I said. I was pretty sure I wouldn't be able to eat it, anyway. My mouth was like a desert, my stomach like a clenched fist.

A few minutes later, it occurred to me that I'd just made him order for me. So much for trying to maintain my independence in this fake relationship. I ran the sink and dabbed a little water around my hairline, to create the illusion of vigorous activity that had just recently ended. Then, I returned back to my seat on slightly unsteady legs.

Ben looked angry. He was reading something, or at least pretending to read it, eyes darting across the page while his lip twitched in an almost sneer.

"Relax," I told him, before I could stop myself. "Nobody's going to believe we just had sex if you look like you're about to blow a gasket."

Right on cue, there was a knock at the door. I glanced up with a frown. I'd vaguely heard Ben order, but I couldn't remember what. It didn't seem long enough, anyway.

"Come in!" Ben sounded slightly out-of-sorts, just enough for the facade we were putting on. By the time yet another fresh-faced intern walked in, he'd managed to arrange his face into an expression that didn't look so angry.

I could feel the knot of frustration in my chest, too, but I thought I did a pretty good job of hiding it behind an expression of guilt and embarrassment. The poor intern practically dropped the food and ran, blushing bright red as she processed the sight in front of her.

"That's all, really?" I muttered, after the door slammed shut. "How do you know she'll even tell anyone?"

"Oh, she will." Ben's mouth twisted as he dug into the bag. "I made sure to find out who the biggest gossip is. The whole office will know within ten minutes."

I poked at my food, but could hardly taste it. The room was tense, but not like before - it wasn't the pleasant kind of tension that seemed like it would end with explosive pleasure, but rather the kind that might end with a chair going through one of those gorgeous windows.

The irony of the situation didn't escape my notice. Everyone in the office, by Ben's estimation, now thought we were basking in some not-so-furtive afterglow, when in reality, I wanted to tear my hair out from frustration.

That was it. I couldn't let this happen again. As much fun as it might've been in the moment, if it wasn't going to go any further, I had to put a stop to it.

No more funny business.

"I should probably go," I said, quietly, after moving the food around for what felt like ages.

Ben nodded, tersely. "I'll call you tomorrow."

No more funny business. And that was *final*.

I sat with my phone in my hand for a long time.

I had to tell my parents. The longer I put it off, the harder it was going to be. Before I hit the button, I took a series of deep breaths, rehearsing my story over and over again in my head. It felt so *wrong*, doing this, but I kept reminding myself it was for the greater good. My parents wanted me to be successful, and this was how I was going to accomplish it.

The conversation was full of awkward pauses, long silences, and confused questions. They sounded hurt, particularly my mother, but not as much as I'd feared. I realized that I was still hearkening back to those days when I was still the center of their world.

Not that I wasn't, now. But it was different. On some level, they could accept that I'd moved on, that there were important parts of my life that they hadn't been privy to.

"Are you sure, honey?" my mom kept saying, with concern in her voice. "I mean, how well do you really know this man?"

I had to keep reassuring her with lies, telling her how well I'd gotten to know him - the *real* him, and how much he appreciated being with someone who didn't care about his money. How kind and considerate he was, how smart, how successful.

While most parents would have been thrilled to hear that their daughter was seeing a billionaire, I could tell that wasn't a selling point for mine. They were thinking of the people they'd known, the people we'd both known. They thought they already knew him. And despite how hard I tried to convince them they were wrong, I knew they weren't.

Not really. Ben might be charming, he might seem different, but he wasn't. He lived in a bubble. Hell, I'd seen it firsthand. He snapped his fingers, and whatever he wanted just appeared. Who else in the city could get a lunch order that fast? And how? It didn't even seem humanly possible, but to him, anything less was unacceptable.

So it wasn't really his fault. You'd have to be some kind of saint to avoid getting caught up in that lifestyle. After all, he was born into it. So he had no perspective - of course he didn't. He could hardly be expected to. But that didn't make it any less irritating.

My parents didn't want to get off the phone, but I finally managed to pry myself away with a lie about how busy I was. Really, I had nothing to do for the rest of the day. Ben obviously didn't want to be around me, and that was definitely for the best. As much my brain flew into wild fantasies of showing up at his house, preferably wearing something skimpy under a long coat...

Okay, so maybe "busy" was a lie. But I was definitely in need a freezing cold shower.

Chapter Sixteen

Ben

It wasn't the first time I jerked off in my private bathroom, but it was the first time I really felt guilty about it.

I never should have let things go so far. But she was intoxicating, standing so close, talking about what we'd *theoretically* look like if we'd just had sex. How was I supposed to pretend like I didn't want her?

So, after she was gone, I took matters into my own hands. It was a bittersweet relief. Was it going to be like this for our entire marriage? I was pretty sure I wouldn't survive. Or at least, not without doing some serious damage to myself.

I'd already decided it was too risky to keep seeing other people while we were married. Discretion could be bought, to an extent, but so could information. Daria and her bloodsucking lawyer would leave no stone unturned. I wasn't going to end up like Eliot Spitzer.

But of course, that meant two years of celibacy. I hadn't actually thought about that, and now I was cursing my own blissful state of denial. It would be one thing if Jenna wasn't so fucking sexy. It would be yet another thing if she didn't obviously want to get into my pants. But with those two things combined, I didn't know how long I could hold out.

I'd practically *dared* her to kiss my neck. For God's sake. Why was I so desperate for her to touch me? Why did I think I'd be able to stop there, and get away unscathed? *She* certainly had no willpower. If my phone hadn't gone off, that little game of chicken would've ended with her ass on the bathroom counter and her legs wrapped around my waist. The only way she could possibly get sexier was if she was screaming my name.

Get a grip, Chase.

I laughed at myself, the way you laugh when you hit that spot on your elbow too hard. The way you laugh when a massage therapist digs into that spot next to your shoulder blade where you carry the weight of the world. The way you laugh when you just got the wind knocked out of you.

It wasn't funny. Not at all. Especially not because I couldn't stop picturing her raised eyebrow, her sardonic smile, if only she were still here. If she could read my thoughts.

Get a grip? Looks like you just did, Mr. Chase.

Oh, this was bad.

I gave myself a few days to get some distance. The concept of a "cooldown period" was something that had eluded me with Daria, so I had high hopes that it would help me behave more like a human being this time. No one at the office asked me about Jenna, but I did get a lot of knowing looks. Some of the interns seemed more nervous than usual.

"Why is everyone so jumpy, Carol?" I asked her, when I stopped to drop off some inter-office mail.

She gave me a long-suffering look. "She's an unknown factor, Mr. Chase. There's nothing more frightening than an unknown factor."

If only she knew.

"Well, throw them a pizza party or something, will you? It's making me nervous just to look at them."

Carol looked at me over her glasses. "A *pizza party*, Mr. Chase?"

I hesitated, halfway back to my office. "What, do people not like pizza anymore?"

"These are MBA students, Mr. Chase. Not a church youth group. Of course they like pizza, but they're not going to like the implication. They want to be treated like adults."

"Fine," I said, irritated. "An Adderall party, then. Whatever it's going to take to convince them it's business as usual. They're making *me* nervous just looking at them."

"Doing something radically different to the status quo seems like the opposite of that," she said. "Just give them time. They'll adjust."

Easier said than done. I was about to grind my teeth into a powder as it was, and the last thing I needed was a bunch of jumpy interns. On second thought, an Adderall party was probably a bad idea.

Right on cue, my jaw popped audibly, and I realized I was clenching every muscle in my face. I made a concerted effort to relax.

And then, my phone buzzed with an incoming

message.

I thought we should probably see each other soon.

Jenna was reaching out to *me*? What the hell happened?

My fingers were typing before I had a chance to overthink it. *Run out of batteries?*

I pictured her smiling and rolling her eyes, but blushing a little, prettily, because well, you know.

Don't flatter yourself. I just thought it would look suspicious if we spent too much time apart.

She was right. There was even a party coming up that would be a perfect opportunity for us to appear in public together, and I'd be stupid to pass that up. My presence wasn't mandatory, but it would certainly get the buzz going.

I hit the "call" button and held the phone up to my ear. She picked up on the first ring.

"Just to get this out of the way, I'm wearing old sweatpants and a Snoopy tee-shirt," she said. The sound of her voice sent a wave of warmth through my chest.

I tried hard to ignore it. "Are you doing anything on Friday night?"

Jenna made a small noise of acknowledgement while she flipped through her calendar. "I have Laura until six o'clock," she said. "Will that work?"

"Sure. We'll be fashionably late." I cleared my throat. "I can pick you up right from the Thornes. I'll have your dress sent over there, if you think you can get ready while you're watching her."

"Okay." She swallowed audibly. "Can't I just wear the same dress as before?"

I chuckled. "But why *would* you?"

"I don't know. You seemed to like it." She was keeping her tone innocent, but that just made it more alluring.

"It wasn't the dress," I said.

For a moment, my heart stopped beating, then picked up again at double-time.

Did I actually say that?

"I think it was the dress," she said. I could hear her shifting, sighing, like maybe she was reclining in bed. "At least, a little bit."

All right. Okay. So, where was the harm in admitting we were attracted to each other? It wasn't like we didn't already both know.

"The dress just made it harder to ignore," I said, glancing at my desk phone, and stabbing the "Do Not Disturb" button. Of course I had a Do Not Disturb button. The whole *"Carol, hold my calls"* thing was just for show.

"Ben?"

"Hmm?"

"I lied. I'm not wearing a Snoopy tee-shirt."

My mouth was very dry. "What about the sweats?"

"Nope." She sighed, softly, then laughed a little. "I'm wearing that dress. I really like it, you know."

Shit, shit, shit. I was instantly hard, instantly throbbing, instantly *wanting*.

"Do you like the dress, or do you like remembering the way I looked at you in it?" My voice was slipping a few octaves lower, quieter, without meaning to.

"Both," she said. There was another rustling noise, like she was sitting up. "We probably shouldn't do this, right?" Her voice was regretful, but I didn't like the tone of finality.

"It's fine." I glanced over my shoulder, as if anyone could see me from the other skyscraper windows. "What could possibly be the harm? Other than you running out of batteries, of course."

"No, I'm sorry," she said, in a rush, "I really can't do this. I'm sorry. I didn't mean to tease you. I just..."

"It's fine," I reassured her, even as I cursed silently, gripping the arm of my chair so hard my knuckles turned white. "We'll just pretend this never happened."

"Thank you," she exhaled. "I'm sorry. I have to go."

This time, I did it right at my desk, and I didn't feel guilty in the slightest. She started it, after all.

But still, there was vague sense of unease, settling into my chest just as soon as the momentary bliss of release faded. This was bad. This was very, very bad. Things were spiraling out of control.

Once I'd washed my hands, caught my breath, and reassembled myself into something presentable, it still took me a few minutes to remember the Do Not Disturb button. I pushed it warily, and the whole thing immediately lit up like a Christmas tree.

"Sir?" Carol never buzzed directly into my intercom unless it was an emergency. I braced myself.

"Yes?"

"The senior partners want to know when you're planning on showing up for the board meeting."

Shit.

True to my word, I didn't mention it.

Not with my words, at any rate. But when I looked at her, sashaying down the staircase in that sleek black dress that flowed like water over her curves, I couldn't think about anything else.

We almost had phone sex. We almost had phone sex. We almost had phone sex. You called me specifically with the intention of turning me on. You wanted it. You wanted to have phone sex. With me.

I didn't exactly blame her for chickening out. Not after how quickly I'd cut off our real-life encounter that almost ended in disaster. Blissful, messy disaster. It was understandable. She knew, as well as I did, that it was a Bad Idea to really get involved.

The dress dipped down low in the front, and even lower in the back, but she wore it unselfconsciously. Her attitude was no different than it had been last time she'd climbed into the backseat of the limo beside me.

"Hi," she said, scooting in and kissing me on the cheek. Her hand cupped the side of my neck, pulling me closer. My whole body tensed, before I forced myself to go with the flow. She was right. We had to put on a show for Tim, too. Not that he'd talk. But the more people who were convinced, the better.

"Hi." I didn't want to talk - *couldn't* talk to her without bringing up the one thing I wasn't allowed to discuss. My jaw ached, my head ached, fucking everything ached. Including, yes, *those.* It didn't matter how many times I came thinking about her lounging in that dress, in bed, touching herself. I still wanted more. Needed more. I'd thought I was prepared for tonight, but I already felt like I was on a hair-trigger.

All I could think about was putting up the partition, and dragging her over my knee for a well-deserved spanking. She might not have meant to be a tease, but oh, she was. She'd be so wet for me, my punishment sending her to heights she didn't even know existed. I'd spank her and finger her until she was sobbing with the need for release, and then I'd lick her off my fingers and send her into the party aching and empty. Give her a taste of what it was like to really be teased. I'd be in agony too, but it wouldn't matter. Seeing her meet all of my high-society so-called friends with flushed cheeks and rubbery legs, with the smell of her arousal smeared all over her thighs, would be worth it.

Of course, I wouldn't be able to deny her all night. Eventually I'd pull her into some secluded (but not too secluded) room and fuck her senseless, with my hand on her mouth so no one would hear her scream.

"Are you okay?"

I jolted back to reality.

"Yes," I lied, shifting in my seat. She was pressed right up against my thigh; there was no possible way to adjust my ridiculous erection without her noticing. Whether or not she could see it now, I didn't dare speculate. "Just had a long day. Somebody pissed in the senior partners' Cheerios."

"Well, you don't look it," she said. "Guess that witch hazel really works, huh? You'll be the belle of the ball."

She was grinning, but there was a real appreciation behind her voice. I wished I had the presence of mind to enjoy the complement. I did look good. But all I could think about was my dick.

"No, I'm pretty sure that's you," I said.

"Right." She rolled her eyes. "Amongst all the

billionaire heiresses and their top-dollar plastic surgery, I'm sure I'll shine like a diamond."

She had no idea how true it was, but I couldn't find the words to explain it to her. Especially not now. We still had nearly half an hour left in our trip, and that was assuming some kind of divine intervention with the traffic. How could I possibly survive?

I started balancing chemical equations in my head.

By the time we arrived, I'd managed to will myself down to half-mast, and Jenna had subtly scooted to towards the other side of the car. I took a deep breath and reassured myself that this night was going to be just fine, even if it didn't end with my fingers in her mouth and my -

"We're here," Tim announced, just trying to break the awkward silence. I thanked him, and jumped out of the car to open Jenna's door before she had a chance to. This time, she actually let me. Mindful that my groin was at eye-level as she slid out of the car, I kept the door between us so she wouldn't notice the lingering effects of my little fantasy.

It was a pretty nice venue. Nothing special, but I could tell from Jenna's expression that she'd never dreamed of setting foot in a place like this. It positively dripped wealth and excess, without being outright tacky. But it was very old money. High ceilings, crystal chandeliers, gold accents, even a damn cherub fountain out front.

Jenna was gaping. Wanting to steady and guide her, I laid my hand gently on the small of her back. The *naked* small of her back. She shivered a little at the touch of my hand, like it was too cold for her sensitive skin. My dick twitched.

Nope. Nope nope nope.

I moved my hand to her arm and returned to my equations.

We breezed through introductions predictably, as I slowly grew to hate everyone in the room for staring at her like that. There was an air of suspicion, of *this one doesn't belong.* But there was something else in many of the men's eyes, and I hated that even more. Why the hell didn't I choose a more modest dress? Sure, she would've ended up looking like a schoolmarm compared to the rest of the women here, but at least I wouldn't be left wishing I'd strapped a knife to my ankle. Appreciating a beautiful woman was one thing, but some of these assholes were just being *disrespectful.*

"Everybody's staring at me," she murmured, as we made our way around the room.

"Told you," I said. "Belle of the ball."

She laughed softly. "I'm sure that's not why. They think I'm a gold-digger."

"They're not thinking about anything except the way you look in that dress," I said, heatedly. "Trust me."

Her little giggle warmed something in my chest. "Even the women?"

"Especially the women," I said. "Every single one in this room is at *least* bi-curious right now."

"I'd say the reverse is true for you, but I don't know if you'd take that as a compliment." She grinned at me. "So I'll just say you look damn good, Benjamin Chase."

"Thank you," I said, sincerely. "Now, how does a drink sound? There's an open bar."

"Seriously?" Her eyes widened. "God damn it. No one gets more free stuff than the people who need it the least."

"I've been saying that for years," I told her, heading for the glittering wall of expensive liquor. "If there were some way to donate all of this Grey Goose to the starving orphans, believe me, I would."

"Vodka martini," she said, when she reached the bar. "Dirty. So dirty I should be arrested for drinking it in public."

The bartender smiled politely. "Very good, ma'am."

"I was hoping for a laugh, but you know, that'll do," she muttered, as I settled next to her. Our hips were almost touching, again. I was struck with the insanely innocent urge to just hold her hand.

A moment later, I realized I could. Should, even.

But I couldn't bring myself to do it.

"Laughing wouldn't be professional," I said. "You'll probably want to try your standup routine on someone else."

Just as we got our drinks, I felt someone clap me on the shoulder. As the vodka sloshed over my shoes, I turned around, irritation written across my face.

"Hey, my man! I'll talk to you later!" the culprit called out, as he disappeared into the crowd.

I turned to Jenna, ready to answer her unspoken question in the form of a rant, but she was still staring after him. Her mouth was hanging open slightly. "You know *Spencer Holloway*?" Her voice was tinged with awe.

Briefly, I racked my brain for a reason why she'd know that name. "Yes," I said, looking nonchalant about it. He was certainly a bigger deal than I was - richer, and more influential, so it was only logical she'd be a bit star-struck. Still, a little twinge of jealousy wormed its way through my chest. "Why, are you a fan?"

Jenna's eyes were like saucers. "He owns two of the biggest film studios *in the world*, Ben. Did you seriously not think to mention that you happened to know the guy who controls half of the film industry?"

I'd actually forgotten. Spencer put more of his effort into the telecom side of things, so we'd never talked about his entertainment empire. From what I understood, he was mostly hands-off.

"I don't think he pays too much attention to all that," I said. "It was just a series of lucky acquisitions. Why, do you think he'll give you career boost?"

"He could give me a *career*," she hissed. "Period. At least introduce me to him."

Honestly, I was surprised. I'd never seen this side of her ambition, and I'd always assumed she would have too much misplaced pride to care if I had any useful industry connections. Instead, she was like a shark who smelled blood in the water.

"I'll do you one better than that," I said, smoothly. "But you have to do something for me."

She frowned. "Don't get the wrong idea. I'm not looking for any special favors. Just a chance to talk to him. If I can't win him over on my own merits…"

Oh, *fuck* no. Spencer Holloway could charm the clothes off anyone. Literally. I couldn't let them be alone together, or I risked the whole thing blowing up in my face. Hell, just a picture of them with their heads together at a party would be enough to raise Daria's suspicions. I wasn't the jealous type, but I never let her near him. I didn't like to tempt fate.

I shook my head. "I'm here to tell you, that'll never work. Let me handle this. It's a once-in-a-lifetime opportunity, you don't want to botch it. I'll give him your reel, but he won't pull any strings for you unless he really likes it. He doesn't owe me any favors. You won't be getting any special treatment - just an opportunity. No different than this, except he'll actually remember it, because he'll ideally be sober at the time."

Her eyes narrowed as she stared at me, considering this.

"Fine," she said. "So what do *I* have to do for *you*?"

"You already agreed to do it," I said, mildly. "Doesn't matter what it is."

"Oh, come on." She rolled her eyes. "We're not doing playground rules. That was clearly a conditional agreement."

"No playground rules? What *is* this, Thunderdome?" I protested. She just glared at me. "Agree right now, or it's no deal."

"You don't play fair," she said. "You know if I don't like it, I'll just walk away, right?"

I knew. I knew all too well.

"That's fine," I said. "But you know I'm a reasonable man. Do we have a deal?"

"Yeah." She smiled, secretively, lifting her empty glass. "We've got a deal."

Oddly enough, Jenna didn't stay glued to my side the entire night. She actually started talking to people, and at times, we drifted far enough apart that I lost track of how much she was drinking. But after a few hours, when I ran into her again, the shine of her eyes made it all too obvious.

"I think you might've been right about the women in the room," she purred, sauntering up to me with an unsteady gait. "I've been getting some eyes."

The mental image was enough to send me spiraling back down to the same insanity that had overtaken me in the limo. I shook my head to banish the thoughts. "I'm tired of everyone in this room staring at you like they want a piece of what's mine."

A moment later I realized what I'd said, but Jenna didn't correct me. "Oh, don't pretend like you wouldn't love it."

"Honestly? The only thing I'd love right now is something I probably shouldn't talk about. Since we're in public, and you're drunk, and all."

"I'm not *drunk*," she insisted, in the way only drunk people do. She seized my hand, taking the opportunity to draw little circles in my palm with her finger. "I could stand to go home, though."

"That's probably for the best." I had to get away from her. This wasn't a fun game anymore, now that I knew there was no chance of a satisfying ending. She was too far gone. She needed to go home and sleep it off, and hopefully forget about how many times I tried to devour her with my eyes.

We said our goodbyes, as quickly and discreetly as possible - not that she was the only one there who'd overindulged, but I didn't want her to feel embarrassed in the morning.

Tim had the town car waiting, and I bundled her

in before taking my seat.

"Time to take you home," I said, as I held her seatbelt buckle steady for her. She still managed to stab the metal connector into my hand several times before hitting home.

"What about our deal?" She was pouting. "I want to know what it is."

"We'll talk about it tomorrow," I insisted. "Tonight, you need some rest."

I'd planned for her to come home with me, very visibly, so no one could mistake our inevitable trajectory towards cohabitation. But now, it didn't feel right. I'd never take advantage of her like this, no matter how much I'd spent the night salivating over her. But it didn't look good - did it?

"I don't wanna go home," she protested, flopping against me. "It's cold there. And too quiet."

"Turn up the heat." I dutifully removed her hand from my thigh. I'd spent so much of the evening in a haze of denied arousal that it hardly even affected me anymore. I wasn't sure if my dick would ever go completely limp again. I wondered if this was the sort of scenario you should call a doctor about.

She just giggled.

"Did you want to take her home, boss?" Tim was stoic, as always. God love the man.

"NO!" she protested, loudly. "I wanna...I don't wanna go home."

Her hand was creeping up my thigh again.

We were dating. It wasn't weird for me to take her home falling-down drunk. No one would think I was an asshole. Good boyfriends were *supposed* to do this.

"No, that's fine, Tim. She'll stay at my place

tonight."

"Yaaaay," she said, softly, her head resting heavily on my shoulder.

For a long time, the car was completely silent except for the soft, abstract humming of road noise.

"Were you thinking about spanking me?"

My whole body jolted to attention. I frantically stabbed the button to raise the partition, although I wasn't sure why I cared so much.

"*What*?" I hissed, pulling her hand off my thigh again.

"Earlier," she muttered. "In the car, when you got all hot and bothered. Were you thinking about spanking me?"

Oh, God. Was it that obvious?

Hell. She asked. With any luck, all of this would fade in the morning anyway.

"Yes," I said, gruffly. "Among other things."

She smiled, eyes still closed. "I don't know why, but I like that."

I know why.

"I don't want to talk about this right now," I said, that frustrating throb rising in my groin again. "I've been fighting to keep my hands off you all night, and now I'm fighting to keep *your* hands off me."

"I'm sorry," she whispered. "I know I shouldn't. It's just...it's nice to pretend." She sighed. "But we have to talk about it now. Now's the time when it's safe. I know you won't let anything happen. You're an ass, but you're not that kind of ass."

"I won't," I assured her. "But that doesn't give you free license to torture me with what I can never have."

"Never?" she repeated, opening one eye. "What

makes you say *never*?"

My heart was throbbing now, too, as much as I didn't want to admit it.

"I don't know," I said, cautiously. "Just a safe assumption, I suppose."

"Never is a long time," she said. "Can I tell you a secret?"

I had a feeling I was going to regret this. "Yes."

She grinned. "I think you're gonna have to buy me a new dress every time we go out. It's this Pavlovian thing. Every time I put on the other one, I get all..." She made a series of vague hand gestures. "A-flutter. You know what I mean."

Unfortunately, I did.

"And now this one's gonna have the same problem," she whispered. "You know how I can tell?"

Please don't say it. Please don't say it. Please don't say it.

"I know I should bite my tongue." She sighed, gripping my bicep like she was drowning, and I was her only lifeline. "But damn it, Mr. Chase, *I want you so bad right now.*"

I groaned out loud, letting my head hit the back of the seat.

Chapter Seventeen

Ben

It didn't take as long as I'd feared to get her trundled into bed, with a bottle of water and ibuprofen waiting for her on the nightstand. She was sleepy and pliant by the time we got home. Her eyes shone with trust, which I hadn't earned, but would never dare betray.

Of course, I had my limits. I let her kiss me goodnight. Once. On the lips, but no tongue.

And once I was locked in my own bedroom, I didn't even bother to shuck off my jacket or loosen my tie before I sought the relief my body so desperately craved. My clothes had felt like a prison all night, chafing against my skin, my collar too tight, and my jacket might as well have been asylum-issue. But now, with my back against the door, all I did was unzip with shaking hands and bring myself off with a few vicious strokes.

It was embarrassingly quick, even considering the ordeal I'd just been through.

Ordeal. All I did was spend the evening in the

company of an attractive woman. I was thinking about it like I'd been through a war. What the hell happened to me? When did I become such a pathetic sex fiend?

I couldn't let this happen again. Another night like this, and I'd actually lose my mind. It was like junior high all over again. I had no self-control, and no ability to think beyond the various ways in which my body craved to connect with hers.

As if that wasn't enough to make me feel like a waste of space, there was the way she reacted to me. And the fact that it just felt right. Of course she liked me. Of *course* she wanted me. That was the way it should be.

Look, it's not like I was some caveman, but I grew up watching the same movies everybody else did. Work hard, get smart, triumph over those who want to drag you down, and you win a girl.

Every. Damn. Time.

Her wants and needs, hell, her personality, didn't even seem to enter into the equation. She was always just sort of wandering around the sidelines with a vacant smile on her face, waiting for some poor schmuck to discover that the power was inside him all along. And then, boom, the bra and panties went flying off.

I knew the real world didn't work that way, but nobody ever bothered to explain how it *did* work. So I guess when I met Daria, and she seemed to already like me for some inexplicable reason, I figured my work was done. I didn't have to keep working to hold her interest; I'd won her already.

But you should know better, Chase! You're a God damn billionaire scientist - what's wrong with you?

Hell, how should I know? The smartest men in the world turn stupid when women are involved. It's a proven fact. What chance did I have?

Amazingly, by the time I came downstairs, Jenna was already awake.

I'd taken my time getting ready, assuming she'd be asleep well into the mid-morning. But I'd forgotten that conversation with Maddy that implied they'd once both been veteran drinkers, and even if Maddy had fallen behind because of her pregnancy and breastfeeding, that didn't mean Jenna had.

I froze in the kitchen doorway when I saw her, perched on one of the stools. "Good morning," she said. "I made coffee."

She had, indeed. While her face stayed mostly buried in her own mug, I could feel her eyes glued to me as I navigated my way around the kitchen, looking for...something. How was it that *I* was the one feeling embarrassed?

Now that I knew her size, I'd bought a few more outfits for her and stocked the guest room she'd chosen. She looked phenomenal in dark jeans and a simple cream blouse, which was no surprise. But seeing her in that dress last night had opened up a whole new level of appreciation for her beauty on all levels.

"No rush, but I wanted to talk about the terms of our deal," she said, matter-of-factly. "Whenever you're feeling up to it." Her eyes narrowed a little. "Speaking of which, are you feeling okay?"

"Fine," I said, pouring a cup of coffee. "I know

you probably don't remember this, but..."

"I remember last night." Her voice was remarkably calm, and it was like she was watching me for a reaction. What the hell? Why did this woman leave me feeling so unsteady? I was supposed to be the one in control. "You put up that asshole alpha male front, but you're really a perfect gentleman." She smiled.

"Thanks," I muttered, staring into my coffee. "But I don't know if that really qualifies as gentlemanly." A sudden thought came to me, and I glared at her. "Were you *acting*?"

Her cheeks went slightly pink. Finally. "Maybe a little," she admitted. "I did have quite a few drinks, though."

"Oh, my God." I buried my head in my hands. "Well, I know who I'll be nominating for the Oscar."

"Come on, don't take it like that." She reached out and nudged my arm. "It was only, like, thirty percent played-up."

"Which thirty percent?" I looked up, blearily. "Or do I not want to know?"

Her mouth twitched. "A good magician never reveals her secrets."

"Fuck me." I gripped my coffee mug. "You're not a magician, Jenna."

"We'll let the Academy be the judge of that," she said. "When you're ready to talk turkey, meet me in the library."

Well.

That settled that. I had a few ideas of how could sweeten the pot, so to speak, to merit the extra favor on my part. Given her behavior, it seemed appropriate to pick the most devious one.

Two could play at this game.

After a series of deep, calming breaths, I walked into the library and sat down at my desk. She watched me with mild interest, until I folded my hands and spoke.

"I thought of a way you could lend some credence to our relationship," I said. "But as a fair warning - you're not going to like it."

Shrugging, she waited for the bomb to drop.

"You know a little bit about the lifestyle I lead. I have friends there. Professional associates, even, although we follow unspoken rules of conduct when it comes to keeping business and pleasure separate. There's one club in particular that I typically visit, at least once or twice a month. If you come with me, nobody will doubt our relationship's real. My ex-wife still knows a lot of the people there, and word travels fast in the community. If you show up by my side, that's practically half the battle."

She crossed her legs, leaning forward as if she was a journalist about to uncover a particularly juicy tidbit. "You want me to *play your submissive*?"

She was smiling, a little. She wasn't running away. I shifted in my seat, suddenly overwhelmed with an image of Jenna in a beautiful little collar, connected to a delicate silver chain - and me on the other end, showing her off to the club.

"I'll be honest," I said, trying to slow my racing pulse. "I was expecting more of a fight."

"It makes sense, though. I mean, your ex-wife might believe I've cured you of your wickedness, but it seems like an easier sell if she thinks *you've* corrupted *me.*" There was something playful in her tone, but I also knew it was rooted in her actual feelings about my proclivities. "So, what are the terms?"

I considered for a moment. "Twice a month, I'll take you to the club that I frequent. It's a social event. You won't have to do anything except be there, and you won't be expected to watch anything that would make you uncomfortable. We'll mingle, we'll let ourselves be seen, and we'll go home."

She was chewing on her lip again, a rosy blush rising up her neck and slowly spreading across her cheeks. "What do you mean, I won't have to watch anything that would make me uncomfortable?"

Shit. I shouldn't have even brought that up. The live scenes were a small part of the gatherings I went to, and she wouldn't ever encounter them unless she went snooping around in the back rooms. I was losing ground, and fast.

"I mean, whatever insane orgiastic scene you're picturing with Tom Cruise and Nicole Kidman, that's not going to happen here." I was recovering quickly; her face relaxed a little. "It's just a chance for like-minded people to have a few drinks and unwind. No one will bother you. The Doms won't even talk to you, unless they have my permission."

Her brow furrowed again. Damn it, I was losing her.

"It's a sign of respect," I said, practically tripping over my own words. "It's not because you're a woman, it's because you're my…"

Wow, was I ever getting ahead of myself.

"…it's because they'll *think* you're my submissive," I modified. "Doms don't talk to subs, as a rule, unless they've been given permission."

She folded her arms, stretching her legs out in front of her as she leaned back on the sofa. "It sounds complicated."

"It's actually very simple," I said. "The thing is, when you're out in the world - just interacting with people, trying to navigate this massive tangle of cultural mores and personal hang-ups, it's a complete nightmare. There are all kinds of power structures and unspoken rules and expectations. But then you step into my scene, and everyone's open about it. There's an actual rule book, and we've all agreed to follow it."

"But what if somebody doesn't like the rules?" She cocked her head slightly. "They can't possibly be one-size-fits-all. Not really."

"Then you make your own." I shrugged lightly. "The only unbreakable rule in the lifestyle is respect. Respect other people's boundaries, respect what they're doing, and respect how they want to be treated."

Jenna was hugging her knees into her chest, leaning forward again. I had a feeling the constantly changing poses were a reflection of the confusion in her mind, and I could only hope she'd come to a favorable conclusion.

"Sounds like a utopia," she said, with more than a hint of sarcasm.

"I'm not saying it's perfect," I conceded. "There are people involved, so of course, sometimes things go wrong. But no one who causes trouble is allowed to stay. We take care of each other. At the end of the day, we're all just human beings trying to navigate the same hostile world."

"Oh, that's inspiring. I feel like putting a ball gag and a saddle on somebody kind of undermines that, though." She held her thumb and forefinger about a millimeter apart. "Just a tiny bit."

There was no outright hostility in her tone, but I still didn't appreciate her being so flip. Gritting my teeth, I tried to remind myself how difficult it was to wrap your head around kink for the first time.

"It might look silly to you, but I promise you, it means something to them."

Taking a deep breath, she watched me carefully for a moment. Her eyes travelled over my body, and I noticed that little flash of desire again.

Don't tempt me. I'd love to show you exactly how meaningful all of this can be.

"So what does domestic discipline mean to you?" she asked, softly.

Hands resting on my knees, I leaned forward to meet her eyes. "Will my answer affect your decision?"

"Maybe." She shrugged. "I'd like to get to know the man I'd be spending the next two years of my life with."

There was no point in being anything less than honest.

"It's not about what it means to me," I said. "It's about what it means to *her*."

"So you get nothing out of it? I don't quite believe you."

"I didn't say that. But when I see her come alive, the freedom she can feel because I've given it to her…"

"I don't understand. How is it freeing when someone else is trying to mold you into a version of yourself that they want?"

I had to laugh. She was so far off in her understanding - I mean, how did someone get to adulthood without being able to wrap their head around human sexuality? Shaking my head, I tried to explain exactly how wrong she was. "Is that what you think this is? It doesn't work like that. Not at all. They tell me what they don't like, what they want to change. And after that, it's up to them to confess. Unless they've asked for me to monitor them, it's one hundred percent honor system."

She was even more confused now, her eyebrows knotting in that fiercely cute way that certainly didn't fit her personality. "I'm not going to pretend like I'll ever understand this, but for whatever reason, I trust that you're not a maniac." She sighed. "And I'll play the role you need me to play. Who knows. Maybe it'll give me some material."

What the hell game was she playing?

"All right," I said. "Well, that's settled, then."

"Good," she said. "Thanks for the clothes."

"They're all yours," I said. "But I'd suggest leaving some here, for these kinds of occasions."

She nodded. "When did you expect me to move in? I mean, we're working on a pretty tight timetable here."

"I think it should wait until after the wedding, don't you? Otherwise it's an awful lot to worry about, all at once."

"Does anyone get married these days without living together?" Jenna gave me a skeptical look.

"Sure," I said. "I'll buy a toothbrush, and you can tell people you're *basically* living here, if that helps."

"Well. I have an audition today," she said,

standing up. "So I'll talk to you later - all right?"

I didn't want to let her leave. I wanted to demand an explanation for why she'd so gleefully given me blue balls, just to prove a point to herself. It wasn't fair. There were about a thousand ways I could've proven to her that I was a decent human being, that *didn't* involve dangerous priapism.

But that would probably fly in the face of the whole "decent human being" thing.

"All right, break a leg," I told her, as she gathered her things and prepared to walk out of my door one more time.

Why, why, why was she tormenting me with something I couldn't have?

Maybe it was just her way of seducing me. She wanted a taste - of course she did. I wasn't being conceited. I knew what I looked like. Back in college, I used to get plenty of offers for modeling underwear, or something equally ridiculous. For a while, when I was obsessed with fitting in, I actually posed nude in the art department. The figure drawing classes loved me. I acted like I needed the money, even though nobody was fooled. I never actually cashed the checks. It was just something to do - and I enjoyed watching the way the students' eyebrows would raise slightly when I shrugged off my robe.

I always thought that would come back to haunt me someday, but so far it seemed like everyone had forgotten. Everyone except me, at any rate. There was probably some unspoken honor code of posing nude for art classes.

I found it endlessly interesting which students drew me with the tattoos, and which ones left them out. They were only partially done back then, nowhere near as complex or vibrant as they were now.

If Jenna drew me, I had a feeling the tattoos would come first.

She liked bad boys in college. That was one tidbit I'd managed to glean from Maddy, and it certainly rang true so far.

After some thought, I picked up my phone and called Daniel.

"Hmm?" He always answered the phone so *professionally* when he knew I was calling. I grinned.

"Good morning to you too. Busy?"

"What do you think?" he groused. "If this isn't about a flood or a wildfire, I'm hanging up."

"I can't talk about it over text," I said.

"Why?"

"Because you'll just delete it."

He groaned. "You realize that's the equivalent of hanging up on you. Which I'm about to do."

"Wait!" I insisted. "Remember the Silo?"

There was a long silence.

"Hanging up now," he said.

"No, no, no. Please. Just hear me out. Jenna's willing to give it a shot. This is a one-in-a-million thing. She's not really...kinky. But she wants to try, for me. Do you have any idea how valuable that is?"

"Some," he said, dryly. "But the answer's no."

"Come on. Dan. I would've done it for you. This will be so much easier for her if she's around at least one friend she can trust." I put on the most sincere tone I could manage. "I really, really like this girl. I think she's the one, man. I've never felt this way about anybody since Daria...I didn't even feel this way about

Daria. It's real. If she can learn to love this too…"

The line was silent for a while, but he hadn't hung up. "I never would've asked you to do it for me," he said, shortly. "Not if I knew you'd left. We had this discussion, Ben. That's not who I am anymore."

"But it is," I insisted. "You think Maddy wouldn't enjoy a little bit of being shown off on your arm?"

"That's my wife you're talking about," he growled. "Be careful."

I sighed, pinching the bridge of my nose. "Relax. Will you at least ask her? For me? Make it like it's all my fault. Like you never enjoyed going there at all. I'm twisting your arm. I bet you'll be surprised by her reaction."

"You're on thin ice," he warned.

"God damn, okay!" I raised my palm in a surrendering gesture, as if he could see me. "Forgive me for allowing the possibility that your wife enjoys a bit of the rough. She did marry *you*."

"What did I *just* say?"

I was feeling cheeky, but I decided not to push it. "That your wife's a lovely, understanding woman who will certainly want to help me out with my predicament."

"I really am hanging up now," he said.

"Thank you," I half-shouted, as the line went dead.

Well. It could have gone worse.

Jenna would certainly view the whole thing a lot more sympathetically with her friend by her side. Even though I loved the community at Silo, and trusted most of them, there was no guarantee that everything would go smoothly. If something spooked her, I wanted

Maddy to be there to smooth things over. I wasn't going to risk my whole plan blowing up just because of some stupid hiccup at a fetish club.

I was asking for trouble, suggesting this. I'd known that at the start. But giving Jenna this little initiation into my world gratified something deep inside me, and I couldn't just pass up this opportunity.

Of course, if she ended up too intrigued, I'd have a whole new set of problems on my hands. But that was a risk I'd just have to take.

Chapter Eighteen

Jenna

I was in way too deep.

My little stunt on the way home from the party was supposed to be a test. I needed to know. Now, I wished I hadn't found out, because if I thought he was the kind of absolute scumbag who'd take advantage of a very drunk girl - well, that would've made it a lot easier to hate him.

Instead, I saw his tender side, his sense of responsibility towards his fellow human beings. The fact that he respected women, respected *me*. At first, it was fun to watch him squirm, but I quickly found myself wishing I hadn't been so convincing.

I didn't know why he'd been so worked up in the first place - maybe his pre-party state stood him up, or something. He was looking at me like he wanted to eat me alive, and I wanted to let him. But that would be irresponsible. Complicated. Messy. Wrong.

By the time he let out that tortured groan in the car, I was in even worse shape than he was. I was almost sure of it.

It was nothing a few furtive sessions of self-gratification in his guest room couldn't cure. Or so I thought.

I really *was* a little drunk. Enough so that I could say the things I said without embarrassment, but not enough to wonder why they came so easily, rolling off my tongue like the truth.

In the cold light of day, sober and all too awake, I started to wonder.

Yes, I wanted him, but I could control myself. Couldn't I? I was an adult. We were both adults, but in the backseat of that town car, just for a moment there, it felt like we were horny teenagers. Completely hormonal, and completely out of control. I didn't like feeling that way. At the same time, it was strangely thrilling.

That was half the reason why I'd agreed to go to the stupid club, or whatever it was. I had no idea what to expect while I was there, but at least it would be something new. And I'd be with him. People would look at us and assume we were together, and I was quickly finding that to be an oddly intoxicating experience. Did I really look like I could be a billionaire's girlfriend?

Ben sure seemed to think so. And hell, in the absence of anything else, I was willing to take that as a complement.

"You sure you don't want a ride home?" Maddy asked me, for the fifth time.

She'd gotten home a little early, but I could never actually leave until my bus came. It wasn't that much of a burden, but one of them always offered.

215

"Seriously, I like the bus." A lie, but I sold it pretty well. They were already being too damn nice to me. "It's fine. I just wish they came a little more frequently."

"Don't worry about it," she said, with a dismissive wave of her hand. "You can wait here for as long as you need. I just need to go talk to Daniel about something."

"Of course."

She disappeared up the stairs, and I heard the low murmur of Daniel's voice floating down. I couldn't distinguish the words, but when Maddy spoke, it was much clearer.

I felt bad, sort of, but they weren't making any effort to be quiet.

"Wait, what?" she said. "*What* kind of club?"

My heart skipped a beat. Had Ben asked them to come along? Of course, it would make sense, but after his conversation with Daniel at the bar, I figured that negotiation was over.

I would be really nice to have a friend there - someone with more than a passing knowledge of this world. But not if it was going to cause a big fight. I already felt guilty, even though I knew it wasn't even close to my fault.

"Wait, no," Maddy was saying. "I didn't say if I wanted to do it. Why would you assume I didn't?"

Daniel's voice was a little louder, but still too low on the register for me to understand.

"Of course I like it being our thing, but if it wasn't a problem for you to be out at the clubs before - why now?"

More indistinguishable sounds.

"Oh, come on. That's ridiculous."

"It's not ridiculous!" Finally, I could hear Daniel clearly. "I just want you to be safe. And happy. You don't know what it's like to be out there in the community, it's not something you ever asked for. It's not something you wanted." There was a glimmer of self-annoyance in his tone. Were all of these guys conflicted about their desires? Ben didn't seem to be, except sometimes, he almost did. It was a strange paradox.

"Daniel," she said, a little more softly now. "I love what we do. I love all of it. I don't need to hide it, and I don't need to be hidden."

"So, what then?" He sounded frustrated. "You want me to show you off?"

"Do you *want* to show me off?"

"Of course!" Daniel practically shouted. "Of course. Part of me wants that. The other part of me wants to kill any man who looks at you. So you can see my problem."

Maddy's voice got softer. "I wish you'd say that more often," she said.

"What?" He sounded slightly amused. "Threaten murder?"

"Not specifically." She sighed. "It's just...it's nice to know that you still get jealous."

It was time for me to leave. But something told me that Ben and I wouldn't be going to that club alone.

I didn't really know what to expect when I opened up the package on my doorstep. Once again, Ben was having my dress sent over - but this time, it was for a very exclusive club called the Silo, and I was supposed

217

to pretend like I understood anything about kink beyond reading the Wikipedia articles for BDSM and the Folsom street fair.

I figured this wasn't one of those latex dress places, but beyond that, I had no idea what the standards were.

Not as revealing as I expected. That was the first thing that popped into my head as I surveyed the cream-colored, knee-length cocktail dress, decorated with a criss-ross of black ribbon. It was a subtle nod to bondage, I assumed, but about as classy as fetishwear could get. The artfully ripped fishnet stockings were a little less classy, but I had to admit they made my mouth water a little. I'd always kind of secretly lusted after edgier fashion choices, but I never felt like I could pull it off. I mean, where do you sport a pair of fishnets? The grocery store? A Christmas Eve party? Now, I actually had an excuse.

There was something heavy in the bottom of the box, and I pulled them out with slightly heightened anticipation.

Boots.

I frowned a little. I thought the dominants were supposed to be the ones wearing boots. All the pictures of subs I'd seen, they were barefoot, or in really impractical spiky heels. But if I needed to wear something I could actually walk in, maybe boots were the stylish sub's natural choice.

And, oh, they were nice boots. I was still a vanilla girl, through and through, but who doesn't get a few goosebumps at the sight of a nice pair of "fuck-me" boots? And these were definitely fuck-me boots. Considering how relatively demure the rest of the outfit was, I was surprised.

They were tall, but not too tall, stopping just short of my knees, lined with silver buckles along the sides. Not quite goth and not quite punk, but oh so beautiful. I wondered if Ben had picked them out personally.

I spent an inordinately long time getting ready, experimenting with my hair a thousand different ways before I just settled for "down." Should I text Ben and ask him how he wanted it? Was that how this worked?

Damn it, why couldn't any of this be easy?

My boots, at least, were solid and reassuring. I liked the sound of my own footsteps. In the mirror, I thought I looked like a kid dressing up for her creepy older boyfriend's Halloween frat party. But if this was how Ben wanted me, this was how he'd get me.

When the car finally arrived, I stood nervously at my front door for a minute, fiddling with my lipstick before I finally shoved it back into my only formal purse (it was black, luckily) and stepped out onto the porch with a reassuring *thunk, thunk.*

Ben was standing on the curb already, waiting for me. Judging by the look on his face, he was hearing The Cars' "Moving in Stereo" in the back of his head. It was nice to see him a little slack-jawed over me, but the frequency of it definitely made it seem less like a complement, and more like a constant state of being.

He, meanwhile, looked very much like his usual self - but with a bit of a sinister twist. As I got closer, I realized that his tie and his high-collared jacket were both made of dark, supple leather. He was holding a pair of matching gloves in his hand, and his pants seemed to fit a little differently than usual. Everything about him screamed *alpha male*. I couldn't quite put my finger on all the subtle differences, but this wasn't a businessman dressed for a day of work. This was a predator on the prowl.

I wanted him to devour *me*.

Stop it.

Shaking my head, I settled in for the ride. Ben seemed lost in thought, but I found him more captivating than usual to look at. This was another side of him entirely, one I'd never seen when he was just talking about this stuff. It was something words couldn't quite capture.

From time to time, he lifted one hand to the side of his face and sort of prodding at his jaw, gently, wincing a little bit. I wanted to ask he was all right, but he seemed lost in another world.

The club wasn't far, but it was tucked away in a corner that was safe from prying eyes, with plenty of room for cars to make pickups and dropoffs in relative privacy. There were two bouncer-types near the end of the cul-de-sac, watching for photographers and any suspicious characters who tried to get too close, I imagined.

Ben checked his phone as he approached the door. "Guess they're already inside," he said. "Just stay close to me."

That sounded ominous.

The door leading in from the outside was nondescript metal, blending into the grungy city surroundings. But inside, there was a small, elegant foyer with two massive oaken doors that must lead to the rest of the club. Two more bouncers nodded to Ben, who nodded back, his hand resting at the base of my spine. I wondered if he had any idea how much that simple touch affected me.

Inside the double doors, everything was reds and blacks, low lights and pulsing music. But somehow, it wasn't overpowering. There was something in the air - a hint, a promise of sin, but not quite enough to be unbalancing. I actually felt very calm, and moment later I realized it might have something to do with the music, which thumped at just about the pace of a low-key heartbeat.

"Over here." Ben led me towards the massive bar, and I realized Maddy and Daniel were standing there. I almost hadn't recognized them in the dim light, with my attention so scattered by everything around me.

Daniel was dressed similarly to Ben, but it was my old friend who caught my attention. She was absolutely stunning, like some dark medieval princess, in a jet-black corset dress that accentuated her soft hourglass curves, and something I initially mistook for a choker before I remembered where I was.

Right. Collar. That was a thing that *people* wore.

It was just a simple strip of leather with a little silver padlock dangling from it, like a pendant. But I could tell from the way she held her head that she was proud of it.

"You look phenomenal," I told her, still slightly awed. It wasn't just the getup itself, of course, but the utterly self-actualized way in which she wore it. I glanced at Daniel. There was still that hint of anxiety and defensiveness lurking around him, but he couldn't tear his eyes away from her.

He was so *proud*.

"Thanks." Maddy grinned. "You look pretty good, yourself. Where'd you get those boots?"

I shrugged. "They just showed up. Ask the mysterious benefactor over there."

Ben and Daniel had their heads together, talking quietly, and it didn't seem like a fight was about to break out. So I decided to leave them alone.

"I'll make sure to find out later," she said. "I don't know what the hell I'd do with them. I doubt Daniel's going to want to come back here."

"You might be surprised." I surveyed the rest of the room for the first time, noticing the variety of people mingling there. Most of the men were wearing very similar variations on formalwear with some leather accents, but there was much more variation in the way the women dressed. Some were much more revealing than others, but I did see quite a few corsets. None of them looked as good as Maddy.

"Can you breathe?" I asked her.

"Oh, yeah. Of course. It doesn't have whale bones in it, or anything." She smirked. "It's actually pretty comfortable. I got it from a very fancy costume place. I told them I needed Morticia Addams cosplay."

"*Cara mia*," said Daniel, appearing out of nowhere. His mouth twitched into a dark smile, and I watched Maddy's whole body language change, subtly, and yet not so subtly, melting to him. "A word."

She followed him to a quiet corner, and I managed to tear my eyes away.

"So, that's going pretty well," I said.

"Very well," Ben agreed. "So well we might not see them for the rest of the night. That wasn't exactly my plan, but hey, whatever gets their marriage revitalized, or whatever."

I grinned. "I don't know that it needs revitalizing,

but let 'em have their fun. This place isn't so bad. I don't know if I'd want to hang out here all the time, though."

"I don't," said Ben. "But it's always been a good place to meet people. No one gets in without being thoroughly vetted. And it's nice to hang out somewhere where everybody already knows your dirty little secrets."

"Huh. Like Alcoholics Anonymous," I said, without thinking.

Ben snorted. "You might want to avoid that analogy when you're talking to other human beings."

"Sorry." My cheeks were instantly burning. "I didn't mean..."

"I know you didn't," he said. "Except you sort of did, didn't you?"

I shrugged, uncomfortably. "I mean, sexual paraphilias are considered by some people..."

"Please," he said, his eyes growing suddenly hard. "Don't start with 'it's a mental disorder' thing. Studies show people who practice BDSM are more mentally healthy than the rest of the population at large. Not that any of that matters, because if something scares people or intimidates them, you don't want to let any pesky facts get in the way of fear-mongering."

Maddy and Daniel returned from their corner, without actually having disappeared into one of the mysterious back rooms, where I assumed all kinds of debauchery took place.

Ben was angry, and I had a feeling I wasn't going to talk my way out of this one. Nor did I want to, really. I wasn't exactly alone in thinking this whole thing was more than little bit weird.

"Oh my God. Dan. Look." Ben jerked his head towards the front of the room. "Three o' clock. Who let *him* back in here?"

I followed his gaze, spotting a tall, ruddy-faced, lanky man in a white suit. He had a stringy brown ponytail hanging down his back, and an ill-fitting fedora perched on his head. Judging by his hand gestures, that very hat was the main substance of whatever argument he was having with the bouncer.

Finally, he handed it over, stalking into the room in a huff.

"Oh Jesus," Daniel muttered. "With the hat, again."

"The dress code is very clear," Ben explained, glancing at Maddy and me. "No hats. He's been fighting that since day one. He finally got himself banned a couple years back when he made a stink about some other meaningless bullshit, but apparently somebody decided it was a good idea to let him back in."

"Danny!" Fedora guy bellowed, coming over to clap both men on the shoulder. "Benji! I haven't seen you in ages."

He turned to both of us, and the men sidled closer, as if on cue. Daniel's arm wrapped around Maddy's waist, slowly pulling her out of fedora guy's tractor beam.

"Milady," he said, offering me his hand. I shook it, gingerly, which seemed to put him off. "I don't believe we've met. I'm Master Jordan."

"Jordan," said Ben, firmly. "You don't have to call him Master if you're not his sub."

Jordan's lip twisted into a sneer. "Since when do

you make the rules, Benji?"

"I'm just explaining the etiquette," he said, calmly. "It's her first time."

"She under your protection?" His eyes had a hungry glint to them, and I didn't like them at all. His attitude and his bearing stood out like a sore thumb among all these people, subtle and classy and respectful, in spite of (or perhaps *because* of) the setting. I wanted to tell him to fuck off, but the whole scene was so new to me, and I didn't want to charge in here like a bull in a china shop and offend everybody.

I mean, not unless he gave me a *really* good reason.

"Yes," said Ben, stiffly. "But she's just testing out the waters."

"Well, you'd better snap her up quick," he half-smiled, half-sneered. "She's going to be very popular around here."

Ben's lips thinned. "Thank you for the advice," he said.

"I mean, she's got it all." Jordan's eyes slid over my body, and I shivered. "But especially those breeding hips."

My mouth falling open, I took half a second to try and formulate my nuclear-level fuck off response before I saw the fire flash in Ben's eyes - and his body lunge forward, his fist connecting with Jordan's swollen face.

Crack.

Jordan let out the most undignified scream imaginable, pitching forward with both hands clutching his injury. Two huge men in suits immediately descended on us from God knows where, creating a physical barrier between Ben and Jordan. Moments later, a very important-looking woman in a sleek pantsuit appeared. Her flint-like eyes darted around the room, before she made a beeline for Ben.

Maddy and Daniel were still standing, frozen, on the sidelines. Maddy's hand was halfway covering her mouth, and Daniel had a darkly satisfied smile on his face when as he watched Jordan disappear through the doors of the club.

"He never should have been let back in here," the woman in the pantsuit said, touching Ben's arm. "Is your hand all right, Mr. Chase?"

"Yes, thanks. I aimed for soft tissue, mostly." He managed a slightly shaken smile. "I shouldn't have gotten so carried away."

"Please, don't apologize," she said. Belatedly, I realized she must be the manager. "I'm sure it was justified. It's pretty clear at this point that his actual fetish is harassing women, and he's not even smart enough to avoid the ones who came with someone who's got a killer left hook." She smiled at me. "Or who might have a killer left hook themselves, given the opportunity. Welcome to the Silo, miss. I'm very sorry about this incident, but please don't let it color your opinion of the place. My name is Lucy, I'm the manager here. If you need anything, please don't hesitate to ask."

"Thank you." I wasn't sure what else to say. I was still reeling from the suddenness of it, and all I wanted to do was sit down in a quiet corner and try to figure out what it all meant.

"Come on," said Ben, as if he could read my mind. "Sit down. I'll get you a drink."

"No thanks," I said, softly. "I just need to breathe for a minute."

"Okay." He sat down nearby, but not too close. "I'm just going to stay here, unless you want me to go."

"That's fine," I said, glancing at him. "Thank you."

"I should've kept him away from you," Ben said, shaking his head. "There's no particular honor in the fact that it escalated to violence."

I smiled. "All the same, it was pretty impressive."

"Yeah?" Some of the color was coming back into his face. "You think so?"

"Absolutely. You could probably have your pick of these women tonight."

He glanced around, following my line of sight. "Any woman in the room?"

"Sure," I said. "I mean, word's going to spread fast, even if they didn't see it."

"*Any* woman?" He smiled at me, and I finally caught his meaning.

I cleared my throat. "That's not what I meant."

"I know," he said. "I just wanted to make sure you realized what you said."

"I seldom do, until it's too late," I admitted. "Listen, I still feel really bad about that whole...mental illness thing. I shouldn't have said it. It was dumb. I'm just some naive girl trying to understand shit that's beyond me."

"You're not naive," he said. "And you already understand a lot more than most people do."

On impulse, I reached out and grasped his hand. He was a little puzzled, for a moment, then he smiled.

"Seeing as we're a couple and all," I said, softly, scooting closer. "We should probably look like one."

227

"Right." He stroked my hand, absently, with his thumb. "Maybe we should put on a little bit of a show."

Guiding me to my feet, he laid his hands on my waist and turned me to face him.

"I think I should kiss you now," he said.

"I think you should, too." My breath started to quicken.

"Good," he murmured, his hand stroking the side of my face. He leaned in and kissed me, gently at first, and then I felt the tip of his tongue nudging against my lips. Asking for permission. They parted, without any conscious decision on my part, welcoming him in. Warm and soft, but demanding, he utterly possessed me in less than a moment. His hand curled around the back of my neck, gentling me. Steadying me. Instinctively, I pressed my body tighter against his, letting us melt together in the midst of the crowd.

I swayed against him, but he held me steady.

When he finally broke away, his eyes looked dark and heavy. His body's reaction to the kiss was unmistakable. I wondered if I said the right thing, would he take me into one of those back rooms and teach me exactly how much fun this could be.

He gave me one last look of pure longing, and then broke away. He adjusted his jacket and took a deep breath.

I asked a question to break the silence. "What does that mean? Being under your protection?"

He made a slight face. "I only said 'yes' because I thought it would make him go away. Some people take it seriously, or basically just use it to mean mentoring, but I've never liked it. Just because someone's entering the space as a woman, or as a potential submissive, doesn't mean they should need a Dom's protection."

The words made sense, but the idea of him... *protecting* me, whatever that actually meant, made me shiver a little. In a good way.

"It does sound a little medieval," I admitted. "But if it keeps people like Master Jordan at bay, you can tell anybody anything you want."

I wondered if I'd live to regret saying that.

The irony didn't escape me, either - the guy who was basically into 1950s roleplay thinking that something was condescending towards women. Ben was a lot more complicated than he seemed at first glance.

Then again, so was Maddy. So was Daniel. So was all of this.

If I managed to get through the next few years with my sanity intact, it would be a miracle.

Chapter Nineteen

Jenna

I just couldn't forget that kiss.

Ben was haunting my dreams even more than usual, now. And even though I'd fulfilled at least part of my end of the bargain, I hadn't even started thinking about how to get my reel ready for him to give to Spencer Holloway. I knew it was something I needed to put together, sooner rather than later, but I'd been so caught up in everything that I barely had time to think about it.

The next morning, I didn't have anything on my schedule, so I started by searching for demo reel production companies and briefly snorting coffee out of my nose when I saw the cost. I could afford it, but not comfortably - I didn't like relying on Ben for anything, just in case something imploded, so I wanted to have plenty of savings stocked up. I had to be free to walk away at any time. Even with my generous nanny's salary, a professional demo reel from a well-reviewed company was going to take a chunk. And after I was done with my ridiculous New York City rent, utilities, and meager grocery bill, I just wasn't comfortable with the projected result.

I decided to give research a break.

A little while later, I found myself absorbed in a completely different kind of research.

Still, my brain was struggling to accept everything that Ben was. Everything that he wanted. As much as the newness excited me, my dreams taking on a darker edge with every passing night, I still couldn't quite accept that this was just another version of normal. How could it be? People were supposed to treat each other as equals. If someone truly wanted to be inferior, there had to be something a little bit warped in their brain. Didn't there?

All the words, all the complicated explanations and philosophizing, were starting to hurt my brain. So I did something I hadn't really done before - not on purpose, anyway.

I started looking at the pictures.

At first, I found a lot that made me cringe. Women who looked sad and downtrodden, with strange implements on their bodies and ugly words written on their skin. There was lots of overexposed amateur photography, and plenty of hardcore porn with ball gags and tears.

I could never be that person. No matter how open-minded I became, I could never quite look at this and see the beauty in it. Whatever it was Ben saw, I was sure it would always elude me.

Suddenly, I saw something different.

There were other pictures out there, more artistic, more carefully done. I clicked through one of the image search results and found a whole blog devoted to "the art of BDSM."

Of course there were professional photographers who did this sort of thing. I knew about Mapplethorpe. But I hadn't realized how popular it was, how many hundreds of thousands of pictures were out there that evoked something the blunter stuff completely missed.

I scrolled and scrolled, until I saw something that made me stop dead in my tracks.

There was a man in a suit, fully dressed, but barefoot, sitting in a comfortable armchair with his feet planted in a wide, authoritative stance. But the focal point of the image was the naked woman curled up in his lap. His arms surrounded her, just holding her in this quiet moment. Whatever had happened to get them here, it didn't really matter. This moment was just for them. So calm. So peaceful.

My breath caught in my throat, my heart beating faster as I stared at the picture. Despite her nakedness, it wasn't blatantly sexual; strictly speaking, the staging was almost platonic, but it was still the most erotic thing I'd ever seen in my life. It was like I could feel his care, his devotion, radiating from the image. His confidence. How much she'd pleased him, just by being there. Submitting to him. It was achingly beautiful.

All the reading I had done, all the frowning, confused research, and I'd somehow missed the most important thing. The crucial truth at the heart of it. The reason why.

Like a lot of people, I'd assumed all the roleplay and the posturing and the implements were ways of keeping distance. I'd seen that theory put forward plenty of times, and I'd never had a reason to disagree with it. But the intimacy of the moment captured in this picture told a very different story.

Finally, I managed to tear my eyes away. Some of the pictures had little stories underneath them, and I started to read, letting the words sink in deeper than before.

There was a common thread in all of them. The Dom was so attentive, so focused - but never on his own pleasure. Only on hers. I'd been told, I'd tried to understand, but until now, I didn't. I couldn't have, until I was ready.

I couldn't remember anyone ever *trying* to arouse me. Anyone ever deliberately touching me, in a way that was anything other than grasping and taking. I sat there curled up in my chair and I remembered the first time a boy touched me inside. I was a junior in high school. His fingers were rough and bruising, inelegantly demanding. He said he was trying to "get me ready" and I didn't understand what that meant. Was I supposed to be enjoying it? What was wrong with me? Was I broken somehow?

When I got a little older, got into college, I ended up meeting the man who was "the best I ever had." That was the title I'd assigned to him, anyway. But now I could remember him - more skilled than a high school boy, but still impatient. Still clumsy. Unhappy with my response and always coaxing me, pushing me, wanting more than I could give him. I started faking it more often than not, so I wouldn't feel like such an inconvenience.

I wasn't sure if I wanted to laugh or cry. All this time I'd been reluctant to examine the memory, knowing it would tarnish. Everything these people were sharing and writing about - it was so far removed from anything I'd ever experienced. I didn't think it was possible. But I knew what they were writing was real. Every word pulsed with authenticity.

Was this something I could have?

With him?

Just the thought of it was enough to make my heart race. The way he'd kissed me...if the lovemaking was even half as intense, I'd probably explode into a cloud of lust.

But there were the practical considerations. Such as, we weren't really together. He didn't want that. He'd made it very clear. Things would get too complicated, and then where would we be?

Hell, I didn't know. I was just trusting his judgment. Why was complicated *bad*? Why didn't he want to be with me, for real? It wasn't for lack of desire. I'd felt the proof of that, pressed against my thigh.

Grown men didn't get hard-ons from lukewarm kisses from women they were only pretending to like. I might have a sad, hollow excuse for a sexual history, but even I knew that.

I was tired of playing games, but this was what I'd signed up for.

Ben called me out of the blue, while I was sitting on the floor watching Laura set up her Little People village.

"Hi," I said. "I'm working."

"With the baby?" His voice sounded a little bit strange. "Tell her hi for me."

"I'll make sure to do that," I said, dryly. "What's going on?"

"This is embarrassing," he said, "but I need a favor."

A beat. I cleared my throat.

"...okay?"

He was - sleepy? Or...slightly tipsy, or something. "I've got to have my wisdom tooth out."

I blinked. "Now? Aren't you about thirty-five?"

"Thirty-three," he said. "Although I'm not sure why that's relevant."

"Don't you usually have that done when you're like...fifteen?" I crawled over to rescue a firefighter who'd rolled away, under the sofa. Laura's frown of concern turned into a smile. "Or is that only for commoners?"

He sighed. "I might've...procrastinated."

"Oh, for..." I stood up, walking the length of the room while I shook my head. I seemed incapable of talking to this man without pacing. "Okay, so, what?"

"I need a ride," he said. "My driver, Tim - his grandmother got sick and he's got to leave town for a while."

"Oh. Well if you talk to him, tell him I'm sorry to hear that." I thought for a moment. "What about Carol?"

"She's busy that day," he said. "On vacation. In the Bahamas. Requested it over a year ago. I'm not that much of an irredeemable asshole. Besides, you're supposed to be my girlfriend."

I really didn't like the tingle that ran through me at that word. "What if I already had a vacation scheduled in the Bahamas?"

"That would be strange," he said. "Seeing as you're my girlfriend."

Right.

I actually felt bad for him. The guy had no family, at least no one local, and

"Tuesday," he said. "Nine o'clock in the morning. It's uptown. There's a parking garage. I'll pay for it."

"I should certainly hope so." I worried my lower lip between my teeth. "You know I don't have a car, right?"

"I'll rent one for you," he said.

"Uh, don't you have like twenty cars?" I didn't actually know. I just assumed.

He laughed a slightly dopey laugh. "Just because I'm rich, I must have twenty cars? I don't. Who the hell drives in this city?"

"So you *don't* have a car?" I was slightly bewildered. "I mean, besides the one Tim drives."

Laughing again, he took a moment to respond. "I have cars. Just not twenty. Not even close."

Oh, boy. What was he on? I rolled my eyes as I replied. "Well, it seems like just one would be enough to avoid renting."

"You are *not* driving one of my cars," he said, firmly. I could practically hear him crossing his arms.

"You sound like a spoiled child," I informed him. "But, fine. Sure. Of course. Like I'm going to pass up an opportunity to hear your twilight sleep ramblings."

I wondered if he'd considered that. With a sharp intake of breath, he seemed to think about the possibility for the first time.

"Don't blackmail me," he said, finally. "You wouldn't like me when I'm blackmailed."

A burst of laughter came out, before I could stop it. Laura glanced up at me in alarm. "Are you high right now?"

"A little," he said. "I couldn't sleep last night, so I went to the doctor and he gave me something for the pain. It's pretty strong. I forgot how strong it is."

"Don't drive anywhere," I warned him. Suddenly, I remembered how he'd seemed to be in pain before we went to the club. "Was that what you were poking at, the other night?"

"It's been bothering me for a while," he admitted. "I guess I was hoping it would go away on its own."

"Sure, that's what usually happens with dental problems, right?" I snickered at him.

"Yes!" he said, defensively. "If you ignore them for long enough, they just rot and fall out. Problem solved. But this one's a special case. It's stuck in there. Apparently I need a surgeon. It's complete bullshit, if you ask me. How does a tooth even get this fucked up? I think there's a conspiracy involved. I knew I shouldn't have turned down that offer to join the Illuminati."

"You're not making any sense," I told him.

"*You're* not making any sense," he grumbled. "By the way, I have very good oral hygiene. This is just one of those...one in a million medical errors."

"Okay, sure," I said. "But for the record, an impacted wisdom tooth isn't exactly one-in-a-million. I had all mine taken out when I was a kid."

"Conspiracy," he mumbled. "See? Told you. How do you know for sure they wouldn't have grown in? The dentists have us by the balls, I'm telling you."

"Right, well, make sure to let me know when you've finalized all your theories on that," I said. "I have to go. I'll talk to you later."

Why was I so *worried*?

Sitting in the waiting room, I twisted a loose thread on my sleeve, over and over and over again. I wondered if I should have worn something more glamorous to take my billionaire boyfriend to the dentist. Would I pass as the appealingly unsophisticated girl-next-door type, a breath of fresh air after a lifetime of models and heiresses?

A family came into the crowded waiting room, four of them, and they searched silently for a place to sit together. Everything on my side was taken, but there were two sets of two empty seats on the other side, bisected by a completely oblivious couple. The family was too polite to say anything, and they split, glancing at each other awkwardly over the couples' heads. I fumed silently, fighting the irrational urge to jump up and scream at them for failing to notice the *blindingly obvious*.

Ben was going to be fine. It was a routine procedure, so common, so simple. But I'd looked over his shoulder when he signed the waivers. I knew all the things that could go wrong, simply because of the anesthetic. I knew they were just covering their asses. But they still needed his signature, just to make sure that he understood. There was a chance - however small, however insignificant - that he wouldn't wake up again.

Stop thinking like that.

I stared at the TV, slowly nursing an irrational hatred for everyone involved in the production of *Days of Our Lives*.

After what felt like an eternity, the nurse with the clipboard finally called my name.

"Ms. Hadley? You can come back now."

She looked relaxed enough, so I didn't hold my breath as I followed her to the recovery area.

"Everything went great," she said, leading me to his cot. He still looked mostly asleep, pretty peaceful, and only *slightly* like a chipmunk. "He's pretty groggy. You might have to stay with him for a while. Some people come out slower than others. Do you know if he's usually like this?"

I shrugged uncomfortably, like the nurse somehow knew my secret. "No, I...I mean, he's never been put under since I've known him."

"Well, if somebody can watch over him for the next couple of hours at least, that'd be ideal. He might have a little trouble with his balance for a while, and he'll have to be careful with eating. His stomach might reject anything he eats for a while. It's no big deal, except you're not going to want to clean up the mess."

"Right," I said. Of all the things I'd imagined myself doing to scrape by in New York, cleaning up a billionaire's puke certainly wasn't among them.

Then again, neither was any of this. But I had to draw the line somewhere.

Ben made a small noise, stirring and opening his eyes slightly.

"He won't remember any of this," the nurse said. "And even after he seems 'awake,' he probably won't remember most of that, either. And anything he says is likely to be complete gibberish. The best thing will be for him to just sleep it off."

She rattled off a few more instructions, reminding

me a few more times that he wasn't going to remember anything. After she left, Ben seemed to come back to consciousness a little bit. He worked his mouth open and closed a few times, and made a slight noise.

"You want something to drink?" I asked him, holding up the bottle of water. He nodded, and I tipped a little into his mouth. He swallowed with difficulty, his eyelids heavy.

"I don't feel very good," he muttered, his head falling back on the pillow.

"Well, that's understandable." I patted his hand, unsure of how I should try to comfort him. Nobody was around, so I didn't feel like I needed to put on a show. Would his ex-wife's lawyer really come around and interview the dental staff, anyway?

He groaned softly.

"The nurse said you'd probably throw up," I told him.

"I won't," he said. stubbornly. "I've been under general before. I don't throw up. They always tell me I will, but I don't."

He sounded so belligerent. I grinned in spite of myself. "Okay. But you need to be careful about eating, anyway."

"Fuck careful," he muttered. "Order me a pizza."

I glanced at the room, and then back at him. "I'm not ordering you a pizza to the surgeon's office," I told him. "You can't chew it, anyway."

He groaned again.

"I'll get you a milkshake on the way home," I promised him. "After we go to the pharmacy."

The nurse was passing by, and she laughed. "If you're planning on having kids, this is pretty good practice."

I smiled wanly.

Fighting the traffic wasn't quite as bad as I'd anticipated, and Ben had already arranged for the valet at his place to return the car to the rental agency. Ben wasn't swaying anymore, so I let him walk up the stairs on his own, slowly, guiding him towards the sofa in his library once we got inside. Getting up another flight of stairs seemed like an unnecessary hassle.

He laid down gingerly, groaning.

"Want something to eat?"

He shook his head. Right. With oral surgery, it was unlikely he'd want anything for a while. It had been so long, I forgot.

I perched on the arm of the sofa, awkwardly, wondering what the hell I was supposed to do now.

"Hey," he mumbled.

"I'm here," I told him.

"Is it normal to remember some of the surgery?"

I almost wanted to laugh at the way he sounded with the gauze still stuffed in his mouth, but I didn't. "I don't know. Maybe. Could you feel it?"

"No," he said. "Not really. I think I just woke up at the very end."

There was a moment of silence.

"I have a Tesla," he said.

I processed this for a moment.

"Okay," I replied. "Like, the car?"

"No, like the scientist," he muttered. "The fuck do you think?"

"No need to be a dick about it." I got up and settled down in the chair across from him. "Although, on the plus side, I guess that means you're feeling better."

"I feel *great*," he said. "I feel like that Pink Floyd song. *Doo doo doo…a distant ship, smoke on the water…I turned to look, but the child was gone…*" He hummed, very off-key, waving one arm like a drunk conductor, while I nearly doubled over with laughter.

"I don't think that's how it goes," I managed, as he drifted off. "So you've got a Tesla, huh?"

"You seemed interested in my cars," he muttered. "When I first asked you for a ride. I thought you might be curious. It's very pretty." He sighed. "We should take it for a spin sometime."

"Okay, sure," I said. "Just as soon as you can remember all the actual words to 'Comfortably Numb.'"

Very slowly, he lifted up his arm, and flipped me off.

The room settled into silence again, and

"You know why I picked you?" His eyes were closed, and I had no way of knowing if he was really talking to me. Or to anyone. For all I knew, he was seeing nothing but pink elephants and babies crawling on the ceiling.

Even so, my heart started racing. "No," I said. "Why?"

"Because," he said, slowly. "You really do."

If I prodded him, I'd probably make him forget what he was going to say. But I had to know.

"I really do *what*?"

He sighed. "Shine like a diamond."

It took me a while to remember what I'd sarcastically said at that party, when I was feeling inadequate next to all the elegant and wealthy women who vied for his attention on a daily basis.

"I saw it right away," he said. "You're different. Maybe that was a stupid reason, and I should've picked somebody ordinary. Everything would be easier. But I didn't. I picked you."

Smiling, I leaned back in my seat. "I'm sure none of the women you've been with are *ordinary.*"

"I guess that's true," he muttered. "Maybe I'm the ordinary one."

I laughed. "Not a lot of ordinary people have Teslas and private drivers."

"Daria hated it too," he muttered.

I was trying to keep up. "Daria?"

He didn't answer, but I realized that must be his ex-wife. He'd never called her by name before.

"My money," he said. "She hated it, too. Eventually, she hated me."

There was genuine sadness in his voice, and I felt terrible in spite of myself. "I'm sure she didn't hate you," I said.

"I wasn't enough for her," he mumbled. A moment later, his voice became louder, clearer. "I'm never enough for any of them." He faded a little more. "Never enough."

I waited patiently, sensing he wasn't quite finished. The nurse had told me it would all be nonsense. I had to keep that in mind. I should just walk away and let him sleep, but I wanted to hear it. Even if it was all total garbage, I had to know.

"The only reason I take control is because I don't know what else to do. Anything else...terrifies me. Of course I have to give them all the power. That's the hell of it. That's the thing that keeps me awake at night. They can always walk away, and of course that's how it has to be. I'd never really want it any other way. But still..." he sighed. "I can't stand it. Any of it. I drive them away because it feels inevitable. Because I just can't see any other end to it."

I swallowed hard. "I wasn't your fault, with Daria," I said. "She made a choice."

He laughed softly. "Of course it was. I made it impossible for her. You know how I can get, and you barely even know me. Cold. Sarcastic. I made myself unlovable, and then I blamed her for not loving me. Imagine trying to live with me at my worst, twenty-four-seven. I was never outright hostile, and that was the worst part. I made her feel like a bad person for wanting to leave me, so that's what she became. Everything she did, everything she became...it's all because of me. It's what I deserved.

"And that's why I didn't fight it," he said, his voice still faint but unmistakably clear and coherent. "Because deep down, just like the rest of them...I wanted to accept my punishment." His mouth twitched, but didn't quite become a smile. "I thought if I didn't fight it, if I let her...metaphorically, you know, stomp all over me in stiletto heels, I thought that would be enough. That I'd rest easy after that. I thought I'd feel better. She had the power to make the guilt go away. Or at least make it bearable. But of course, she didn't.

"She didn't owe me that. Nobody did. But I still haven't forgiven her. I need it. I need it, and I can never have it. It's never as easy as it seems. But I guess that's why I'm so good at what I do. Every submissive always says I'm the best she's ever had...and I know what you're thinking, but I can tell when a woman's lying to me. I'm the best, because I know exactly what they're after. Seeing somebody else experience that release - it's the closest I can get to experiencing it myself. I'll be chasing it forever, but I'll never find it."

His eyes opened, suddenly. A ghostly smile was tugging at his mouth, but his lips seemed too sluggish to give in. "And that's it. Pathetic, huh? I've been trying to punish myself for so long, and it's only at the last minute that I realized I didn't want it. Like jumping off a bridge. That's the real reason why it took so long. When I'm sober I won't even be able to admit it to myself, but that's the truth. I thought maybe if she really did get my company, that would do it. But now I've realized it's not going to be enough. It's never going to be enough. Because forgiveness is something you have to *give* someone. I can't take it by force."

He was starting to drift off again, his eyelids fluttering closed. I wanted to say something, to comfort him, even if he'd forget all of this in a few hours. I just wanted him to stop drowning in his guilt, even if it was only for a little while.

A moment later, he exhaled softly, and I realized he was asleep.

Chapter Twenty

Jenna

Once Ben was recovered, he took me out to dinner at one of those restaurants with reservations booked out for a year. We hadn't spoken since the day of the surgery, and I didn't know if he remembered anything he'd said while he was coming out of it.

"It must be nice to be eating real food again," I commented, across the dimly-lit table.

He looked very sharp, of course, and it was hard to reconcile this version of Ben with the guy who'd tried to sing Pink Floyd on the sofa. Not a single hair was out of place.

Smiling, he took a sip of his drink. "Nicer than I realized. You don't know what you've got until it's gone."

"So I've heard." I glanced around, feeling like everyone was staring at me.

"Not this coming weekend, but the one after," he said, with a secretive smile, "I'm taking you out of town. I already cleared it with Daniel and Maddy. When we come back, we'll officially announce our engagement."

He said all of this very matter-of-factly, leaving no room for protests. Not that I would have, but I wasn't used to being *told* what I was going to do.

"Where?" That seemed like the next logical question.

The corners of his mouth quirked up farther. "That would be telling. Same weather as here. Bring a swimsuit."

Fine, I could play that game. "So we should probably talk about the wedding, huh?"

The food arrived, and he seemed more than a little taken aback that I wasn't demanding answers about the trip.

"I've got some portfolios," he said. "A few wedding planners that come highly recommended. You can pick your favorite, or just close your eyes and throw a dart. From there, they can pretty much handle everything, and they'll just come to you with a few choices while they handle all the logistics."

"Wow," I said. "So this is how the other half lives."

He poked at his risotto. "I don't think hiring a wedding planner is particularly glitterati."

"Well of course, you wouldn't." I smiled at him, but he just gave me an irritated look.

I figured there was a fifty-fifty chance we'd end up killing each other on our romantic little getaway.

"I'm so going to enjoy arguing about the logistics of our wedding with you," I said, swirling my wine.

"Oh, darling." He leaned back in his chair, smiling indulgently. "I love it when you talk dirty to me."

He had a private plane.

Of *course* he had a private plane. What were we, commoners?

The urge to roll my eyes at everything was extreme, but I managed to suppress it. And yeah, it was pretty convenient that I didn't have to take off my shoes or shuffle in a line of whining kids with my luggage that had a perpetually broken wheel. I mean - it was nice. It was impossible to keep any level of detachment or cynicism when I walked up the pristine steps, into the beautiful, spacious cabin, and sank into the plush leather seat.

I glanced at Ben as he sat down beside me. He'd never known *any other life*. This was his reality. Had he even set foot on a commercial airline?

"It's too bad we couldn't take the big plane," he sighed, leaning back in his seat. "But we're flying into a matchbox airport, basically. We'll just have to make due."

I looked around me, taking in the ridiculously plush surroundings. "You're...kidding, right?"

He glanced at me sideways, a grin tugging at his mouth. "A little bit."

I laughed, drawing my knees up to my chest. The seat was practically big enough for me to curl up like a cat and nap in the sun. "I've never even flown first class before."

Ben made a dismissive gesture. "Not worth the money. Once you fly private jet, you never go back."

"Oh, my God." I turned to look at him, unable to hide my smile, even though I sort of wanted to smack him. "Do you have any idea how you sound?"

Leaning back in his chair, he gestured for the attendant. "People are going to hate me no matter what, so I might as well deserve it." His eyes sparkled. "Mimosa?"

"What the hell." I sat up and accepted a flute from the silent attendant, thanking her, to which she only nodded politely. "I don't understand why you won't just tell me where we're going."

"More fun this way." His eyes darted to mine, as he sipped his drink. "Besides, I like the little wrinkle in your forehead when you're trying to figure something out."

This seemed like dangerous territory, but the warmth of the champagne spread in my stomach and I forgot exactly why. I probably should have eaten breakfast before we left.

"I'm sure I won't be able to guess," I said, trying to gently deflect. "I mean, you were content to take the small plane, which means it can't be very far. If we were taking an overnight trip, I'm assuming you wouldn't settle for any less than a flying Ritz Carlton."

"The lady knows me." Ben grinned. "You're correct about that part - it's a short flight."

"So we're staying in the northeast." I frowned at my empty champagne flute. When did *that* happen? "That narrows it down, but not by much."

"You won't get it out of me," he said. "I promise you that. I'm very stubborn."

I snickered. "*No.* I hadn't noticed."

For a moment, our eyes locked, and his smile almost made me forget what we were really doing.

What *were* we really doing? How was I supposed to behave, on a romantic getaway with a man I was not actually romantically involved with?

I tore my eyes away from his face, determined to

be the first person to break the contact. I was afraid of what would happen if one of us didn't, and I didn't quite trust him to do it.

"I know this is a little bit strange," said Ben, softly. His tone had taken on a serious undercurrent, something I seldom heard from him. "And I'm sorry for that. If there was an easier way to do it..." He hesitated. "But anyway, I thought you'd enjoy this trip. Even if it's...awkward."

I stared at the wall in front of me. "Why does it have to be awkward?"

"It doesn't," he said, quickly. "But I know things could get...you know. If the lines blur. It's understandable."

My heartbeat was quickening, and I didn't exactly know why.

He cleared this throat. "I mean you're - well. You know what you are. You're trying to be an actress, for God's sake."

I blinked, trying to follow his train of thought. "So?"

"So, you know what you look like." He was staring at the floor. "You're about to make a career out of being irresistible."

Laughing in disbelief, I sat up straighter. "There's a little more to acting than sex appeal, Ben."

"Maybe so." He glanced at me briefly, then back at the floor, barely hiding a smile. "But when I look at you, I'm not thinking about how much I'd like to give you an Oscar."

There was a buzzing in my head, growing ever louder with each passing moment. How was I supposed to pretend like his words weren't affecting me?

"What *do* you think about?" I asked, my voice a little husky. Damn it. I didn't mean to sound so alluring.

Or maybe I did.

"Oh, *no*." He laughed, gesturing for another drink. "Your honor, I refuse to answer that question, on the basis that it might incriminate me."

Shit. I was completely out of my depth. Flirting was one thing - although I was fairly out of practice, these days - but flirting with a guy I was already going to marry, for completely practical reasons? And one who I absolutely, categorically *could not stand* as a human being?

Hell, what could possibly go wrong?

"That's disappointing," I murmured, smiling down at my lap. Another mimosa appeared in front of me, and I let my eyes linger on Ben's hand as he set it down, his fingers long and nimble and -

Damn it.

"Trust me, it's for the best," he said. "You'd either kill me, or..." He cleared his throat. "Well, I'm not sure. But either way, I'm pretty positive it wouldn't be appropriate for the venue."

"You just had to take the small plane, didn't you?" I leaned my head back, glancing sidelong at him. His eyes widened slightly.

"Remember that conversation we had about boundaries?" he asked me, softly.

"No," I said, smiling.

This was totally harmless, right? What could possibly go wrong? We were only about to spend a week together, probably in a romantic bed and breakfast in the mountains somewhere, probably with just one bed, because otherwise how would *that* look?

"Just to be clear," said Ben, after a moment's silence. "Are we talking about killing me, or...some other option?"

"Let's just see where the night takes us," I said, archly, loving the look on his face.

He slumped a little in his seat. "You've really got to stop this," he said. "A man can only take so much."

"Oh, I'm sure you can take a whole lot." I grinned. "Mr. Perfect Billionaire who's always in control."

"Nobody's perfect," he said. "For instance, I've got a snaggletooth."

He bared his teeth in a smile and pointed, to demonstrate. I had to laugh. One of his canines was slightly askew, now that he'd invited my scrutiny - just enough to prove that he hadn't been genetically created in a lab. "Yeah, wow, it must be very tough for you. I bet all the supermodels can barely look at you, Elephant Man."

He actually looked a little bit taken aback, like he'd shared something he didn't tell most people. I almost felt bad as he cleared his throat, frowning slightly.

"I just mean, it's not a big deal," I explained. "I never noticed it. People are always like that, with their so-called 'flaws.' Nobody can see them but you."

"I guess," he said. "But it doesn't really matter, does it? Either way, I act like the guy with the snaggletooth. People might not see it, but they see the self-consciousness. I've gotten better at hiding it, but that doesn't mean it's gone."

It took all of my strength not to laugh out loud.

The idea that someone like Ben, who could have made his fortune in underwear modeling if he hadn't been born a billionaire, was insecure about *one tooth* - it was pretty hilarious.

But to him, it was real.

"Why don't you get it fixed?" I suggested, gently. "Not that you need to, just...maybe you'd feel better."

He made a face. "You should already know the answer to that. I hate dentists. Orthodontists. Whatever. If they want to fuck with my teeth for a living, I don't want to know them. Unless, of course, I'm in pain, then we can make a deal."

"Fair enough." I crossed my legs. "Well, I like it."

He raised his eyebrows slightly. "Yeah?" he said, softly, looking like he actually believed me.

"Yeah," I said. "It's got character."

Rolling his eyes, he took the last sip of his drink. "Oh, sure. Okay. Thanks a lot for that."

"I'm serious," I insisted, surprised to find that I was. Now that he'd pointed it out, it was part of the whole package that was Ben - and if I was being honest, probably my favorite part. He was just too damn perfect otherwise, but with the snaggletooth he looked...*cute*. Approachable. I just couldn't figure out a way to say that, without offending him.

Suddenly, I realized that was why so many of his smiles were lopsided. He was trying to cover that tooth. Like he actually thought that it mattered to people.

"If you just displayed your tattoos all the time, you know, nobody would be looking at your face," I suggested, half-jokingly.

"And you claim to be so vanilla," he said, reaching

down to unfasten his cuffs. "Little Miss Tattoo Fetish. Here." He started rolling up his sleeves. "You can look, but don't touch. Like a museum."

"No flash photography?" I grinned. This was the closest I'd seen them, and I found myself trying to focus on the individual elements of the design. "Are there stories, or is it just art?"

"Yes, and yes," he said. "But the stories don't matter anymore."

I wondered about that. Slowly, just because he'd told me not to, I reached out and traced a little spiral design with my fingertip. "What's this?"

"It's a Triskelion," he said. "It's an ancient symbol. Has a lot of meanings." His eyes met mine. "You're not very good at following rules, are you?"

"It's like a Wet Paint sign," I confessed. "Somebody says *don't*, I just want to do it more."

Ben smiled, closing his eyes and letting his head rest on the back of the seat. "You and I could have so much fun together. I love a good battle of wills."

I didn't know what to say to that.

Chapter Twenty-One

Jenna

The sign said, WELCOME TO THE FINGER LAKES WINE COUNTRY.

Upstate New York. Of course. Maddy had spoken very highly of the wine that came from these regions, but I'd never been. It was breathtakingly beautiful, dappled sunlight glowing on the water, with a lovely little cabin all to ourselves.

The gravel crunched beneath my feet as I walked up to the rustic front door. I wanted to admire the place, but I only had eyes for the man standing on the porch. In his three-piece suit, still minus the jacket, with those sleeves rolled up so enticingly to show off the wildness he hid from the world, he looked like a wet dream.

Any willpower I had left was fading fast.

Inside, there was a beautifully appointed kitchen with a variety of wine bottles already laid out on the counter. Ben went to them immediately, selecting one from the middle and examining the label. "What do you think, a nice Syrah? Or is it too early for proper drinking?"

"It's never too early to drink in wine country," I said, hunting for stemware. Once I found it, and satisfied myself that it wasn't dusty, I set out the glasses for him, and he poured.

I should've eaten something - a small snack, at least, and there was definitely a basket of crackers or something in the corner, but I was standing very close to Ben and suddenly I didn't want to go anywhere.

"It's good, isn't it?" He swirled his glass. "I don't know that much about wine, but *I* think it's good."

"Well, it's an acquired taste," I said. "Luckily, I've acquired a taste for much worse. So this is quite nice."

He chuckled. "Well, my taste can't really be trusted either. I'm adaptable." He took another sip. "Eager to please, you might say."

"Oh, sure, that's you all over." I rolled my eyes. He was obviously driving at something, but I wasn't going to let him get there too easily.

"There's a lot of things you don't know about me," he said, resting his hand on the counter. It was the one with the big silver watch on it, and the tattoo that I'd so recently fondled. "I wouldn't rush to judgment so quickly, until you have all the facts."

"Okay, fine," I said. "I'm sure you'll have plenty of time to present all sorts of facts over the weekend."

He was trying to hide a smile, a little secretive grin, but he wasn't quite succeeding.

"What?" I demanded, sidling up to him. The air still sparked with the flirtation between us, and I was reluctant to let it go. The alcohol made me just clumsy enough that I went too far, and bumped my hip against his.

It was *an accident...right?*

"Nothing," he insisted, his smile only growing. If he noticed my little slip-up, he didn't react - at least, not outwardly. But I was pretty sure I felt the tension in the room grow thicker. "I'm not gonna say it."

"Come on," I wheedled, stopping just short of fluttering my eyelashes at him. But I *was* shameless enough to purposefully reach past him for the bottle of wine, turning sideways so that we faced each other. I knew this dress was doing all kinds of favors for my cleavage, and it just seemed wasted if I didn't show it off a little.

And yeah, he noticed. His eyes flickered down a little bit, just like any human being would when confronted with a faceful of boobs. His tongue flicked out to wet his lips slightly, and he took a deep breath before his eyes returned to my face.

The smile came back.

"Nah," he said. "Not unless you tell *me* something."

I cleared my throat. For some reason, it was suddenly hard to remember words. "Okay," I said, grasping the corkscrew in my fist. "Go ahead, I'm an open book."

He turned slightly, his hip leaning against the counter, so we were face to face, just inches apart. "Then why is your face the same color as your lipstick?" he asked, showing off that ridiculously adorable snaggletooth. Warmth pooled in my belly. "A lovely shade, by the way."

My throat was very dry. "Matches the blood of my enemies," I quipped. "Wine makes me flush. That's all. Don't flatter yourself."

It wasn't exactly a lie, but that certainly wasn't why I was blushing. Oh well. He didn't need to know.

Judging by the look on his face, he already did.

Smug prick.

"Okay," He shoved his hands in his pockets, looking me up and down. I managed to suppress my little shiver - just barely. But the weight of his gaze really felt like a caress, as ridiculous as that sounded. "I know I said I wouldn't bring it up again, unless you wanted to talk. But I gotta ask…"

Instantly, my heart started racing. I was so not ready to discuss this again. Not with him. Especially not after the out-of-control fantasies I'd been having lately.

"…have you thought about it since?" he finished, his eyes glinting slightly.

He didn't have to say anything else, and he knew it. We both understood.

My fist tightened around the…wine…opener… thingy.

Holy shit, he makes you stupid.

"Yes," I said, my voice coming out just barely above a whisper.

Ben's eyes widened, softened, and then his smile grew a little bit. "*Yes?*" he repeated. "A one-word answer? That's all I get?"

I nodded.

"Fine." He shrugged. "Your turn."

"You know what I wanted to ask you." I took a deep breath, trying to calm my heartbeat. "I wanted to know what you were thinking. What made you smile."

"I was just thinking," he said, slowly, his eyes dragging across my body again. "If we were really a couple, and you touched my tattoos after I specifically told you not to, I'd have to give you one hell of a spanking."

I almost dropped the thingy.

With a sudden movement, I turned back to the counter, grabbing the wine and trying to stab the... fucking...*whatever* it was called into the cork. I couldn't deal with this. I absolutely could *not* -

"Ow," I hissed, when the sharpest part of the implement slipped and scraped down the side of the bottle, catching my hand in the process.

Ben intervened. "Here," he said, grasping both items and smoothly removing them from my grip.

Corkscrew. Right.

Screw.

Damn it, I was losing my mind. My pulse was thudding so loudly in my head, it was a wonder I could still hear anything else.

"Are you okay?" he glanced at me.

"Yeah," I said, staring down at my hand, blushing furiously. It was just a superficial scrape. Just a stupid, clumsy slip-up, because all I could think about was Ben's hand resting firmly on my back, pushing me down onto the kitchen table so he could deal out the spanking that I deserved.

Bullshit, I don't...

But it didn't matter if I deserved it. I *wanted* it.

The question came out in a rush, before I could stop myself. "Is that really how it works? I thought they got to decide when they get spanked."

"It depends." He set the bottle down, and I could feel him looking at me, even though I refused to meet his eyes. "I don't think you should have anything else to drink right now, do you?"

Yes. No. I don't know.

"Maybe not," I conceded.

"Jenna, look at me."

I did, swallowing hard.

"Is it the wine that's making you act like this, or is it something else?" He smiled a little. "I've seen you drink a lot more than this before, and you never acted so…"

It's because of you. I'm drunk on you.

Damn it, if I said that out loud, I'd never live it down.

"It's just weird," I said, a little too loudly. "Us. Alone together. I barely know you, and pretty much all I know about you is what kind of sex you like. That's kind of strange, isn't it? I mean, it's hard not to think about it."

I wasn't sure if I was making any sense, but he seemed to accept that. "Jenna, if there's anything else you want to know about it, feel free to ask me. That offer always stands. I'll tell you anything you need to know, to feel comfortable with me."

Well, I was certainly never going to be comfortable. But I appreciated the gesture, nonetheless.

I had so many questions, still. After that long conversation at his apartment, I still felt like I had no idea what it was like, being his lover. How could I possibly hope to play the role if I didn't even understand something so basic?

"I guess I do still have questions," I admitted. "I didn't really want to ask, it seems…awkward…I don't know." I twisted my hands together, wishing I was still holding the stupid corkscrew so I'd have something to do with them. "But if I'm supposed to pretend like we're a couple, I need to know what it's *really* like."

He raised his eyebrows. "You want details? You might have to dial it down to something more specific. I'm not much of a raconteur."

I considered for a moment.

"What do they call you?" I cleared my throat. "I mean, you know, your uh…your submissives? Do they have a special name for you?"

"I wouldn't call it special." He grinned. "I ask them to call me Mr. Chase, or Sir. They can make other suggestions if they want, but it has to be respectful."

A few less-than-respectful ideas popped into my head, and I giggled slightly. "What about them? Do you call them something?"

He nodded, looking thoughtful. "Each one gets their own name," he said. "It has to fit the situation. It has to fit them. I'm pretty good at coming up with something - it's one of my less marketable talents."

"Oh, boy." I laughed, leaning against the counter. The lighthearted tone of the conversation was putting me more at ease, but it didn't do much to relieve the tension winding up in my body. I wanted…I didn't know what. I just *wanted*.

"You think I'm kidding?" He shifted his weight a little, using the opportunity to close some of the small gap between us. Maybe he thought I wouldn't notice, but I most certainly did. "I've got a list of references you can call."

"I guess I don't know what constitutes a good nickname," I said. "Of course they're going to say they like it. That's part of the game, isn't it?"

"Trust me." He winked. "I can tell if they like it."

"What does *that* mean?" I was pretty sure the temperature in the room just went up by about ten degrees, and there was suddenly a lot less oxygen to be had.

"You know what I mean." His voice was a little softer, a little lower. We were getting into a dangerous territory now. "I know you wanted details, but I don't know if you want *that* many details."

I swallowed hard. "You're telling me you're so good at coming up with pet names, that it's actually a turn-on?" I was trying very hard to keep my voice light. "I mean...okay, sure. I guess."

"You're so skeptical." He eyed me. "Don't make me prove it."

My pulse was racing. I *wanted* him to.

God damn, did I want him to.

"A businessman like you should know," I said, arching my eyebrow, while the sensible part of my brain raced to catch up with whatever the hell I was doing. "You gotta put your money where your mouth is."

"Oh, well then." His mouth twitched. "If that's how we're playing it. But I'm not giving you a pet name for free. You have to earn it."

I couldn't look him in the eyes. The fingers of his left hand, his dominant hand, were slowly moving, the thumb rubbing against the tips of the other fingers absentmindedly. Like he was getting ready for something.

"How?" I whispered.

"You know how." His voice was low and husky.

I swallowed hard. "A spanking?"

He nodded. "Just a spanking. No funny business." He rested his hand on the center of his chest. "Cross my heart, Jenna."

For a moment, I just stared at him. Was I ready to accept what he was offering?

"What do you say?" He looked me up and down, one more time, the heat of his gaze almost palpable on my skin. "Are you ready to accept your punishment?"

I wavered, literally and figuratively, a deep blush spreading across my cheeks, and down further. My chest flushed hot as I watched him and tried to imagine his hand connecting with my backside.

"Hmm," he said, a soft noise that went straight to the heat between my legs. "Are you sure?"

I nodded.

He took a step closer, smiling at me. Our eyes were locked, and I couldn't tear myself away if I tried. "There's no going back. Once I tell you, that seals the agreement. Understand?"

I nodded.

"Out loud," he said. "I need to hear you say it."

"Yes," I said, my voice barely above a whisper. "Yes, Mr. Chase."

Abruptly, he closed the gap between us, standing so close that our clothing brushed together. But not quite pressing against me, just close enough to hear my breathing, to inhale my scent. His fingers ghosted along my jaw, my neck, like there was something about me that he needed to absorb before he could decide.

"You're so damn beautiful," he whispered. "You smell good. I bet you taste good, too." I could hear his smile.

"Thought you said no funny business," I managed,

breathlessly.

"Fuck. So I did." His fingers paused by my throat. "Sorry about that, *sunshine*."

It wasn't so much the name itself, but the way he said it - my lips parted and I actually had to stop myself from making an embarrassing sound. Really?

Really. He really was that good.

"It's okay," I whispered.

"It's not okay," he murmured. "I'm a man of my word. I promise I won't break it again." He exhaled. "Go over to the island, there. Up against the countertop, with your back to me."

It seemed to take ages to get there, my heels clacking on the polished floor.

"Bend over, and close your eyes."

His voice was like honey, luring me into a sense of calm, in spite of what was happening.

"Put your palms flat on the table," he murmured.

"What should I do with my head?"

"Whatever's comfortable," he said. "You may keep it up, or you may rest one cheek on the wood."

He spoke with a real authority, not the false bravado I'd seen him display in public. Every cell in my body *wanted* to obey him, before my brain had a chance to intervene and question what the hell I was doing.

Before I knew it, he was very close. I felt the warmth radiating from his body, the gentle weight of his hand resting on my bottom.

"Ready?"

All I could do was nod.

At the first hit, I cried out.

It was more from surprise than from pain. And

though there was a sharp unpleasant sensation, the *thud* of his hand vibrated through my body in a remarkably pleasant way.

Instantly, I came alive. My nerves were singing, a soft buzz of arousal growing between my legs. I could feel myself pulsing all over, from my toes to my fingertips, wanting him to hit me again.

"Okay?" he asked me, softly.

I nodded, still unable to speak.

Smack.

This time, I wasn't startled, but I couldn't muffle the little groan of pleasure that came from the back of my throat. Shit, was *this* what I'd been missing my whole life? I would've gladly crawled around the house naked for a month, in exchange for just a few minutes of feeling like this.

My head was swimming. Were there really people out there who got to feel like this every day? Any time they wanted? Could Ben tell how aroused I was? That wasn't part of the plan. This was supposed to be no funny business.

We were pretty fucking far from that possibility. He'd half-stolen my breath by now, and I was sure he could hear it. He spanked me three more times in quick succession, and I heard his harsh exhale that I *hoped* meant he was feeling something too.

"Do you think you deserve a good girl spanking?" he asked me, his voice a half-whisper that went through to my core. I shuddered.

"No," I muttered, fingers squeaking against the wood as I tried to brace myself for the next hit. "I've been disrespectful."

Smack.

"But didn't you used to think I deserved to be sassed?" His hand lingered this time, resting on my throbbing ass. I purred.

"You did," I whispered. "But I hardly gave you a chance to make it right. I was unfair."

I squirmed, and he hit me again. This time, my throaty moan was completely unmistakable.

I was undone.

Hearing him breathing behind me, feeling the heat of the connection between his skin and mine, separated only by my skirt, I tried to imagine what he looked like. Were his eyes dark with anticipation? Did he lick his lips?

"I'm not sure this is a good enough punishment," he said, punctuating with another smack. "What do you think?"

All I could do was pant, trying to gather my thoughts enough to give some kind of coherent answer.

"Is it supposed to feel like this?" I whispered, finally.

He chuckled, a low rumble in his chest. "How does it feel?"

With a slight movement, he bumped up against my hip, and I felt a heady rush at the urgency of his arousal, searing against me.

His fingers traced a path up the back of my neck, the blunt ends of his fingernails scraping gently along my scalp, before he grabbed a handful of my hair and tugged sharply. He let it go slack a moment later, but my skin still throbbed. The sensation jolted through me like a lightning strike, and I melted even more.

I was a mess.

"Is that too much, sunshine?"

I shook my head, tears springing to the corners of my eyes at the sudden tug on my hair. He wasn't letting go. And I didn't want him to.

My legs shook underneath me, and I was sure I wouldn't be able to hold myself up much longer. Whimpering, I pressed my cheek harder into the table, like that could somehow transport me out of this moment of torturous anticipation.

Suddenly, he pulled back and spanked me again. This time, all pretense was dropped.

"*Mr. Chase,*" I moaned, feeling my ears start to burn a moment later.

He laughed, his hand lingering tantalizingly on the base of my ass - where he'd just have to slide his fingers a little bit lower to touch me where I needed him. He smacked me again, lightly this time. I managed to repress my reactions to a slight shudder. His body was suddenly very close to mine, bending over me, caging me in. His hot breaths gusted past my ear, and I felt goosebumps rise all over my skin. His hardness was so close to my aching core that I wanted to scream.

I moaned helplessly, squirming beneath him, more aroused than I'd ever thought possible.

"I wish I could touch you." The sound of his voice vibrated through my back. "Find out if you're as turned on as I am. You have no idea how much." He exhaled. "But I can't. That's a damn shame, isn't it?"

I just whimpered.

"Of course, I have my suspicions." With a subtle movement, he ground himself against me. I tried to choke back another moan, with little success. "But I can't really know, can I? Not without some *funny*

267

business."

Slowly, he stood up, backing away just far enough to slide his fingers under the hem of my skirt. Pushing it up, inch by inch. "Just stop me if I go too far, sunshine. Okay?"

I nodded.

"Okay?" he repeated. His fingers were still, burning into my skin.

My voice was barely recognizable. "Yes, Sir."

This time, he didn't stop until my skirt was bunched all the way up around my waist. I felt him kneel down, slowly, until he was eye level with the one place on my body that craved him the most.

"You ever have a man beg to taste you?" he murmured. "Because I gotta say, I am *damn close.*"

I almost cried out in frustration.

"But I wouldn't, of course," Ben went on. "That wouldn't be very *dominant* of me."

He stood up, suddenly. I felt the heat of his body retreating, and my heart dropped into my stomach.

"No!" I shouted, standing up so quickly I almost lost my balance. My legs felt like jelly, and everything between my legs was puffy and over-sensitized and my nerves were frayed down as far as they would go. I turned to face him, my skirt still rolled up, my hands balled into fists. "That's not fair!"

"Not fair?" His eyes glinted. "Oh, sunshine, who ever told you this was going to be *fair*?"

With a sudden movement he captured both of my wrists in his hands, holding them immobile in front of me. I struggled halfheartedly, but I was no match for his strength.

"You're torturing me," I whispered. "Why would

you do that?"

"Torturing?" He raised an eyebrow. "What *torturing*? You've been telling me for months that you don't want this. That you think it's weird. That I'm basically a caveman for enjoying it. Now, suddenly, you want it all? You want to throw yourself in over your head and fucking drown in it? Doesn't work that way. You've been teasing me for so long. Flirting with me, knowing what kind of man I am. *Knowing* that I want to put you in your place. Well, this is it. This is what you wanted." He was breathing hard, staring me down. "I'm in control now, sunshine. Now, do you wish you'd never rubbed your tits on my chest?"

I glared at him. It was impossible to tell how much of this was supposed to be a game, but I didn't want to play anymore.

"You're in control?" I repeated, hating how much my voice shook.

He didn't answer.

"Let me go," I said, quietly.

He did. Without hesitation, he released my arms, stepping back, some of the wildness leaving his eyes. He worked his mouth open and shut a few times like he meant to speak, but I didn't give him a chance. On legs that felt like they might give out at any moment, I walked towards the foyer, grabbed my purse off the coat hook, and made it to the door before he spoke.

"Jenna, wait."

I stopped.

"Please," he said.

I turned around, slowly.

His face was twisted with regret. "Shit, Jenna, I'm sorry. I don't...I don't do this. Like, ever." He raked his hand through his hair. "There's always negotiations beforehand. Fucking *contracts*, for Christ's sake. I'm not good at spontaneous. I thought..." He let out a long breath. "I thought that's how you wanted me to be."

I folded my arms across my chest, watching him. He was still visibly aroused, and my body had an instant reaction to the sight, winding me even tighter than before. But I just took a deep breath and watched him squirm.

"I just want to ask you one more question, Ben," I said. "Can you be a Dom without being an asshole?"

He let out a tight laugh. "I have it on good authority that I can't breathe oxygen without being an asshole. But if it means you'll stay...I can *try*."

"Good," I said, taking a step towards him. "'Cause I was just bluffing."

This time, he laughed for real, crossing the room in a few long strides and capturing me, with his arms around my waist. "You've got a hell of a poker face, sunshine."

"You have no idea." I pressed my hips against his, loving the little groan that escaped the back of his throat.

He kissed me, hard and fast, just giving me a little taste of his mouth before he withdrew. "Get back in position, babe. We've got unfinished business."

Laughing breathlessly, I went back to the table and practically hurled myself across it. "That's not my name, Sir."

"Yeah, sometimes I like to mix it up a little bit." He pulled my skirt back up, letting his hands linger on my ass. "God *damn*, you are beautiful."

"You know it's not the names, right?" I gasped as

his fingers strayed between my legs. "It's the *way* you say them."

"It's both," he replied, kneeling down behind me. "But I'll accept that as a compliment anyway."

Giggling, I squirmed at the feeling of his hot breath on my skin. "Are you going to beg?"

"That was just a figure of speech. I don't beg. Ever." He brushed his lips against the sensitive skin on my inner thigh, and I shivered all over. "But if that's a sticking point, a man might just *ask very fucking nicely*."

I laughed, then whined a little as his teeth grazed me through the soaked fabric of my panties. "Consider this an open invitation to taste me whenever the hell you want, Mr. Chase," I breathed. "But a girl does like to hear *please* and *thank you* every now and then."

"All right, then." He nuzzled against me. "*Please* might I grab your panties between my teeth, so I can get them out of the way and make you scream my name until you lose your voice?"

I really hadn't thought it was possible to be more aroused than I already was. But I was wrong.

"Yes," I managed.

"*Thank* you."

He made good on his promise.

My knees buckled, pleasure rippling up my spine and making me cry out helplessly. Scrabbling for my grip on the table, I tried to hold myself up, but a moment later his hands planted firmly on the backs of my thighs. He was pressing me hard against the wood, and I'd have bruises, but all I cared about was his tongue.

It was shockingly intimate, for a man I hadn't even planned on kissing tonight. Let alone *this*. I realized that until moments ago, we'd never even kissed for real, not in private - but every kiss we'd shared in public had more meaning than we'd wanted to admit.

I was spiraling out of control already. It was almost embarrassing, the way my body had responded so quickly to him, so relentlessly captivated by everything he did. But I didn't even know how I could have hidden it. There was no artifice. With the first impact of his hand on my ass, he'd lit a fire under me that I'd never be able to forget.

Thrashing and moaning, I tried to keep myself still underneath him. But it was impossible. With his face buried between my legs, all I could do was hold on for the ride.

The man knew what he was doing. I had to give him that. He stopped for just long enough to lick his lips and whisper, "tell me when you're about to come. Talk me through it. I want to know."

I nodded breathlessly, and he went back to his task. I didn't know why, but something about his request just pushed me higher, until I could feel the inevitable tremors begin.

"Mr. Chase," I moaned, "I'm about to…"

He made a soft, encouraging sound as his tongue continued its movements.

"I'm…" I panted, struggling to find words. "Oh, God. Ben, I'll…"

I froze. As my inner muscles twitched and tightened, I felt a *gush*. There was just no other word for it. I couldn't stop it, couldn't do a damn thing about it - and with his relentless tongue continuing to suck and swirl, in spite of the fact that I must have just soaked his face with my juices, there was no stopping what came next.

So I just kept talking, like he'd asked. "I'll come if you keep doing that. You're going to make me…"

My heart almost stopped.

"Come," I gasped, as my world shattered. His tongue was perfect, *he* was perfect, coaxing me through it. I came and came, my body jerking and shivering and finally collapsing, only the counter still holding me upright.

He stood quickly, grabbing me by the waist and spinning me around.

"*Fuck.*" I was still catching my breath, but my face flamed with embarrassment. I didn't know what the hell just happened to me, but I knew it wasn't exactly normal. At least, not for me. "I'm sorry."

"You're sorry?" He shook his head, bewildered. "For what?"

"*That,*" I said, staring at his face while he swiped his sleeve across his chin. "I, um…"

He was smiling - the built-in smug was back. Well, fuck me.

"Stick with me, I'll give you all kinds of new experiences," he drawled, pulling my body tightly against his. "You ever tasted yourself on a man's tongue before?"

"Of course." My face was still burning.

"Not like this, you haven't."

His kiss was fervent, possessive, and yes - unlike anything I'd felt before. I clung to him, wanting to somehow absorb all the things that made him irresistible.

Still drunk on pleasure, I slipped my hand around

to his front, trying unsuccessfully to find the pull of his zipper. He sucked in a breath as I gave up and just closed my hand around his stiff length.

I swallowed hard, still not knowing all the rules.

"Can I..." I started, trailing off as my courage waned.

"Can you...?" he encouraged, with a smile.

"You know," I insisted, my voice wavering almost to a whisper.

"Do I?" he teased. "I can't give you what you want unless you use your words."

All kinds of filthy phrases ran through my head, but I was suddenly so timid. What was wrong with me? Why couldn't I just put what I wanted into words?

His patience was wearing thin.

"You want me in your mouth, sweetheart?" he murmured. His hand lifted my chin, his thumb parting my lips and silently asking for entrance. "Show me. Show me what you want to do."

Obediently, I sucked and swirled, lavishing his thumb with the attention he so badly needed elsewhere.

"Good," he said at last, breathless, pulling his hand away. "Get on your knees, I'll let you have a taste."

He was long and thick, and throbbing-hard, so much pent up desire, and I wanted all of it. Every single drop belonged to me.

When I took him in my mouth, he let out a long, heavy sigh. His eyes fluttered closed, but he opened them again, looking down at me. His fingers toyed absently with my hair.

"I always knew you'd look so perfect like this." His Adam's apple bobbed as he swallowed, heavily. "But it's better than I imagined."

The last time I'd done this for a boyfriend, he'd almost winced away from it, telling me over and over again that I didn't *have* to, really, it was fine. He'd made me feel defective for *wanting* to do it. But Ben was stroking my hair, eyes burning into mine, making no secret of his desire for my mouth. I could feel it vibrating through his body to mine, a message just for me, not a demand, but a gift. Allowing me the honor of pleasuring him.

Ridiculous.

Except it wasn't. My mouth watered, and I gave him what we both wanted.

He tasted good. Like salt and desire and masculinity. I loved feeling the pulse of his skin in my mouth, against my tongue. I moaned, and his fingers clutched my shoulder at the vibration of my voice.

It was so beautifully intimate. I never wanted to be anywhere else.

More than intimate; I *owned* him. In that moment, I held everything in my hand. I was kneeling at his feet, but I had never felt more powerful in my life.

I reveled in everything. The feel of his thigh muscles twitching and tensing under my hands, the way his body subtly rocked towards mine, but he held himself back. His inked-up arms in my peripheral vision. The unmistakable unique scent of man, of *this* man, so close to my nose, the natural musk of his body for once not overpowered with something that came out of a bottle.

His soft, shaky groan sent a warm feeling spiraling

through my stomach. "Baby, if you don't slow down, I'm gonna defile that pretty little mouth of yours." His breathing hitched, eyes darkening. "But if you..." He swallowed hard, Adam's apple bobbing up and down. "If you don't want it, you've got about thirty..."

I swirled my tongue around his swelling tip, and he shuddered all over.

"...mmm, make that about *ten* seconds..." His voice broke over the last word. "Oh, fuck. Fuck." Eyes squeezing tight, hands clenching my shoulders, he cried out, a sudden burst of incoherent sound that made my core clench with need all over again.

"*Fuck*," he breathed out, as I swallowed and released him.

A moment later, I let him pull me to my feet and wrap his arms around my waist. "I'm afraid to ask why you're so God damn good at that," he rasped, nuzzling his face to mine. Instinctively, I kept my mouth away from his, knowing most guys were squeamish about that kind of thing.

"I certainly haven't had much practice." I laughed a little. He was just flattering me.

"Hey." His lips brushed my cheek. "Let me kiss you."

"Sorry," I muttered. "Didn't think you'd want to, after..."

"Oh, so it's good enough to be in your mouth, but not in mine?" He captured my mouth, spearing his tongue inside to drive the point home. I moaned against him, still quivering from my climax, feeling weak and delicious wrecked. Finally, he released me, even more breathless than before. "You've sucked off some real assholes in your day, sunshine. I bet I don't even rank."

Laughing, I pulled away just far enough to see his face. "I never said you did. Assholishness isn't relative. And some people are ruder in bed than others."

"I mean technically, we're nowhere near the bed," he said, sensibly. "You think this is good, I'll treat you like damn royalty in there."

I sighed. "Well, thanks for being nice about it, anyway."

"Being *nice*?" he repeated, his eyes flashing with irritation. "What's that supposed to mean?"

"I know I can't possibly be that good at it," I said. "But, you know, I appreciate you pretending like I was."

His eyebrows shot up. "You know, I should just be angry at whatever one of those past assholes made you feel inadequate, but I'm actually offended. Believe it or not, it usually takes me some time to finish like that."

"That was definitely not *no* time," I protested. "I mean - it wasn't *too* long. I mean, it wasn't a short time either, it just…"

"Slow down before you hurt yourself." He grinned. "You've got a peculiar effect on me in general, sunshine, that's no secret. But you're also really fucking good with that tongue of yours."

"Thanks." I was blushing all over, but I found I didn't care. "You, too."

"See, that I believe," he said. "You gotta learn to accept compliments."

"Is that an order?" I blurted it out without thinking.

He stopped, midway through zipping his fly back

up, and cocked his head slightly. "That depends," he said. "Are you *taking* orders?"

I took in a deep breath. "Maybe," I said, at last.

His face lit up.

"Maybe is a start."

Chapter Twenty-Two

Jenna

Nothing was different.

But at the same time, *everything* was.

After we'd cleaned up and composed ourselves a bit, we had a light dinner with some more wine, and ended up retreating to bed long before the sun went down. We undressed each other, slowly, and he kissed every part of my body until I was panting. Then he stroked me to a slow, dizzying climax with a single finger - I think mostly because I dared him that he couldn't, or maybe he just wanted to prove that he could. The specifics were a little bit hazy.

I returned the favor after that, halfway draped across his body, stroking him leisurely, feeling him throb desperately in my hand as he murmured sweet filthy nothings in my ear. "Are you trying to kill me, sunshine?" he'd whispered at one point, his eyes glassy and his whole body tense with the need to climax.

"Maybe a little," I whispered back.

It was a terrible pun, but when his body finally gave in to my teasing pace, what with his broken moans and his hands clawing the sheets and his hips bucking three inches off the bed, he somehow didn't have any room to complain.

We fell asleep after that, tangled together, naked under the sheets. It felt right, even when I woke up to him snoring directly into my ear.

I woke up gradually, to the sunlight streaming in through the windows.

"G'morning." Ben's voice was still rough with sleep, his smile as crooked as ever. He rolled over and pressed his lips to mine, the tip of his tongue flirting with the space between them. I pulled away.

"My mouth tastes like old socks," I muttered. "Let me brush my teeth first."

"Don't care." He pulled me close again, and I surrendered, letting him in. To my surprise, he didn't recoil, but only kissed me deeper. Finally, he pulled away.

"I don't taste any socks," he said.

"Fine. But I'm going to brush my teeth now, anyway." The moment my feet hit the floor, I remembered I was naked. I glanced back at Ben, watching me with appreciative eyes.

Oh, what the hell.

I took the journey to the bathroom and back without a stitch of clothing on, and I couldn't remember if I'd ever done that in front of a boyfriend. Certainly not in front of a casual lover. I never really liked being completely naked, all at one time. The vulnerability was unnerving. But his warm gaze made me feel like I was wrapped up in a cozy blanket.

A blanket that wanted to fuck me, but still.

"How come we never had sex before?" I asked

him, when he came back from his own morning routine.

"Oh, boy," he said, climbing back into bed and slinging the sheet haphazardly over his waist. "You want a checklist?"

"It wasn't because you didn't *want* to," I said.

"Of course not," he said. "I think that's pretty obvious."

"Well, what then?" I sat up, instinctively pulling the sheet up with me, to cover my chest. All of a sudden, I didn't want to be naked anymore. I noticed his eyebrow twitch at the sight, but I only clutched it tighter.

"What, are we in a PG-13 movie?" He half-grinned, flicking his side of the sheet away so that his naked body was exposed. "Not anymore. You might as well join the party."

Rolling my eyes, and pretending I didn't want to stare, I let the fabric drop to my waist. "That's all you get, sorry," I said. "I'm chilly."

"Yes, I can see that." His tongue flicked out briefly to run along his lips. "This actually might be counter-productive for a conversation, but what the hell. I'm always up for a challenge. Could you repeat the question?"

"Why," I said, snapping my fingers to get his line of sight away from my breasts. "Why didn't we do this before?"

"Oh. Well. You kept insisting you didn't like spanking." He shot an incredulous look towards the sound of my fingers. "Really? Are we going to pretend like you're not trying to catch an eyeful yourself? Just take a picture, it'll last longer."

Laughing, I feinted towards my phone. "Really?"

"Shit, I mean, yeah," he said, reaching down. "But at least let me get it photo-ready first. I don't want my dick to end up on Reddit all half-mast."

"Just once," I said, "I'd like to get through five minutes of conversation with you, and *not* feel the need to roll my eyes."

"Ah," he said, letting go of himself with a hint of disappointment in his tone. "You were kidding. Well. Sure, I mean, no big deal. This can wait. It's not like I'm staring at an incredibly sexy half-naked woman, or anything. I'm sure it'll just go away on its own."

Tossing my phone down on the bed, I gave in to the urge to glance. Just once. Damn. What the hell was I talking about? Something to do with... spanking... "What makes you think I'd post your dick on fucking *Reddit*?" I demanded, as a cover.

He shrugged with the shoulder he wasn't currently leaning on. "Dunno. Isn't that what the kids do these days?"

Right. I remembered now. "Stop evading. I want to know why you didn't want to let this happen. It didn't have anything to do with spankings."

"You're right," he said. "I knew you'd let me spank you if I asked nicely enough, and I knew you'd end up loving it. You weren't scandalized when you saw that stuff on my computer, you were *fascinated*. Give me a little credit - I know the difference. Nobody gets that worked up over something unless they're, you know, *worked up* about it."

"I really don't think that's true," I said. "But, fine. Great. You admit it. But you're still evading. I still don't have an answer."

Ben shook his head. "Do you really want to sit here talking about why we didn't have sex before, when we could be doing it *right now*?"

I swallowed hard. "Like…regular sex?" I blurted out, before I could stop myself.

He laughed like that was the funniest thing he'd heard all week. "What kind of sex do you think I have?"

"I don't know." My face was burning. I snatched up the sheet again, feeling the sudden need to be covered. Or as covered as I could be, when it came to him. "I don't know if you do vanilla."

"Babe, I do *all* the flavors." He slid closer, doing an exaggerated eyebrow waggle that brought out a little giggle in me. "If you know what I mean." He paused, frowning. "I'm not sure what I mean. Point being, though, I do in fact have 'regular sex.' This -" here, he gestured down towards the one part of his body that drew my attention like a beacon "- isn't because I'm thinking about spanking you or tying you up or dressing you in a silly little maid costume that doesn't even cover your ass. I just want you." His voice went a little lower, a little quieter, growing husky and stoking a subtle fire inside me. "However you'll take me. And sunshine, I want to give you all the answers. I do. I want to talk all day and all night until you're satisfied that you understand every corner of my mind. But right now, I can't think straight. You know why?"

I did. But I wanted him to tell me, in vivid detail.

"I need to fuck you." He rolled onto his side, pressing our bodies together, kissing me again until I could hardly remember my name. "I've waited too damn long," he whispered, breathless, his forehead resting against mine. "So have you. Let's make up for lost time."

I nodded, forgetting for a moment how the mysterious process of *talking* worked.

Pulling away from me just long enough to grab a condom from the beside drawer - when did *those* get there? - he ripped it open with his teeth and sheathed himself hastily. His fingers quested between my legs, dipping inside, finding me more than ready.

"Fuck," he whispered, pulling back replacing his fingers with the blunt head of his erection. We both groaned as he sank inside, slowly, until he was buried.

He started slowly, as my body adjusted, but soon we were both frantic, the bed creaking loudly beneath us in protest.

My body tingled all over. Slowly just slightly, he grabbed my leg just under my thigh and lifted, until I gasped at the angle of his thrusts. I hooked my knee over his shoulder and clutched the sheets until I screamed.

We spent most of the day visiting wineries, tasting the varietals and answering polite questions about what we did for a living. I learned to hate the little condescending smile people gave me when I said I was an actress, but had to answer "not yet" when they asked me if I'd been in anything they'd recognize.

But the wine was good, and after a few visits I stopped caring so much if they judged me. We almost ate lunch at a bistro attached to one of the vineyards, but an assortment of olives and overly fancy cheeses wasn't particularly appealing. We went down the road in search of heartier fare, finally stumbling across a diner in the middle of a gravel lot.

"Have you ever eaten in a trailer before?" I asked him, as we approached the rickety screen door.

"Of course," he said. "You haven't lived until you've eaten in a diner with aluminum walls."

The food was deliciously greasy and satisfying, and I marveled at how Ben managed to eat a bacon cheeseburger without getting even a single stain on his gorgeous suit vest.

I kept bumping his foot under the table by accident, and eventually it become on purpose. After lunch, we took a canoe around one of the smaller lakes, gliding around the water until sunset. Of course we had dinner reservations at one of the fanciest places on the waterfront, but it didn't quite live up to the greasy spoon.

I felt fuzzy-headed and strangely exhausted by the time we got back to the cabin.

"Why don't you head off to bed?" Ben suggested, rubbing my neck lightly. "I've got a little bit of work to go over. I'll be up soon."

I took his advice, wondering what on earth could be so important that he'd let me go to bed alone.

When I woke up, the room was completely dark. At first, my arm reached out to feel for Ben beside me. He was still absent, so I reached for my phone and squinted at the time.

It was almost three in the morning. Way too late for a woman on a supposedly romantic getaway with her supposed fiancé to be sleeping alone.

What could possibly be so important? Of course

this was all for show, but at least I was taking the opportunity to really go on vacation. I supposed Ben didn't have that luxury, but something told me he'd probably passed out on the living room sofa with his face in some extremely boring spreadsheets.

I should rescue him. I owed him that, at least.

Padding down the stairs, I soon heard the slow, steady sound of his breathing that indicated I was at least partially right. The papers were spread out on the coffee table, along with an assortment of beer bottles and candy wrappers, and he was sprawled across the cushions just as I'd suspected. Smiling, I knelt down to shake him gently awake.

He blinked sleepily at me, then scrunched his face up and yawned.

"You're gonna have a hell of a crick in your neck," I murmured. "Come to bed. Nothing you're looking at here is more important than getting some decent sleep."

"Sleep?" He was a little more awake now, but his voice still sounded rough and lazy. Warmth spread through my chest. "You're trying to lure me back to bed with the promise of sleep? You're gonna have to do better than that."

I laughed, grabbing his hands and pulling him to his feet as he stood. "Right now, what you need is sleep. We'll get to the other stuff later, when you're well-rested enough to enjoy it."

He mumbled a protest, raking his hands through his hair and stumbling his way up the stairs. "And you're not coming?" he groused, pausing halfway up. "How is *that* fair?"

"I'm just going to clean up your mess and turn off

the lights," I called after him. "Go to sleep, Mr. Chase."

After I'd picked up the garbage, I paused to look at the papers. They didn't seem to be in any particular order, and one of them had already wrinkled slightly when it picked up condensation from a beer bottle.

I didn't mean to snoop. I was done snooping. But he'd left it out in the open, and I couldn't help but notice some of the words.

They had something to do with clinical trials. That wasn't surprising, but there was something that gave me pause. I certainly didn't understand enough about clinical trials to grasp all of the intricacies of it, but there were some words I recognized: Huntington's disease. I was certainly no expert, but I knew it was a serious degenerative disorder.

I also knew enough from the references to previous trials that Chase Pharmaceuticals must have been pouring a *lot* of money into this research. As I paged through the report, I tried to understand why. It was devastating, but as far as I knew, pretty rare. I wouldn't have expected a profit-focused business to put so much into it.

Unless, of course, there was a personal connection.

Once again, I was struck by how little I really knew about Ben. If this was a passion project of his, he must have known someone with the disease. I knew that both of his parents had passed away, but I didn't know how.

And Huntington's was genetic. If one of his parents had it, there was a fifty percent chance he had it too.

My mind was racing. It was all speculation, and

wild speculation at that. But the fact that he was keeping it so quiet... I'd Googled Chase Pharmaceuticals before and found no mention of it. This wasn't corporate altruism. It was personal. He didn't want anyone to know, because he wasn't doing it for publicity.

Suddenly, I felt a rush of guilt. I shoved the papers into the briefcase and went back upstairs, fighting to put the paperwork out of my mind.

Chapter Twenty-Three

Jenna

The next morning, he wanted to go to the beach.

Well, first, he wanted to give me something that he called a *good girl spanking*. I didn't know what that meant, but I had to admit I liked the sound of it.

"It's just a little gentler," he told me. "I won't say it doesn't hurt, but it doesn't sting. You get a nice warm-up first, and then, when you're good and ready, whatever reward you choose."

"I have to choose just one?" I pouted.

He grinned. "Don't be greedy."

I managed to put aside the memories of what I'd discovered last night, letting it fade so that it seemed like nothing more than a bad dream.

In the end, the little noises I made as he "warmed me up" proved to be too much to resist, and he let me have my reward a little early. Taking me hard and fast, bent over the bathroom counter, he smacked my bottom with every other thrust, groaning at the way I clenched tight inside with every impact. When he gripped my hair by the roots and pulled my head up, making me meet his eyes in the mirror, I came so hard I saw stars.

After that, I shouldn't have been embarrassed by the way he looked at me in my bikini. Maybe embarrassed wasn't the right word, but I was a little afraid we'd get carried away in public if he didn't stop.

In the end, he managed to control himself, and we staked out little outpost at the beach without incident. He wanted to go into the water, but I was content to stay by the sidelines and watch him. This turned out to be a pretty good choice. The only thing better than Benjamin Chase in low-slung swimming trunks was Benjamin Chase in low-slung swimming trunks, and *soaking wet.*

After a while, he returned, glancing around him like he was suspicious of something.

"I feel like someone's watching me," he said. "As much as I'd like to blame it on my rockin' bod, I think it's very possible I'm actually being watched for some other purpose."

"Typical," I muttered, smiling at him. "Everything's gotta be about you, doesn't it?"

I was just teasing, but it seemed to rattle something inside him. He glanced at me, stretching out on his towel. "You always act like you know rich people so well," he said. "What, did you major in Poli Sci?"

"I grew up in a resort town," I told him. "Working. Cleaning houses. Me and my parents. So I've known plenty of people like you before."

He smiled a little. "All of our dirty little secrets. Did you ever try to blackmail anyone?"

I couldn't help but laugh. "It was tempting, but

no. Nothing really all that juicy. Just a lot of random mess, and a lot of pill bottles. All par for the course."

Nodding, he stretched out further, resting his head on the towel. "We used to visit one of those every summer. It was nice. I remember I always annoyed my parents by asking who lived in our house when we were gone."

I snorted. It was funny to imagine little Ben Chase, being just as clueless about things as I was. Not understanding the meaning of money. The influence he automatically held over everyone like me.

"I always wondered what it would be like," I said. "We always had to take our vacations in the off-season, of course. Nothing fancy. Usually we'd go camping. About as far as you can get from a luxurious seaside getaway. But I liked it, because it was different."

Ben nodded. "Not as many boys, though, I imagine."

Grinning at him, I rolled over on my side. "Believe it or not, that wasn't really my primary concern when it came to picking vacation spots."

"You're telling me you never fell in love? Not even for one summer?" Ben shook his head. "That's the saddest story I've ever heard, Ms. Hadley."

In spite of the sun, I could feel my skin tighten with goosebumps. I *liked* it when he called me that, and I had no inclination to figure out why. "No," I said, simply, trying to ignore the rush of feelings twisting in my stomach. "You really think I would've been allowed to fool around with billionaire's kids?"

"What? Your parents didn't approve?" He looked confused.

"*Their* parents," I corrected him. Shit, was he

really that clueless? "I guess they really didn't want their sons spending time with the cleaning lady's daughter. I can't imagine why."

Rolling my eyes, I flopped down on my back. It was impossible to have a normal conversation with this guy. Our experiences were just too different, despite the odd little ways in which they seemed to cross over.

"Mine wouldn't care," he said, simply. "I'm surprised anyone did. That kind of thing went out of fashion a couple decades ago. Actually, I'm pretty sure my mother had some romantic fantasy that I'd end up with a girl who was *below my station*. Too much Jane Austen, I think."

Curiosity tickled at the back of my mind. "Well, did you?" I hadn't really asked him any questions about Daria. He didn't seem to like thinking about her, let alone talking about her - but I found myself wondering about the history.

"Not really," he said, shortly. "Well - I think it's a shame you never mingled with the tourist kids. They might've learned something from you."

"I didn't say I *never* mingled." Memories were coming back, still surprisingly vivid and strong, after all these years. "I did. For a while. But I learned better, pretty quickly."

Almost twenty years, and there was still a hole in my chest. It ached and burned just as badly as it had back then, when I was still so young I didn't understand the difference. I didn't know why some kids were only around during the summer, and why they went away. When we were all playing in the sand, we seemed the same.

Back then, there was a boy. He was older, by a

mile, it seemed, back then - but in reality it was probably just a few years. I was of the age where a few years makes all the difference.

"Young love," Ben teased me, gently, bringing me back to the present. "I knew it. Why lie about a thing like that?"

"Gross." My fingers were digging absently into the sand, unearthing a little twig to pick and twist between my fingers. "I was like, six years old or something. It wasn't like that. I just...you know, I thought we were going to be friends. But his parents put a stop to it."

"Maybe they just didn't like their creepy kid hanging around with a six-year-old." He was grinning, propping himself up on his elbow to take a swig from his beer. "Probably did you a favor."

"He couldn't have been much older than eight," I protested. "There was literally no reason to keep us apart, except..."

Ben laid back down, this time, his shoulder a little closer to mine. At first I thought I might be imagining it, but I was certain. I could feel his closeness, even through the baking heat of the sun.

"Did he tell you? Maybe his friends were just making fun of him for having cooties, and he used his parents as excuse." Ben tilted his head back, stretching slightly. "Kids do that. They're surprisingly conniving."

"No." I wanted to stop talking about it, to stop remembering, but at the same time, it almost felt...*good*. Like picking off a scab that had been left for too long. "*My* parents told me. Said his dad came and talked to them. I kind of felt guilty, even though I didn't know I was doing anything wrong."

"And you never heard anything from him?"

"Nope. He acted like I'd never existed. Probably forgot about me immediately." I sighed, trying to conceal how much the whole thing still affected me. "I stayed inside for a while, and just avoided everybody as much as I could. I didn't want anyone to get in trouble. Before long, he was gone, and that solved that problem. The next year, I'd figured out how to mingle without being one of them. I just started reading a lot of books, staying away from all their games. I don't think I ever saw him again, but he'd probably changed so much I couldn't recognize him."

"They do grow up fast, at that age." Ben sounded oddly thoughtful. "I don't have a whole lot of clear memories from back then. You must've been unusually sharp."

"I guess so."

He was silent for a while. "Either that, or it hurt you more than you want to admit."

His voice was soft, almost understanding. Like he wasn't about to make fun of me for still carrying the wounds from a pre-school shunning.

"It's hard to explain," I admitted, surprised to hear the sound of my own voice. I wasn't planning on telling him, I just…started to talk, and then I couldn't stop. "It was never that easy for me to make friends. And not just because half of the kids I knew were millionaires, and only came for a couple months a year. Even the ones I knew all the time - the other townies, I just couldn't relate to them. Or they couldn't relate to me. I don't know. It was just hard." I sighed. "That boy…I don't even remember what he said to me, just that he made me laugh. He helped me build my sandcastle, and it was like we just understood each other. I don't know. It's stupid."

Ben's voice cut through the fog of memories. "It's not stupid," he said. "It meant something to you."

"We must've spent the whole day together. But when he went to get some more supplies, some tools so we could build taller turrets and really make that thing into the grandest castle that had ever been built - he never came back. My mom came and fetched me. She was so mad that I'd wandered away from the other kids, from where the lifeguard watched. But more than that, she was mad that I'd been spending time with one of the tourist kids. At first I didn't want to believe her. She said he was just...I mean, I didn't understand it at the time. Kids always think everybody is sincere. But when I think back on it now, I guess she was trying to tell me that he was setting me up for a fall. Toying with me. He wanted me to think that he could trust me, so he could tear me down. I have a hard time believing it, even now, but it's like you said - kids are conniving."

"Not like that, they aren't." I could hear the frown in his voice. "Do you think maybe it was just *your* parents that had the problem?"

I paused.

No. It couldn't be. My parents were the most kind, generous, compassionate people I'd ever met. Sure, they held a little bit of a grudge against the tourists, but who wouldn't? They blew into town and left a mess in their wake, sustaining the economy, but at what cost? It was hard to really appreciate someone when you were scrubbing their spoiled toddler's crayon stains off the lily-white walls of their five million dollar beach house. Especially when they "forgot" to leave a tip.

"I don't think so," I said, turning his words over and over again in my mind.

"You don't sound completely convinced," he said. "And maybe this'll sound particularly asshole-ish, coming from me, but hear me out. Being rich might make most people a tiny bit insufferable, at best - but being poor doesn't make you a saint, either."

I bristled. "My parents weren't *poor*."

"I didn't say they were." He let out an irritated sigh. "You know what I meant."

"Yeah, I do. But I happen to think the way my parents felt about people like you was pretty damn well justified."

"Maybe it was," he said. "But maybe they owe you an apology for ruining what could have been a really nice friendship."

I lay there next to him, fuming. What gave him the right to try and explain away the past? Of course he wanted the rich kid's parents to be blameless. Just because his mom and dad were apparently so open-minded and tolerant, he found it hard to believe that anyone had those issues.

He could sense my irritation. Satellites orbiting earth could probably sense my irritation. "I'm going to cool off," he said, heading back for the water.

As I watched him walk down the beach, I let my mind wander back to what I'd seen in his paperwork. After a long night of research, scrolling down page after page on my phone and squinting at the tiny text, I'd learned a lot. Very little of it was encouraging. If my suspicions were right, then there was a genetic test available that would tell him whether he had the disease. He wouldn't have to wait for symptoms to show up. But many people with a family history chose not to. They preferred to live their life as normal.

I couldn't imagine it. Every stumble, every tremor, wondering if that was it. The beginning of the end.

No, I'd have to get the test. Even if it meant knowing the worst.

Which path had Ben chosen?

Was I even barking up the right tree, at all? Or was it all just wild speculation, completely off base from reality?

I couldn't ask him. I couldn't even bring it up. Not today, not when the sun was shining and the lake was shimmering, blindingly bright. Even with my sunglasses on, I could hardly look at it.

What if this was real?

Would it matter?

I hated the thought. I hated wondering. It *wasn't* real, so it didn't matter. Whether or not he had the disease - it was horrible to think of, I didn't want him to have it, I didn't want *anyone* to have it. But even if we stayed friends after our little arrangement, by the time it started to affect his life, we would have drifted apart.

But still, I couldn't help but wonder.

Would you let it change the way you felt about him? If you knew he was sick?

Of course not. Of course it wouldn't. If I really loved him -

If.

If I really loved him. Because I didn't. Because this wasn't real.

Ben was walking into the water, letting the little

waves lap up past his chest, dunking his head down and shaking off the droplets from his hair as he came back towards me. He flopped down on his towel, sprinkling me with lake water.

Ugh.

"You know that water's like, ninety percent duck poop, right?" I let my mouth twist into a lighthearted scowl, while my mind stayed in the shadows.

"That seems a little high," he said, turning towards me, grinning that lopsided grin. "Do you have the studies on that?"

This wasn't real. It never would be real.

So why did the thought of someone else caring for him - *someone else* being there for him, at the end -

Why did it make me want to scream?

Chapter Twenty-Four

Jenna

"It's just...this is so different from anything I've ever done." I was frowning at the table, twisting a cocktail napkin between my hands. "Obviously dating is always nerve-wracking at first, but whenever I settle in with somebody, get into a routine, it's...simple. Relaxing."

Boring.

I didn't say it out loud, but I probably didn't have to.

Ben noticed I was on pins and needles, and he wanted to talk about it. I appreciated that, but I wasn't going to tell him what really upset me. Naturally, he thought it had to do with the new development in our relationship. Like, the fact that we actually *had* a relationship now. Not a romantic one, strictly speaking, but it was something.

"That's all." I shrugged. "I'm just not used to being...on my toes."

"You prefer your routine," he said.

"I, uh..." Did I? That sounded so horrifically

mundane. "I wouldn't say I prefer it. It's just what I'm used to."

He chuckled. "Well, that's the definition of a routine, isn't it? But we're certainly not following any kind of routine now."

There it was, again. Although I'd started out this trip by repeatedly reminding myself that none of it was real, now, I began to resent that fact. I hated being forcibly reminded of it. It wasn't that I wanted to pretend it was real, I just didn't want to think about it anymore.

"I know that," I said, irritably. "I just…"

"Jenna, hey." Ben's voice was soft, persuasive. I looked up at his face. "If you don't want to do this, we can stop. But I just want you to know it's normal for this stuff to bring up all kinds of emotions you don't expect. We spend most of our lives trying not to be vulnerable, avoiding it at all costs, and then…"

And then some kinky billionaire comes along and makes you do things you never knew you wanted.

It felt like losing headway, on a battle that was never mine to fight. I didn't want this to be political. And maybe, even if it was, I had nothing to be ashamed of. After all - this was my choice.

I'd proven that on the very first day, within minutes of our arrival. He told me that he was in control, but I knew that was just a fantasy. The moment I broke that spell, the moment I walked to the door, it was clear. I held all the cards. He only wanted this if it was given willingly.

When he first tried to argue for his altruism in all of this, I'd practically laughed in his face. But now I understood. It wasn't exactly selfless. It gratified him, but only because it gratified something in me.

There was a part of me that I never knew existed, something I'd had to suppress just to survive. I imagined most people did. The helpless part, the part that doubted, the part that just wanted to bow to someone's authority. *Be a leader, not a follower.* But not everyone could be a leader, all the time.

If I was going to follow somebody, I could do a lot worse than Benjamin Chase.

"I don't want to stop," I told him. "But I think we need to hash things out, before we keep doing this."

He nodded, slowly. "Right," he said. "Spontaneity's been fun, but it can always end badly." He smiled, a little sheepishly. "I just didn't want to scare you off by unrolling some big contract or checklist. It doesn't always have to be like that. We can just talk."

I cleared my throat and glanced at him. "You mean, we don't need to get it notarized?"

He smirked - meanwhile, my brain, my stupid overactive brain, couldn't help but wander to the thoughts of paperwork that did need to be notarized. Like divorce filings.

My heart twisted in my chest. Already, it felt like something inside me was breaking.

We're not even married yet.

"You brought something, didn't you?" I made a vague gesture. "You know...supplies. Toys. I don't know what you call them."

Was I imagining it, or was there some extra color in his cheeks? "I did," he said. "If you want, you could..."

"Look at them," I finished. "And we'll start there.

If I have any questions, I'll just..."

"Right," he said, standing up. "I'll, uh, I'll go get them."

I stood up. "Maybe not in the living room?" I suggested, a little hesitantly.

"I don't want there to be any pressure," he said. "But if you think the bedroom won't be too, um..."

There's not a room in this house I haven't pictured you fucking me in.

I flushed. Now was not the time to have that conversation.

"It'll be fine," I promised him. "Lead on, Mr. Chase."

He glanced at me over his shoulder, with an unreadable expression. A moment later, I was following him up the stairs, trying to drag my eyes away from the tight muscles of his ass, bunching under those jeans he wore so well. I liked him best in suits, I thought, but the casual clothes were a delicious little vacation into a whole other world.

He could have made anything look good. I wondered if he'd wear an outfit *I* picked out for him. Did it go both ways? What if I wanted him to dress up for *my* fantasy - as a professor, or a priest?

My whole body instantly felt hot. Where did that come from? I didn't have any...fetishes. At least, I didn't *think* I did.

Still, there was no denying a nice pair of glasses, or a well-fitted cassock, looked pretty damn hot. Maybe we could talk about that later. But I was *not* dressing up as a nun. Maybe a naughty Catholic schoolgirl...hey, it could work in both scenarios.

Already I was starting to feel unsteady, a little

tingle in the pit of my stomach warning me that this was going to escalate fast. Maybe sticking to the living room would have been a better option. We hadn't had sex there - yet. The kitchen, arguably one of the least sexy rooms of your average house, was right out. Obviously. I'd never be able to look at a stove hood again without remembering his tongue buried between my folds.

Back in reality, Ben was carefully unzipping an innocent-looking black bag that he'd plopped on the bed. I crossed my arms, in a mostly futile effort to hide the stiff peaks of my nipples. I didn't want him to think this little exercise was turning me on - no, picturing him as a professor with compromised ethics, spanking me over his desk with a ruler - that was what really lit my fire.

I wondered if he had a ruler in there.

I realized he was waiting for me, so I dug in.

Handcuffs. That was standard enough. I pulled them out and examined them - heavy, well-made. I frowned.

"These are police issue," I said, glancing up at him. He was hiding a smile behind his hand, but not very well.

"Yeah," he said. "I don't do things halfway."

Well, I could admire that. My fingers closed around something else that felt like some kind of whip or flogger, but when I brought up a handful of what I grabbed, I realized it was zip ties.

A little creepy, and not so sexy. But way less danger of losing the key. I could kind of appreciate that.

"For more realism," he explained. "They hardly

use the metal handcuffs in real life anymore. Some people actually care about that kind of thing."

I snorted. "You do a lot of cop roleplay?"

It wasn't really a fantasy of mine. Then again, until earlier, I hadn't realized that I had any fantasies. This one might be a little too real-life scary for me, but I wasn't ruling it out. I knew the zip ties were technically more realistic, but they didn't really make me think cop. They made me think mafia, or…serial killer…

Holy hell, was I really more on board with a serial killer role play than a cop role play? What the hell was wrong with me?

"We don't have to…I mean, none of that is really my specialty anyway." Ben was misreading my hesitation, thinking I was already unnerved. And I was, a little - but only by the images in my own brain. "This is all stuff I like playing around with, but all I really need…" He paused, swallowing audibly. "….is you."

He was standing a little closer now, looking painfully sincere.

"That's sweet," I said. "But I know it's not entirely true. And that's okay. I'm just…there's a lot to think about. Nothing here scares me."

Not quite right. He just didn't understand *what* I found scary.

How could I possibly have all of these parts of myself, locked away, somewhere, for years and years - without knowing? Why had no one else ever woken it up?

What *was* it about this guy?

I reached in and grabbed something solid.

Wooden. I knew what it was before it came out of the bag.

A paddle. From the way he inhaled, sharply, and the way his body twitched a little, I could tell this one was important to him.

It made sense. He was into spankings, punishments, rule-following - but this really seemed like it would sting. I preferred his hand. Then again, maybe this wasn't always about what I preferred.

"Do you ever use your belt?" I heard myself ask.

"I..." He swallowed again. "For punishments? Yes. I have. Would you..."

"Might be worth trying," I said, lightly, setting the paddle aside.

I wished he would relax. I didn't like him this way, tense and watchful, embarrassed by his own interests and slightly terrified of my reactions.

"Sit down," I said. "I mean, if you...if you want to." I cleared my throat. "What I mean is, you're making me nervous, and not because of your little bag of tricks."

He let out a burst of laughter. "I'm sorry," he said. "I just - you know, this is new to me. Typically we work these things out long before anything starts."

Everything carefully regimented, carefully planned. It made things easier. I was a liability, in more ways than one.

Still, I couldn't figure out why he cared so much. As much as it made my stomach roil to think about it, I was sure he could go and find anything he absolutely needed after we were married. If I wouldn't do it, he'd find someone who would. Discretion shouldn't be an issue. There had to be a million people out there who would be in even worse-off shape than him, if anyone found out what they did in private. Plenty of people must cater to that kind of thing.

"You know, if you…" I felt bile starting to rise up my throat, and I tried again. "I don't want you to feel like you can't…"

He watched me, curiously.

I took a deep breath. "What I mean is, obviously, the terms of our arrangement don't preclude going elsewhere to have needs fulfilled. Right?" I watched his face carefully - other than a little twitch in his jaw, there was no reaction. "I mean, I won't. But you…" I clutched the edge of the bag. "You can. Obviously. Not that you need my permission."

He shook his head, finally walking to the other side of the bed and perching carefully on the edge of the mattress. "No," he said. "Too risky. That goes for both of us."

We hadn't talked about it. I honestly hadn't even considered it, because it hardly mattered one way or the other. It's not like I was going to stumble across the love of my life in the next two years. I'd be lucky if I stumbled across someone whose company I could stand for more than a few minutes, with my track record lately.

Just my luck, my fake fiance was turning out to be quite a lot of fun.

But now, I felt guilty. Anything I wouldn't agree to do with him, he'd just have to…go without? Something told me a man like Ben wasn't used to going without.

"There's no pressure," he said, quickly, as if he was following the same train of thought. "I don't want you to feel like you have to live up to some standard, just to keep me happy. I wasn't expecting any of this, so..."

"Me neither," I admitted. I reached into the bag again to cut through the awkward silence. This time it actually was a flogger, leather, I thought, feeling soft and supple on my hand. Depending on how it was wielded, I imagined it could either tickle lightly or sting like a bitch. And everything in-between.

I understood that pain could be exhilarating. I'd even experienced it a little bit myself, but I was pretty sure I couldn't be classified as a masochist. The spanking was something special.

"Are you a sadist?" I asked him.

He watched me for a moment, like he was trying to gauge my reaction before answering. "No," he said. "I just feel like the sweet tastes sweeter, once you've had something bitter."

Laughing, I reached into the bag again. "You know, I won't run for the hills if you just say yes."

"I'm not," he insisted. "It's not the pain. It's the control."

This time, I could tell he was being honest.

I found scraps of silk that could probably be used for blindfolds, or bondage. Elegant rope that was dyed deep black. There was a pair of surgical scissors, the kind that are smooth and flat on one side for safely removing bandages. Or, in this case, zip ties or bondage rope in a hurry, if needed - at least that's what I imagined.

Or...clothes?

At the bottom of the bag there were a few small things, themselves encased in little silky sacks, which made my pulse race a little bit. I picked up one of them, feeling the shape through the fabric.

A plug. I knew what that was for.

Flushing deeply, I dropped it back into the bag and reached for the last thing. Beads.

Okay, that wasn't so bad. Not something I was ready for, I thought - but still, nothing scary.

"No ball gag?" I looked up at him. He was watching me with rapt attention, but the question seemed to surprise him.

"I'd much rather use my hand," he said.

I tried very hard not to think about a scenario where he'd have to muffle me. Certainly not while he was pretending to be a priest.

Certainly not.

Careful, Father, everyone will hear...

I swallowed hard, looking back down at the implements on the bed. As luck would have it, the one fantasy I was obsessed with now didn't fit any of this. Maybe we weren't so well-aligned after all. Maybe the spanking had just been a lucky coincidence.

"Tell me what you're thinking," he urged.

Tie me up and pretend to kidnap me.

Oh, right, I had *one* fantasy that would make use of the zip ties. But as much as it quickened my heartbeat, I didn't know if it was a good idea. For one thing, even though I trusted him, it was pretty serious to basically lay my life in someone's hands. For another, it might scare him away.

After all this, now I was the one worried about frightening *him*.

"We don't have to talk about it right now," he said, finally breaking the silence. "If you need some time to think..."

"Do you ever pretend to be somebody you're not?"

I was blushing, deeply. And it was a stupid question. I'd worded it terribly.

"I mean, obviously you roleplay. As a cop, anyway. But I mean like...someone different from who you really are."

No, that was still terrible. Why couldn't I just bring myself to say it?

He was half-smiling. "I'm certainly not a cop. And I've been a priest before, if you need someone to absolve you of your sins."

Holy shit. His voice got a little deeper when he said that, and I felt heat coiling deep inside. "Well, I don't think you have the right outfit for that," I said, mortified at how husky I sounded.

His smile grew. "They don't *always* dress like that, you know," he said, edging closer to me. "Sometimes they just look like normal people."

My mind was racing. No, I couldn't dive into it. Not here, not now. I needed time. I needed to breathe.

Suddenly panicking, I stood up. I couldn't figure out why my brain wanted to claw its way out of my skull, but I just had to get out. Out of this room, out of this house.

By the time my tunnel vision cleared, I was on the front porch, leaning heavily on the railing. Ben must think I was insane. Or worse, he'd think that he did something wrong. Shit. Why couldn't I just be honest with him? Why couldn't I tell him what I was thinking, instead of panicking and running away?

I hated my inability to confront this. The fear, the

anxiety, whatever it was.

The fear that I wasn't good enough.

That was what it was. Whenever I tried to roleplay, or *perform*, it triggered that fear. That inadequacy. I was so sure that my dreams would never come true, that my career ambitions were all stupid and pointless, that I couldn't even act for fun.

I had to stop running away from it.

They tell me what they don't like about themselves, and I help them fix it.

The solution to my problem was right in front of my face.

When I turned around, I half expected to see Ben standing in the doorway. But he wasn't there. Heart hammering with anticipation, I went back up the stairs, finding him right where I'd left him. All of the toys were packed away, and his head was bowed, deep in thought.

I took a deep breath, walked in, and kneeled at his feet.

Chapter Twenty-Five

Ben

Stupid, stupid, stupid.

I was so fucking stupid. Here was this girl, this completely vanilla, completely inexperienced girl, and I practically dumped a bucket of sex toys on her head. Expecting...what, exactly? That she'd instantly turn into an insatiable sex kitten?

No, I just wanted to give her a gentle introduction to my world. I didn't even care that much about any of these props, all I wanted was her sated and smiling in my arms again. However it took to get there, that was fine with me.

I didn't need ropes or cuffs, not even a paddle or a belt. If all I ever used was my hand, and I got to hear her ragged moans again, I'd never wish for anything else. How could I? She was perfect.

Just my luck, I'd chosen a pretend fiancee who melted at my touch like we were born to be together.

Why did things have to be so complicated?

After what happened in the kitchen, I knew I couldn't go back. Spending the next two years pretending to be her husband, but unable to do the things I wanted with her - utter torture. And maybe, maybe she'd still be down with vanilla sex. But that wasn't going to be enough. Not when I'd remember how she mewled and squirmed every time I spanked her.

When she first ran out of the room, I thought about following her. I ached to make sure she was okay, but at the same time, I didn't want to put any pressure on her. I split the difference and looked for her out the window, and could just barely see her on the porch, leaning out over the railing. She was still upright and she wasn't vomiting, didn't appear to be hyperventilating. Fine. So I wasn't needed.

I sat back down and packed up my stupid toys, one by one.

I expected her to come back in, eventually, probably apologize, which I would wave off. I'd put a brave smile on and tell her everything was okay. Because it was. I would make it okay. I just had to figure out what that meant, first.

What I didn't expect was to look up and see her kneeling at my feet.

I worked my mouth open and closed a few times, failing to find any words that would fit the situation.

"I'm tired of running away from what I need," she said, softly. "Punish me."

An eternity passed.

"Jenna…" I searched for the right words. "You don't have to…"

Her eyes blazed, and I drifted off.

"Ever since I came to New York, I've been scared," she said. "I guess it's been there my whole life,

I just pretended like it wasn't. I acted like I was confident and I couldn't fail. But I know that's not true. And ever since I got here, I've been setting myself up for misery. You know how I ended up at that stupid porno audition? Because I never even bother submitting to the ones that seem too *ambitious* for me. I was going for something that seemed like it was *on my level.*"

She smiled, bitterly, then went on.

"That's how I've been thinking, ever since I came. And when it seemed like you were about to start some roleplay, I freaked out. Because I'm afraid to do the one thing that I really want to do. If I suck at roleplay then I suck at acting, and if I suck at acting, it's all over."

She stopped, breathing quickly, and I found myself mesmerized by the rise and fall of her chest.

"Acting is all I have. It's all I've ever wanted to do. The stakes are too high - so I just run away from it. I have to stop running away, and I need your help to do it."

My heart was racing as I stared at her. Holy shit, she actually wanted it - and for the right reasons. She understood why I did what I did. She needed my discipline, wanted my discipline, and I was ready to give it to her.

Take a deep breath, Chase. Count to ten.

I had to consider the ramifications. We weren't really together. Sure, I wanted it to seem authentic, but this was going way, way too far.

But it was too late. I couldn't put a stop to this now.

"Are you sure?" I asked her.

She blinked, slowly.

"Yes."

There was no doubt in her voice, in her expression. Inside, I thrilled.

I fought to keep my face neutral. "All right," I said, slowly. "Give me a minute. Let me think up a suitable punishment."

She nodded, smiling a little. "Should I leave you alone?"

I shook my head. I was afraid if she walked out of the room, she'd never come back. Not that I thought this was some moment of insanity, but it certainly wasn't her usual thing. I didn't think she'd regret it. But given enough time, she might try to back out. Especially given her checkered past with the subject.

I could do the obvious. A straight up, "you messed up and now I'm punishing you" spanking. Followed by wild sex, of course. That was a given. But there was another scenario that popped into my head and just wouldn't leave. But it might be too much, especially considering the source of her anxiety and what she'd just gone through with her last audition.

Still, it was worth a try.

"Would you be willing to try an experiment with me?" I asked, finally.

She nodded, eagerly.

"Here's my idea," I began, taking a deep breath. "I want to roleplay. But it's going to be easy. You'll just be yourself. I'll be a casting director. You're coming in to read a scene in which a husband spanks his wife, for disobeying him." I heard her breathing quicken, saw her eyes widen slightly. "But he doesn't find your read convincing enough. However, he likes you...so he's determined to raise the stakes until you can prove that you're right for the part." I swallowed, my throat suddenly dry.

For a moment, the only sound in the room was her rapid breaths. She sat up straighter, pulling her shoulders back so that I had no choice but to notice her arousal through the thin fabric of her shirt. Outwardly, I stayed calm, but my fingers gripped the edge of the mattress.

"I think you forgot one character detail," she said, at last, with a secretive smile. "The casting director... does he wear Magnum XL condoms?"

"If you play your cards right, maybe you'll find out." I felt a rush of relief; then excitement, anticipation zinging through my veins.

"So." She was biting her lower lip, a little gesture that I normally found endearing. But now, it went straight to my dick.

"You need a safe word," I said. "To end it, if you need to. At any point."

She frowned. "If I use it, doesn't that defeat the whole purpose?"

"No. Jenna, listen - it's important that you understand what this is for. I'll push your boundaries for you, but I'll never break them. You have to respect your own limits, so I can respect them. If you feel a little uncomfortable, if you feel nervous, that's one thing. But if at any point in time you feel like you *can't* continue, like you *need* to stop - that's what it's for. To keep you safe. To keep both of us safe."

I could tell she didn't really know what I meant by that, but the beginnings of understanding were dawning across her face. She still didn't look happy

315

about it, but I knew if things went too far, she'd be happy we had this conversation.

"So, how do you pick a safe word?" She licked her lips, and I had to resist the urge to kiss her.

"Any word is fine, as long as it's something you wouldn't say naturally during the encounter. Mostly it's meant to take the place of 'no' or 'stop,' in case it feels right to say those things as a part of the scene."

She smiled faintly, her eyes darkening a little in a way that made my pulse quicken in response. "Do you think that's going to feel right to say those things?"

"Maybe," I said.

It seemed wrong to wink, although she certainly looked intrigued by the idea.

"I like...caramel."

She grinned.

"Oh, very funny." I lifted her chin with a firm hand, reminding her who was in charge. "Is that caramel with a K?"

"If you want." She fluttered her eyelashes. "Anyway, it's not going to matter. I won't use it."

My grip tightened, ever so slightly. "Promise me that you will, if you need to."

"Fine." She took a deep breath, and I finally felt she was serious. "Fine. I'll use it if I need to."

I nodded, letting her go. "So, go out into the hallway. Give me a few minutes, then come up and knock on the door. From that point on, unless you need to safeword, we don't know each other. You're Jenna Hadley, aspiring actress, and I'm Benjamin Chase, casting director. That's Mr. Chase to you, of course."

She stood up, arms folded, gnawing on her lip again. God damn it, how was I supposed to focus on my role when she was driving me to distraction, just being *her*?

"Can I ask you for a couple more notes, before we start the scene?" she asked.

I had to laugh a little bit at the double meaning of scene. "Sure."

"Should I pretend like we're in a normal casting office, or...?" Her eyes flicked to the bed.

"I'll leave that up to you." Smiling, I gestured towards the door. After a moment's hesitation, she went.

A few minutes. Not that she was going to count - and she was probably going to give me a lot less than one hundred and twenty seconds. That would feel like an eternity to her, waiting out there. I could use some time to gather my thoughts, to prepare a real performance, but I didn't have it. Not now. Hell, I had no guarantees she was even coming back in the room.

In the end, all I did was tuck my hard-on up under my belt so she wouldn't be distracted.

Showtime.

Right on cue, she knocked. I put on exactly the kind of smug expression that I imagined casting directors wore all the time, which wasn't too much of a stretch.

"Welcome," I said, looking down at an imaginary clipboard in my hand. "You must be...?"

"Jenna Hadley," she said, with a pretty blush and bright, eager eyes. I shook her hand, letting the skin contact linger just enough to remind her what we were doing. "It's so good to meet you. I didn't get any script or materials ahead of time, but your assistant told me -"

I silenced her with a raised hand. "Yes, that's fine.

We'll go over all of that in a minute. Please, sit down."

She looked around the room as if she'd never seen it before. "Um...sorry, did you want me to sit on the bed, or...?"

"Wherever you like," I said. "I know this setting is a little unorthodox, but I find it helps people relax. Give a more...natural performance."

Her face scrunched up a little bit, in that wonderful way of hers. "Oh...okay. I guess, um..." She perched on the edge of the mattress, and I took the chair on the opposite end of the room. All I wanted to do was close the distance between us, pop the button on those not-quite-Daisy-Dukes and *feel* exactly how excited she was for myself. But I had to do this right.

"So...what am I reading?"

I cleared my throat. "It's very simple, you won't even need a script. I'm more interested in your reactions, and your ability to ad-lib in a scenario so it seems natural. Most of the film will be scripted, but it's easy enough to find somebody who can parrot lines like they mean it. I want to make sure you can bring something special to the table. Not just the ordinary stuff."

"Okay." Her whole body was practically humming with nervous energy, and I wasn't sure how much of it was put-on. Either way, I could hardly wait to kiss her breathless while our bodies crashed together on that very bed where she was sitting so primly.

Patience, patience.

"Well, you'll be playing the role of a 1950's housewife," I told her. I let my eyes roam her body, lingering on the tanned expanse of her bare legs. "You're not exactly dressed for the part, but..."

She blushed deeply. "I'm sorry. They didn't..." Swallowing hard, she found her voice again. "It's hot out. I just wanted to be comfortable."

"There's nothing wrong with that," I reassured her, trying to make my voice soothing, but not too soothing. After all, this whole thing was predicated on me playing the part of a sleazy casting agent who didn't mind taking advantage of a vulnerable actress.

Or maybe I was going about this the wrong way. Maybe he wasn't normally like this. Maybe there was just *something about her*...

I shifted in my seat, as if I was trying to go back to acting like a professional. "My apologies, Ms. Hadley. I only meant that I'll understand if it takes you a little extra time to get into the right mindset."

She cleared her throat. "So...what exactly is going on in this scene? What am I ad libbing to?"

"Your husband's just come home." I glanced back down at the phantom notes in my lap, wondering if she noticed the straining erection running up the length of my zipper. She was doing a good job of pretending not to look, anyway. "Earlier, you discovered that he's been lying to you about some bad investments that he made. You're angry, but you know he was just trying to shield you from worrying. When he walked in the door, you didn't have his martini ready, like you always do. He was upset, and you lashed out, because of course you didn't make it because you know that he lied...but you don't want to admit it." This was way too much backstory. I had to get to the point. There was a damn good reason I wasn't a real screenwriter.

"So," I said, "deeply upset by your disrespect, he's turned you over his knee."

Time froze.

Her reaction was perfect. Eyes widened, jaw dropped slightly, breathing quickening. She crossed and re-crossed her legs, shimmying a little on the bed like she couldn't get comfortable. I knew the feeling.

"Um…"

"Is something wrong, Ms. Hadley?" I asked - a little sternly.

"Oh, no, it's just…it's not what I expected." She let out a nervous laugh. "That's fine."

My eyes narrowed. "It doesn't seem fine, Ms. Hadley. Are you offended by the content of the scene? If so, we can end this right now."

"No!" she exclaimed, quickly. Then, softer: "No. I'll do it. So you just…you want me to react as if I'm being spanked?"

I nodded. "Your husband's name is Howard. Work from a basis of 'no, Howard, please! Stop! You're hurting me!' Et cetera, et cetera. But bear in mind, the most painful part is that you've disappointed him. It's really not about the spanking at all."

"Oh…right. Okay." She took a deep breath, screwing her face into a slightly pained expression. "Howard, no! Please - stop. Don't."

I hid a grin behind my hand. She was doing a spectacular job of being awful.

Before she looked up, I rearranged my face into a look of bored disappointment. "Hmm. Let's try that again, shall we?"

"Sorry," she muttered, squirming again. God damn it, if she didn't stop that…

"Sit still," I commanded, before I could think better of it.

She gasped, looking up at me. "I'm...*excuse* me?"

"Sorry. I just mean, please try not to squirm. It's very distracting." I tried to look irritated. "Let's just get on with this, okay? Try to really put yourself in the headspace."

"I'll try," she said, biting her lip. I *throbbed*.

You could cut the tension in the room with a knife. In spite of my order, she was still rubbing her thighs together a little, and I knew exactly why. The seam of those jean shorts was pressing *right* where she needed it. That wasn't quite fair.

"Again, Ms. Hadley," I said. "You can...assume the position, if that makes it easier."

Her eyes went wide as saucers, face turning bright red. "Position?"

"You know." I made a meaningless gesture. "Like you're really being spanked. Whatever that means to you."

"Uh...is that really necessary?"

"No," I said. "But if this next read doesn't blow me away..."

"Okay," she said, quickly. She stood up, situating herself so that her hands were flat on the mattress, and her ass was in the air. But not facing me, of course - she was sidelong, and while I appreciated the view, I was feeling a little shortchanged.

"Go."

"Oh, Howard...please, no," she moaned. "You're...you're..."

I growled, stopping her. "You sound like you're enjoying it. What the hell are you doing? Why are you wasting my time like this?"

She jumped upright, unshed tears shimmering in

her eyes. "I'm sorry, I don't know how to do this! What kind of audition doesn't even have a script? I can't..."

"It doesn't sound like you want this part," I said.

"I do." Her tone was desperate. "I just, I don't think I can do this. I can't just *pretend* like someone is spanking me."

Taking a deep breath, I surveyed her. A perfect performance. Body quivering, eyes watering, and ready to do anything I asked.

Ready for me.

"Here's the thing, Ms. Hadley," I said. "Jenna. I like you. I think you're right for this part. You have a great look, a vintage look. People are going to eat that up. But I can't give you the part if you don't convince me you can do this scene. It's pivotal to the role. If you think the problem is that you can't just *imagine* being spanked...well, we can fix that." I gestured towards my lap. "I'm willing to go out of my way for you, Jenna. Don't make me regret this."

"I..." She took one step towards me, staring, her hands balled into fists. "I don't think..."

"Not many people would do this for you," I said, smoothly. "Probably no one else in this town, in fact. This is your lucky day, Jenna."

Breathlessly, she walked over to me, pausing when she drew close. "What should I...?"

"Lay across my lap." At the feeling of her body heat, I almost groaned, thrusting my long-suffering hard-on into her taut belly. But that wouldn't be consistent with the role. She slid around, trying to find a comfortable spot, and I bit the inside of my cheek to keep quiet. To keep my body still. It was almost impossible.

She twisted her head around to look up at me. "Is this okay?"

"Yes, Jenna, that's fine." I laid my hand on the soft denim that covered her ass. "Do you think you'll be able to get the right experience while you're wearing these? In the film, you'll be spanked through panties only." Her breath caught in her throat. "I think it's best to go for authenticity, don't you?"

"I'm not sure," she whispered.

"I think it's important for the role," I told her, smoothly, reaching under her pelvis to undo the shorts. In spite of her command performance, she couldn't hide how badly she wanted me to touch her there. She whimpered softly, arching into my touch as my fingers ghosted past the top of her panties. I returned my hand to her ass. With one sudden movement, I yanked her shorts down and smacked her lightly on that soft, vulnerable skin, now protected only by lacy black panties that stood out in stark contrast, making my mouth water.

She yelped, squirming on my lap. "Oooh...Mr. Chase...I mean, Howard...?"

I spanked her again. "You still sound like you're enjoying it. I'm going to keep spanking you harder until you seem like it's actually upsetting you, instead of turning you on."

Jenna made an outraged noise. "Turning me on? How dare you, Mr. Chase? I don't know what kind of girl you think I am, but..."

"I think you're the kind of girl who prances into an audition with hardly anything on." *Smack*. "I think you're the kind of girl who picked your outfit today solely based on whether you thought it would make me hard." *Smack.* "Well, congratulations." I rested my hand on the small of her back, holding her firmly in place while I thrust against her quivering body, letting her know exactly how much I wanted her. "You succeeded. Do you feel that, Jenna?"

She nodded, making another tiny whimpering sound. "I'm so sorry, Mr. Chase," she gasped. "I didn't meant to...I just thought...please, don't punish me anymore."

"I'm not punishing you, Jenna." I caressed her ass, where a slight blush had started to appear from my tender loving care. "I'm trying to help you. But I can't help you, if you can't act like a woman ought to when she's being punished. Not like a whore."

A sharp intake of breath. *I went too far.*

Her fingers tightened around my thigh, holding on for dear life. "I think you like it when I act like a whore," she said, softly, shimmying her ass under my hand. This time, I let myself groan. If she kept doing that, this was going to get very embarrassing, *very* quickly.

"Stop it," I ordered, harshly, smacking her once more. "This isn't about what *I* want. If *you* want this part, then you'd better muster up some tears."

She squirmed again, and I almost abandoned the whole thing. The temptation to pick her up and toss her over the bed, and give her what we both wanted so badly - it was almost overwhelming.

Almost.

"Don't make me use my belt," I said, darkly.

She laughed - low and throaty, and very, very aroused. It was so obvious, in every movement, every breath. She was about to combust, and it was all because of *me*.

"You wouldn't," she whispered.

"You sound so confident," I whispered back, letting my fingers drift up her spine and tug lightly on the ends of her hair. "You're right - but only because it doesn't fit the script. We have to be authentic, don't we, Ms. Hadley?"

"Mmm." She turned her face towards me, slightly, her hair falling down just enough to almost cover one eye. Licking her lips, she sighed. "We do, don't we? But you haven't told me what happens after this scene."

"I'll tell you…when I believe your performance."

I spanked her again. Hard. She yelped and cried out, she whimpered, she begged, but she never said the safe word. At one point, I hesitated, fearing she'd forgotten it. But as she lay there, panting, I could still feel the desire thrumming through her body. Even when the tears came, she never stopped wanting it.

"Howard, please!" she nearly screamed. "Howard, you're hurting me. I'm so…I'm sorry…"

She choked off in a sob that sounded *so goddamn real*, but I knew it wasn't. We were connected now, and I could feel her reactions in every breath and every movement.

Finally, I stopped. We were both panting, and I was going to have bruises from where she gripped my leg.

"You want to know what happens next?" I whispered, my hand resting where it last landed, fingers dipping tantalizingly close to her molten heat. "He realizes she's a liar, because she really loves being spanked. He fingers her until she comes. *So. Damn. Hard.*"

She gasped, whispering yes under her breath. I wasn't sure she even realized it.

"Then," I went on, "he throws her down on the bed and he fucks her senseless. What do you think, Ms. Hadley? You wanna seal the deal? You want one last chance to prove yourself? *Guarantee* you get this part?"

"Yes, yes," she nearly sobbed. "Oh, God. Ben…"

I was going to let that slide. My fingers dipped down where she wanted them, rubbing her through the damp lace. She'd soaked through, leaving a wet mark on my jeans. I grinned viciously. "Looks like you've made a mess on my pants, Miss Hadley. You'll have to be punished for that later, don't you think? It's only fair."

All she could do was moan and quiver, her body drawing bowstring-tight as I rubbed her hard and fast. This was no time for teasing. She was ready to explode, and so was I.

Within moments her eyes went glassy, her body convulsing on mine as her fingers dug into my leg muscle so hard I winced. But I could hardly feel any pain. She gushed, like she had before, utterly soaking through my jeans and crying my name as her limbs quivered and jerked.

I didn't give her a chance to recover before I stood, picking her up with me, and dropping her on the bed like I'd promised. She sprawled, still gasping, while I fumbled with the fucking condoms and tried to undo my jeans one-handed. Weak and boneless, she still managed to push her panties out of the way while I sheathed myself and loomed over her.

I sank in deep with one smooth, quick thrust. She let out an unearthly moan, locking her ankles around my waist and tilting her pelvis to meet my every movement. I'd thought this wouldn't last long, but now that I was finally where I wanted to be, it was like my body wanted to prolong the experience as much as possible.

She was so tight, her body stretching to accommodate me. I sank in deep again, all the way, and paused with my forehead resting against hers.

Fuck me, I was in trouble.

Everything about her was perfect. Every cell of my body, except for that one intelligent part of my brain holding court in the very top of my skull, was utterly and completely in love with this woman. I was having feelings for her - very real feelings, not just the usual *I'm about to come so everything seems like a good idea* feelings.

More like, *this could be real if only we hadn't met when I was looking for a fake wife* feelings.

God damn it.

God damn it.

God…

I came inside her, and it felt like the beginning of the end.

Either that, or the end of the beginning.

I could never be quite sure.

Chapter Twenty-Six

Jenna

I woke up curled in Ben's arms.

After our utterly explosive roleplay, he'd tenderly washed me in the shower, then dried me with a fluffy towel and bundled me up in bed. It was our last day in wine country, but as long as I stayed burrowed under the covers with him, I could pretend this might last forever.

We took a short hike after breakfast, breathing in the last few lungfuls of fresh air at a picnic lunch on the water. Ben threw bread crusts to the ducks, and I scolded him, and I wished we could stay here for just one more day.

"I actually think I'm going to miss this place," I said, as we loaded our bags into the rental car.

"*Actually*?" Ben echoed. "Why, did you expect something less than perfect from Mr. Perfect Billionaire?"

"I guess I didn't know what to expect." I climbed into the passenger seat, slumping down with my forehead against the window. "But it sure grows on you."

The luxury plane felt a little less welcoming, now that it was taking me back to real life. I sighed, watching Ben pour himself a gin and tonic from the bar before he sat down next to me.

After takeoff, he suddenly shifted, reaching into his jacket pocket. "I almost forgot," he said. "The whole reason we came here."

Curious, I sat up. I'd actually forgotten when he told me at the restaurant before we left, until I noticed he was holding a little black box.

"Oh," I said, then, quieter: "*Oh*."

"It's not much," he said. "I didn't think you'd want something ostentatious."

I opened the box slowly, feeling my throat tighten. The ring was delicate and beautiful, with a few nested diamonds and a little gold design surrounding them. It was exactly the kind of ring I would have picked for myself.

For the love of God, do not get emotional over this.

But it wasn't the ring, not really. The ring was the last straw in my emotional roller coaster of a weekend, and I cared deeply about this ridiculous man and I didn't want him to die young and I really, really didn't want to keep on pretending to love him when it was so close to the truth.

"Sorry if it's…" He made a gesture whose meaning I couldn't guess at. "I don't know. I thought you'd like it."

"I like it," I said, softly. "Should I, um, should I put it on?"

"Before we land, yeah, ideally." Seeing me still

frozen, he plucked the box from my hand. "Here. Let me."

Yes, this felt right. I wanted to keep on pretending for a little while.

As the cool metal slid on my skin, I was struck with an irresistible urge to kiss him.

So I did.

He seemed surprised for a moment, then he warmed to it. I broke away, and he only raised his eyebrows slightly when I climbed out of my seat and stood in front of him. Leaning forward, using his tie for a bit of leverage, I let my body slide down his, loving the site of him slowly understanding what I wanted.

Eyes fixed on my face, he was slouched slightly, one hand still clutching his drink even as it dangled over the side of the armrest. His breathing started to quicken.

"Master may I?" I asked, teasingly, with my hands on his thighs.

He nodded, exhaling sharply.

I didn't think I'd ever tire of the taste of his skin, or the way he sighed and shifted his hips when I did it just right. This time he was more aggressive with me, grabbing my hair and holding my head still so he could control the pace, sliding in deeper than I thought I could take, testing my limits. He was watching me, waiting for the slightest sign that I was overwhelmed, that I needed him to back off. But I timed my breathing and let him take me. It was intoxicating. My whole body relaxed, glowing with acceptance.

When he came, I heard the glass clink to the floor, rolling away, leaving a puddle of gin and tonic in its wake.

"Good girl." He was still breathing hard when he released me. My whole body buzzed with arousal, and a tiny bit of confusion, because I was pretty sure I wasn't supposed to like what he just did. He smiled darkly, grabbing my hand and pulling me to my feet, and onto his lap. I squealed, then sighed, feeling his hand slide up my thigh, and under my skirt. "So you see, I'm not always a perfect gentleman. But you like me better that way, don't you?"

His fingers found their answer, and a short time later, they found me panting and moaning his name.

"You're so beautiful when you come undone," he whispered. "And now, everybody knows you're mine."

I'm yours.

I'm yours.

No one else's. Make me yours for real.

I swallowed all of my thoughts, everything I wanted to say, and just tried to catch my breath.

Jenna

"Have a good trip." I threw my arms around Ben's neck, hugging him tightly, even though no one was watching.

"I won't." He smiled wryly. "Can't stand these speaking engagements. But at least I've got you to come home to."

Even though we hadn't moved in together, I agreed to stay at his place and watch over the cats and bring in the mail. Harry and I were fast friends, and the more timid ones had started to venture out into rooms that I was in, but only if I sat still for a very long time.

I saw him out to the car, kissing him goodbye, and felt a very real tug of longing in my heart.

Back inside, I typed:

I miss you

And let it sit in my outgoing messages for an hour before I deleted it.

He'd given me the assignment of watching the movie *Secretary*, so I made myself a frozen dinner and settled in. Harry watched me curiously, not understanding why I was here alone.

"Sorry, buddy, I'm all you get for a couple days," I said.

The movie captivated my attention, and afterwards I spent a lot of time thinking about it. There was one scene in particular, when the main character was walking home, having just been given the order to do so. She talked about how it made her feel loved, just following his orders. It made her feel more connected to him.

I knew exactly how that felt.

Ben called me after he'd settled in at his hotel. Even though we often went a long time without speaking, I found myself counting down the hours until my phone rang.

I was feeling frisky. The movie had something to do with it, a few very steamy spanking scenes leaving me longing for Ben's hand. He must have been able to hear it in my voice, because his own tone warmed, growing a little more teasing and playful as we talked.

"What's wrong, sunshine?" he asked, with a smile. "I can tell you want to say something, but you're biting your tongue."

I had to gather my courage for a moment.

"One time, you promised me that if you had my number..." I trailed off, hoping he'd remember.

"Oh." He chuckled, quietly. "I was kidding. Mostly."

I licked my lips, which suddenly felt very dry. Damn, he wasn't going to make this easy. "What, you want me to ask?"

"Yeah, I want you to ask." I could *hear* the smug. "You ask, or you get *nothing*, sunshine."

Taking a deep breath, I swallowed the rest of my dignity. "Send me a picture. Please."

"You want a dick pic, sweetheart?" He was grinning. But I could hear the sound of his zipper. "Will you be good, the next time I see you?"

"Yeah." My heart was beating so fast, and suddenly I couldn't catch my breath. Why did I care so much? I'd seen it, I didn't need a picture. But I wanted him to do something for me. Something naughty, something transgressive, something dirty and sexy and *wrong*.

I expected him to ask for something in return, but he didn't. I just heard him pull the phone away from his ear, and I heard the shutter noise when he did what I'd asked for.

My phone buzzed in my hand, against my head, and I looked at the screen. My breath caught in my throat. God damn it. I *wanted*.

"How come you're so far away?" I asked him, softly. "I want..."

"Tell me what you want." His voice rumbled down the line, low and sexy, making me tingle all over. I wanted to tell him, wanted to put it into words, but my tongue felt tied. "Do it, sunshine. Do it for me."

"I..." I choked, the words swirling in my head but refusing to come out. Shit, why wasn't I better at this? Why did I freeze up when it came to Ben?

Because it matters.

Because you care what he thinks of you.

I hated the realization, and I tried to push it away. But there was no denying. The stakes were too high. I hated it when he thought of me as naive, virginal, and my inability to have proper phone sex was just another mark against my record. Ironically, that made it impossible for me to go with the flow.

"Come on," he coaxed. "I know you can do it. Tell me what you want. Do a good job, make it sweet, and I'll give you the reward you deserve when I get back home."

Oh, it was tempting. What did he mean, exactly? I pictured him nestling his head between my legs and almost whimpered out loud, but bit it back. Why? What was I afraid of? Hadn't he cured me of this, back in wine country?

"Come on." he sounded frustrated. "What's wrong? Just talk to me. I want to hear your voice."

And that moment, I did the worst possible thing I could have.

I hung up on him.

Guilt roiled in my stomach. It had been almost sixteen hours - not that I was counting - and he hadn't called back. I knew he was angry, and he had every right to be, but I wished he'd stop torturing me.

For all he knew, maybe my phone just cut off.

Maybe it died, and I was frantically trying to get it fixed.

Yeah, right. Too damn convenient. He knew exactly what he was doing.

And I had a hell of a punishment coming.

Chapter Twenty-Seven

Jenna

Ben was due home tonight, and I was a bundle of nervous energy.

Just then, my phone buzzed with a text message.

Black skirt, white blouse, nothing else.

An interminable minute passed. Then, another message.

Be home soon. Assume the position.

My face burned. I knew exactly what that meant. After watching *Secretary* at his behest, it was clear - I was to bend myself over his desk, hands flat on the wood, waiting for my punishment. And I was supposed to do it now, even though he'd offered no definition for "soon."

He wouldn't know the difference. I could wait until I heard his key in the lock, sit and read comfortably, or have a glass of wine to help my nerves stop jangling. But that wasn't what he told me to do.

Heart pounding, throat dry, I undressed, and found the clothes he requested. The tight skirt on my bare skin felt positively sinful, and by the time I'd finished, pulling my hair up into a bun because I felt like it completed the look - I was *ready*. My body responded automatically to the ritual of following his orders, knowing he'd be touching me soon.

But maybe not in a way I liked, considering how our last conversation ended.

Slowly, almost reverently, I walked towards the library. My thighs rubbed torturously against my growing arousal. Without being told, I knew I wasn't supposed to touch myself. I wasn't supposed to do anything except assume the position, and wait for him.

I wondered if I was supposed to be facing out, or facing in. He hadn't told me to move his chair, so I walked around to the front of the desk and stood. Stared. Waited. For what?

There was no reason I had to do this now. There was no reason I had to do this ever. I could go back to my room and change into my pajamas and text him and tell him *I'm sorry, I can't do this anymore, it's not you, it's me.*

I had all of these choices, but even as I stood there, seemingly suspended in indecision, I knew I wouldn't take any of them.

I would do exactly what he told me to do.

And I did.

The sound of my own breathing was harsh in my ears. The rest of the house was eerily quiet, and I thought about getting up, going to turn on a TV somewhere just to have some background noise. Just so I wouldn't hear my own heartbeats. He'd have no way of knowing that I hadn't simply left it on by accident.

No.

The command was in my head, so clearly, as if he'd murmured it right in my ear. I felt as if his hand were actually pressing me down into the wood, his hips against my ass, immobilizing me.

Already, I could feel some of the guilt unknotting itself in my chest. Knowing he'd be pleased with me, following his orders, lessened some of the agony I'd been putting myself through since I hung up on him.

Since I ran away, again, like I'd promised I wouldn't. I'd asked him to punish me if I did.

This was all for me.

The clock was behind me, and I was thankful there would be no temptation to look. I didn't want to know. I just wanted to wait.

Every nerve was singing, my whole body on high alert. I'd never felt more peaceful and more vibrant at the same time, panting with anticipation based on just a few words on a screen.

I thought back to the first time I'd seen the words *domestic discipline*, and I almost wanted to laugh.

Almost.

When I heard his key click in the lock, my heart jumped into my throat. Instantly, I was trembling all over, a whimper lodged in my chest, trying to leap out.

All of this without him touching me, without me seeing him or even hearing his voice. His absence was even more powerful than his presence.

I heard him walking in, then I heard him speak - to someone? Was he on his phone?

When I heard another voice, my heart almost stopped.

"Right over here, or you want me to take them upstairs for you?"

There was *someone else there*. A stranger. What in the *fuck*? He let someone else in to carry his luggage, knowing that I was in here waiting with my ass practically hanging out of my skirt?

"No, this is fine," Ben replied. "Thank you."

"My pleasure," said the other man. "You have a good night, sir."

"Thanks, you too."

The door clicked shut, and I breathed again.

For a moment, all I heard was soft noises, indistinct rustling, and it was impossible to tell what he was doing. Then there were footsteps. Closer, closer... then right past. I heard a few more unidentifiable sounds, then a few seconds of running water. More footsteps.

He was in the doorway.

Slowly, ever so slowly, he approached.

I felt his hand on my back first, sliding, up and over my shoulder, and down past my collarbone. It took me a moment to realize what he was checking for, and I lifted my torso slightly to accommodate his hand engulfing my breast. He squeezed lightly, exhaling, tweaking my stiff nipple just a bit between his fingers. I stifled a moan.

His other hand rested on my ass. Sliding down, to the hem of my skirt, fingers curling under and questing and feeling for the panties I hadn't worn, as per his instructions.

I waited for something, for a *good girl*, or maybe I didn't get one since this was all a prelude to a punishment. Still, didn't I deserve something for doing all this? For waiting so patiently?

His hands still seared into my skin, but they

weren't moving. I held my breath.

After an eternity, he spoke.

"I didn't tell you to put your hair up."

Damn it. Pulse pounding, I struggled to find my voice. I'd felt a little cheeky, doing it - knowing he might disapprove, but he hadn't give me any specific instructions for my hair. So how could he get angry at me?

"You didn't say I couldn't."

His voice was hard, quiet. "I very clearly said a black skirt..." His hand tightened around one cheek of my ass. "...a white blouse..." His fingers pinched my nipple again, and I gasped. "And *nothing else*. But you're wearing a hair band."

"A hair band isn't clothes," I whimpered, trying to figure out why the hell I wouldn't just let him win. It was pointless, arguing with him - especially when all I wanted was to finish the punishment and get on with the rest of our reunion.

God, I'd missed him. I just wanted to feel him inside me, feel his mouth on mine, his teeth scraping my neck, my collarbone, as he lost control.

"I didn't say don't wear any other *clothes*, I said don't wear *anything else*. Period. That includes hair bands. Jewelry. A fucking watch." He growled, pressing his body against mine. He was so hard it must hurt. How could he hold himself back for so long? I was about to lose my mind. If I were in control, I would have jumped on him within five seconds. *"This isn't that difficult."*

"I'm sorry," I whispered, finally. "I didn't think. I just wanted to keep my hair out of my face."

I knew, without being able to see him, that he was

shaking his head. "Too late. You could have apologized when I asked you, but you had to give me sass." With a sudden movement, he released his grip on my flesh, leaving me throbbing, somehow cold and overheated at the same time. His fingers plucked at the hairband, pulling it free and tossing it aside. Then he grabbed a handful of my hair and tugged, gently. Then harder. He released it, stroked the side of my face, and slowly made his way towards my lips. I opened my mouth obediently, taking his fingers inside and sucking eagerly.

He exhaled in a quiet groan. A thrill of triumph went through me. *Not so cool and composed now*.

"I'll let you pick your punishment," he said, roughly. "More spankings, or no orgasms for a week?"

"How many more spankings?" I asked, breathlessly.

There was a smirk in his voice. "Does that really matter?"

Of course it didn't. I would endure any amount of punishment, if it meant a relief from this incessant pressure between my legs.

"Spankings," I whispered, in defeat.

He didn't waste any time.

I cried out, the impact jolting my whole body, stinging my skin and lighting every nerve on fire. It went on for as long as I could bear, and then a moment longer. I realized I was stronger than I thought.

One foot nudged against my ankle, gently kicking my legs apart. I knew what came next. Whining with anticipation, I arched my lower back as far as it could go, presenting myself to him like an animal in heat. I heard his low, dark chuckle as he unzipped.

I would never tire of this feeling. The skin on my ass throbbing with heat and pain, everything between my legs slick and swollen and screaming for attention.

"Very pretty," he rumbled, grabbing my waist and pulling me tight against him, so his hardness was trapped between my cheeks. "But not like this, tonight. I need to see your face."

He turned me around, hoisting me up onto the desk so that my ass just barely hung over the edge. It was the perfect height. I wondered if he'd chosen it for this. He kept my legs hoisted up with his arms, knowing he'd be able to take me deeper that way.

The soft noise he made, sinking in deep, was almost as good as the feeling of being completely filled. Briefly, he leaned over me, one hand stroking the side of my face, trailing down my body in a slow worshipful path. "I missed you," he murmured. "It was hell, these last few days. Not being able to hear your voice." He slid in and out, slowly, reveling in the sensation.

"You could have called," I said, softly. I was still feeling raw, rejected, because even though I understood his annoyance I didn't think there was any reason to give me the cold shoulder.

"So could you." He punctuated with a deep thrust, pinching my nipple between his fingers. I keened, rocking my hips against his body.

Of course, he was right. I'd been too much of a coward.

"I'm sorry," I whispered.

"I'm sorry too." He let my legs slide down, gently, so he could lean over and kiss me. "No more silent treatment."

Nodding in agreement, I gave myself over to the

feeling.

As we climbed higher together, spiraling, losing ourselves in each other, I let myself believe.

As my awareness shattered, I gave myself over to forgetting.

Chapter Twenty-Eight

Jenna

I sat on the edge of the bed, heart pounding, waiting for him.

Although Ben had assured me last night that my punishment was over, he still wanted to "rectify the problem." I didn't know what that meant, but my nerves were frayed to the breaking point.

Finally, he walked into the room. He was wearing a dark gray suit with the vest, but without the jacket, sleeves rolled up, looking positively mouth-watering. He knew exactly how to make himself look irresistible.

He also had an armful of something, which he set down on the bed. I realized it was a set of four leather cuffs, meant to fasten me spread-eagled to the bed. My body reacted instantly, warming from the inside out.

"What's this?" I asked, softly.

He smiled. "It's time for your master class in acting. Do you trust me?"

I sucked in a breath. "Yes."

"Will you tell me if you need to stop?"

I nodded.

"Tell me what you think I'm going to do," he said, his voice low and tempting, as he leaned ever-so-subtly towards me.

I swallowed hard. "Tie me to the bedposts, with my arms and legs spread." I looked to him for approval. "And then, I have no idea."

He chuckled. "Very good. Are you ready?"

Butterflies filled my stomach. "Yes."

Quickly, efficiently, he fastened each of the cuffs to the four corners of the bed, and then to me. They were surprisingly plush and comfortable against my skin, but all I had to do was move an inch to remind myself that I was tied down.

"Your first lesson," he said, circling the bed, "is proper phone sex."

"I don't..." Blushing furiously, I tried to squirm out of the restraints. It was useless, of course, and I didn't really want out. I just wanted out of the situation, out of my own skin - my own stupid inability to do something as simple as talk dirty. "I really don't know how."

He quirked an eyebrow at me, his hand still resting casually on his lap, drawing my gaze and driving me slowly insane. "You're an *actor*, Jenna."

Helpless, I just stared, my eyes pleading with him to end this game. It was ridiculous. It was horrible. And I was going to make an even bigger fool out of myself than I had on the phone.

"I'm not, though," I said, softly. Surrendering to the realization, I went limp on the bed, my head flopping back on the pillow. "I never will be. And you're really not helping."

"I'm not trying to help you," he growled, standing

up suddenly and striding over to me. He knelt down by the bed, lowering his head to just inches from mine. With two steady fingers, he guided my face towards his. "You're doing this for me, and only for me. Do you understand? I want you to do this. I need you to talk to me like you really want me. I have to hear the filth spilling from your lips - everything I know you're thinking, but you can't bring yourself to say."

My breath caught in my throat. His words went straight to my core, and I clenched and heated at the sound of his voice. "Yes," I whispered. "I understand."

"Good." He rose, pacing around the perimeter of the bed with his hands behind his back. "Now. Because I'm feeling particularly generous tonight, I'm going to guide you."

Guide me? What did that mean? And how pathetic was it that an aspiring actor actually needed help?

I always did suck at improv.

Taking a deep breath, I watched him pace, marveling at the way his body moved under his suit, the whispering of the expensive fabric as he walked the same path over and over again. Finally, he glanced at me.

"Close your eyes," he said, quietly.

I did.

Instantly, I was hyper-aware of his presence, as if the inability to see him just made him loom larger. His presence filled the room, palpable, stealing my breath. I tried to calm my rabbiting heart, but it was impossible. No audition had ever made more nervous than I was now, so painfully self-conscious, trying to please a man who didn't even care about me.

That's not true. You know it's not true.

"Keep your eyes closed." The sound of his voice flowed over me, smooth like silk, and I sighed. Trying to relax. "If you think you'll be tempted to open them, I can blindfold you. Do you think that will be necessary, sunshine?"

I shook my head.

"Answer me out loud." His tone was firm, leaving no room for protests or excuses. "Say 'yes, Sir' if you understand." I could hear the capital S, just the way he said the word.

My heart threatened to burst out of my chest. "Yes, Sir." I took a deep breath, trying to remember the original question. "No, Sir. That won't be necessary."

"Good." There was a smile in his voice. "Tell me how you feel, sunshine."

"I..." I'd started speaking, because I felt compelled to, but I had no idea what I was going to say. "I'm nervous. I'm scared of what's going to happen."

"Why?" He sounded very close now, like he'd knelt down by my head again. "Are you scared of me, sunshine?"

Every time he called me that, my heart skipped a beat. "I'm not scared of you," I whispered. "I'm scared of disappointing you."

His fingers brushed against my cheek. I was right - he was close by. My body jumped slightly, not anticipating the touch, but I soon warmed to it. "You don't need to be afraid of that. You can't disappoint me, as long as you *try*."

I didn't quite believe him, but I just nodded. "Yes, Sir."

"Sunshine."

I shivered, unable to suppress it.

"What was that? Do you like it when I call you…" He hesitated, and again, I could hear him smiling. "…sunshine?"

Swallowing hard, I answered him. "Yes, Sir."

His fingers travelled down my chest, running along the neckline of my dress, leaving a tingling trail of sensation along my sensitive skin. "I like it when you call me Sir," he confessed. "I think I have a similar reaction. Are you feeling a little less nervous, sunshine? Are you feeling a little *warmer*?"

I nodded, forgetting his order.

"*Tell* me," he commanded, raising his voice just slightly.

"I'm sorry, Sir," I said, breathlessly. "Yes, Sir."

"Good," he said. "Me, too. But I'm going to need something more than that, I'm afraid. You'll have to paint me a picture with your words. Can you do that for me, sunshine?"

"I can try," I said, honestly. "But I don't…I don't know where to start."

Suddenly, he stood up and withdrew from me. I felt the loss of his body heat, his presence, the scent of his cologne mingling with his skin. It was unlike any other smell in the world, and it made me remember the heavy sting of his palm on my ass.

Say it. Tell him.

Taking a deep breath, I spoke.

"I like the way you smell."

That didn't sound quite as good as I'd hoped.

I heard a warm chuckle from across the room. "That's a good start," he said. "Go on."

"Your cologne, I mean," I rushed out, wishing I could see him. My eyes were squeezed so tightly shut, and all I wanted was to watch his face as I tried to arouse him with my words. "It reminds me of the first night we were together. When you…spanked me."

My face flamed hot at the word spanking. It was still so embarrassing to say out loud, no matter how much my body craved it.

"What else did I do?" he asked, his voice a low, masculine rumble that heated my skin. The heat was growing, a little tingle between my legs.

"You…your mouth." I tried again. "Your tongue. You licked me. Until I came…"

He made a soft, encouraging sound.

"…all over your face. You made me squirt. I was embarrassed, but now it's all I can think about sometimes. You made me lose control completely, and I loved it. I loved how much *you* loved it."

"Tell me how you feel now, sunshine."

He sounded a little breathless. I wondered if I'd succeeded in my task.

"I'm so…" I shifted slightly, feeling the tug of the cuffs, and loving them. Loving this. "I'm so…"

Turned on? No, that didn't sound very sexy.

"I'm so wet," I whispered, finally, my blush coming back with a vengeance. "I feel like my heart's beating between my legs. I wish I could touch myself." I sucked in a breath. "I wish *you'd* touch me."

"Tell me, sunshine," he murmured, suddenly sounding very close again. "Do you think you could come like this? If I talked to you, told you all the delicious and depraved ways I want to use your body, how thoroughly I'm going to *own* you - do you think it would push you over the edge? Just the sound of my voice, and nothing but your imagination?"

My whole body shuddered. I was on the verge already, listening to him. I nodded, my power of speech stolen. Luckily, he didn't seem to care this time.

"Open your eyes," he whispered.

I did, slowly.

He was looming over me, his shirt hanging loose on his shoulders. He shucked it off while I watched, and my eyes drifted to his belt. I saw the telltale bulge there, and knew I'd won.

I must have looked smug, because he shook his head at me as he crawled onto the bed, kneeling between my legs. "You did well, sunshine, but don't act so triumphant. You're completely irresistible, even without your sexy voice tempting me. I got a hard-on just from looking at you, all tied up like a present just for me." He grinned, glancing down at the juncture of my thighs. "Goodness, you weren't lying about this, were you?" Almost dispassionately, he slid his fingers under the fabric of my panties and quested inside. "You really *are* aching for me, aren't you?" He said this very softly, looking up at me with clear eyes devoid of any games or meaningless flirtation.

"Yes." I whimpered, tilting my hips, trying to draw his fingers deeper. "Please, Sir."

"Please, what?" He licked his lips, his Adam's apple bobbing noticeably as he swallowed. "*Tell* me, sunshine. You have to tell me, or you don't get what you want."

My head was swimming. I wanted *everything*. I wanted all of him at once, his fingers, his tongue, and the promise that throbbed between his legs. I couldn't tear my eyes away, although he hardly seemed to notice it anymore. He was completely focused on me, his eyes dark and predatory.

I was struck with a sudden desire, one that surprised me. I had him here, at my disposal, but I didn't want him to touch me. I wanted him to touch himself.

"Please," I said. "Untie my right hand."

He looked at me curiously, but he went and did as I asked, leaning over me to do it. I breathed in that scent of his, closing my eyes momentarily as I lost myself in everything Benjamin Chase.

"The next time you go out of town, I want to be able to picture it," I told him, feeling my heart start to race again. I just hoped he wouldn't be offended, or upset, or...something. "I want us to do it now, like we'd be doing if we were on the phone. It'll make it easier for me, next time I have to do it for real."

He looked at me for a moment, and then he smiled.

"Very well, sunshine," he said, softly. "That's fair. You may touch yourself until you come."

Instantly, I buried my hand between my legs, fingers gliding over heated flesh. I watched him as he unzipped, rushing to catch up with me. It was a beautiful sight, so much more captivating even than I'd imagined - watching the way his hand moved, the little hitches of his breathing, everything I missed when I was the one doing it. With my hand on autopilot, I was free to watch, to just drink him in. There was no hint of arrogance when he was like this, losing himself in his own pleasure. His eyes would close from time to time, blinking heavily, but his gaze kept drifting back to my rapidly moving hand.

With a sudden motion, frowning a little, he reached out and grasped my panties firmly. Shocked, I froze for a moment, as he yanked them down and away.

"There," he muttered. "Got a better view, now. Continue."

I giggled, then sighed as I followed his orders.

Now that he could see my fingers disappearing between my folds, he was losing control - and fast. I moaned, my hips jerking of their own accord, and the thick scent of my arousal filled the air. I saw his nostrils flare, and I knew he'd noticed it too. We were moving in concert, daring each other higher and higher, every little sound and movement pushing us closer to the precipice.

It was so terribly intimate, and we weren't even touching.

I teetered on the edge, but something held me back. I didn't understand. Biting my lip, sighing, I tried to relax and let it happen. Ben was almost lost to the world, but he slowed, stopped, though the expression on his face told me how much of an effort it took.

"What's wrong?" he rasped, his eyes searching mine.

"I don't know," I admitted, a frustrated sob welling up in my chest. I wanted to, I did, more than anything, I needed release. Every part of me ached for it.

"Stop," he commanded.

My wrist ached. I pulled my hand away, a heavy sense of defeat in the pit of my stomach. He loomed over me, his hand replacing mine, a feather-light touch that still made me gasp. He rubbed slowly, gently, in little circles that had me twisting and moaning within moments. His shaft bobbed in the space between our bodies, stiff and neglected, but his only focus was on me.

"Let go, sunshine," he murmured. "When you're ready, just let go. You've been holding this for so long. You don't have to anymore. Pour it out. Let yourself shatter. I'll be here." His lips brushed my forehead. "I'll be here."

He wasn't just talking about now, tonight. He was talking about all of it. Everything. The fear, the insecurity, the pain and the anger and all the clutter that got in the way of just *being*. This wasn't just a release for my body, it was a release for my soul.

That was his gift to me.

"Please," I gasped, opening my eyes, only then realizing that I'd closed them. His face was inches from mine. His fingers still moved, relentlessly, and my body began to shudder in ways I couldn't control. "Stop. Please."

He did.

My whole body throbbed. I was ready, but I wanted, *needed*. I couldn't find the words to ask, reduced to one raw exposed nerve, and I had nothing but the ability to reach up with my one free arm, trembling, my fingers digging into the taut muscles of his ass. With all the strength I had left, I pulled him to me.

He sank inside me with a groan, his eyes clouded with lust when he managed to drag the lids open again and look at me. "I won't last," he warned me, quivering with the effort of holding back. "Are you ready?"

I managed to nod.

"What do you need?" His words sounded thick and heavy on his tongue, like he was drunk on me. "Is this enough?"

I nodded again, my inner muscles quivering and clenching. *So close.*

With a growl, he began a brutal pace. One hand captured my hip in a bruising grasp, and with the other, he held himself up, giving the leverage he needed to pound and pound and pound so hard the bed shook.

On the first thrust, I was already lost.

My climax swept me up like a riptide, and instead of one swift peak, it carried me along in ecstasy, until he was spent, and further, achingly sweet, achingly perfect. When he stilled, shuddering with release, I moaned softly. The embers were still burning, achingly intense pleasure still radiating.

"More?" he murmured, his fingers finding the place just above where we were joined. "Are you not finished, sunshine?"

Breathless, boneless, I nodded. Hoping he understood.

He caressed me, catapulting my body back to those heights. I didn't recognize the feral sounds I was making, and I could feel my back starting to ache, all of my muscles quivering, my eyes rolling back in my head as I came. And came. And came.

When I finally went limp, the last few aftershocks jerking my exhausted limbs like a puppet on a string, he sighed.

"So beautiful," he whispered. He smiled, his lips against the side of my head, almost kissing but not quite. He was still so hard inside me, just as hard as when we'd started.

"Are *you* not finished?" I managed to whisper, teasingly, having caught just enough of my breath to form words. It was a stupid question. I could feel his seed inside me, but God, I wanted more. I never wanted this to stop.

A quiet chuckle, as he moved his hips a little. I gasped, another little aftershock shivering its way across my skin. "I almost think I could fuck you again. Would you like that, sunshine?"

Was he serious? I stared at him.

"*Would you?*" he repeated, with a tiny thrust.

"Yes," I moaned. "Of course, I just didn't think…"

"Neither did I." He pulled back and slammed his way home, with a groan that sounded ripped from deep inside his chest. "*Fuck.* But here we are." He nibbled at my ear, and I cried out, my body pulsing with bliss.

It was pure sin, feeling him slide so easily with our mingled wetness inside of me, knowing there was something about me that defeated his very biology and made him need beyond need. I was his own personal Viagra, and I cried out his name until I really and truly lost my voice. He didn't stop until my pleasure started to mingle with too much pain, my body resisting against the onslaught of sensations I'd endured tonight. He saw the change, the way I bit my lip a little too hard, my forehead knotting in a silent wince. Pulling out, he knelt over me, stroking himself and asking me softly where I wanted him to mark me.

The answer was easy.

Everywhere.

It took a long time, but he did. Chin, neck, chest,

stomach, all were anointed, before he collapsed beside me, chest heaving. He untied the remaining knots with shaking hands. A string of creative curses spilled from his lips as he wound his arms around me, not caring that he spread the mess across our skin.

"Darling," he whispered after a long silence. "If I have a heart attack in the next few minutes, will you promise to put my dick away before the EMTs get here?"

I giggled.

If this was aftercare, I didn't need it. I was pillowed in bliss, ignoring the stickiness that dried on my skin and feeling nothing but a warm glow. All the same, I *liked* it. We snuggled together, and for the first time, I allowed myself to forget.

I allowed myself to pretend.

Darling. It was just a figure of speech. But it sounded so good, coming from his mouth. Like he actually meant it.

Like I really was his darling.

Chapter Twenty-Nine

Ben

I fell in love with Jenna Hadley, and there was no point in pretending it wasn't true.

I'd accepted that weeks ago. But I resisted telling her, even as I laid my plans to completely blow her mind. She had no idea that my little business trip was actually a research expedition, and I'd arranged everything. Our honeymoon was going to be perfect. There was just one minor setback.

"That's sadistic," was Daniel's very helpful input.

"Thanks," I said bitterly, stirring my drink. "But it's not that easy. What am I supposed to do, just tell her?"

He nodded. "Much better than letting her wonder and wait. Why would you put someone through that kind of agony? She's crazy about you, Ben. Are you blind?"

"You can't possibly know that," I said.

"You're right," he said. "Maybe she's really the greatest actress of all time. But Maddy tells me what she says about you."

But she's lying to Maddy.
Unless, of course, she's not.

"It's not quite that easy," I said.

"It is that easy," Daniel insisted. "Just open your mouth and form words with your brain. Maybe your tongue gets involved at some point. I don't know. I don't control your life."

"But you *wish* you did."

"You've got to admit, things would go a lot more smoothly for you," he said, without a hint of irony. "That was a double entendre, by the way."

"Oh, the tongue thing? Yeah, you're very subtle. I knew I should've called Wozniak instead." I crumpled my napkin up, bitterly.

"Wozniak wishes he had my game," said Daniel, seriously. I had to laugh, Sometimes, he was a hilarious drunk.

"I just don't want to dump it on her all at once," I said.

"What the hell do you think your plan is, then? It's a thousand times worse. She's definitely going to cry, and she'll probably hit you."

"Happy tears," I said. "Happy punches."

"You *idiot*." Daniel looked at me with a sour expression on his face. "You really don't get it, do you?"

"Feel free to enlighten me." I sat there, head in my hands, staring at the insides of my eyelids.

"No." He was using the kind of tone that a less authoritative person would bow down to, and that irritated me more than anything. "You'll just argue with me, and we'll both waste our time, and in the end you'll be even more convinced that you're right."

"I won't say a word," I promised him, looking up to meet his irritated gaze. "Just tell me what you're thinking, because I have no idea what I'm doing."

A smile was slowly forming on his face. "You have no idea how long I've waited to her you say that."

"Oh, my God." I let my head thump down into my hands again. "*Shut up.*"

"I thought you wanted to hear what I was thinking."

"I'm going to kill you," I said. "Slowly. I know where you sleep."

There was a moment of silence.

"You're afraid," he said, simply. "You see her taking the same path Daria did, and you think she'll eventually go somewhere you won't be able to follow. Your conscious mind is resisting the comparison to your ex-wife because they're really nothing alike, the circumstances couldn't be more different, but the fight-or-flight part of your brain can feel it. That's why you panic. You're afraid to have her, because you're afraid to *lose* her."

"I didn't lose Daria," I protested. "She walked away."

"Then what are you afraid of?" He cocked an infuriating eyebrow at me. "Don't tell me you're not. I know it when I see it."

"That's because *you're* always scared, Chicken Little," I griped. "So you smell it everywhere. You're just projecting."

He was making a lot of sense, but I really didn't want to admit it. My only excuse for my fear was the fear of losing my company - but I couldn't tell him about the settlement, he'd never let me hear the end of it.

"Right. I'm the one who's scared," he grumbled. "Just because I'm paranoid doesn't mean the sky's *not* falling, you know."

Jenna *must* already know. She had to. How could she have possibly missed it? The paper-thin justification of our fake marriage hardly explained anything we'd said or done in the past few months.

And if she didn't, well, the honeymoon would be an even bigger surprise than I'd planned. That wasn't a bad thing.

Was it?

Chapter Thirty

Jenna

As the wedding insanity began to ramp up, with more and more last-minute emails from the planner making sure I was okay with this type or flower or this minor color variation, I made more of an effort than usual to stick to a routine. I had to retain some semblance of sanity, and caffeine was always the first step.

So that's how I found myself in my favorite coffee shop, ordering my usual, on a morning like any other. With the minor exception that it was the day before my wedding.

It still didn't feel real. Not even close. I knew the venue - a beautifully remodeled vintage movie theater, complete with the lush red and gold accents - and I'd signed off on the invitations, the cake flavors, the damn place card designs. But all the time, it felt like I was sleepwalking through someone else's life.

And things were about to get a lot more surreal.

"Excuse me," said a voice from behind me, as I sat down at my table. I looked up. There was a woman standing there, her gaze fixed on me, like she could read my life story off of my face. "Are you Jenna Hadley?"

I cleared my throat. "Can I ask who you are?"

"I'm Daria."

For a moment, it seemed like the whole world fell silent.

I don't know what I expected. She was tall and beautiful, curvy, with the smoky eyes of a French movie star. I could see how Ben would fall for someone like that.

"Daria," I echoed. "Do I know you?"

She smirked. It was almost a mirror of Ben's, but not quite. "Don't play dumb. It's a bad look on you." She sat down, gracefully. "I have to admit, especially considering the timing, I was suspicious. But I'm not anymore."

I cleared my throat. "Suspicious?"

She smiled at me, sympathetically. "Did he really not tell you? Well, *that* I can believe. He certainly doesn't like to talk about things that don't paint him in a flattering light." With a single gesture, she beckoned the server, and he came. "One cup of chamomile tea, please."

I watched her, trying to understand. Was this all a test? Did she really believe a word I was saying? Did I seem nervous?

Hopefully, no more nervous than was appropriate for the situation.

"I'm Ben's ex-wife," she said, finally, frowning a little. "Jesus - really? How much hasn't he told you?"

I swallowed hard. "I know everything I need to know."

"Oh, honey." She reached across the table and patted my hand; I withdrew like a snake had bitten me. "You think that now. Someday you're going to regret trusting him. Believe me. Why do you think he didn't mention me?"

"Maybe you don't matter to him anymore." I felt bad, saying it. But it was the only way to convince her that I really didn't know who she was. "He's moved on. It must have been a long time."

"Oh." She smiled down at the table. "Did he tell you that you were the first woman he ever loved? He told me the same thing. Of course, when I met him, he was nineteen. So it was probably true."

Nineteen. He was practically a kid. They both were.

"Did he tell you about the Huntington's?" she asked me, her eyes suddenly piercing.

My heart plummeted.

"He told me about his mother," I lied. "That's all." I prayed that wouldn't be a fatal miscalculation.

Daria's mouth thinned. "But he didn't tell you about himself?"

"No," I admitted. Something about her expression told me that she'd been in the dark, too - at least for a while. "But he said he'll tell me when he's ready. I can understand if he doesn't want to take the test…"

"He got the test," she said, simply. "When he was ten years old. His father gave him the choice, which is borderline criminal, if you ask me."

My heart thudded audibly in my chest. "Was it…?"

She shook her head. "He wouldn't tell me," she said, with a bitter smile. "How's that for fucked-up?"

I swallowed hard. "Really? That doesn't seem…"

"Fair," she finished for me. "No, it doesn't. Seeing as it would've had a pretty profound effect on my life. I only found out about the Huntington's through some pretty clever investigative research. I didn't tell him right away. When I finally asked him, he admitted it ran in the family - and that he *knew*. He knew whether or not he was going to get sick. But that was all he'd tell me. He was angry, but I never asked about it again. I think that was when I knew it was over. The fact that he'd hide something like that from me. I kept trying to make it work, but I just couldn't forget. It was as good as a lie, to me. You don't think to ask someone - when you first start dating, you know, 'oh, by the way, do you have a neurodegenerative disorder that you're not telling me about?'"

I exhaled softly. "Maybe he doesn't."

"Maybe," she said. "Then why hide it? Don't tell me you haven't wondered the same thing."

I had. Of *course* I had. I hated that I had, that me and Daria shared so much in common. I wanted to snarl at her for invading his privacy like that, for trying to involve herself in something so deeply personal. But I was on the verge of doing the same damn thing. How could I possibly go on, not knowing?

"I've noticed you two together," she said. "I think Ben expected me to turn tail and run to another city when things fell apart, but I wouldn't be smoked out. We still pass each other on the street, and he always sees me, but he always pretends not to. He loves you, Jenna. And I can tell you love him. I just want you to know, that's not always enough." She blinked heavily. "Some things can't be repaired."

"Is that a threat?" I demanded.

"No," she said. "It's a statement of fact." She exhaled, slowly. "A regret, if you will. We both did a lot of things out of spite, but I hope he came out of our relationship a better man. He thinks everything I do is for some evil ulterior motive, because that's the story that suits him. But if I could see him be happy, I'd sleep a little easier at night." She smiled, faintly. "I know I seem like a stalker. If you don't know the whole story, it certainly comes across that way. But we were obsessed with each other, at an age when that means something. It's hard to disentangle. I might have been the one who walked away, but he was the one who left. Long before we were ever apart, there was nothing left between us. But we had to cling to the only thing we knew."

I stared at her, trying to understand. She wasn't exactly stable, but she wasn't completely off her rocker, either.

"I'll leave you alone now," she said. "Just know that whatever he tells you, I wish you nothing but the best."

What was the meaning of that? Was she just trying to put me off my guard, or had I really fooled her so well?

Of course, with the way I felt about him, maybe it was that obvious. Maybe it showed on my face every minute of every day.

If someone had asked me, a week ago: do you believe in "one true love?"

Of course not. It's such a stupid concept. Out of all the millions of people in the world, the idea that there's just one person with whom we can be truly happy - is there anything more absurd?

But I felt like I'd found it, in the strangest way possible. The only problem was I didn't know how I could possibly hold on.

I was pacing my apartment, trying to wrap my head around the reality of all this. Daria's voice echoed in my head, her unwanted questions and advice making my brain ache with the impossibility of accepting it all.

My phone buzzed with a text from Ben.

Got your something blue?

I answered him, quickly.

I'm not superstitious.

A moment later, my doorbell rang. The man himself was standing there, with a roguish smile, and as soon as I stepped back to let him in, he whipped out a box from behind his back.

"I'm going to go ahead and guess this is blue lingerie," I said, taking it from him.

"A gentleman never tells," he said, with a flourish. He was in a playful mood, and he probably expected a little stress-relieving quickie, but I was in no mood - a fact that he quickly noticed, as I brushed past him to rummage aimlessly in the fridge.

"What's wrong, sunshine?" He followed me, slowly, letting me keep my distance.

"I wish you wouldn't call me that all the time," I muttered.

He leaned against the counter. "Sorry," he said. "I'll try to save it for more special occasions."

I sighed, wanting to apologize, but not knowing where to start. My encounter with Daria was just too damn weird. I needed to process it first myself, before I foisted it on him.

"Nothing," I insisted.

"You know," he said, with a hint of a smile, "there's a little something they call stress relief spankings. I could…"

"No," I said, flatly. "Thanks. I appreciate it, really. But no."

"Come on, Jenna." He leaned forward, earnestly. "Just tell me what's wrong. It's been ever since the Finger Lakes trip, and I thought you just didn't want to leave. But something's eating at you."

I swallowed hard, suddenly feeling too raw and vulnerable to keep hiding it.

"I saw your paperwork," I said. "The Huntington's. It was your mom, wasn't it?"

His lips drew into a tight line.

"There's a reason I don't talk about it," he said. "And I think it's actually a pretty obvious one."

"Sorry," I said, well aware that I didn't sound sorry. "But I thought it's something you would have told me. Even if we weren't…" I shook my head, vigorously. "I know it's none of my business. I know that. I really, really do. But you wanted to know what's been bothering me, well, that's it. I hate the thought of you getting sick. I hate the thought of not knowing. I hate the thought of *you* not knowing."

"I took the test," he said. "If the outcome had any effect on you, I would've shared it. But it doesn't, either way. So drop it."

I'd never heard him sound so harsh. Instantly, guilt pooled in my belly. I had no right to pry, no right to ask invasive questions about his illness. Or lack thereof. He was right, it had no effect on me. I had no right to be upset.

Because it wasn't real. I just had to try and remember that.

"I'm sorry," I said, softly, unsure if he was even hearing me. He was lost in his own world, absorbed in some kind of deep anger and resentment that I'd triggered with my stupid nosiness. "You're right. It doesn't have any effect on me. I was just worried about you, but I should've kept my mouth shut. It's just..."

He still showed no sign that he even knew I was talking.

"...it's just that I really *care* about you," I said, at last, instantly regretting the words as they left my mouth.

Ben let out a bark of laughter. "And this is how you show it?" Raking his hands through his hair, he finally looked at me. "Look. I understand it's upsetting and overwhelming. It's hard to deal with. Right? You don't really know how to wrap your head around it. So just imagine how I felt, watching my mother die. Imagine how I felt, wondering if I'd go the same way. Imagine how upsetting and overwhelming that was. Imagine how hard that was to deal with. There's a reason I don't talk about it, and it's not because I'm afraid of my feelings, or trying to be mysterious, or brooding, or whatever fucked-up reason you think it is. It's because I don't want to. I don't want to think about it. I've dealt with it already, and I'm done."

Tears were trickling down my cheeks, and I couldn't hope to stop them.

"I'm sorry," I whispered again. "I didn't mean to upset you, I just…"

I just love you. That's all.

Fucking stupid. What was wrong with me? Why wouldn't I just let it go?

Because it's real. Even if he doesn't see it…

"I know," he said, finally, his voice a little quieter. "I know. I know you didn't mean it. It's just, everybody thinks it's their business. And I hate that. I can't stand it. That's why I kept the research quiet. I knew it would be obvious if I made it public, that there was some kind of personal connection. Because it's true: there's no money in a cure. Especially not for such a rare disease. I'm doing it because it's a tiny drop in the bucket, but it's something I can do. It's people I can help, that nobody else is going to bother helping. It's something. It's not for me."

In spite of everything, my heart leapt a little bit in my chest. "It's not?"

He sighed. "I don't have it, Jenna. I don't have the gene. I've known that since I was ten years old. My father knows. I never told anybody else, because it's none of their business. I'm not dying. At least, not any faster than anybody else."

Relief flooded my system. I struggled not to show it, unsure of how he'd react.

"We don't have to talk about this anymore," I said, fighting to keep my voice from trembling.

"Of course we don't," he said, with a sarcastic smile. "You got the information you wanted, right? Now you can sleep easy at night. Because you'll never have to go through what I went through. Now, you can just move on and forget that people die horrible deaths before their time." He roughly finger-combed his hair again. "I'm sorry. This is just something I've been living with for as long as I can remember. It's hard to have any kind of normal perspective on it."

"You don't have to apologize," I insisted, even as I shivered at the chilliness of his attitude. I understood, or thought I did - as much as anyone possibly could. But I couldn't really know what was going through his head. I couldn't know what it was like to be ten years old, and see your mother die.

"I know I don't," he said. "But you're not going to calm down unless I say I'm sorry, so, I'm sorry. I don't know what I'm sorry for. I'm sorry I didn't share every painful part of my life with you. I'm sorry I didn't want to talk about it. I'm sorry."

"Daria found me," I blurted out.

He stopped, and stared. All the blood drained from his face.

"God," he said. "Jenna, I'm..." he exhaled tightly. "I'm so sorry. I really am sorry. I didn't think she'd..." His eyes darted wildly around the room. "What did she say to you?"

"Nothing important," I lied. "Nothing you need to worry about. She just wanted to wish us well."

He could tell that I was lying, but he didn't know what to say to make me tell him the truth.

"I'm sorry," he said, again. "If you want to talk about it - if you need to ask me anything, I..."

"No, it's fine," I said. "You're right. You should probably just go."

Shutting the door after him, I gave myself a

moment to breathe before I started crying.

Chapter Thirty-One

Jenna

My wedding day went by in a blur.

Not the happy kind of blur I think you're supposed to have, where it's just so joyful you can't find the place in your mind to hold the memories. More like the kind of blur that leaves you feeling like you've got some kind of flu, or a brain fever, or you've just been spun around in one of those astronaut training machines and you're no longer sure which way is up.

I finally saw my parents at the theater, a few hours before I was whisked away to start the insanely complex process of transforming me into a bride. I didn't understand why it had to take so long, but apparently, it was very important that I look exactly like a living, breathing wedding topper.

"Hi, honey. "My mom hugged me tightly, smiling, a little apprehensive. "We're so happy for you."

"This must be the lucky guy," my dad said, with forced joviality.

"Very lucky," Ben agreed, turning on the charm.

I saw my parents sitting there in the first row, my

father clasping my mother's hand. Confused, apprehensive, but happy.

Happy for me.

We spent some time on meaningless chit-chat, and I learned all about what they'd been doing. Their eyes were filled with unasked questions at first, but as time passed, I saw them begin to relax. They noticed something between Ben and me, probably the same thing that Daria noticed. They weren't so suspicious anymore. The worry began to fade.

Everyone knows it, except for us.

It was a funny thought, except it wasn't funny at all.

Looking back, I could hardly remember walking down the aisle. I knew I did it, because I had to assume no one carried me. But the specifics, the vows, none of it registered, except for the way Ben looked at me.

That was all I could see, standing there, as the officiant droned on. It looked so real. It looked so much like he really wanted to be spending the rest of his life with me.

My guess about his gift was right. It was a dark blue lingerie set, simple enough, just panties and a bra. But I wore it, for him, because I wanted to. I wanted to see his face when he finally undressed me on our fake wedding night.

I had to focus on that, because I couldn't wrap my head around anything else.

Finally, the ceremony ended. I only had a few minutes to compose myself before I had to appear at the real party.

The reception was teeming with faces, strangers

and friends, family I hadn't seen in years and people who might just be crashing the party, for all I knew. I didn't manage to spot my parents, which was probably just as well. I needed to gather my thoughts.

I sidled over to Maddy and Daniel, as Ben seemed to have been drawn into the tractor beam of some work acquaintances I wasn't particularly anxious to meet. Daniel was talking to a tall, elegantly-dressed woman who shared his clever eyes and unruly hair.

"Jenna, this is my sister, Lindsay," he said.

"Congratulations, it was a beautiful ceremony." She was giving me a gently appraising look as she shook my hand. "I hear Ben's quite a catch."

I nodded, smiling in a way that felt appropriate for the situation.

Maddy drifted over, grabbing me by the elbow. "Sorry, I just have to borrow the bride for a second. If anyone asks where she is, just tell them to wait for the ransom note."

"Got it." Lindsay's knowing look was starting to unnerve me.

I let Maddy steer me into one of the endless side-rooms, sitting me down in a chair and handing me a bottle of water. "Drink," she said. "You look like you're about to keel over."

"Thanks." I sagged with my elbows resting on my knees. Heart racing, head pounding, stomach churning - it was no wonder I looked like hell.

"I know the feeling," she said. "It's overwhelming, especially when things move this fast." She patted me on the shoulder. "You want me to leave you alone?"

"Actually, could you get my mom?" I didn't know why, but I felt like seeing her face would help me somehow.

"Of course." Maddy disappeared, and a few minutes later, my mom rushed into the room.

"Oh, honey," she said. "Are you okay?"

"I'm great, Mom," I said, forcing a smile. "It's just been a really, really long day, and I didn't get enough sleep, and I'm feeling a little overwhelmed by everything. It'll pass. I just wanted to have a chance to talk one more time, before I go back out into the craziness."

"Of course." She sat down next to me and covered her hand with mine. "I'll admit, I was pretty confused when you told me and your dad about this guy, and how you'd apparently fallen in love with him at the drop of a hat. But I see it now. I don't get it, but then again, your dad and I only knew each other for six weeks."

She laughed.

"Six weeks?" I repeated. "I never knew that."

"Well, we didn't want you to think it was a good idea." She smiled. "The good old 'do as I say, not as I do.' But obviously, it works out okay sometimes."

We sat in companionable silence for a while.

"So, where are you going on your honeymoon?" she asked me, suddenly.

"I don't know," I said. "He won't tell me."

"Oh." My mom smiled. "That's so romantic. Just call me when you land, okay?"

Sitting with Ben in the back of the limousine, as we

waved goodbye, I didn't know what the hell to say to him.

"I'm sorry about everything," I blurted out, finally.

He sighed. "Me too, Jenna." Reaching for my hand, he clasped it tightly, stroking his thumb in little circles the way he always did. "You don't have to talk about Daria if you don't want to, but I'll be happy to listen. I'll be happy to explain anything you want to know."

I shrugged. "I don't think any of the specifics matter that much," I said. "Except, we don't really have to be afraid of her."

"I was never afraid," he insisted.

"Okay," I said, quietly. I didn't believe him, but I was going to let him pretend.

A small silence passed.

"So," I said, with the beginnings of mischievous smile. "Where are we going?"

His eyes darkened. "What did I tell you about asking me that?" he growled. "Just wait until we're alone, Mrs. Chase."

Chapter Thirty-Two

Jenna

"I thought you liked surprises."

"Whatever gave you that impression?" I twisted around in my seat, as if that could somehow help me see through the blindfold. "This better be worth it, Mr. Chase."

"Oh, trust me, Mrs. Chase - you'll be thanking me later."

I could hear his wicked grin. It made something twist in my chest - longing, confusion, and that overwhelming desire to just *ask* him. To lay all of my cards on the table, so I could find out how he really felt about me. We'd been playing this game so long. I just wanted to know if it had become a tiny bit real for him, too.

The sex was one thing. Obviously, our connection in the bedroom was electric. I couldn't deny that, but I needed more. I didn't know how I was going to survive the next two years if I had to pretend it was just about spanking and hair-pulling and explosive encounters driven purely by lust.

All this time, he'd been so secretive about the honeymoon destination. I'd pleaded, cajoled, and earned myself more than a few punishments in the hopes that he'd crack. Just once. But he'd stood firm, right until this very moment, after we landed in *some airport* and he put on my blindfold and led me into a car.

It was a short flight, but I didn't think he'd be taking me to wine country again. That was too obvious. He had something amazing planned. Maybe we were just catching a connecting flight to Paris or Japan or something. There were so many corners of the world I'd never seen.

I felt the momentum slowly decrease, and then the car shut off.

"We're here," he said.

So, not a connecting flight then. I frowned, waiting for him to open my door for me. Like so many things that started out as totally unnatural to me, it had become a habit. It was a small thing, but it made him happy. I could compromise. Even if I thought it was a little too caveman, I knew enough of his real personality to understand it wasn't about that.

The door popped open, and he took my hand, leading me out into the fresh sea air.

Instantly, the smell brought me back.

He could have left the blindfold on for the rest of our honeymoon, and there would be no question in mind. I was back home.

Back in Cape Cod.

I took in a deep breath and let it out, slowly. The memories rushed back, powerful and heavy. Tears threatened at the corners of my eyes.

Whisper-soft, his fingers untied the blindfold and pulled it away. I blinked rapidly, trying to conceal my feelings, hoping that my watering eyes would pass for shock at adjusting to the sunlight.

I whirled around, taking it all in. This wasn't just any beach, this was *my* beach. I would recognize it anywhere. Some of the houses had changed, the landscape, but not enough to fool me. This place was everything that had made me who I was.

My forehead crinkled as I stared at him. He was beaming at me, hands thrust deep in his pockets, just enjoying the fruits of his labors. And I couldn't really blame him for that.

"How did you..." I took another deep breath, letting it out slowly. "How did you find out? Did you ask my parents?"

He shook his head, extending his hand to me. "Come on," he said. "I want to show you something."

We walked up the beach, slowly, my heart hammering in my chest. There were so many things I wanted to say, but I couldn't possibly find the words. I never would have guessed this would be the perfect honeymoon, but somehow, he'd just known. This was the place I needed to go back to.

For a moment, I was struck by the strangeness of it - returning back here, not as a townie, but as one of the tourists I'd resented so much. It was hard not to imagine how they'd think of me - whoever was in my parents' place now, in mine, cleaning up after people like me, not understanding that I used to be one of them.

Because now, it didn't matter. I'd married into enough money to keep them at my beck and call.

Something like regret twisted in my chest, then I glanced at Ben. The sunlight gleamed through his hair, and my heart thumped even faster.

I didn't care about the money. All I cared about was him - and that was dangerous.

All along, I'd grown up knowing that a rich boy could break my heart. I had to stay away. I knew better. I'd done so well, on my mother's warning. And then, I went ahead and fell in love with one anyway.

How monumentally stupid was I?

"Come on," he said, leading me towards a little copse of trees. Some long-forgotten memory stirred, deep inside my mind, but I couldn't quite reach it. The details were too hazy, and if I tried to put it into words, it slipped even further away, like a dream after hours of waking.

All that was left was the feeling itself. Something poignant and bittersweet.

My heels were sinking into the sand. "Wait," I said, letting go of Ben's hand. "My shoes."

He waited as I took them off, carrying them in my other hand as he grasped mine again and kept on urging me forward. I laughed a little as my toes sank into the sand. "What's so important?"

"You'll see," he promised.

We'd almost reached the trees. I looked over my shoulder, grasping again for the memory.

It's gonna be the biggest best sandcastle in the world

My throat constricted. This was where it happened - this was the exact spot where I first learned that very important lesson about rich boys. Of course, Ben couldn't know that. He just thought he was doing something very sweet and thoughtful, and he was. But

I felt that same wave of loneliness wash over me again, bringing the tears back to my eyes.

The sand gave way to dirt, and suddenly we were in the long shade of the trees. The sun was setting, and I wanted to lose myself in the beauty of it. But there was a great yawning emptiness inside me, because no matter how good things were now, I was destined for the same heartbreak again. He'd leave me. They always left.

"Jenna," he said, softly. "Look."

He was pointing at a tree trunk. I stepped closer, my eyes still adjusting to the relative darkness. There was something carved in it. Blocky, unsteady letters, darkened with age but still starkly visible in the wood.

BW

SK

There was nothing else, just those two sets of initials stacked on top of each other. But it all came rushing back.

We took a break from building the castle when the lifeguard called adult swim and said we were too close to the water. We had to get out of the way. He didn't want to have to watch us. So we left, going into the woods, and he didn't care, just as long as we didn't drown on his watch.

The boy had a pocketknife, and I thought that was very cool and a little bit scary. I wasn't allowed to have one of my own. He showed it to me, and I gasped and told him to be careful.

He wanted to make a mark in one of the trees. A memory

of the day, and how we built the best sandcastle to ever be built.

"What should I carve in it?"

I giggled. "Batman."

All day, he'd been calling himself Batman. I really didn't know who that was, except that he wore a scary rubber suit. I didn't like Batman, but I liked him. So if he called himself Batman, that was okay with me.

He shook his head, his messy hair falling down over his eye. "No. That's not what Batman would do. You gotta use your secret identity."

"So? What are you gonna put on it?"

Grinning, he dug the tip of the knife into the bark. "B.W.," he said. "For Bruce Wayne. That's what people call Batman whenever they don't know he's Batman."

"What about me?"

"You can be my sidekick," he said.

"I don't wanna be your sidekick." That made me mad. I knew what a sidekick was - less. Not as strong, not as powerful. Not fair. I wanted to be as cool as Batman.

"Fine," he said. "What about, if you were Catwoman?"

Catwoman. I wasn't sure I liked that, but it sounded better than being his sidekick.

"She's smart, too," he said. "Sometimes she's bad, but sometimes she's good. She's probably just as smart as Batman." He didn't like saying that, but he was trying to make me happy. I nodded enthusiastically.

"Okay. I'm Catwoman. What's my secret...identity?" I had to sound the word out carefully.

"S.K.," he said, starting to carve. "That's Selina Kyle. Don't forget it, okay? Next time I see you, that's what I'm gonna call you." He flipped his hair out of his eyes. "And what are you gonna call me?"

"Bruce," I said. "Bruce Wayne."

"That's right."
The sun beamed through his hair, and I smiled at him.

Ben's voice cut through the memory.

"Please tell me you remember."

I stared at him. Shorter hair, thinner face, and yeah, he was a few feet taller. But there was no mistaking it now. He'd brought the memory back to me, and I knew who he really was.

"Bruce," I whispered, stepping towards him, although my feet felt like lead.

"Hey, Selina." He was holding back his smile a little, but it still broke through. "It's been a while."

"Not so long," I said, softly. His fingers brushed against my cheek, feather-light, before they came around to cup the back of my neck. *Possessive.*

"I told you I'd come right back," he said. "How come you left?"

Tears welled in my eyes, and I didn't even think to be embarrassed. "Your parents were supposed to hate me."

"My parents didn't give a shit." His eyes locked with mine, and for once, they showed me everything. No artifice, no false bravado. The memory of childhood had stripped away everything dishonest about us, all the walls we'd put up in the many years we'd been apart.

A sob welled in my throat. I felt stupid, so stupid, for believing what my mother had told me. I knew all she wanted to do was protect me, but she'd torn me away from the one promising friendship of my childhood.

Suddenly, it all made sense. The connection we

felt back then, the way he could always make me smile, just with a glance. The way we understood each other without having to speak. We'd both become different people - but really, nothing had changed at all. The way I felt about him now, and the way I felt about him then, suddenly mingled in a tidal wave of feelings that threatened to pull me under.

"There was a monsoon that night," he said, softly.

"I remember." I nodded, trying to swallow the thickness in my throat. "Washed away everything we built."

"I was here every year after that," he said. "But I could never find you again. By the time I was old enough to figure out how to start asking questions, I realized I didn't know anything about you. Were you here on vacation? Were you one of the townies' kids? I had no idea. And you grew up...your face changed..."

Taking a deep, shaky breath, I let my hands unclench by my sides. "How long have you known?"

He half-shrugged, his hand still clasped around the back of my neck. "I didn't remember, at first. I'll admit that. Not as clearly as you did. But when you told your story, it brought something back. I had to do some digging. I came back here, that weekend I was 'away on business.' I had to see for myself, and make sure my memory wasn't playing tricks on me. As soon as I saw this tree, it all came rushing back."

Somehow, I'd completely forgotten about the tree. Our fake names carved there, one on top of the other, as if they were waiting for a plus sign and an outline of a heart. But it hadn't been like that - not back then.

"Something's missing," I said, softly. Wondering if he'd understand.

His face broke into a lopsided grin. "I was hoping you'd say that."

Releasing me, he turned towards the tree, reaching into his pocket for something. I swallowed hard and watched as he unfolded the little pocketknife, and the blade glinted in the moonlight.

Carefully, painstakingly, he carved the little plus sign that signified our connection. Then came the heart, a big swooping design, slightly lopsided. Slightly imperfect.

Just right.

I giggled, stepping close to his side as he put the knife away. "I think you might need to see a cardiologist, dear."

"Fuck you." His arm slid around my waist. "Go ahead, you try to carve a decent heart with a twenty-year-old pocketknife. I'll be waiting."

My arms circled around him, silently, just holding him and feeling his body pressed against mine. Deep inside, there was a peace that hadn't been there before. A sense of calm. Belonging. I *hadn't* been rejected, all those years ago.

I didn't know what that meant for the future, but it brought closure to my past.

"I thought that was a pretty good gesture," he said, softly. A little teasingly. "Don't I even get a kiss?"

My whole body thrummed. "I want to," I admitted. "But if I kiss you now, I don't think I'll be able to stop."

"Oh, Mrs. Chase." His lips brushed against my temple, hot breath giving me goosebumps all over. "Didn't you notice how empty the beach was? I've had it closed for a private event. Nobody's here. Nobody's *going* to be here, all night." His hand slid down a little lower, to cup my ass. "Just us."

I laughed. "You closed the beach? Oh, the billionaire's kids must be *pissed*."

"They'll get over it," he said, spinning me around so that we were pressed together, face to face. "Someday, they'll understand."

Swallowing hard, I glanced at the tree. "Right here?" The idea excited me, and I was almost afraid to admit it. "Would that be horribly wrong?"

"Why?" His fingers travelled up my back, coming to fiddle with the clasp on my dress. "Here is perfect. Less sand. I don't know if you've had beach sex before, but…"

"We were just kids, last time." I swallowed hard. "This place…"

"Yeah, but now we're all grown up." He stepped back a little, letting my unfastened dress sag, threatening to fall and exposes my breasts, but not quite. His eyes raked up and down my body. "And *how*."

Giggling, I made a show of holding up the fabric to preserve my dignity. "Okay, *now* you're making it weird."

"This place is ours," he said, his eyes heavy-lidded as he swooped in to kiss me. Well - almost kiss me. He stopped just millimeters from my lips, to murmur. "It belongs to us. The memory. And we can do whatever we want with it. I know you don't want to lose the innocence from back then. It's not going anywhere. It'll always be like that, no matter what happens now." His hand grasped my hip, firmly. "Let's make some new memories. Ones we *won't* tell the grandkids about."

It was a joke. Just a joke, a thoughtless little innuendo that absolutely didn't mean a damn thing about his intentions for the future. I knew that. But when he said it, I couldn't help but feel a thrill at the idea he might actually want to start a family with me.

That he wanted this for real. Not just for show.

He kissed me, and all thoughts scattered. I clasped my arms around his neck, holding on for dear life as my knees buckled against him. I had no resistance left. Nothing. I just wanted him to touch me, and I wanted to spend a little longer pretending.

We sank to the ground, somehow, the delicious bulk of his body holding me down. The thrill of that sensation hadn't lost any of its newness, and I moaned into his mouth, trying to lose myself in the moment. Wanting to. But there was another, stronger desire that was threatening to overwhelm me, and I needed to know. Even if the answer would break my heart.

His hand was sliding up my thigh, under my skirt. I froze, then squirmed away. His hand stopped and slowly withdrew.

As I struggled to prop myself up on my elbows, he pulled back, letting me up. Confusion and lust warred in his expression, and I felt terrible.

"I can't do this." Tears shimmered in my eyes, and I felt a horrible knot of guilt in my chest. But I had to stop. I couldn't keep pretending. "I'm so sorry. I'm sorry, Ben. I thought I could, but I couldn't."

He stared at me, and I could almost see the gears trying to turn in his lust-clouded brain. "Can't do what?" he asked, finally.

"I can't keep pretending." The tears were spilling down my cheeks, and I hated it, hated my weakness. "I don't know what we're doing here, Ben, and it's killing me."

For a split second, he looked confused. Then he laughed.

The sound twisted in my chest, as I tried to understand. Did he think it was funny, that I'd actually fallen in love with him?

"Jenna," he said, still smiling. "Jenna. How much more clearly can I telegraph this for you? I brought you here. I carved a *heart* around our names. What do you want me to do, rent a sky-writing plane? 'Cause I will. If that's what it takes, I'll do it right now." He feigned reaching into his pocket. "I know a guy."

"I'm sure you do," I hiccuped, staring at him. "Ben, I...I don't know. I'm never sure if it's *real*, when you act like..."

When you act like you love me.

He was still laughing. "Jenna." He leaned forward, capturing my face in his hands. "I love you. I loved you the first time you shot me that *fuck-you* glance at the grocery store, although I didn't know it back then. I've been falling more in love with you every damn day. Have you really not noticed?"

I stared at him. "Was this whole thing just a ploy?" I demanded. "A convenient excuse to get close to me?"

I wasn't sure how I'd feel if it was. I mean, we were here now, weren't we? I was in love with him, wasn't I?

Now that I could admit it to myself, I didn't even have to frame it as a question. There was no doubt. I loved him more than I'd ever thought possible, every ridiculous line and every lopsided smile. I loved him because he didn't give a shit, because he'd punch a highly-respected member of the fetish community right in the face for disrespecting me. I loved him because he knew exactly how to touch, how to kiss, how to *ignite*. I'd never thought I would feel the way he made me feel.

When it came to him, I was helpless. There was no resistance, no hesitation. Just the slow fire creeping through my veins, lighting me up inside. He didn't just touch me, he *worshipped* me.

Of course he loved me back. How could I have missed it? He'd been telling me all along, with every whisper of his fingers against my skin. His lips, his tongue, every part of his body had betrayed him - if only I'd been paying attention.

"It wasn't a ploy." He looked offended. "I didn't know. I didn't know, until we were sitting by the water at that restaurant in wine country, and I looked at you and I realized..." His face softened. "I wanted this forever. I wanted it to be real. And when I saw you walking down the aisle in that white dress, it felt real. I knew it *was* real, at least for me. And I was so glad I'd arranged this - I needed a way to show you, something you wouldn't be able to ignore."

My heartbeat was thudding so loudly in my ears I couldn't even hear myself think.

Ben was smiling. "But apparently, you needed a little more clarification. So there it is. Should I go ahead and hire that skywriter?"

I swallowed, hard. "Maybe later," I said, hearing my voice go husky and feeling utterly powerless to do anything about it.

"Thank God," he breathed, pitching forward to

crash his lips against mine. I squealed, then sighed - or would have, if his mouth wasn't devouring mine. He pushed me down into the ground with the weight of his body, his hips pinning mine, the hot, hard length of his arousal impossible to ignore.

"I'm a patient man, Mrs. Chase," he murmured, pulling away just long enough to let me catch my breath. "But even I have my limits."

Mrs. Chase. The full realization jolted through me, and suddenly I couldn't get him out of his clothes fast enough. This wasn't just for a few years, not just for long enough to convince the world, to fulfill an obligation. It was forever. He wanted it. He wanted me. Not just for tonight - forever.

He laughed softly as I tore at the buttons of his shirt, capturing my wrists and holding them tight. "Not yet," he murmured. "Turn over, sweetheart."

I couldn't help the little breathy mewl that came out of my throat. "Is this a good girl spanking?" I whispered, wriggling amongst the twigs and leaves as he pulled up my dress.

"Have you been good?" His hand caressed my bottom lightly, bringing out the goosebumps.

"Yes," I practically moaned, anticipating his first gentle swat.

He was pretending to consider this, his fingers tracing the edges of that lacy dark blue thong. "These don't look like good girl panties."

"I'll be so good," I whispered. "Please."

"That's not how this works." He gripped a handful of soft flesh, squeezing just tightly enough to make me moan again. "You don't get to make withdrawals based on promises of future behavior. The question is, *have* you been good?"

I nodded, momentarily forgetting how to make words come out of my mouth.

"Hmm." He let go his bruising grip, then stroked gently again. "I suppose I can overlook a few minor transgressions. Just this once. For our wedding night."

And with that, the ritual began. He warmed me up, just the way I wanted, just the way I *needed*. Until I was molten, until I whimpered and begged. Finally, he grabbed my hips and lifted me up, just holding me against him for a moment. The fabric of his pants, tented by his erection, rasped against my sensitive flesh.

"I know this is our first time as husband and wife," he whispered, pressing himself harder against me. "I know it's supposed to be missionary position with candles and scented bubble bath, but God..." He sighed. "I want you like this. Is that terrible, sunshine? Taking my new bride like an animal in the woods?"

If it was terrible, then I was terrible too. Far from wrong, it felt *right*, so perfectly intimate even if it meant I couldn't see his face. I didn't need to. His body told me everything I wanted to know.

Clutching the moss and leaves underneath me, I ground against him. Hoping he would understand, because I didn't know what to say. I'd forgotten how to do anything but need.

With a soft growl, he pulled away just enough to unzip and slide himself against my entrance. Teasing, just a little, but not too much. He was desperate too, but he knew every little enticing touch, every moment he denied me, just dialed my pleasure a little higher. It was for me. It was all for me.

He cursed softly as he finally sank inside, so deep, ripping a groan from deep in my chest. "*Aaah*. Sunshine, you feel so good. I love you like this." He picked up a steady rhythm, his little sighs and groans punctuating each word as he spoke. "I love seeing my marks bloom on your pretty little ass while I claim you. Make you mine again. So many different ways to do it, and I never get tired of any of them."

I could hear the smile on his lips, now. "And I like it when you do this." He spanked me, lightly, and my whole body clenched. With a little, laughing groan, he smacked me again. "*Fuck* yeah. But I have to be careful with that if I want to last."

My whole body was alive with sensation, every inch of my skin tingling. Darkness fell slowly as we moved together, driven by deep love and primitive lust, rutting like wild things amongst the trees and dirt. I felt like I could no longer breathe without moaning his name.

I'd lost all sense of time when he slid one hand up my back and gripped my hair, tugging just the way I liked. "Touch yourself, baby," he whispered. "Come for me."

He didn't have to ask twice.

I was spiraling out of control in moments, my fingers flying, and his hand clamped over my mouth just in time to catch my scream. The beach might be deserted, but there were still houses within shouting distance. As my whole body jerked and shuddered, somehow, just as I hit my peak, I heard him panting and cursing as he tried in vain to hold himself back. But my clenching core was insistent, milking his pleasure from him. Hearing him tumble unwillingly into his own climax only made mine stronger, and we both writhed together as we slowly tumbled down the other side.

Moments later, still breathing hard, he pulled away from me and I whimpered at the loss of feeling.

"Shhh." He sat down, gathering me up in his arms and pulling me into his lap. "Shhh, I'm right here." He chuckled softly, his lips against my temple. "One of these days I'll learn to control myself with you, sunshine. Your wicked little body doesn't want that, but I'm gonna win. One of these days."

"Can't exactly help it," I murmured. "You make me feel so good. Besides." I opened my eyes, smiling up at him. "I like it when you get all flustered."

"Yeah. I noticed." He frowned slightly. "Hey, did I ever punish you for that little phone sex stunt?"

My heart throbbed at the memory. "Of course. You don't remember?"

"Not *that* one. The first time." He raised his eyebrows. "When I was *at work*, you little hussy."

I laughed. I'd actually forgotten about that ridiculousness. "I didn't mean to. You're the one who called me, remember?"

"Yeah, because you texted me first. Just laying there in bed, wearing that dress. Are you telling me that's not what you wanted?"

"Not at first," I protested. "But your voice is just so sexy…"

"Stop it," he growled. "That's not going to work. You started off joking about what you were wearing. You knew exactly what that would do to me."

"Yeah, well, do you have any idea what a state I was in when I visited your office?" I countered. "You deserved a little quid pro quo."

"Quid pro..." He rolled me towards him slightly to give me a little smack on the bottom. "Are you fucking kidding me, woman? The state *you* were in? I'm surprised I didn't do any serious damage to myself after you left. I might have a repetitive motion injury from all the times you left me high and dry."

"That was almost always your idea," I reminded him, laughing, my head snuggled safely against his chest. "If your phone hadn't gone off that day in your office bathroom...I was about to drop to my knees right there and mark you with my lipstick where it *really* counted."

He groaned, hugging me tighter. "Stop that, sunshine. I really do need some time to recover, tonight."

"I'm glad it happened the way it did, though." I sighed into his partially-unbuttoned shirt. "I'd be afraid to change anything."

"Me too." His lips brushed my forehead. "I fucking love you, Mrs. Chase. More than sand castles and Ben & Jerry's. More than anything in the whole damn world. I wish I'd never let you go, but at least I found you again."

Tears glistened in my eyes again, and this time, I let them fall. "I love you too," I whispered. "I didn't even realize how much I've been missing you, all these years."

"Me neither." He laughed softly. "Isn't that crazy? I know I'm just projecting the way I feel about you now, but I could swear I was in love with you then. Somehow. Even if I didn't know what it meant."

"I know." I wanted to believe it was real, even if it

couldn't possibly be.

"Promise me one thing." He stroked the tangled hair back from my face. "Don't ever leave me again. Okay? Or I'll have to put a collar on you with a bell."

"That doesn't sound so bad," I purred.

I felt his chuckle reverberating through his chest. "You're impossible," he whispered. "I love impossible."

"I know," I whispered back.

The stars were coming out, one by one, and then suddenly, all at once. As I watched them appear, cradled in his arms, I truly realized for the first time something I'd known all along, without really *knowing*.

The stars were always there. Bright and beautiful, their vibrancy only hidden in the daylight. But they were never gone. Not really. They were just waiting.

I'd waited such a long time. Now, it was my turn to shine like a diamond.

Thanks for reading! If you enjoyed this book, you'll love Melanie's New York Times bestselling romance novel:

HIS SECRETARY: UNDONE

I'm about to throw an ashtray at my boss's head.

Turns out, the mind behind my favorite, steamy romance novels...the ones I only read in private...the ones that are my only escape after a long day of dealing with The Boss From Hell? It's not Natalie McBride, the sweet, rural housewife.

It's him.

That's right: my boss, Adrian Risinger, the thirty-three-year-old, maddeningly sexy, pissant billionaire "bad boy" who thinks he runs my life. He is also the author of all my deepest, most secret fantasies. And to make matters worse, he needs me to impersonate "Natalie" at a series of book signings and conventions. But, of course, that's only if I want to keep my job.

On second thought, I'm going to need something heavier than an ashtray.

Get it now: Bit.ly/SecretaryUndone-Landing

For exclusive content, sales, and special opportunities for fans only, plus a FREE romance serial for subscribers only, please sign up for Melanie's mailing list at MelanieMarchande.com. You'll never be spammed, and your information will never be shared or sold.

You can also friend her on Facebook: Facebook.com/Melanie.Marchande.3

And LIKE her page: Facebook.com/MelanieMarchande

Made in the USA
Lexington, KY
02 January 2016